GLORIOUS BOY

GLORIOUS BOY

a novel

Aimee Liu

🐓 Red Hen Press | *Pasadena, CA*

Book design by Mark E. Cull

Library of Congress Cataloging-in-Publication Data

Names: Liu, Aimee, author.
Title: Glorious boy : a novel / Aimee Liu.
Description: First edition. | Pasadena : Red Hen Press, [2020]
Identifiers: LCCN 2019022868 (print) | LCCN 2019022869 (ebook) | ISBN
   9781597098892 (trade paperback) | ISBN 9781597098472 (ebook)
Subjects: GSAFD: Suspense fiction.
Classification: LCC PS3562.I797 G58 2020 (print) | LCC PS3562.I797
   (ebook) | DDC 813/.54—dc23
LC record available at https://lccn.loc.gov/2019022868

Publication of this book has been made possible in part through the financial support of Ann Beman.

The National Endowment for the Arts, the Los Angeles County Arts Commission, the Ahmanson Foundation, the Dwight Stuart Youth Fund, the Max Factor Family Foundation, the Pasadena Tournament of Roses Foundation, the Pasadena Arts & Culture Commission and the City of Pasadena Cultural Affairs Division, the City of Los Angeles Department of Cultural Affairs, the Audrey & Sydney Irmas Charitable Foundation, the Kinder Morgan Foundation, the Meta & George Rosenberg Foundation, the Allergan Foundation, the Riordan Foundation, Amazon Literary Partnership, and the Mara W. Breech Foundation partially support Red Hen Press.

First Edition
Published by Red Hen Press
www.redhen.org

For my own Glorious Boys—

Marty, Dan, Graham

The Andaman Islands lie in the Bay of Bengal, between the 10th and 14th Parallels of North Latitude, and between the 92nd and 94th Meridians of East Longitude. . . .

. . . In 1788–89 the Government of Bengal sought to establish in [these] Islands a penal colony associated with a harbor of refuge . . . now called Port Blair.

—Maurice Vidal Portman, 1899
A History of Our Relations With the Andamanese

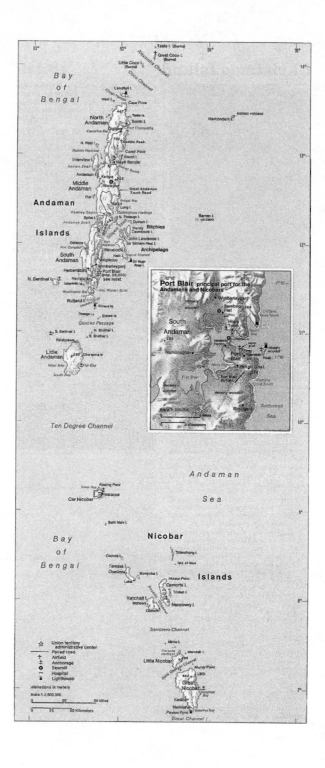

Bay
of
Bengal

North
Andaman

Andaman

Islands

South
Andaman

Middle
Andaman

N. Sentinel I.

Little
Andaman

Ten Degree Channel

Port Blair principal port for the
Andamans and Nicobars

South
Andaman

Port
Blair

Andaman

Sea

Car Nicobar

Bay
of
Bengal

Nicobar

Islands

Sombrero Channel

☆ Union territory
administrative center
┼ Paved road
✈ Airfield
⚓ Anchorage
✿ Sawmill
⊕ Hospital
♦ Lighthouse

elevations in meters

Scale 1:2,500,000

0   25   50 Miles

0   25   50 Kilometers

Little Nicobar

Great
Nicobar

The fish in the water is silent, the animal on the earth is noisy, the bird in the air is singing,

But Man has in him the silence of the sea, the noise of the earth and the music of the air.

—Rabindranath Tagore, *Stray Birds*

He considered his own identity, a thing he had never done before, till his head swam. He was one insignificant person in all this roaring whirl of India, going southward to he knew not what fate.

—Rudyard Kipling, *Kim*

PART ONE

I

March 13, 1942

When Shep lifts the blackout shades, a thin film of gray invades the bedroom, exposing his annoyance. He's overreacting, Claire tells herself. The deadline for boarding's not till two o'clock. It's just that he needs to get down to the jetty early to oversee the transfer of his patients and hospital equipment onto the *Norilla*, and until last night, he'd assumed that she and Ty would come with him. Shep cannot understand why his wife still needs more time to deal with *her* field specimens, when he finished crating his yesterday.

They pull on their clothes in silence rather than argue the point again. She does have their books, Ty's things, and the family essentials in hand, but Claire has a bad habit of saving the most painful tasks for last, so her study's still piled with field journals, artifacts, and her attempts to decode the language of the forest tribe that's become her second family over these past five years. A family she's being forced to leave without even saying goodbye.

But it's not just that. The sorting of their household staff—especially Naila's fate—has also taken more of a toll on Claire than she lets on. As she and Shep now pass Ty's room on their way up the outside stairs, she winces at the memory of the girl's impassive face last night when they told her she couldn't come with them. Their gentle Leyo will surely take good care of her, but Naila has been through so much. She doesn't deserve this.

"You really don't think we could sneak her aboard?" Claire asks as they cross the terrace.

Shep sighs and stomps a warning foot before cracking the kitchen door. Vipers and scorpions are always a concern when entering the out-buildings.

"And then what, Claire?" He rummages for tea and biscuits—the cook left days ago. No need to remind her how fraught their own future is. Who knows where he'll be sent from Calcutta, or where she and Ty will land, or what else the war has in store, now that it's finally caught up with them.

She follows him in, strikes a match under the kettle, and wrestles with her conscience. Naila is thirteen years old, an orphan, but she's not their child, and she does belong here. Port Blair is the only world she's known. Also, she's not at risk the way they are. Even if the Japanese should land in the Andamans, most of the locals are so deeply steeped in resistance to the Raj that they would welcome the soldiers of Britain's enemy as liberators—"Asia for the Asians," an old and passionate refrain among these erstwhile freedom fighters.

None of that would stop Shep from bringing Naila with them, though, were it not for the Commissioner's evacuation edict: *Europeans and official personnel only. All local-borns to remain.*

Colonial rules. A tyranny of injustice, not to mention ineptitude. For years every official in Port Blair has insisted the enemy couldn't possibly push this far west. Not even the news from Pearl Harbor rattled this conviction. Last month, three navy green fighters with small red suns emblazoned on their sides scatter-shot the airfield, and still the Brits denied danger. No one was even scratched, according to the Commissioner. And Shep was right there with him. He came home from surveying the damage—a few small craters, some broken saplings—and told Claire the bombardiers must have been blind. Three weeks later, Rangoon fell. Now everyone's changed their tune, and poor Naila's got to pay the price.

"We've provided for her as best we—" Shep breaks off at the sight of Ty trudging through the morning mist in bare feet and blue pajamas.

"Hello, old boy!" He swings the child into his crooked elbow and plants a kiss on his cheek, which Ty promptly wipes off when Shep sets him down.

"Biscuit?" Claire puts on a smile and holds out one of their last McVitie's, but Ty's lower lip thrusts into a pout. As usual, their four-year-old's inexplicable speechlessness dares them to read his mind.

"Toast?" She tries again.

"Big boat ride today." Shep prefers distraction, but this morning Ty resists him too, and the familiar clutch of frustration is barbed with panic as Claire pictures the three of them sailing into the future alone.

"Where's Naila?" she asks.

Ty brightens, turning to point as the girl reaches the top of the stairs and lurches into view. She's dressed in haste, her green skirt backwards, pink blouse untucked, that cap of soft unruly black curls framing the fear in her eyes.

Relief floods her face at the sight of them, and Claire feels another pang. Until Shep overruled her yesterday, she'd argued in favor of keeping the girl in the dark. It would have been hard enough if they'd waited until they reached the jetty, but Shep thought Naila deserved some time to prepare herself. He was right, of course. And Naila received their plan with a grace that Claire never could have anticipated. But that grace is gone now, replaced by the lingering tremors of a child's alarm. She must have thought they'd abandoned her already.

Ty scurries over and gives a little hop as Naila salaams to Shep and Claire. "Sorry," she says, sounding shy and breathless. "I am sleeping when Ty Babu—"

"It's all right," Claire says.

Shep gestures for her to join them in the kitchen. "Ty was trying to tell us what he wants for breakfast."

Naila leans down to look into the boy's eyes. They confer for a couple of seconds in their silent, exclusive language.

"Toast, please," she translates, coming up.

Ty nods and takes her hand, and Claire pushes back a tide of emotions that would do none of them any good.

Her husband's silence, unlike her son's, is easily interpreted: We must get on without Naila, but how?

"All right," Claire says. "The bread's a little stale, but it should toast all right."

The children set to drawing with chalk on the terrace while Claire gets their breakfast going and Shep downs his. Then she walks him out to the forecourt, where his driver, Narinder, stands waiting beside the Morris.

The blue air smells of night jasmine. Shep inhales. "Can we take this with us?"

She hears sorrow and resignation, the end of an era in too many ways to count. She removes his pith helmet and smooths back his damp ginger forelock, then replaces the topi, only straighter. "We'll come back," she tells him.

He gives her a not-quite-reassuring squeeze.

"We'll be down at the dock by noon."

"Earlier," he says, his tone stiffening.

"You're not going to let them leave without us."

"I shouldn't be letting you stay here now."

"I know, I know. Commissioner's orders. No exceptions. We'll be there, Shep."

He shakes his head and is off without a kiss.

No sooner has he gone, however, than the morning twists sideways. Ty climbs into the empty boxes. He empties out the full ones. He breaks a glass and tries to hold the shards up to the sun. The day's heat rises.

It's only natural, Claire keeps reminding herself. How can a four-year-old be expected to grasp the threat of war? He thinks this is just a game. And why should she ruin these last hours for Naila by fighting Ty, why shatter this last bit of peace?

She sends them down to help Leyo move Shep's specimens up from the greenhouse while she finishes packing her study. At ten Narinder will be back for her and Ty and the last of her boxes and Shep's plants. *Hurry,* she admonishes herself, but time turns glassy and slow as she focuses at last on her field pieces.

Each of the shell bowls, reed baskets, pandanus mats, and arrowheads that line the floor tells a story, connects her to a different soul, a unique moment of discovery and change within herself. The straw headdress Chief Kuli wore to greet her and Shep on their very first visit to the Biya camp. The woven sling little Artam rode as an infant, just seven months before Ty's birth. The conch in which Kuli told her to listen to the voice of the Biya god Biliku, a god who often over these years has seemed much wiser and kinder than her own.

How patient and accepting the Biya have been with her. Especially in the beginning, putting up with her callowness, her naive arrogance and presumptuousness. The thought of her initial view of this tribe as anthropological subjects now makes her wince. She'd come to the Andamans mistaking youthful ambition as a virtue, and it took her a long time to realize that ambition is worthless unless it's rooted in human understanding. Had she been a quicker study, perhaps she and Ty would have that understanding now, as he and Naila so instinctively do. It's a painful irony that she communicates better with the Biya—even when they, too, are speaking silently—than she can with her own son.

But she and Ty have a long future in which to repair their bond. Soon these objects could be all she has left of her Biya friends and mentors. While no one on this island now can be certain of their fate, the Biya's numbers began to decline decades before the war started.

What if she never comes back? This is the thought that derails Claire when Naila and Ty appear in the doorway, Ty making straight for the arrowheads, which are sharp enough to hurt him.

Reflexively, she grabs her son's arm. He replies by punching her hard in the chest.

Claire pulls back and holds still, as she's trained herself to do in such moments, waiting for Naila to glide between them and apply her mysterious powers to soothe whatever injury Ty believes his mother has inflicted. Instead, Naila gives a little gasp. Glancing down, Claire notices the circle of blood where the stone in Ty's fist pierced her shirt.

Her son watches from Naila's sheltering arms, his green eyes bright with attention now as the wound begins to throb.

"Mem—" Naila starts, but Claire waves her away.

"It's nothing. Really." She meets Ty's gaze. He studies her with a detachment that hurts far more than the scratch. She forces a smile, and he shrugs as if tolerating a truce.

"Please," she says to Naila, then hears herself begging. "Just keep him out of the way."

The girl takes Ty's hand, and he presses against her, quiet now, his hair a halo of wavy darkness against her crumpled blouse, his face the same warm brown as her arms. They grimace in unison, and then, for no reason that Claire can discern, they grin.

Urchins, the two of them, she thinks. Like brother and sister. Unlike either of his parents, Naila always knows what Ty most wants: to memorize sunbeams and trace the clouds, to match each bird to its song, to draw the botanical names of plants, even if he can't speak his own.

She dreads ripping them apart almost as much as she yearns to share in their closeness.

"Ten minutes," she says. "I just need ten more minutes."

Naila circles her chin and crooks her pinky in a signal that lights the boy's whole small being. Then the two turn to leave. Joining hands they skip in unison out into the sun.

❦

Shep surrenders so deeply to the stupor of duty that when the *Norilla*'s horn blasts, he loses his balance. Catching himself on a wooden bollard, he checks that his final batch of crates has started up the gangway. He's seen to that all right. What he's failed to notice is the chaos thickening on the jetty behind him. The scene is a frenzy of Burmese, Indian, and Eurasian officials and their families, everyone who's allowed to leave desperate to get on board with their belongings, while the local remainers taunt the Indian soldiers and police who'll be left with them "to keep order."

He glances at his watch—twelve thirty—and searches back over the throng. Claire and Ty should have been here at least an hour ago, but he resists the alarm that needles through this calculation. The crush must have held them up in the square.

It practically requires hand-to-hand combat to get back through it. Every few feet, exhausted couples block his path squabbling over heaps of possessions that exceed the emergency restrictions, and the light-fingered locals threading around them don't help. One of his own porters earlier tipped a box of surgical supplies into the drink, no doubt with a plan to retrieve it as soon as the *Norilla* sails. If the Japanese ever do land here, those scopes and scalpels will be worth more than gold. The potential end of British rule in these islands makes everything fair game for those staying on.

He takes a breath and presses forward, but the dread that the horn unleashed keeps rising. Why can't Claire *ever* just follow the rules?

"On the *next* ship, then!" A squat Indian matron is shouting at the MP who's threatened to confiscate her trunks if she doesn't move them back off the pier.

"God willing," comes the young Sikh's beleaguered reply.

Shep elbows past. The real question is, why are they still here at all?

Hubris. Delusion. Fantasy. Did he and Claire honestly believe the war wouldn't find them, that their respective ambitions justified putting their lives—and Ty's—at risk? Possibly, but it was his own cowardice that tied the knot. The prospect of abandoning his wife and son terrifies him even more than the inevitability of being called up.

A sudden spasm compels him to check that the gangway's still down, and in that instant the *Norilla* appears as a towering gray Gulliver bedeviled by Lilliputians. The mooring cables groan against the wharf's pilings, and the midday heat makes the hull seem to tremble.

He blinks. Or was it that the balance he and Claire struck together might be too fragile to survive anywhere other than "paradise"?

At last he's through the worst of it. He stands on the curb of the fore-shore road and scans the crowded waterfront, but the only car visible amid the jam of rickshaws and lorries is the police superintendent's jeep, which careens to the platform and disgorges two reluctant plantation managers who seem to embody Shep's guilt.

Sunburnt and unshaven, still in jungle kit, the men look like they've come straight from the toddy shack. One Shep recognizes as the widow-er of an elderly woman who sailed from Calcutta with him and Claire when they first arrived in this tropical backwater. The wife succumbed to dengue not long afterward, and this bastard didn't even see fit to notify the authorities.

"Dr. Durant!" Assistant Commissioner Alfred Baird hails him with a sheaf of his inexhaustible lists. "Your specimens get on all right?"

"Specimens." Shep needs a moment to realize that the well-meaning major is referring to his botanical samples. "Yes, but . . ." He shades his eyes against the sun and traces the route to Middle Point. "I'm still waiting for Claire and Ty."

Baird's voice spikes. "Why in God's name—"

Just then Shep spots the large red knob of the Morris winding down the hill. His hand twitches as he points to the car. "It's all right."

By the time the vehicle reaches the backup of vans and carts above the square, his pulse has returned to normal. The car halts. Claire jumps out and pushes ahead on foot. But even from this distance her spasmodic haste and rudeness—blindly shoving people and animals alike out of her way—telegraphs her desperation.

He's never seen Claire behave like this. And why is she *alone*?

Inside a giant banyan grove on the other side of the hill, the only audible sound belongs to the cicadas. When he first showed her this hiding place, Naila's father said the cicadas kept time for the gods, but Naila thinks now the gods must be deaf to need such noisy timekeepers.

Her father counsels her, *Listen, beti, and watch the shapes, the size and color of the sound. Don't be so quick to judge, then even the screech of the cicada may bring music to your ears.*

She shakes her head. The gods *are* deaf. And her father is dead. Would he offer the same advice if he'd heard Mem and Doctor Shep last night?

You know we'd take you if we could.

This evacuation is just a precaution. We'll be back before you know it.

Leyo has promised to look after you.

When the doctor placed that wad of rupees into her hand, she held it like a dead fish. Then he gave Leyo a bigger wad and advised him to spend it on whatever he could best use for barter because the money might lose its value after the British are gone.

Beside her now, Ty rouses, then sits up, abruptly awake, and starts to stand.

"Not yet, *beta*," she calms him. "Let's find the pictures in the tree."

Obedient whenever he likes the game, Ty drops back onto their blanket. She points to the cutwork of branches and leaves high above the mosquito net, and together they trace the dark shapes of two children holding hands, a pair of butterflies. When they narrow their eyes, the shapes change places, and suddenly patches of sky press blue elephants and lizards through the banyan's fretwork. Ty loves the way he can make the outlines blur and light explode, the pictures jiggle and change, just by squeezing his eyes. Once his mind ignites, he is like a motor that will run forever.

Naila makes sure he has reached this zone, then summons her parents again. They lean into her memory through the blue gateway of their quarters before the days of Mem and Doctor Shep. Her father's face is broad and square with a fine chin dusted with whiskers beneath his scruffy mustache. His smile seems never to leave his face, no matter how heavy his cares, and in the thickness of his black hair a crescent of white sweeps above his left eye.

Her ma liked to say pa wore the moon on his temple. She would take his face between her hands and hold him in her gaze.

Naila feels their lips against her forehead as a hot breeze stirs the leaves. *Go with love, Daughter.*

"But go where?" she begs out loud.

Ty begins to hum, so softly that she can barely hear him beneath the cicadas. After a few seconds she recognizes the same Bengali lullaby that her mother used to sing, that she herself often hummed to Ty when he was a baby.

So dear you are to me,
How could I ever let you go?
So dear you are to me,
No one else must ever know . . .

II

1936

"If you want to be the next Margaret Mead," Shep had agreed, "the Andamans do seem ready-made."

They were sitting on the grass in New York's Central Park in the summer of '36, having known each other less than a week. Her hair cropped short, her limbs still coltish, Claire looked, Shep would later tell her, like Louise Brooks without the eye makeup. He, on the other hand, was twenty-eight, more Ronald Colman than Gary Cooper, but Shanghai-born and trained in London, now headed for his first posting as Civil Surgeon in the most tantalizing place Claire had ever heard of: a barely civilized archipelago in the Bay of Bengal.

"I could skip all the hoops," she plotted, hardly believing her own moxie. "No research grants, no department approval."

Shep whistled. "Can you imagine the reception you'd get from Columbia? Or Oxford, for that matter—if you walked in the door having already conducted your own original field study!"

Could she imagine. She reached across the picnic basket and gripped his hand. This ruddy, disarming Brit had kissed her for the first time just four nights earlier, and in her mind, she was already halfway around the world with him, plunging into uncharted territory. It was madness. But he was nothing if not a willing co-conspirator. They'd spent every available hour since that kiss laying the groundwork for this scheme.

He leaned over and kissed her again, then threw off his seersucker jacket and rolled up his shirtsleeves. The way he watched her, his sea-glass green eyes were slightly out of sync with his mouth, and this flicker of anxiety warned Claire that Shep wasn't just besotted. He was *serious*—unlike her previous college-boy suitors. Also, trusting and protective.

And vulnerable. She'd need to be careful not to take undue advantage, but what was he offering if not the invitation to take *full* advantage?

Truth be told, she was out of her depth. When they'd met at the 21 Club last week, she'd initially mistaken this raw-boned stranger for a world beater. Asia, England, now America for a just-finished fellowship at Johns Hopkins. His doctor colleagues had brought him up to Manhattan to celebrate his appointment; it was that new. "A colonial port on a tropical island," was how Shep first described his destination. Bully for you, Claire had thought, and was turning away when one of her meddlesome roommates piped up, "Claire here fancies herself the next Margaret Mead. Before you know it, she'll be hunting heads in Borneo."

The gin-soaked glitter of their surroundings had flared, and Claire deflected. Her friends loved to tease her, she told Shep. She'd been drawn to ethnography ever since reading *Coming of Age in Samoa* when she was thirteen, and she applied to Barnard just so she could study with Dr. Mead's own teachers, but she'd never been west of Chicago—or east of Long Island. All painfully true. Claire had graduated less than a month earlier, was only twenty-one and barely qualified for the steno pool, let alone Borneo. The only way she could live in New York was to share a room at the Barbizon with three other girls, and the only reason she stayed in New York was because the alternative was to move back home to Connecticut. With the economy still in tatters, her parents couldn't afford to send her to graduate school, and not even Dr. Benedict's recommendation had been enough to land her a scholarship.

Shep said, "I'm told where I'm headed the tribes date back to the Stone Age." He smiled. "I can't promise that they hunt heads, though."

He was flirting. Nothing more. But he'd gotten her attention. She asked, "What *do* they hunt?"

That seemed to catch him off guard. "To be honest, I've no idea." He looked down at his martini as if he wasn't sure how it had wangled its way into his hand. "I'd never heard of this place until I received my marching orders this morning."

She felt herself redden. "So you made all that up." Again, she prepared for flight.

"No!" His drink splashed across her forearm, and he gasped. "Oh. Sorry!"

Claire watched a kaleidoscope of emotions flash across this stranger's face. Despite his nervous British manners, he seemed to radiate candor.

"It's nothing." She licked off the damage and grinned, but Shep remained as flustered as a nabbed truant. It was his turn to blush—or, more accurately, for the tips of his ears to turn bright pink. "Seriously," she said. "I know times are tough, but sloshing a few drops of gin is hardly a federal offense."

He took a half-step away from her, the packed room offering little leeway. Their friends had vanished. "I didn't make it up," he said. "I just don't know much more than I've told you."

They both were novices, then. She studied his eyes, their clear, open color. By contrast, her own dark gaze must seem furtive, but that didn't appear to bother him. "What do you want?" she asked softly.

A new ripple restored Shep's smile, simultaneously daring and winning. "Everything," he answered. "Don't you?"

Instead of returning to Baltimore with his "mates," Shep had stayed in New York, and they'd seen each other every day since. Getting down to business now in Central Park, he unfurled their blanket under a sheltering maple, unpacked their picnic—two wrapped sandwiches, two cups and one bottle of cola—then handed her the leather-bound volume they'd found in the library that morning: *The Andaman Islanders* by Alfred Radcliffe-Brown.

He was calling this their "research phase." Since he knew almost as little about his destination as she did, he'd suggested they find out what they could together before taking "any next steps." In the process, he didn't need to say, they'd also research each other. Exposed already: this gangly redhead was as methodical as Claire was impatient. Doubtless a good thing, under the circumstances.

"I remember Professor Benedict talking about Radcliffe-Brown," she said, scanning the book jacket. "She called him one of ethnography's big-picture men, but she never described his fieldwork." Claire wished Dr.

Benedict hadn't left already for her own summer fieldwork. Her advice would be worth gold.

She opened to the introduction and gave the book back to Shep. "You first."

He hesitated, as if this might be some sort of test. She said, "I can picture it better if you read it to me."

"Ah." He stretched his long legs and leaned back against the maple's trunk. Then he cleared his throat and began to read with the buoyant lilt of a radio announcer. "'Viewed from the sea, the islands appear as a series of hills, nowhere of any great height, covered from sky-line to high-water mark with dense and lofty forest . . . The coast is broken by a number of magnificent harbours. The shores are fringed with extensive coral reefs—'"

Claire scowled. "Sounds like paradise."

"What's wrong with that?"

She blurted without thinking how it might strike him, "I'm not looking for a holiday!"

"No," he replied quietly. "I can assure you, Claire, you needn't worry about that." He seemed on the verge of saying something more and different, but instead returned to the book. "'The Andamanese belong to that branch of the human species known to anthropologists as the Negrito race. They are short of stature with black skins and frizzy hair—'"

"Wait," Claire stopped him. "Let me see that." Until this moment, she'd assumed the Andaman islanders must resemble Polynesians—like Margaret Mead's grass-skirted Samoans. The image that now formed in her head made her search for the book's photographic plates. Though grainy and faded, they confirmed her mistake. In picture after picture, men, women, and children glared back in hostile defiance. They looked more African than Asian, and far wilder to Claire's eye than Mead's smiling islanders. The Andamanese wore necklaces and loincloths, and little else. Their chests and backs were threaded with patterns of scars, and their hair resembled black fleece shorn close to the skull. Some sported tattoos of clay. A couple of the men held bows and arrows longer than the hunters were tall. One girl had a skull strung to her back.

Claire wondered whatever had possessed her to think she was qualified to communicate with these people, to make this preposterous journey. At the same time, her longing to do just that struck her dumb.

She flipped back to read that the Andamanese were likely related to
the aboriginal inhabitants of the interior of the Philippines and the Malay Peninsula. They'd been isolated on these islands off Burma for thousands of years. Even though Europeans had begun scouting the islands
in the 1700s, many Andamanese tribes in Radcliffe-Brown's time had
yet to encounter a westerner, and he was the most recent ethnographer
to study them.

That was it, she thought. That was the prize. To meet these people
would be like entering a time capsule. Like starting life over. Erasing everything that came before.

"Claire?"

She looked up with a sense of shifting lenses to find Shep studying
her the way her father used to when she was little, when they went out
searching for fossils or egret feathers, just the two of them. His expression
curious. Hopeful. Forgiving.

She dropped her gaze. "It says Radcliffe-Browne was the only trained
anthropologist ever to study the Andamanese. Many of these tribes were
already dying out, and that was thirty years ago."

A paper boy stopped in front of them, belting out the evening head-
lines: "Louie Meyer wins Indy in four! Mussolini declares Italy an Empire! Remington Rand Strike, Day Five!" It seemed to Claire he was ring-
ing a gong. Time! Time! Time!

Shep finally bought a paper just to get rid of the kid. Then he shook
his head, as if having a silent conversation with himself. Without meeting
her eyes, he retrieved the book, flipped back to the introduction, and held
it for her inspection. "There's something else you need to consider, Claire."

Confused by his sudden gravity, she read where he was pointing: "'The
islands, save for the clearings of the—'" She looked at him. "'Penal Settlement'?"

He closed the book and lowered it to his lap. "Port Blair—the town
where I've been posted—was founded as a place to send India's political

prisoners. It's the only modern settlement in the islands, and technically, it's a penal colony."

Claire's bewilderment must have shown. He said, "I guess you Americans would call the inmates revolutionaries. The Indian nationalists call them freedom fighters." After the Sepoy Mutiny of 1857, he explained, the British Indian government decided to distance the leaders of the insurrection from their followers. "I expect the remoteness of the Andamans was their appeal for this purpose. Back then the place had a rather sordid reputation."

"But that was . . ."

"Eighty years ago."

"So this is ancient history."

"Not quite." The concern in his voice told her this was the real test he'd been dreading. "After the convicts finished building the settlement, the British put them to work on a jail, where the violent criminals could be held while their more peaceable comrades were sent to work the island's teak plantations and sawmills. The jail was completed around the time your Mr. Radcliffe-Brown arrived."

"I don't understand. You're making it sound like some sort of tropical gulag."

"Well, in a way I guess it was. Back then, anyway. But once the hardened types could be confined in the jail, the general atmosphere calmed down and the port began to flourish."

Now, Shep explained, the town of Port Blair was populated by Burmese and Indian convicts who'd been released for good behavior. These former prisoners had to remain in the Andamans but were otherwise free to marry or import their wives and children. They'd built settlements along the coast, started farms and businesses. Many chose to work as servants for the civilian and military administrators. "The officials live on an island that's set up as a cantonment across the harbor from the town. That's where the main hospital is—where I'll be based. The British there call it the Paris of the East—though I assume that's somewhat in jest."

"The Paris of the East," Claire deadpanned. Shep seemed to expect her to recoil at the notion of moving to a penal colony, but Port Blair sounded more bizarre than off-putting. Trouble was, she didn't yet know enough to know how to react. In Claire's experience, the history of the British Raj, the Sepoy Mutiny, the Indian Independence Movement, even that famous little man Gandhi amounted to no more than exotic newsreel images. If she had to pick a side, Shep was correct that she'd probably line up behind the freedom fighters, but it didn't sound as if it would come to that. Anyway, her primary destination was not this port or penal colony or whatever it was, but those "dense and lofty forests," where she envisioned herself spending most of her time among the islands' true and rightful inhabitants.

Why, then, did Shep look so sheepish?

"Am I supposed to be afraid?" she asked.

"It's not that." He chewed on the inside of his cheek. "But there are bound to be tensions . . . It's different from China, of course, yet I expect there'll be parallels. Colonial attitudes die hard in Asia, and the Brits aren't always as benevolent toward their 'loyal subjects' as they pretend to be." He scowled, perhaps remembering his childhood in Shanghai. His freckles and ginger cowlick sometimes reminded her so much of her brother, Robin, that Claire had to look away.

Whatever colonial tensions might await them, she sensed that they weren't what worried Shep most. No, he was more worried about her, afraid that she might not turn out to be the go-getter he imagined, the partner he needed as he returned to a world that obviously filled him with ambivalence. And she was hardly equipped to reassure him.

She leaned closer and placed her palm on *The Andaman Islanders*. "If Radcliffe-Brown could work his way around this wrinkle in paradise, then I ought to be able to, too."

She waited for him to meet her gaze, then reached for the bottle of cola, opened it and, ignoring the cups Shep so thoughtfully had arranged on the blanket, took a swig and passed him the bottle.

Shep returned her gesture with a smile as a streetcar clanged on Fifth Avenue. They watched two miniature sailboats collide on the pond in front of them, a group of children playing blind man's bluff on the hill beyond. Claire considered asking why Shep had pretended to know next to nothing about Port Blair, when he obviously knew plenty, but she let it go.

At length he took her hands. "I'll help you, you know. I mean, as much as I possibly can—what do you think?"

She held very still. "Are you suggesting we take the next step?"

A wave of relief—or, no, it was more like elation—charged his grin. "What's that thing Americans say?"

"What thing?"

"Like, *you're on.*"

"*You bet?*"

He shook her arms like reins. "You bet."

Four weeks later they were married in a small, stifling ceremony at home in Connecticut. Her father wept and her mother sat characteristically stiff and dry-eyed, a Yankee stoic through and through. Shep's sister, Vivian, sent a whimsical topiary elephant and best wishes from Sydney, where she was based as a foreign correspondent. Shep's parents, from their retirement village in Wales, sent proxy wishes in the form of a funereal tower of gladioli. After all, the bride and groom were bound for a penal colony.

Innocents, the two of them. Naifs willfully twisting omens into romantic curiosities.

Their first night at sea, Shep recited Kipling. They were lying stripped and spent, surprisingly yet deliciously renegade in their abandonment on the *SS Ormonde*'s upper deck. Lounge chairs like shadow sentinels stood guard against the August torpor, which had followed the ship from shore.

"'We've painted The Islands vermilion,'" he sang, soft and jubilant as Claire traced the Pleiades to reorient herself.

"'We've pearled on half-shares in the Bay,
We've shouted on seven-ounce nuggets,
We've starved on a Seedeeboy's pay.
We've laughed at the world as we found it—
Its women and cities and men—

From Sayyid Burgash in a tantrum
To the smoke-reddened eyes of Loben.'"

Dawn burnished the eastern horizon. She placed her ear to her new husband's heart and wondered at the whoosh.

Shep's geography was pale and angular next to her own softer honeyed flesh, and his exuberance soon yielded to a more studious intimacy. Back in the pink light of their stateroom he'd trace the curve of her jaw, the hollows behind her knees, the moles arrayed in the shape of a mouse just below her left breast.

Claire squirmed under this microscopic mapping. One night she caught his hand. "You touch me like I'm much more valuable than I really am."

But there was that fraudulent voice again. She felt as if she were trying to walk atop a giant ball. Could she pull it off, should she? Some part of this cavalier act must be true.

Another part was necessary. She lacked the nerve to make her admission without cover of jest. So, she lay back in the swirl of bedclothes, flung an arm above her head, and waggled her hips like a floozy. "Maybe I should have confessed up front, but then I thought, you're a worldly man."

Shep grinned too needily. He made the sign of a cross over her unclothed body before touching her hipbones, elbows, ribs. "*Semilunar fascia, serratus magnus, brachialus anticus, latissimus dorsi.*" The beautiful anatomical terms floated like an incantation of forgiveness.

"You're not secretly Catholic."

"Just a reverent doctor." He would not be rushed. He kissed the hairline scar across her sternum, the bitten cuticles of her right hand. He grazed the cap of short dark hair, each imperfection with his lips, his teeth.

"Tell me something I don't know about you."

He sighed and lay back, stared at the ceiling as if at a cinema screen. At length he said, "Back in Shanghai I used to make quite a pest of myself at the apothecary stalls. I'd pretend they were opium dens, and I was king of the devils."

"You mean, I've married a bad boy?"

He grinned. "You sound hopeful!"

"How exactly were you a pest?"

"I wanted to try everything. Ticked off the merchants to no end. They didn't dare shoo away little white boys—no telling who my father might be. On the other hand, they were bound to catch bloody hell if I got sick from their herbs and potions."

"What was the attraction?"

"Ah. Those places were everything I was forbidden. Dark and smelly and dank. Native and scary. The ginseng roots looked like shrunken scrotums."

"That appealed to you, did it?"

"When I was nine," he said as he stroked her thigh, "I didn't yet appreciate the importance of healthy testicles."

She slapped his hand. "Is there a story here?"

"Well. There were these botanical buttons that looked like stars and tasted like licorice. I pinched one and swallowed it as soon as I got home. Turned out, it cured constipation in thirty-four minutes flat. Vivvy timed it. You should have seen my father's face when I told him."

"Why on earth did you tell him?"

"More the fool, I thought he'd be interested. He threatened to sack the cook for taking me into the native quarter, and I got the belt, but that only taught me to keep my experiments secret. Lo and behold, other heathen cures worked better than any dose of Father's Kaputine, Piso's, or Cheracol."

She saw, finally. "You won."

He didn't answer, but then said, "It's the work I really want to do when we get to the Andamans, Claire. Those forests are like one great undiscovered apothecary shop. They could well contain the next medicinal miracle."

"Your very own treasure hunt." She gave her husband a kiss. "That makes two of us, I guess."

He raised himself up to look down at her. "Now you."

"Now me what?"

"Tell me what you should have confessed up front."

And though she'd rehearsed this a hundred times, still she fumbled for a way in. She pulled the sheet over her nakedness. "My parents. It's not what you think."

"What I think . . ."

"I mean, they're sad to see me leave, and maybe they blame you for taking me away, but it's not just that. Or, not just you. See, I had a little brother. He died when I was eleven. Drowned in the pond behind our house."

She'd never spoken of Robin like this. She'd never needed to. Her brother was no longer mentioned at home, and her other suitors had all been intent on pretending that life was a lark. The Depression did that to some people, but maybe not in China. And Shep wasn't a suitor anymore.

So, before he had time to react, Claire pressed ahead. Robin was eight years old. He wanted to play with her and the girl who'd come home with her after school, but Claire was jealous because this friendship was new and her gawky little brother embarrassed her, so she told him to get out of her room. The pond looked frozen but wasn't. Robin went out and never came back. Her parents insisted it wasn't her fault, but she knew better. She and the girl who'd been there that day could not so much as look at each other afterwards.

"For months I couldn't even face the mirror, much less talk about Robin." Ten years ago was one hundred twenty-seven months. "I remember he stuck out his tongue as he was leaving. Licorice was his favorite candy. His tongue was black with it."

Shep didn't move. "You loved him," he said. Not an exoneration, but not a question. An offering.

She thought he'd go on about a life without risk not being worth living, about her brother never intending to saddle her with guilt, about the mistake it would be to forever blame herself. The old, useless exhortations, which only her father had ever had the heart to even attempt.

Shep said, "Want to tell me about him?"

The answer that came to her startled her. "Someday."

He took her hand and cradled it, open-palmed, as he would a bird being willed to fly, and she knew she would forever remember this sensation, the spare architecture of his bones, solid as a bridge. A doctor's hand, she thought then. Surgical. Confident. She didn't yet know the truth of him, that his heart was his liability. Back in London, he'd nearly lost a child on the operating table because he couldn't bring himself to amputate the little girl's leg when there might yet have been a chance to save it. Five years old, that child was, her family too poor and too brown to justify a specialist, as if she deserved to be a practice case. Shep, only a resident, froze, unable to make the first incision, failing to recognize the sepsis hurtling through his patient's bloodstream. His chief surgeon had to step in, and this might have ended Shep's career but for the influence of his father, a Royal Medical Officer. Shep's "fellowship" in America was a form of exile, his posting to the Andaman Islands no plum but a booby prize that he was struggling to make his own.

Claire knew none of this that night in their stateroom on the *Ormonde*. Had he told her, matching her confession in order to placate or absolve her, or simply to come clean, would she have judged him weak? Or, would she have resented "his" child's survival and his own reprieve? Would just that much have broken the spell, or would she have loved him that much more for his ungodly humanity? He was wise not to trust her, not to take that risk. If he truly wanted her.

He did. She could tell that much even then without question, the way he held her, as if she were the lightest being imaginable. This was his true dare.

So she flipped her palm and touched his wrist, the tapestry of blue veins over pale stalks of bone, the weft of fine creases beneath an almost imperceptible nap of fine golden hairs. The pulse beneath the surface, proof of life in his skin. He watched her, waiting.

The nerve, her father had whispered. Another summer, four years earlier.

They were standing in front of Gauguin's *La Orana Maria*. Hail Mary. Polynesia, landed in New York City. Claire was in her first year at Barnard then, providing her father with a ready excuse to escape his

Depression-soaked law offices in Stamford for the illusory reprieve of Manhattan. The two of them explored museums the way they used to comb the beaches and woods of Connecticut after Robin. For uplift, he would say. Which was a good description of Claire's response to Gauguin's sinuous lines, rounded colors, and worshipful gestures, the serenity of the naked boy riding his mother's shoulder and the quietly mocking reverence of halos on a South Seas Madonna and child. While other museumgoers cleared their throats and muttered about shame, Claire longed to dive into that heat and lust and lose herself.

The painter's nerve, for her father, involved something else. As a boy, Tyler March would weave baskets out of willow peelings like the Algonquin Indians. Left alone he probably would have become a naturalist. *Like Thoreau, or Muir, or, God help me, Mr. Darwin.* Instead he became a probate attorney, like his father before him. He used to tell Claire his weakness was his reliance on the helping hand. She never believed him until she saw him in front of that painting, rivers pearling in his sad gray eyes, envy making him hoarse.

She'd heard his longing again in her ear when she repeated the words on her wedding day: *I do.* But her first view of the Andaman Islands put the lie to her own nerve.

First, a small uninhabitable pincushion of palm trees appeared on the turquoise sea. Then a massive green monolith rose behind it, like a waking dinosaur. The behemoth's coat of forest green undulated, dense and vast as a creature in its own right—a creature intent on driving the slender white snake of beach back into the ocean. This was North Andaman, the top of the island chain that would terminate for them in the south at Port Blair.

"There's no one there," she said, stunned by the confounding shimmer of beauty, humidity and primeval heat that seemed to pulse from shore.

"No see-ums," Shep quipped, but his heart wasn't in it, either.

Claire gripped the bulwark, fighting a spasm of nausea. His arm wound like a question mark around her waist. It didn't help.

Who did they think they were fooling? Both of them, impostors.

Over the next six hours the shoreline remained relentlessly wild. They spotted a couple of isolated coastal villages, but even these looked deserted. Then a distant lighthouse blinked. Atop a bluff beyond, a regimental block of concrete rose, spiked with gleaming antennae.

"There." Shep looked up from the gazetteer spread-eagled in his palm. Hope and relief cracked his voice as he pointed to the outer bank of Ross Island, their new home.

The hillock stretched like a long green breaker at the entrance to a harbor that abruptly bristled with boats. A mirage is how Claire would record this first impression. A miniature replica of a world she thought she'd left behind. A dark gothic church with a soaring steeple. The semblance of a town square and parade ground. Victorian houses along the ridge, with gabled roofs and wide verandas, pale gingerbread trim. The colonial residents themselves were scarce, but small brown figures in white uniforms appeared and disappeared among the towering shade trees. Their numbers multiplied toward the southern end of the island, where the western architecture yielded to a dark brick scramble of shop houses and the humanity of a bazaar. The Hindu temple on the waterfront resembled a multicolored stack of Life Savers.

The Ross cantonment was the seat of British power for the entire Andaman archipelago, but to reach it, they had first to continue across the harbor to disembark on the "mainland," where Port Blair proper stretched like a lizard's claw out of the forest's interior. There, white-washed bungalows like those throughout India ranged along the slopes, and high on the lizard's outmost knuckle stood an imposing fortress with rose-colored crenellations.

"The Cellular Jail," Shep said.

Claire gazed up at the pink castle walls. Inside—reputedly—the Raj's most hardened convicts sweltered. By design, the whole port functioned as one vast concentration camp, but since the inmates' dominant crime was their will to fight for independence, Claire felt far more disgust for their British overlords than she did any fear of the prisoners themselves. The anxiety playing across Shep's face told her he'd been dreading this reckoning as much as she'd been refusing to think about it. He was now working for those overlords, after all, and she was their subject by marriage.

"It's strangely picturesque," she offered. "Maybe things won't be so bad."

As if in confirmation, traveler's palms waved like giant hands welcoming them to Phoenix Bay Jetty, where the mood seemed downright festive. There, Europeans and Indians and everything in between—soldiers, civilians, and pukka sahibs, barefoot Indian and Burmese women wearing scarlet, turquoise, and canary yellow—called to arriving passengers. Children and pye-dogs scuttled around waiting rickshaws. Cries of *Jao!* and *Boy!* skittered across the harbor.

Suddenly the deck tipped, the anchor splashed, and Claire's gaze was thrown down and back toward the stern, where a dozen manacled convicts, who must have made the crossing inside the ship's bowels, stood waiting for a tender to take them ashore. A single voice had begun to chant, "*Inquilab Zindabad! Inquilab Zindabad!*" The others took it up. *Long live the Revolution!*

Claire and Shep had heard this and other nationalist slogans rising in the distance and behind closed gates during their weeklong stop-over in Calcutta, but this one now was chased by the sickening thwack of wood on flesh and bone. The victims screamed as the others fell silent. A rear gangway lowered. The prisoners shuffled onto the bobbing tender, prodded by their armed guards.

Shep took hold of Claire's elbow. She heard his voice climb. "Steady on, darling. No apologies, no regrets." It sounded like a plea.

They took a little wooden ferry back to Ross Island and tried to put the prisoners' cries behind them as they walked to the top of the ridge. There they landed in front of the low red gate to the Civil Surgeon's bungalow.

Shep flipped the latch, and they stepped through to a vivid green lawn ringed with coconut palms, birds of paradise, flaming heliconia, and orchids of every description. The bungalow itself had freshly whitewashed walls and a wide triangular red tin roof with gables at either end. A deep columned veranda ran the length of the house, overlooking the sea.

It was late in the afternoon. Thick stripes of jade-green ocean laddered to meet the sky. The air had a queer golden vitality, like jazz music made visible.

"We're home," Shep said, as if testing the gods.

"We're home," Claire answered, taking his hand.

"Welcome to paradise, my love."

The following morning, about an hour after Shep ventured across the yard to report for duty at the hospital, the servants arrived, shyly peering in the front door. Som was a careworn middle-aged man with a trim salt-and-pepper mustache and slicked-down hair emblazoned by a white streak over one temple. He seemed as reticent as his much younger wife, Jina, was bold, her confident warmth somehow enhanced by her red-stained teeth. Shep had hired the couple sight unseen, on the recommendation of his predecessor, who described them both as island-born and nominal Christians, descended from convicts but not criminals themselves and therefore worthy of trust.

When Claire invited them inside, Som bobbled his head in that Indian way that she'd learned could mean *Yes, Good, I understand, I'm pretending to understand, If you wish, If I must,* or *We shall see.* Jina's broad smile, however, spoke to Claire more directly. She held her muslin sari over her head and whispered to her husband in Urdu, the lingua franca of Port Blair.

Claire liked them for their sweetness toward each other and for their curiosity about her and Shep. It was decided that Jina could manage the house and cooking. Som, whose English was almost nonexistent, would handle gardening and maintenance. They'd live in the two-room servant quarters out behind the kitchen.

Only after all that was settled did Som beckon his daughter from the shadows where she'd been waiting across the yard. His and Jina's reference had not mentioned a child, but after her initial surprise, Claire found herself enchanted.

Naila was a very petite eight-year-old, with dark eyes almost too large for the delicate face that framed them. As she took in her new *memsaab*'s wrinkled shorts, the unpacked bags and parlor furnishings of the civil surgeon's bungalow, she seemed both shy and precocious, amused and critically attentive.

"But what will she do for school?" Claire asked. It was the first question that came to mind. Education was not a foregone conclusion for girls in India, and there was no school on Ross Island, since any European children here had long ago been shipped "home," but she could hardly accept this bright little girl *not* being educated on her watch.

Jina pushed the child back a step and signaled her to lower her eyes. "Aberdeen school on mainland, Memsaab."

"By boat each day?"

"Certainly, Mem."

"But who will take her?"

"She herself, Mem."

Claire, at once relieved and impressed by this plan, smiled at Naila, who clearly understood every word. She looked less Indian than either of her parents, more Burmese, or possibly Andamanese. Her hair was a glossy black and springy, cut nearly as short as Claire's own. Her nose was broad and flat, a little ungainly, but her figure was as fragile as her mother's was full, her eyes behind their long, thick lashes as lively as her father's, her skin a lovely pekoe color. Not pretty, exactly, but obviously perceptive.

When Claire put her palms together in an awkward salaam, Naila replied with a curtsy.

In the days that followed, Claire invited Naila to help shelve the library and was pleased to see the girl eagerly leafing through each book before placing it. She seemed particularly fascinated by the photographic plates in *The Andaman Islanders*. Apparently, she'd never encountered any native Andamanese herself, though one picture, she said, resembled the layabout Porubi in Aberdeen Bazaar. "But," she added, "Porubi at least is keeping his clothing on."

Claire noted the disparagement in her voice. She wondered where it stemmed from.

"What is this book, Mem?"

"It's the story of the people who lived in these islands before you or I or even your parents were born, Naila. The people whose ancestors came here first. They still live in the interior, you know. Have you never seen any yourself?"

"The naked people."

There was that same disapproval, but this time flatly matter-of-fact. Claire asked, "Is that what you've been taught to call them?"

Naila swayed her head back and forth like her father. She told Claire that everyone in Port Blair—Europeans and locals alike—viewed the naked people as pests because they were strange and dirty and ugly to see, uncivilized. When the British began to build Port Blair, they fought the largest of the tribes in the Battle of Aberdeen and nearly wiped out the Great Andamanese entirely. Teacher Sen said the surviving forest people still raided settlements and plantations up north, and some of the most remote islands had tribes that were said to be cannibals. Most of the naked people still used spears and arrows, however, so they were no match for British guns. The girl wrinkled her nose at the picture of an aboriginal couple seated rigidly, perhaps ritualistically, back to back and staring in opposite directions. "They are not looking real."

Eventually, Claire would deduce that Naila's father himself had a grandmother from the forest, but she'd died before he was born, and he and Jina never mentioned her, instead instructing Naila to say that she had Tamil ancestors, dark people from south India being racially preferable to the indigenous Andamanese, and "local-born" designating a class meaningfully distinct from "native." Prejudice in British India, Claire would learn, was actively transferable and widely embraced.

She persevered with Naila. "The Andamanese tribes have lived here for thousands of years. They've survived in the forest without schools or farms or motor cars. Without hospitals—or prisons, either." She tapped the book the girl was still holding. "The man who wrote this is called an anthropologist. It's his job to learn how they survived."

"Are you antha-ro-po—"

"Not yet. But I'm trying to figure out how to become one, and I hope the Andamanese can help me." She glanced up. "And you, Naila? What do you want to be when you grow up?"

The question caught the girl off guard. Her grandfather had trained as a chemist before his arrest, but as the son of a convict, her father was forbidden to receive a proper education. He often told Naila that she was different, and India, too, would soon be different. Great leaders like Gandhiji were working to persuade the British to send the freedom fighters back to their home states, and once that happened, their local-born children and grandchildren also would be allowed to leave these islands and make a different future for themselves.

In Calcutta there is a street called College Street. Someday, daughter, you will go there to study and you will make us so proud. And her mother agreed, *You go to school, you learn with all your might, and one day you will cross that water.* Jina would fling her arm at the horizon as if scattering seed. *Daughter, you—*

Naila never let her mother finish. She was drawn to maps and books about the world beyond the sea, but she'd never spent even one night away from Port Blair or apart from her parents. She didn't want to become someone different than she was, especially not if it meant she must leave those she loved.

Claire said, "Well, I'm not so sure who I'm going to be, either, so let's try to help each other figure it out." She extended her hand.

Naila slid her fingertips tentatively along the outstretched palm.

Claire clasped Naila's fingers. "Friends?"

The child stared at their joined hands and answered in a voice so grave, she sounded apologetic even as she echoed, "Friends."

The next week, Shep discovered that the hospital *chowkidar* belonged to one of the island's forest tribes. Though still in his teens, the boy spoke excellent missionary English, and he also knew the native uses for all the local flora. Young Leyo was being wasted as night watchman, so Shep hired him to help Som establish a medicinal garden. Then he sent him over to see if Claire would like him to tutor her.

Would she!

"My people," Leyo told her. "Biya people."

His features resembled those of Radcliffe-Brown's subjects, but he'd evidently accommodated to the western custom of clothing. He carried a cloth sack and wore a white singlet and coral sarong, albeit without shoes. His hair was cropped close to his scalp and parted by a broad straight line shaved from his left temple all the way back and down to his neck. He barely came up to Claire's collar bone.

He had volumes to teach her. "*Aka* Biya," he said grinning. "*Aka* mean *mouth-talk*. Together we *aka* Biya"

Elated at her good luck, Claire asked him to spend an hour with her each morning. But he presented a couple of challenges that she hadn't expected.

For one, he'd spent enough time in Port Blair that his command of his language had been diluted with Urdu. In fact, he told her, the only one left who spoke pure Biya was his headman, Kuli, who lived with the rest of his clan in the forest to the north.

The second challenge was the Biya's entirely separate nonverbal language. To explain, Leyo gestured with his palm to his crown, then his chest. "Spirit talk is for head, for heart; silent, still we hear."

Among the Biya people, if Claire understood him correctly, this silent spirit talk was valued more than the language of words. The language of the spirit was communal and empathic. It was also the language of nature. Leyo told her he'd noticed in Port Blair that neither Europeans nor Indians could speak this spirit language, but in his tribe, newborns learned naturally to communicate through silence with the world around them. Gestures and expressions of spirit conveyed warnings, exhortations, and concerns from the Biya god Biliku, as well as shared feeling, from the heart.

Speech, in contrast, was transactional, used for trade, planning, or resolution of problems. It was needed most when a member of the tribe needed to leave or when the communal bond was threatened by conflict—when dealing with outsiders, for example.

This lesson would alternately console and torment Claire in the years to come, but at this point the concept of talk without words seemed alluring. It filled her mind that same afternoon when she rode across the harbor to shop in Aberdeen.

In the bazaar, languages streamed together. Her fellow foreigners—mostly British, but also French and Dutch and various admixtures—all seemed helpless to understand each other without raising their voices. Likewise, most of the mainland-born Indians and Burmese, of whom there were many more, chattered nonstop in Urdu, Karen, Hindi and Marathi. Among both groups, silence seemed synonymous with isolation or disconnection, with fear or shame. Witness the town vagabond skulking at the entrance to an alley off the bazaar.

She spotted him sitting cross-legged across the street. His skin was so dark that he would have blended invisibly into the shadows but for his filthy red shirt and tattered khaki shorts and those bloodshot eyes, which shone bright and mad within the haggard frame of his face. This was surely the poor soul Naila had called Porubi. Apart from Leyo, he was the only Biya anyone seemed to know outside the forest—and by all appearances he was unreachable as well as mute. Remembering Dr. Benedict's irate descriptions of government agents plying American Indians with whiskey, Claire had to turn away as this Porubi hoisted his own brown toddy jug. Isolation. Fear. Shame. The very sight of him filled her with all of that.

She climbed the whitewashed steps of the Kobayashi Kodak Shoppe and found peace at last. The front of the store was empty. An electric fan whirred from the ceiling. She touched the brass counter bell.

Floorboards creaked behind a black curtain, and a small, trim man and woman wearing matching steel-rimmed spectacles and white cotton jackets came through and bowed across the desk. Claire tentatively bowed back.

"May we help?" The man spoke English as if it hurt his mouth.

"I'm Mrs. Durant," she said. "The new Civil Surgeon's wife."

The woman let out a small exhalation, then bowed quickly again. Coming up she smoothed the tight black bun at the nape of her neck and gave Claire a gentle smile.

"Welcome to Port Blair," the man said. "We are Kobayashi. Husband, wife."

After an awkward pause when they all seemed to run out of conversation, Claire reached into her purse for the films that she'd shot aboard the ship and around Ross. The husband and wife began opening and closing drawers, exchanging and marking packets for the film without exchanging a word. A young Sikh MP entered. Mrs. Kobayashi, still mute, showed him the print he'd ordered, and counted his payment before bowing him out.

When Claire inquired how long they'd lived in Port Blair, Mr. Kobayashi whispered to Mrs. Kobayashi, who smiled at Claire from behind a cupped palm. It didn't seem a complicated question, but apparently it required a conference.

"Five year," Mr. Kobayashi said at last and handed her the chits for her films. "This is a good place. We are happy you come."

Claire wanted to shake their hands, but she found herself instead salaaming. As they bowed her out, Mrs. Kobayashi winked at her, and she felt as if they were enacting some arcane comedy of gestures, but not even this friendly pantomime compared to the silent language Leyo had described. What all the non-natives had in common was dependence on verbal thought; without words, neither reason nor understanding could occur. Not so among Leyo's people.

"We'd call that mind reading," she said when they met for their next lesson. "A power that many equate with magic, if they believe it exists at all."

"Magic." Leyo smiled at the pale palms of his dark hands.

"I don't imagine there's any hope for me."

He looked perplexed.

"I mean, to learn your silent language."

He led her out onto the porch and pointed at the sea, which lay matte beneath a metallic sky, the day's heat crushing the surface like a blotter. "You hear?"

"I hear the waves." A soft concussion from the beach.

Leyo shook his head and stabbed the air. She saw the angry brown spot that he was indicating far to the east, like a divot chipped from the sky. "Big storm there."

"And you can hear that in the waves?"

He grinned. "Big water, big mouth."

"In your camp, everyone can speak the water's language, then?"

"Yes."

"Even little children?"

"Yes."

"And the forest has a big mouth, too?"

He covered his ears, laughing. Then he drew a gestured line from his eyes to the storm at sea to the closer waves, and finally to Claire. He didn't speak a word: Tonight, there would be rain.

The unspoken language wasn't silent at all, she thought. It must be positively cacophonous, once you learned to hear it. She remembered Professor Benedict quoting Chief Seattle's plea to Franklin Pierce: *My words are like the stars that never change . . . Even the rocks, which seem to be dumb and dead as the swelter in the sun along the silent shore, thrill with memories of stirring events connected with the lives of my people, and the very dust upon which you now stand responds more lovingly to their footsteps than yours, because it is rich with the blood of our ancestors, and our bare feet are conscious of the sympathetic touch . . . In all the earth there is no place dedicated to solitude.*

She said, "I am deaf and dumb."

1937

Mosquito boots. Bush trousers. Topi with netting. Field tent. Binoculars. Insect repellant. Snakebite kit. Sulfa, tablets and powder. "What did R-B take?" Shep asked.

Claire had no idea. There was no field manual for ethnographers. But then, their first weekend exploration would hardly qualify as a professional field study.

They'd secured a naval launch to take them up the coast. With Leyo leading, this would shave the two-day trek to two or three hours from the point where they landed. So easy, it seemed like cheating.

"Excited?" Shep asked as they crossed the empty parade ground to the pier. It was that sinister hour before dawn when trees looked black and water red, and the sky seemed at war with itself.

"I'm glad we're doing this together," Claire said.

"You all right?" He examined her with concern.

For a moment, she wondered if he saw through her. She'd lost weight and often complained that the Atabrine he insisted they take against malaria made her feel as sickly as it made them both look. The warning signs screamed, yet she'd admitted nothing, and he'd promised to support her in this work. Now—January—was the coolest month, the safest and most bearable for trekking. The duration was what really worried her.

Three days was nothing, she scolded herself and gestured toward the sky. "It's going to be a scorcher."

Reynold, the naval lieutenant in charge of the boat, had a Cockney accent, sun-bleached hair, and a tan that Cesar Romero would envy. He'd charted every inch of the Andaman coastline, he told them. No one knew the islands better. Then, with a sidelong glance as Leyo secured their packs, he muttered that he'd seen enough of the blacks up north to know never to trust one of them.

Claire beat a quick retreat with Leyo to the canopied bow while Shep stayed aft to occupy Reynold. Fortunately, the lieutenant was a punctual man who obeyed his orders, and as soon as they were off, the noise of the outboard muffled his further remarks.

The sun broke through as the launch sped north past the tricorn bulge of Mount Harriet—as Shep said, a drumlin that only homesick Europeans would think of upgrading to mountain status—and in minutes the lighthouses on Ross and North Point were behind them. The coastline thickened with mangroves and towering ficus trees, the water turning from celadon to cobalt, and the sand burned so white it seemed to percolate under the brooding sky.

Coconut palms lined the beach like sentries as their Indian pilot spouted British names: *Kyd Island. Napier Bay. Neil. Havelock.* The Union Jack snapped in the sea spray.

An hour later they entered the forest, Leyo in his element. Even under their largest pack, his bare feet skipped over vines the size of pythons, shoulders swooped beneath fallen trunks. His close-cropped hair escaped the nettles, twigs, thorns, and creepers that bedeviled Claire and Shep as they stumbled along single-file, struggling for footing on the bottomless sponge that passed for ground, for breath in the gaseous heat of decay that seemed to envelop them.

A hornbill, like some prehistoric aviator, sailed beneath the canopy. A stream materialized to their right. Emerald green monitor lizards followed their progress, and toads the size of rabbits scuttled between the fern fronds.

Gradually, as their eyes adjusted to the viscous light, they began to spot the orchids high in the branches or clinging to trunks, trailing plumes or shooting small explosions of color. Once Shep and Claire got the hang of it, as if mastering a child's game of hidden pictures, they saw them everywhere.

A field guide from the settlement library having served as Shep's primer, he managed to identify even from afar the basic contours of lady's slippers, *Dendrobium*, giant *Vanda*, and the delicate winged grace of *Phalaenopsis*. But these were altogether different species from those that grew near the port. Some blooms here were the size of helmets. Some transparent as ghosts. A few moved as if breathing, though eventually they realized this was because the stems were covered with ants. Some, even at a distance of several yards, gave off powerful fragrances or stinks. And many, suspended from their host trees by nearly invisible threads, appeared to float in mid-air.

Mesmerized to distraction, Claire tripped and went down. Shep was on her in an instant, but she waved him off.

"I'm fine. These damned boots!"

She smelled the change before she understood it. Still prone in the decaying leaves, she caught a whiff of oil and sweat, a shift in atmospheric tempo. In her periphery she had the impression that Leyo's feet had multiplied and wondered if she was hallucinating. Then two pairs of hands gripped her arms, hauled her up, and she saw that the new feet belonged to two small young men—or boys—who looked just like the pictures in Radcliffe-Brown, except for their lively movements. One had tonsured his scalp. The other wore two conical tufts, like horns of hair, rising from his otherwise shaved head. Their eyes seemed huge and wet and black in their lean faces.

The newcomers laughed, bantering with Leyo in the language he'd begun to teach her, except that in their throats the phrases seemed to twitch. They plucked at her hair and clothing, and she and Shep both stood speechless. Fascinated. Confounded. Only when the Biyas' two yellow dogs found them and, tongues in a lather, leapt toward Claire, did Shep snap back into himself. He stepped to shield her and pulled her behind him, away from the others.

"Hang on, old girl," he whispered, and this time she did.

The Biya camp consisted of a narrow clearing with thatched shed-like structures that housed fewer than a dozen people, most clad only in a belt of leaves or shells. The Biyas decorated their skin with dried yellow clay. A few wore twine necklaces, women bare-breasted, and all but the youngest were scarred in distinctive patterns up and down their torsos. None stood taller than five feet.

Claire glanced at Shep, whose delighted expression mirrored her feelings exactly. They had done it. They had entered a time capsule by leaving almost everything familiar behind and discovered a reality so strange and new yet ancient that it made every nerve in her body quiver. Except, of course, that they hadn't actually discovered anything. The Biya had been living here all along. She and Shep were simply catching up.

They needed to appear at ease. She must keep clear mental notes until she could get to her field journal. She had to become what Professor Benedict called an inconspicuous observer. But how?

"Just act natural," Shep breathed as they followed Leyo to the center of the clearing.

"Natural to who?" It was an honest question. Everything from their ground cloths and netting to mosquito boots must seem preposterous to the Biya. As would her desire to study this clan.

Then something released in her. How would she feel if some stranger from an alien world asked to watch her every move? The Biya were no different. *No different.* Treat them with respect and compassion, not condescension. Trust that they know what they're doing, even if you don't. Show the genuine interest of a friend, not the intrusiveness of a voyeur.

An older woman with a frizz of gray hair and a man's blue necktie looped around her broad belly stepped from one of the huts. Leyo embraced himself, then hugged the woman, who responded by patting his face and tugging at his singlet with amused disapproval. He'd told them he had just one living relative, an auntie named Mam Golat. "*Umimi,*" he called her now. Aunt, or great aunt, or adoptive aunt—Claire wasn't sure which, and Leyo didn't immediately introduce them.

Instead he motioned them toward a male elder with pronounced lips and eyes. Kuli was the smallest of the adults, with slender limbs and a sequence of horizontal scars forming a ghostly ladder from right to left up his torso. He wore a headdress of grass that resembled a blond wig and a matching necklace that covered his collarbones. His cheeks were high and wide, his bearing regal, his composure absolute.

Chief Kuli pursed his lips, looked the foreigners solemnly up and down, then grinned and crossed his arms over his chest.

Claire made the same cross, nodding slightly in deference. Shep followed suit, then dug in his pocket for the gifts that Leyo had recommended. A pair of shoelaces. A pair of tin spoons. A candle and a box of wooden matches. *Nothing to eat, sniff, or drink.*

Kuli took the gifts in his leathered hands and raised them level with his chin, then turned them over to Mam Golat. His attitude was so calm and practiced that Claire couldn't help asking Leyo, "Did you tell him we were coming?"

Leyo waggled his hand like an Indian headshake and turned back to confer with the headman.

"How could he?" Shep asked Claire. "He hasn't been off Ross long enough to make this trip, and there's not exactly postal service."

"True," she said. "Maybe Kuli's just naturally hospitable." Or perhaps, she thought, the Biyas' silent language traveled.

Animated conversation now burst around them as the rest of the clan resumed their chores. Talk, Claire, reminded herself, was reserved for problems and planning. Were she and Shep deemed a problem? She listened for the full-throated phonetics that Leyo had been struggling to teach her. Sixteen vowels, sixteen consonants. Amid the clicking and tapping and uvular gulps, she managed to make out only the words for *hair, skin, hands, white, snake.*

The last, on the menu for lunch, was a huge reticulated python being sliced beside the cookfire.

Claire shifted her focus to ward off a wave of nausea and noticed a toddler approaching on a club foot, swaying from side to side. He had a round belly and an amiable smile and seemed to have no sense that his deformity was a handicap.

Shep knelt in front of the child, offering his pith helmet as a plaything. With glee the boy plunked the topi over his own head and peered out like a tortoise from its shell. Shep proceeded to play peekaboo with him while Claire looked around for the child's mother.

There were two possible candidates. One thickset young woman with shaved eyebrows laughed and chided the boy. The other, whose buck teeth gave her frown the quality of a rictus, yanked the child roughly away from Shep, sending the topi rolling and the little boy tottering off toward the dogs. Parenting appeared to be a communal enterprise.

Claire fingered her Kodak. Photographs would help. With images, she and Leyo could discuss the roles and relationships of everyone in the clan.

A young girl, perhaps nine or ten, stood in front of her offering a pithed coconut. In Port Blair, vendors along the beach peddled freshly hacked coconuts whose water was refreshing, if tasteless. This liquid, however, was dark and silty, and Claire only pretended to sip it before handing the shell back with thanks to the girl.

The girl stayed, gawking. Still flat-chested with the pudgy limbs of a child, even she had been scarred. The featherlike markings covered her belly. She wore a dirty white band resembling surgical gauze around her forehead, and her mowed hair was divided like two sides of a brain by a shaved path straight down the middle. Her bright eyes studied Claire with bold intensity.

Claire pointed to herself, spoke her name, then pointed to the girl and lifted the camera. The girl grabbed it.

"Ekko!" Leyo cried and pried the device from her hands.

Claire offered Ekko her compact as a consolation prize. When she showed her the mirror inside, the child was transfixed. Soon the entire clan surrounded them. Claire asked Leyo to explain that the Kodak worked like a mirror in a box. It would borrow the clan's reflections, and on her next visit to Behalla she would give their reflections back to them on paper.

The adults had heard of cameras. Some of their forebears who'd escaped from the old Andaman Home had brought back photographs from their time on Ross Island. Leyo told her that Kuli actually remembered Radcliffe-Brown, who'd spent several months in this area when the chief was young. The others didn't understand why white people wanted to look at the Biya people, but they understood that they some-times did, and soon everyone went back to their chores, except for the club-footed toddler.

Shep whistled to hold the child's attention as he studied his move-ments. "He is called Jodo," Leyo said.

"Where are his parents?"

"His brother Tika." Leyo indicated the younger of the friends who had met them in the forest. Tika looked close to Leyo's own age. He was now squatting beside the girl Ekko.

"Mother Obeyo," Leyo said, causing the bucktoothed woman to scowl up from the root she was mashing.

Shep asked Leyo to translate his request to her. "Jodo is young enough. If we brought him to town, I could operate on his foot. I could make him well enough to walk."

Claire, who was photographing this conference, sensed Leyo's reluc-tance as she released the shutter. Had he flinched? Pursed his mouth? Nothing so obvious as a negative word or even a frown. He would nev-er directly oppose the surgeon of Port Blair. But she could tell that he parsed his words carefully in the relay to the boy's mother, and with good reason from the looks of her.

Obeyo's reply was short and curt and required no translation.

The brother Tika suddenly snatched the compact from young Ekko's hands and ran off with her in pursuit. Leyo said to Shep, "Come. I show you the scorpion flower."

Claire thought her husband would press his case for the little boy now laboring after the two older children. Jodo's locomotion twisted him sideways, so he landed on his ankle as if it were his heel. She knew it could be relieved with a relatively simple operation, but simplicity itself was a culturally relative term.

Shep rose, turning from Obeyo's glower to ask Claire if she want-ed to come with him. She waved him off. Become invisible, Professor Benedict would advise, or at least unobtrusive. She and Shep were less obtrusive apart.

She found a spot of deeper shade by the corner of the long hut and shrank into it, swallowing another surge of nausea. Nearby, the young woman with no eyebrows lifted and dropped a heavy stick into a bowl of seeds.

Her name was Imulu. She might be fifteen, or thirty, for all Claire could tell. Her head was shaved clean around the back so that her remaining hair resembled a glistening caracul skullcap. She had a sturdy build and wore a diagonal sling of woven birchbark across her heavy round breasts. Occasionally she threw Claire an inscrutable glance as the stick fell. *Thunk.*

Claire lifted the camera and, since the woman made no protest, was about to snap the shutter when the rhythm broke and her subject reached into the shadows behind the bowl. An instant later Imulu was hoisting an infant from a bed of pandan leaves.

Claire's pulse quickened as the baby snuggled into its sling and latched onto the young mother's breast. This time when Imulu looked her way, Claire felt exposed, as if this stranger could read her every fear, every pretense that had brought her here and, most clearly of all, the primal condition that was destined to thwart her ludicrous ambitions. Far from the hostile glares of Radcliffe-Brown's Andamanese, Imulu's face bloomed with good-natured derision.

Before she could react, however, Shep reappeared with an armload of blooming white specimens. He looked thrillingly young and happy.

"*Eria kurzii!*" he cried.

Field notes
   January 20, 1937

By most accounts, the trip was a success. This morning I heard Leyo boasting to Som and Jina that memsaab tasted snake in the forest. The story of our great adventure seems to amuse him no end. That we went at all earns us gold stars. That we cut it short earns black marks only in my own book.

I did survive my first taste of snake and one night in the field, but the next day's boar did me in. When I crawled back to the fire after losing my lunch, Imulu grinned as if I were the most pathetic excuse for a female she'd ever laid eyes on. I suspect she'd detected my secret from the start but thought I was too dumb even to know I'm pregnant. At this point in my disgrace, however, I realized that she'd been trying all morning to model the Biya way of motherhood for me, and I had been too dumb to see that these lessons in infant caretaking were offered in charity.

Shep, alas, took one look at my pasty face and insisted we head back to Ross.

It took everything I had to convince him I didn't need to be carried.

I felt better as soon as the stink of boiling pig fat was behind us, but then the trek absorbed me, and only when we reached the beach, as Shep was checking his watch, did I regain the presence of mind to ask how the launch would know to come for us.

He scuffed his boot heel in the sand and told me not to be angry. He'd arranged for Lieutenant Reynold to make a run past the cove each day at four o'clock—just in case.

To top it off, he took me by the shoulders and kissed my forehead. Despite all the layers of grime and sweat and citronella. Had he really asked me not to be angry with him?

Of course, I couldn't get away scot-free. Claire, darling, he said. Damn stupid, all things considered, but now the cat's out . . .

No future field trips for me. Claire, darling. He'd caught me cold being selfish and foolhardy, and many another husband would be far less forgiving. But I don't regret this first foray, brief and fraught as it was. Night in the jungle was a misery of heat and wet and biting, stinging, whining, crawling creatures against which our puny net offered little defense, but we saw the Biya dance. We listened to them chant. Shep up and stomping with the other young men. Leyo's head thrown back in delight as the full moon breached that penny of sky far at the top of the canopy.

I can still feel the quiet pressure on each of my fingertips in turn as Kuli took my hand in his and tried to teach me the correct sounds of the old Biya language—sounds that Leyo gets all wrong. Before I ruined everything, Shep had gone out twice with Leyo and Imulu's husband, Sempe, and they collected more than a dozen orchid specimens while I stayed with Kuli and the women.

I learned from old widow Mam Golat how to boil a boar and how the wily Imulu worked while simultaneously nursing little Artam—

Breast feeding. God help me. Am I ready for this?

If only I'd managed to hold on. If I were Ruth Benedict or Margaret Mead, I'd have been living with Leyo's people for weeks by now. Pregnancy would never hold them back, much less childbirth.

No, they'd give birth right in the field, presided over by the old grandmother and chief. Then they'd mine every minute for cultural significance and write a bloody book about it.

༄

The monsoon was in full swing by the time she went into labor. All through the hospital, pails had been set out to catch the leaks, around which teams of lizards raced, little phantoms against the furred green stains of mildew. Fists of rain slammed against the tin roof as Claire counted through her contractions, and the young Indian nurses hummed as they wiped her brow. The daring giggled at Shep's lanky presence brooding through the hours.

He steadied himself by folding a two-month-old *Times* into birds of paradise, an island diversion he'd picked up from Som. The nurses offered him tea and sweets, as unaccustomed to the presence of fathers during labor as they were to viewing their chief surgeon as a human being.

Claire told him to go tend to his other patients, but his only other patients at the moment were waiting for elective procedures on the mainland.

"You're stuck with me."

"Then do something useful."

"You're irritable."

"You try pushing a watermelon out between your thighs."

"I might have to go back to America to find one."

"Go, then!"

He went. She screamed. Dr. Ratna Bose—the "ladies' doctor"—swept in and monitored Claire's progress with a magisterial wave.

But now she felt abandoned. What if the baby came before he returned? What if something went wrong? It would all be her fault. She knew she wasn't thinking straight, but she couldn't help it. She shouldn't have driven him away.

She began to shiver as the nurses mopped her brow. "Where did he go?"

"It is just as well. Gentlemen don't belong in maternity wards." Dr. Bose parked her fists on ample hips. "Especially gentlemen doctors."

And then she was seized by another spiral of pain and could think of nothing else.

Four contractions later Shep returned, breathless, bearing something in a bell jar. He set the wooden base on the table beside her bed. Under the glass a yellow orchid bloomed with the face of a monkey.

He removed the bell and squeezed the monkey's jaws between his fingers like she and Robin used to do with snapdragons when she was a child. Shep put no words in its mouth. Instead he gently bent the stem so the monkey appeared to dance as he hummed the "Waltz of the Flowers."

The nurses gaped from the doorway until Dr. Bose shooed them away. Claire, weeping, was midway through it before she noticed the next contraction.

"Who *are* you?" she demanded when the agony shuddered off again.

He blazed his dazzling gap-toothed grin. "Damned if I've the foggiest."

One hour later, young Tyler Durant emerged on the crest of a final convulsive push. He let out a polite but voluble cry, measured eight pounds, twenty inches, and had all requisite fingers and toes, plus big pink ears and a velvety shag of chestnut hair, eyes that blinked at the strange world around him as if calculating its weight.

Claire was speechless when their son was placed in her arms. Shep leaned over them both.

"Hallo, young Ty," he greeted their son. "Welcome home, little man."

Naila bonded with the baby right from the start. Bookish and shy, she seemed to have few friends of her own. She preferred to orbit around her parents, and caring for Ty gave her an excuse to stay close. Every day she'd race home from school to help Jina tend and play with him. She'd sit on her haunches memorizing the lullabies that Claire sang, and with the slightest encouragement, she'd chant him ditties in Urdu. She was tender and careful, as attentive as her mother—both of them as gentle as any trained ayah Claire could imagine.

Shep wasn't so sure. "There's a line between servants and family in Asia," he said one night in bed. "It can get blurry, but it's best not to forget it's there."

However well-intentioned, the warning landed like an affront. Claire tried but failed to keep her voice light. "You sound like your father."

For several seconds, she heard only the breath of the surf outside. Then, "That's a low blow."

The sting of hurt surprised Claire. "Sorry. It's something I'd *imagine* your father saying. Remember, I've never met the man."

"And I intend to keep it that way." He rolled toward her, found the tip of her nose and kissed it in truce, but she took note. However much Shep loathed his father, the arrogant colonialist, he might have more in common with him than he cared to admit or even realized.

As far as Claire was concerned, Naila was simply a wonder. One day the child demonstrated how, when she was little, she used to press her face to the kitchen screen so the wires would carve the world outside into squares that made her feel safe. Then, when she started school, her teacher Sen fastened a map of the earth onto Naila's classroom wall, and the crisscross of latitude and longitude gave her a similar sense of security, a way to manage—to bear—the immensity of all that she could not fathom.

Teacher Sen's map became a new screen through which she traced continents, oceans, mountains. *These are our islands*, Naila would repeat and show on Claire's map how her teacher stabbed at the pale blue Bay of Bengal, how he ran his forefinger up and down the spine of green bits marked *Andaman Nicobar Archipelago*. Then he would sweep both palms outward as if to embrace the wall—*but all of this is our home.*

When he spun to face the class—Naila reenacted the movement—Teacher Sen's spectacles often fell from their perch atop his bulging forehead, and he'd catch them with a flourish in his left hand even though he wrote with his right, and he never stopped talking about the miracle of geography as he performed this feat. *Master the map and you master the world. That is how the British did it.*

His other pupils sniggered and picked their noses and ridiculed him behind his back, but Naila understood. The British came from a place that occupied barely one square of the map's screen, while India and Burma spread over more than ten squares. How could people from such a small place rule over a land so far away and so much larger than their own?

Claire had no answer, but Teacher Sen did. *Map mastery.* Like Naila in her mother's kitchen, the British stayed securely at home with themselves, yet by mastering the map, they owned the world on the other side of the screen.

Naila imagined floating invisibly through that screen and descending into scenes she'd glimpsed only in photographs and illustrations. Cities, palaces, deserts, and lakes. Teacher Sen said it snowed where he grew up, in Kalimpong. He tried to describe the towering mountains of his childhood, but for Naila, such natural wonders were as foreign as skyscrapers. She loved to dream of them even if she never expected or would dare to visit them in real life.

She told Claire about the day she came home from school to the news that she and her parents would soon be leaving the house with the blue gate where they had lived since she was born, that they were to move across the harbor to Ross Island to work for the new British doctor and his American wife. To Naila, it felt as if America herself was coming to Port Blair!

America seemed the most exotic country of all. Larger on the map than England and India combined, home to the Empire State Building and the Grand Canyon, to Charlie Chaplin and The Marx Brothers, who sometimes appeared in moving pictures at Aberdeen Cinema. The funny men Naila liked, but she didn't know what to make of the cinema ladies who hiked up their skirts and drove motorcars and kissed men full on the lips. No one behaved like that in Indian movies, let alone in Naila's own experience, but Americans seemed to have bigger spirits even than the British. Would the new *memsaab* also have a big spirit? Her ma had laughed at such childish excitement and said she hoped so.

Claire took the girl's hand and replied that her spirit paled next to Naila's.

The baby appeared to think so, too. One afternoon Claire came out of her study to find Naila alone with Ty in the parlor. Naila, in her blue school uniform, sat cross-legged on the divan with Ty Babu, as she called him, in her lap. Neither the infant nor the girl noticed Claire. Naila was too busy feeding him.

All she had was a bottle of water, but her head tipped birdlike to one side, arms nesting the baby against her. *Beautiful,* was Claire's first thought. *Precious.* But it was more than that.

Naila held that bottle like a sacred object, and as he sucked, Ty kept his gaze locked on the girl's. He caught a red thread from the stitching in her blouse, and the intensity with which he rubbed it, between his thumb and middle finger, made it seem a gesture of devotion.

November 15, 1937

Happy birthday, dear Vivvy!

I'm sending this care of your editor in Sydney, though you're doubtless raising muck up and down the Malay. I hope as I write this that you're having a bang-up celebration.

As for us, it's been rather a turbulent year in paradise. Ty is the highlight, of course. In my entirely unbiased opinion, the boy is abso-blooming brilliant. At five months he swims like a fish and sits like a dog. Any day now he'll be babbling Aka Biya—the language of the people Claire is studying.

Or trying to, between setting up the nursery and fielding congratulatory visits from the cantonment matrons. My bride has become a stunning young mother, and she dotes on Ty, as do we all. Occasionally she grumbles about getting back out in the field, but I remind her that patience is a virtue.

Happily, I'm not quite so constrained. Just yesterday I made an excursion that might interest you, to a convict settlement called Ferrargunj—one of about sixty built around the archipelago over the past half century by released prisoners and their wives. Ferrargunj is one of the few not on the outer coastline. It sits near an inland river, which allows the Ferrargunjians to clear the valuable inland timber and send it by raft down to the sawmill here in Port Blair.

My official purpose was to check on the village dispensary, though "official" is a slight stretch. Technically, these village rounds are the duty of my second-in-command, Lt. Gupta, but Gupta's more British than I'll ever be and seems to consider the convict settlers so far beneath him that he can't be bothered to spit on them. As part of my collegial appeasement policy, I've elected to visit these outpost dispensaries myself. Two birds, as they say. I always take our man Leyo with me and, after I treat a few raging sores and machete wounds and the standard quota of malarial cases, we go orchid hunting.

Yesterday we also had a forest officer to see we didn't lose our way. Not much chance of that with Leyo along, but the forester, one Luke Benegal, was a fine chap, and I was lucky to have them both, since we discovered a giant Grammatophyllum speciosum *in the crotch of an ancient marblewood tree. This particular orchid is not only rare and enormous, but the aboriginals use it as a cure for scorpion and centipede poisoning. It blooms only once every two years, and this one was covered with spears of beautiful leopard-spotted blossoms! The whole thing must have weighed over a ton, but we managed to wrestle off a single root bundle that we could hoist between the three of us. As we staggered back to the boat, Leyo pointed out a dozen more specimens that I'd have given my eye to collect, but this trophy was all we could manage for one day.*

It's how one survives in the Andamans, to cultivate these sorts of fascinations with the local flora and fauna. Our current Commissioner Wilkerson tells me Ferrargunj was named after his predecessor Michael Ferrar, who spent eight years in the Andamans, studied five South Asian languages, and collected over four thousand butterfly specimens! A man cut from the cloth of Kipling's Lurgan Sahib.

I do believe that Claire, too, will make something swell of our time here, once she's able to return to her tribe. You astutely remarked in your last letter that she sounded like my kind of girl. I never knew I had a "kind of girl," but I do now believe she is it. Not fearless like you. Sorry, dear sister, but I'd be terribly intimidated by a wife who wanted to beat the world's drum as loudly as you do. You know I say that with hugest affection, but I'm sure you are not surprised to hear that I love Claire for her quiet tenacity and her youthful formlessness. I don't mean that she is formless—au contraire! Only that she's still coming into herself, you know? She's willing to admit that she doesn't know it all, and between the two of us, we refreshingly know next to nothing!

And you, Viv? Your last missive about the nefarious doings of the Japanese in our old stomping grounds sounded decidedly ominous, and I don't trust you to keep your nose clean if all hell breaks out. Why don't you see about coming here instead?

You could cover our latest Nationalist rumblings. There's talk of another round of hunger strikes brewing at our Cellular Jail—there have been several over the years—and I'm quite in sympathy. All the prisoners are demanding is basic stuff like clean water and light and books, but Mr. Gandhi's now weighing in, too, and he wants the politicals to be sent back to jails in their home states. If he prevails it won't exactly be the end of the Raj, but it might be newsworthy.

And of course, I'd love to introduce you to Claire and our glorious boy. Do come!

Your ever-loving brother,
Shep

Claire loved motherhood. She did. It had simply come too soon. Her only physical outlet was to walk the baby around Ross Island, which took all of an hour, and some days she would pause when Ty was asleep in his pram, and gaze out across the water to the forest in the north and wonder what her other self would be discovering at this exact moment in Behalla. What Kuli could be teaching her, or how that other baby, Artam, was growing. Not that she would trade Ty for any of them, but the Biya beckoned her in a way that motherhood couldn't. While her son represented the future, the Biya represented a world that might soon become extinct. Time was crucial in both cases, but she felt it especially keenly when it came to documenting the Biya, and she'd only just begun to trust the promise of that work when pregnancy intervened. She longed to get back to it.

While Ty was nursing, of course, field work would be impossible, but once he was weaned, it would still be a challenge. As a new father, Shep had become unnervingly protective. Lately, in honor of his paternal role, he'd even cut back on his own expeditions.

Also, there was a new insistence to his affections that could verge on cloying, and the harder he reached for her, the more Claire tended to pull away. It horrified her to admit this, even to herself, but a part of her was responding to both Shep and Ty the way she once had to Robin—as if they somehow threatened something deep inside her that she couldn't even name.

Duty played a role in all this. She should have known it would. There had been a day back in New York. A thundershower. Romantic, she'd thought at the time. To Shep, however, the downpour represented an obligation.

As they'd settled into a coffee shop to wait out the rain, he kept apologizing for his failure to bring an umbrella. "I could kick myself," he persisted, even after they ordered their lunch.

"Sounds like you have an overdeveloped sense of responsibility." The words had bubbled up, amused, scolding—and unrecognizably libertine.

Shep wouldn't play. "Conditioned response is more like it." He fingered the starched white cuff of his shirt, which gaped around his thin wrists. His hands tapered to squared pink nails, their restlessness at odds with their grooming.

The rain had formed silver thistles on the window glass. "My father's a British Royal Medical Officer," Shep said. "In our family, a mistake like that would result in the silent treatment for days."

The silent treatment. *In our family.* His confessional tone had thrown down a marker. Whether he wished to or not, he held himself accountable. At the time, Shep didn't know about Robin's death, and his response when she did tell him later was the soul of compassion. Still, Claire shuddered to think how the British Royal Medical Officer would react if *he* learned what she'd done to her brother. Tread with care, Shep was telling her. Duty, to a fault.

And what could be a greater duty than motherhood?

Evenings at the club, she watched her husband across the terrace, sucking on his pipe. A new habit he'd picked up from the officers, she suspected, to make himself appear more mature. More fatherly.

Their son was their joy, their connection. She adored them both. But she couldn't help herself. When Tom Lutty, the wireless officer from North Point Station, happened to mention that some new field transceivers had come in for use by the bush police, she wanted to know more.

According to Lieutenant Lutty, the devices were small as rucksacks and had a signal range of about eight kilometers. This was approximately the distance from Behalla to the coast.

"How do they work?" she asked, bracing herself for Lutty's effusive reply. The young redhead's father was a Royal Scots Fusilier, his mother Bengali royalty—reputedly a scandalous liaison, though there was nothing remotely scandalous about Tom Lutty himself. He loved his "tinker-toys," as he called the station equipment, and could go on about their technical intricacies, ad nauseum.

Before he got too deeply into the nuts and bolts, Claire figured out what she was really asking. "I mean, how do you talk through them? They're not telephones, are they?"

The wireless officer bit back a laugh. "You never heard of Morse?"

She laid out her plan to Shep that night as they walked back to the house. If Lutty trained them, they could have a lifeline when they went into the forest. All they'd have to do was ask Lieutenant Reynold to run his launch past a point within range of transmission, and whichever of them was out in the field could deliver a daily AOK.

She didn't mention that it had been an afterthought to include Shep in the training, a subtle way of making her point, since *he'd* never seen any need to touch base when he went off without her.

"You're that eager to get back at it?" The flickering gaslight warped his smile. "We *could* go out together, like before."

But the quaver in his voice betrayed him. She said, with some calculation, "You'd leave Ty alone with the servants? Without either of us nearby?"

His distrust of servant loyalty aside, Shep had been just five when his parents sent him and his sister off to boarding school. If not for Vivian, he'd told Claire, he never would have survived it. And one was a far cry from five.

There was a long pause. "I just hate to let you go," he said finally.

She took his arm and pulled him close.

Fortunately, Tom made Morse code fun. He loved puzzles and games, and he seemed to take special pride in his speed of translation. The wireless was a battery-powered kit with an antenna that extended several feet overhead. On clear days they practiced setting it up on the lawn behind the station, with Claire transmitting essential messages such as *AOK* and *SOS*. Lutty would give them a thumbs up or down from the window when he received the correct, or botched, message.

Claire and Shep both needed the chattering keys slowed to the pace of a metronome before they could grasp even the most basic incoming phrases. "It's like music," Claire said.

"Right," Lutty agreed. "Notes an' rests. Rests an' rests. Notes an' notes."

"Patterns." She studied the page of dots and dashes.

"Just listen." Lutty closed his eyes and began to nod as his finger tapped the key.

Shep said, "Sounds like cardiac arrhythmia to me."

But Morse was the least of it. *Frequency, range, call sign, directional, crystal, coil, triode . . .* Claire thought, even machinery has its own language.

At the end of their eighth lesson, after ten straight thumbs up, Tom placed a box phonograph on the window ledge above them and set it spinning with "Goody, Goody."

"Guess he's signing off on you," Shep said as Benny Goodman's clarinet trilled down at them. "Can you jitterbug?"

"Not well."

He called up to Lutty. "Get on down here, Tom, and show my bride what you've got."

An hour later she collapsed, laughing beside Shep on the grass, the exuberant lieutenant still spinning and shimmying solo before a crowd of cheering officers and bemused Indian MPs.

1938

Claire tried to compromise between Ty's needs and her own by ending their morning walks at the little stone library behind the club. The room was usually cool and empty, and apart from the bookshelves, a mahogany table and four heavy wooden chairs were the only furnishings. Each time she lifted him out of the pram—an ancient schooner-like vehicle on loan from Mrs. Wilkerson—Ty would give her a thoughtful blink and stretch his limbs for the scrubbed slate floor. If she handed him his rattle, he'd take it in both hands and examine it end to end, tracking its changing rhythms.

Her quiet, serious baby. Ty's hair had grown into a rich curly umber, eyes a dark mossy green. Though he showed no sign yet of talking, he was stubborn and definite in his likes and dislikes. This she'd known ever since they introduced him to the swimming pool, when he was barely three months old. The entire club membership had turned out that evening to celebrate the end of the monsoon season. The baby was a bonus, and the Ross matrons passed him around like a parcel of light. Marian Small pronounced him The Angel of the Andamans. Rita Wilkerson called him The Cherub. The cantonment's aging wives were as greedy for white babies as they were indifferent to brown ones. Ty's birth even helped to mitigate their disapproval of Claire's career ambitions and willful fraternization with the natives.

Still, five minutes of ogling and lavender-scented goosing was more than enough for their glorious boy. He let out a wail, and Claire and Shep fled with him into the water, where they expected surprise, at best a bit of tentative splashing. Instead, the infant took to the pool like a porpoise. Claire felt the tension leave Ty's limbs as soon as he was immersed. He kicked and chortled and reached for the coral glints of sunset skittering across the waves.

"He's a natural," Major Baird declared. "You've got yourself a real amphibian there."

Ever since, they'd taken Ty swimming almost every evening, and no matter how long they stayed, he would fuss when they pulled him out.

He was like that in the library, too. Focused. Definite. Persistent. These qualities took a new turn, however, one morning soon after his nine-month birthday.

At first, Claire saw nothing out of the ordinary. She set Ty on the floor beside her so she could study the library copy of Portman's Andamanese "history." M. V. Portman was a British officer who'd overseen the "home" for Andamanese captives on Ross in the 1880s. He'd also taken a stab at documenting their languages.

"*Do nga' araulo*," she read aloud. "I am following you. *Do nga' paiti ke:* I am going to shoot you. *Do nga' bilak*: I am going to carry you away. *Do tra' mke*: I wrap myself in it."

A swooshing sound drew her attention to Ty, who'd pulled himself to his knees and was rolling his rattle back and forth. His intensity made her wonder again, why *did* she wrap herself in this work? Why wasn't it enough to be Shep's wife and raise their child? Or, why didn't she just content herself with studying the social customs and arcane rules of colonial society in Port Blair? She could conduct *that* field study without leaving Ross Island.

She had no illusions about her personal affinity with Leyo's people. After last January's abortive field visit, they'd doubtless be happy never to lay eyes on her again. And other than Leyo, who'd spent so much time around outsiders that he was hardly representative, the only other Andamanese in Port Blair was that pathetic drunkard in Aberdeen Bazaar—even Leyo disavowed Porubi as "no good." Whenever Claire caught sight of the man, sprawled in an alleyway or lifting a bottle of toddy to his lips as he leered at her with those bulging eyes, she hurried away in revulsion. Yet it was the very shame and pity that accompanied this revulsion which answered her question now.

Ruth Benedict had aroused that same shame and pity with her lectures on the decline of the Choctaw, Pima, and Cochiti tribes. The parallels were inescapable. Just as the Spaniards had begun killing natives in America in the name of God, and the railroad industrialists had all but finished them off, so here the same British who built this library had begun the killing in the name of the Crown, and the current crop of prospectors were eradicating the Andamanese tribes to clear the way for timber, rubber, and coconut fortunes. The missionaries had done their job here, too. In the 1800s, following the rout of the natives that the British without irony labeled The Battle of Aberdeen, it was the colonial chaplain who devised a scheme to win over the survivors by "civilizing" them in captivity. Claire pictured the Victorian inhabitants of Ross, as well as their Indian convicts and soldiers, ogling the natives on display, much as she herself as a child had gawked at the dioramas of Northwest Coast Indians in the Museum of Natural History. Except that her gawking hadn't led to the Coast Indians dying of alcohol poisoning, measles, and syphilis. Not directly, anyway.

Atonement, then. Was that why she felt this sense of obligation to study and record what was left of the Biya? Atonement for the sins of the white man everywhere, not to mention her father's forsaken dreams, her brother's death, her mother's undying sorrow. Her own unspeakable guilt. Pity, plus shame, equals sin that must be atoned for by sacrifice, study, and work?

Or, was that all just a noble front for selfishness? *Dare to call yourself a scientist,* Dr. Benedict had urged, *and conduct yourself accordingly.* Dare, in other words, to be ambitious, to see your opportunities and seize them. As she had seized Shep and lunged for the Andamans in the first place. Not out of guilt, but for—

Shifting, she kicked Ty's rattle, and looked down to find that her son had crawled all the way to the opposite wall, where he sat on his bottom, blue sunsuit straining across his shoulders as he reached for the open door.

Claire hurried to retrieve him, but she'd only taken a step or two when he sat back and lofted his hands in the air. Facing away from her, his interest had been caught by the light from two stained glass windows across the room. At this hour the tableau of the Peaceable Kingdom streamed in vivid hues onto the door's smooth white panels.

"That's a lion," Claire heard herself say. "And those are his little lambs." Her family had never been much for churchgoing, especially after Robin's death, and she had only a superficial knowledge of Bible stories, but in this case, the moral was clearly a plea for peace.

Ty reached to pet the lion, but before he touched the door his hand cast a shadow, and the color caught his arm. He spent several seconds examining his golden skin, then his shadow. Then he turned and, oblivious to Claire, raised his face to the stained glass. She could almost see his mind working as he looked from the high window, back to the scene projected onto the door. He studied the slanting bars of color in the air, watched the motes of dust rain through them.

Again, he raised his hands, now grasping. The particles spun faster.

"Ty," she said. "Your hand is red. Now it's blue."

The shadow of his arm found the edge of the open door. His lips pursed in silent concentration as he opened and closed his fingers, testing to see if his shadow alone would move the door. When it didn't, he scowled and scooted forward.

Again, Claire thought she should stop him, but the pointedness of his concentration warned her against it. He wasn't interested in going through the door; he was transfixed by the changing patterns of light and color that resulted as he pulled the door toward him and pushed it back. Stretch the lion like a snake, or bunch it into a sliver.

"Look what you can do!" The singsong of her voice sounded idiotic as it echoed off the stone walls. When Ty didn't react, she moved in front of him and knelt down. "Those are shadows, Ty. That's color."

She listened for some response. A coo. A consonant. A murmur at the back of the throat.

For a moment he paused and gave her a long impassive stare. He pulled on a lock of his hair. Without making a sound, he returned his attention to the door.

The pang of rejection this triggered in her was ridiculous. Or was it? Babies were supposed to be distractable, weren't they? And sociable?

Instead, Ty went into his own little world and became all but unreachable. Even when he was nursing lately, his interest would wander off through the window or into the mirror, and he'd fail to eat. Shep said it was normal for some babies to wean themselves early. He was proud of their son's self-sufficiency, and Jina, too, assured them that they were fortunate to have a son who demanded so little, but at moments like this Ty seemed to Claire unnervingly remote. Maybe she should follow Jina and young Naila's example and simply let the child lead.

She pulled up a chair and waited while Ty bent his head in and out of the light stream, tried to lick the color in the air, to grasp the separate spears of illumination. If he was disappointed in the results of his experiments, he didn't show it. Every now and then he rocked forward to reposition himself as the sunbeams shifted, but he never made a sound—or so much as glanced at her for ten full minutes.

Finally, she packed up her notebook and returned the Portman to its shelf. Ty's diaper needed changing, and he ought to be hungry.

Straightening the linens in the pram, she announced brightly, "Time to go, Ty."

No response.

She shook the rattle to entice him, then bent down and caught her son under his arms. "Come on, now, love."

His fist met her eye with a force that detonated her vision. In her shock, she let go, and the baby dropped with a short searing wail.

She was afraid his leg had twisted underneath him, but he quickly scrambled back onto his knees, reaching again for the light.

She got behind him then and unceremoniously dumped him into the pram, whereupon Ty started bawling in earnest.

Tired, Claire told herself. Hungry. She heard her mother's once-confident voice murmuring in her ear. *It's only colic. Don't be afraid. He just needs a little food and comfort.*

She looked around to make sure they were still alone, then pulled up a chair, undid her blouse, and lifted her screaming son onto her lap. It was like fighting a cornered animal. She wrapped her hand around his head, made low, cooing sounds, and pinned his flailing limbs.

She'd watched this scene countless times when Robin was a baby, and her mother's breast invariably brought peace. But Ty kept turning his face away, his decibel level rising. When at last she forced the nipple into his mouth, he bit down so hard he drew blood. Then he spat her out.

All right, she commanded herself as she lowered her wailing son back into the pram and wiped the stain from her skin. Read this signal. Respect his wishes. *Conduct yourself accordingly.* And do not get pulled under.

She would return to the forest for just a few days. Jina and Naila could manage Ty during the daytime—Naila would be over the moon, and Shep, too, would welcome evenings with his glorious boy to himself.

She'd take Leyo with her, of course. They'd test Lutty's code, as planned. She'd get her field work back on track. Claire admonished herself to view Ty's willfulness as a gift, though the persistent throb in her left breast warned otherwise.

April 5, 1938
Behalla

Dear Dr. Benedict,

I should be composing my notes, but I cannot resist this chance to write to you from the site of my first solo field trip. I arrived yesterday afternoon and shall be here four days—a duration that my husband and I had to negotiate, since he's in charge of our little Ty while I'm gone. My hope is to build toward longer visits in future, but for now being here at all seems a kind of miracle.

It's just after sunrise, and everyone around me is moving sluggishly. The heat and mosquitoes this deep in the forest make sleep a dubious enterprise, in any event, so mornings always get off to a slow start, but last night there was much dancing, and the Biya chief Kuli hasn't even emerged yet.

Kuli has a solemn, somewhat sad demeanor despite the rakish way he wears his red headband and shells strung from his belt, but he's a generous teacher. With his help I'm trying to work up an alphabet that at least suggests the core elements of the old Biya language.

The rest of the time, while my guide Leyo and his friend Sempe are out gathering orchid specimens for my husband's botanical research, I try to fold myself into the women's lives. Sempe's young wife Imulu and the elder widow Mam Golat let me come along when they dig for roots, and they've taught me how to roast grubs! I actually managed to swallow one. It tasted like charred fingernail.

I've also been trying to create a field code for the tribe's signs and gestures. So little is spoken, but much is communicated. We'll be sitting around the fire and spontaneously—or so it seems to me— everyone will erupt into laughter as if a joke has been told. Or they'll all get up as if a bell has rung. Leyo tells me the light and the wind tell them when it is time to start a new task, to leave or return, but I suspect a great deal more is communicated through the mischievous looks they exchange—especially at my expense!

Sadly, Jodo, the club-footed child we met on our first visit, was killed by a wild pig three weeks ago. From where I sit I can see the small dark hut where his mother grieves, and I can't help but think that if my pregnancy hadn't cut short our first visit last year, we might have persuaded her to let Shep take Jodo and operate on his foot, and he'd be alive today. I fear that his mother knows this, for she will have nothing to do with me.

But it's the youngest member of the tribe, Imulu's little girl Artam, who is my greatest interest. A toddler now, she eyed me with suspicion when I first arrived, but the others just laughed and patted her leg, tickled the reddish pads of her toes until she forgot all about me. She rarely cries. When hungry, she still rides in the birch sling so she can suckle while her mother goes about her business.

Imulu tolerates my presence. She can be sweet and gentle with her husband and Artam, but otherwise she has a gruff demeanor, and I think she finds me ridiculous with all my nosey questions. Still, she answers as best she can and lets me play with Artam, as she lets everyone. And although the little girl seems to trust and respond to us all with amusement, it's clear that her mother is her base in the world. I so envy their ease with each other.

Artam calls her mother Amimi and her father Amae. I'm still not sure how she (or I) will learn the Biya's "spirit language." So far she seems to be learning to speak as most children do, babbling and imitating.

It's my own son, ironically, who remains speechless. He's ten months old now and has yet to say even ma or pa. Though his tantrums prove that there's nothing mechanically wrong with his voice, he's otherwise almost completely silent. I confess that this perturbs me in a way it doesn't his father. Shep assures me that Ty will speak when he's good and ready, and I can see for myself that the baby's otherwise as healthy as he is temperamental. Indeed, as I watch Ty play with the servants' daughter, a girl of just eight who seems instinctively to understand his every whim, I wonder if the failure might not lie with me.

Professor Ruth Benedict
Columbia University
Department of Anthropology
New York City, New York
July 20, 1938

My Dear Claire,

When I received your last letter, I had to smile. Did you know that Margaret Mead addressed your concerns in her New Guinea papers? Despite parental encouragement of speech in Pere, she found many untalkative children, but the Manus people attributed this to temperament rather than intelligence. Margaret noted that when the quiet children did finally begin to talk, they displayed as rich a vocabulary as the garrulous infants, and often showed even greater comprehension, not only of the words but also of their environment.

Margaret and I have often surmised—based on observations in our own culture!—that there may in fact be an inverse relationship between intelligence and the compulsive need to narrate aloud one's every thought or impulse. I suggest you concentrate on your work—which sounds like it's proceeding brilliantly—and your most intelligent son will doubtless learn to talk at his own pace and in his own unique way, through no fault of yours.

ARTIFACT LOG

- *Biya—cowrie shell ornaments (gift from Kuli 4/6/38)*
- *Biya—Pandanus halter (gift from Mam Golat 4/8/38)*
- *Biya—twine necklace (gift from Ekko 4/8/38)*
- *Jarawa—iron arrowhead (relic, found en route to Behalla 10/17/38)*
- *Biya—rope dog leash (gift from Sempe 10/18/38)*

- *Biya—birchbark nursing sling (gift from Imulu 10/20/38)*
- *Jarawa—red loincloth (found near Behalla 10/21/38)*

November 18, 1938
Ross Island

Dear Dr. Benedict,

Something so extraordinary has happened, I hardly know where to begin. It's both ghastly and wondrous, and I suppose as an ethnographer, I should keep an objective stone face, but it's difficult when I feel simultaneously like ranting and celebrating.

You see, thanks to my darling husband, I've spent an entire afternoon with two members of the Jarawa, the mysterious and reputedly hostile inland tribe. However, the circumstances surrounding this encounter were monstrous.

We have a new and odious police commandant whose territory spans the entire archipelago and whose moral compass stops well short of his heart. This man, Denis Ward, heard that a bush policeman and a couple of hunters were killed up north last week near one of the forest outposts. The murderers most likely were Burmese poachers, who are a scourge in these islands, but Ward went up with his men to investigate and decided, in his infinite colonial wisdom, to wreak vengeance on the natives.

I suspect his Indian deputies encouraged this scheme. There is no love lost between the imported "locals" and the indigenous people here, and because the Jarawa are reclusive and violent when approached, they're the least trusted of all the tribes.

The upshot is that Ward's vigilantes ambushed some fifty Jarawa men, women, and children, opening fire on them as they were crossing the Middle Andaman strait by raft. According to Ward's own (gleeful) report back at the club, it was wholesale slaughter, but to prove what a saint he is, he brought in for treatment an eight-year-old girl who'd been shot in the thigh, along with her mother, who refused to leave her.

Ward insists on calling the mother Topsy-One and the girl Topsy-Two. But . . . now they're under Shep's medical care.

And that's how I wiggled into the act!

After Shep initially treated the girl, Ward put the captives under house arrest with a Bengali sergeant and his wife. Naturally, Shep had to go check on his patient, and I tagged along as his assistant.

Trouble was apparent as soon as the young Bengali wife opened the door. They'd been given no warning, she complained. The MPs had simply dumped these "savages" upon them, forcing her into the role of jail matron and "desecrating" her good home.

Shep pulled rank and insisted she allow him to do his job, but the prisoners' cell turned out to be the size of a broom closet, with bars on the window and chains on the door. It stank of human waste and wouldn't fit the four of us, so while he examined and re-dressed the girl's wound, I tried to calm the matron. There was no sign of her husband.

You would have been proud of me, Dr. Benedict. I assured the woman that her prisoners were as eager to leave as she was to be rid of them. I listened to her opine that Ward should have killed all the Jarawa, instead of "just" fifty. Then I reminded her that all this mother wanted was to protect her child, and I disabused her of the persistent local myth that "these creatures eat human flesh."

All the while, the broom closet resounded with wails and thumps. So finally, I dropped my voice to a conspiratorial whisper. I told the good woman that I'd been studying the local tribes, and I'd found that they were really clever devils. If a door or window were left unlocked, they'd vanish back into the forest without a trace, and this ordeal would be over for everyone. Then I gave her a wink, as Shep and I traded places.

The mother and daughter resembed the Biya, but were smaller, more wiry. They wore their tribe's distinctive red fiber bands wound tightly around their foreheads, arms, waists, and ankles, but nothing else. And their talk sounded much faster and higher pitched than Biya, though that might have been because they were angry and frightened and wanted nothing to do with me.

I felt so awful for them, crouched in the corner, defeated by loss, injury, and exhaustion. Their eyes stared, large and deep in their sockets, and their skin, made darker by the contrast of the girl's white bandages, shone blue-black.

The sun striped shadows through the barred windows, and the morning heat was climbing. A bowl of untouched rice sat just inside the door, beside an empty chamber pot. The stench of urine and feces wafted from the opposite corner, where the prisoners had also flung the hospital gowns in which they'd been transported. Mother and daughter held hands, watching my slightest move.

I tried introducing myself: "Attiba Claire." I had to guess at the pronunciation, but Radcliffe-Brown had given me the word for name.

Then I embraced myself as the Biya do in greeting. At that I detected a flicker of attention.

I knew they had to be ravenous. Shep said they'd refuse to eat anything they didn't recognize, so I'd brought honeycomb, cashews, raw cane and mangoes. It was a good bet. As soon as I showed the contents of my bag, the mother lunged for it. Never moving their eyes from me, the two devoured every morsel. Then, for over an hour, I listened and took notes as they demanded their freedom in a twittering language as distinct from Biya as Gaelic is from German.

I felt deeply privileged to meet these supposed headhunters firsthand, more privileged still as they entrusted me with their pleas and complaints, but that sense of privilege was overshadowed by dread. The girl and her mother closely resembled young Ekko and Obeyo. All share the same ancestry, and the dressing on the girl's leg made it impossible to forget what Ward had put them through—or what he'd do to the Biya, too, if given the slightest provocation.

The mother—Bathana, she called herself—grasped my arm as I started to leave. "Malavu bhedu." She pointed urgently to herself, her daughter, clearly expecting the impossible.

I had to pull away, and the look of betrayal on Bathana's small anguished face took a slice out of my heart.

Outside I found Shep and the sergeant's wife perched on the stairs like old pals. Shep was regaling the woman with tales of Shanghai, buying me time. Would that I'd done more with it.

And yet . . . when I woke next morning to the news that the Jarawa girl and her mother had escaped back into the forest, I felt redeemed.

1939–1940

Selected 1939 field notes:

—Sempe, Imulu, and Artam are the only whole family unit. Every other adult is widowed. Ekko is an orphan. Yet the widow Obeyo alone holds onto her grief. Or is it anger? Darkness, at any rate, over the loss of both her husband and little Jodo. She now wears Jodo's skull, strung by a cord, on her back. Her buck teeth and shaved head accentuate the ghoulish effect, and she refuses to join the nightly chanting and dancing. However, she is the master weaver of the clan, and her surviving son Tika is friendly enough for both of them, so there seems to be an unspoken agreement to leave her be. I have tried on each visit to approach her, but as soon as I come near she straightens her arms and turns her back, refusing even to let me greet her.

—Artam has been toilet trained—in the Biya sense—since my last visit. At that time, she was not yet walking, and her mother would simply carry her away from the clearing and hold her over the foliage in a matter-of-fact fashion, then rinse her bottom with water from a special gourd. Nearly three now, if Artam has an accident in camp she'll be cuffed or lightly spanked by anyone who happens to catch her. The older children dispense ridicule with much pulling of the nose and sounds of disgust, but none of it fazes Artam. What seems to have made the greatest difference is her insistence on accompanying others—including me!—when we relieve ourselves. Then she follows suit. A signal less of culture, I suspect, than of Artam's highly sociable nature. She endears herself to all around her and seems to view us all as immediate family. Her trust of me, so genuine and pure, along with Kuli's welcome and Leyo's support, makes me feel at home with the Biya (all except the grim widow Obeyo) in a way I have not felt anywhere since I was a young child.

—As for the spirit language, the men appear to be the keepers of this code. It is the language that connects them to nature and, through the wisdom of their great god Biliku, to success in hunting, fishing, stalking, and survival—and also, I think, to intimacy. When Artam's father,

Sempe, takes her into his arms he rarely speaks, but he'll raise his face to study the currents of wind in the treetops, and she'll follow his gaze. Or he'll give her a little shake to stop her babbling, and together they'll listen to a sound I can't hear, and then they'll leave camp as if sworn to silence and return not four minutes later with a large rat on the end of an arrow, Artam as gleeful as if she'd shot it herself. The evident strengthening of the bond between father and daughter that occurs during these wordless excursions reinforces my sense that the silent language has evolved out of necessity to link survival with love. It is not easily taught to outsiders, however, and despite the ease with which most of the Biya accept me, this cornerstone of their culture continues to elude me.

—When I asked Sempe if he will actually teach his daughter to shoot, he shook his head as if this were unthinkable, but Leyo says that the tribe is shrinking so quickly that everyone, male and female, must be taught to hunt and defend themselves. I wonder how quickly such a role shift can happen. Young Ekko, around Naila's age, is plenty old enough to learn to shoot, but no one appears inclined to teach her, perhaps due to her temperament. This girl is as vain as any of my Connecticut schoolmates, grooming her hair and nails extensively, and she preens in the compact mirror I gave her on my first visit, while jealously guarding it from the others. If the tribe depended on Ekko to hunt, I fear they would starve.

—Artam is growing bow-legged and pot-bellied, with an almost perfectly spherical head, and short, compressed neck. Now in her third year, she produces full-throated, open vowels, and growls. She clicks her way through the Biya consonants with ease and expresses herself in complete statements. No adult will ever stop to correct her pronunciation, yet she gawks as they talk and sometimes mimics them as a parrot might. She seems instinctively verbal, especially when greeting her mother after the slightest separation. I'm most impressed by Artam's fluid ability to shift from silence when hunting with her father to garrulousness with everyone else.

[For comparison, I note that my own son Ty, just ten months younger than Artam, is already nearly half a foot taller than she, but still speechless. He will grunt and occasionally hum, and his fits of rage remain frequent and loud, but he displays none of Artam's vocal sociability. Where she has a magnetic and nonstop attraction to the people around her, Ty seems immune to humanity's charms—with the single exception of Naila, his preferred companion. With Naila, and only with Naila, Ty communicates effortlessly. Their silent fluency bears an uncanny similarity to the Biya spirit language. Leyo suggests *that Biliku has conferred this gift on them as a kind of birthright. Both Naila and Ty, after all, were born in the Andamans under Biliku's protective gaze. But then, so was Artam, and she converses readily in spoken as well as silent language with both her parents, while Ty resorts to tantrums to communicate with Shep and me.]*

December 20, 1940

Merry Christmas, Dear Mum and Dad!

I picture you curled up with your books by the fire or sweeping snow off the front steps . . . and my mind boggles. Here we look onto a sea of diamonds, wear sunhats and shorts out to hunt for our shabby sprig of Christmas evergreen—a local shrub called casuarina—and pretend our Pimm's cups are mulled wine.

But I've so much to catch you up on! I made a week-long field trip last month. Little Artam, the Biya girl I've written so much about, is a gregarious imp going on four now. What a study in contrasts with our Ty! Where he's deliberate to the point of exasperation, she's impulsive. Where he's silent, she's a chatterbox. Where he's stubborn, she's like quicksilver. In a flash Artam will disappear high up a tree, fearless, or chase lizards along the stream. She loves to dance and jump and freely offers effusive hugs, but she can't sit still for anything like a lesson.

Ty, on the other hand, is a born problem solver. He loves to work with Som's tools to fix the benches in the garden, and with Som and Jina's daughter, Naila, to help pot and categorize Shep's medicinal orchids. He's already solving remarkably complex number and letter puzzles, and he adores music, can hum virtually any melody he's ever heard, with the auditory equivalent of photographic memory.

The one thing Ty and Artam have in common is a love of dogs. Artam affectionately torments the pye-dogs that the Biya keep for hunting, and Ty has turned the Commissioner's Dutch shepherd into such a pal that he actually rides the poor beast's back.

As you can see, we are all healthy and busy. In addition to his routine medical duties—and helping Jina and Naila tend to Ty whenever I'm out in the field—Shep has made tremendous headway in the lab. He's developed an extract of Pleated Leaf for the treatment of sepsis, an infusion of Yellow Finger Orchid roots for headache and diarrhea, and even successfully cured several cases of amoebic dysentery and reversed glaucoma using his decoctions.

The real trick is to document every step and scrupulously preserve his samples. Everything Shep accomplishes here will have to be replicated back in "civilization," before the grand Poo-Bahs of medical science will even think of taking him seriously. He says he'll need at least another year in the Andamans before he can begin to face them. And I feel the same about my research.

Dad, I could tell from your last letter how worried you are. The news we get of the war in Europe is truly alarming, and I'm sure you get boatloads more. I wish we could just wave a magic wand and come to you, but we've been hearing absolute horror stories about the voyage around the Cape—months, it can take, and every day the threat of bombers overhead and torpedoes below. The attempts to fly are even worse, hopfrogging across Africa, landing in blacked out backwaters with no idea when the next plane will take off, much less who will be allowed on it.

Dearly as I'd love to come home, we really are safe and sound here. We both have our work, and I think it's best we stay. Maybe it's not the phony war we all thought, but it can't go on much longer. And soon as it's over we'll hightail it back, with bells on.

D'ekrose moer (That's xox, in Biya!)

Claire

III

June 1941

The orchid garden was deserted. Shep had come over to ask Som to cut him some *Rhynchostylis* pseudobulb samples, but now he stood in the sopping heat, unsure of his next move. Som tended these plants as if they were his children. He'd webbed vines and bark on which to suspend the epiphytic varieties, fashioned a shade roof out of rattan, devised elaborate staking and clipping mechanisms to support the heavy columnar blooms. The orchids rewarded this care with lavish new growth and spectacular color and scent, but if Shep tried to cut his own samples, he'd insult Som and probably mutilate the plants. Despite the delight he took in his botanical research, or maybe because of it, Shep was terrified of harming these exotic species.

Where *was* Som?

Naila's reed-like voice floated from the veranda. *Aah, bi, cee, dee, ee, hef, ghee* . . . Claire used to sing Ty this alphabet song, but now, between the Vanilla stalks that screened him from the house, Shep could see only the girl with his son. And though he strained to hear some hint of accompaniment, there was only a pale humming.

Ty'd just turned four. Still, not a word.

Naila soldiered on alone . . . *eych, ay, jay, kay.*

"Jina?" Claire called from inside the house.

"They are not yet back, Mem."

Shep remembered then. Som and Jina had gone over to Aberdeen for the morning.

"Shouldn't they be home by now?" Claire appeared, her yellow dress a flame in the doorway. "That's beautiful work, my sweet. You're remarkable, Naila. You've taught him all his letters."

She kept her voice light, but Shep could hear the effort this cost her. *They're like sister and brother*, had lately become a wistful refrain. Sometimes when she said this, he could tell she was thinking of her own disastrous history as a big sister. Other times, maternal jealousy over Ty's affection for Naila strained her voice. And sometimes this would stir up questions in himself, which Shep tried to deflect, about his own childhood.

He and Vivvy had once been as close as Ty and this girl, though that was probably because Shep's parents wanted nothing to do with them. He'd always considered himself damned lucky to have Viv on his side, but she hadn't been able to stopper his longing for his mother's affection and his father's approval—she'd never fully *replaced* his parents for him, as Naila increasingly seemed to do for Ty.

Whether Ty's bond with Naila was related to Claire's intermittent absences, or to the same complex of factors that kept Ty from talking, or perhaps to something Shep himself had done wrong, he had no idea. But it made his head spin and his heart hurt as he watched Claire struggle to connect with their son—struggle without ever admitting how much her child's rebuffs hurt her. Ty was no more communicative with him, but Shep held a firm conviction that the boy would grow out of this phase and bond with them in time—especially once they'd left Port Blair and returned to a world where he could see how happy families were supposed to live.

The problem may have seemed more personal to Claire because of Ty's temper fits as a baby. They'd persisted for over a year, and Shep suspected that Claire blamed herself for them. One minute, Ty was engrossed in some activity—rolling a ball, or splashing water, or studying a dragonfly—and the next, he'd simply erupt. Screams. Fists. Spitting and kicking. The amount of energy he expelled in each episode could have lit up Ross Island all night, and the tantrums did seem to occur on Claire's watch, usually just days before she was scheduled to go back into the field. At one point, Shep thought she might be provoking Ty so she could tell herself he wanted her to leave him. Then, about two years ago, a night came that crystallized the toll this was taking on her, and Shep realized he was reading the situation all wrong.

He'd arrived home from the club too late to help. The bedtime battle was over, and Claire was spent. He found her on the veranda, where Naila and Ty were playing so contentedly now. He remembered two punk sticks glowing like eyes in the darkness. Claire sat jackknifed on the steps, arms wrapping her knees. Sheet lightning lit up the east, but otherwise all was dark and drenched in liquid heat.

Shep sat down beside her, was reaching to touch Claire's shoulder, when the night ignited with rain, and she sprang away from him into the slanting needles. Head flung back and cheeks streaming, she lifted her right hand as if it were burnt and fisted it at her breast. A crack of voltage silvered the yard, crowning her with an illusion of pearls, and he saw she was weeping. With frustration, with sorrow or yearning, or all of it, he didn't know, but he loved her more in that instant than he'd ever thought possible.

In the next downbeat he was around her, undoing her hands, peeling off her wet dress. Tuning his lips from her sternum down between the bared wings of her rib cage, he breathed the trembling out of her until she calmed and turned home to him, and he never doubted her again.

After that night, the edge of tension that had been hardening between them for months softened and let go. At the same time, a shift occurred in the household so subtle that Shep might not have noticed, except that Ty's tantrums subsided.

It was as if Claire had surrendered without acknowledging defeat. She took another series of steps back from Ty, and Naila glided deeper into the space she created. No words were exchanged, to Shep's knowledge, no roles formally changed, but now whenever Naila was home and Ty became frustrated, the girl provided his distraction. If Claire couldn't make her son listen, Naila would cock her head and smile, and the boy would come along. Naila had such an uncanny ability to intuit whatever Ty wanted or needed, Claire would say it was as if the children had their own spirit language.

Shep and Claire told each other they were lucky that *someone* in the household knew how to read their son's mysterious mind. Lucky that this arrangement allowed them both to pursue their other ambitions while he was still so young. And yet, Shep thought, it would be so much better for them all—especially for Claire—if Ty's Someone weren't a servant.

A mosquito landed and sucked at his arm. He shook it off. The heat had stupefied him.

It was too late for lab work anyway; he needed to get over to Haddo for rounds. As he headed back to the hospital, though, he glanced with longing at the local boys down fishing off the rocks. The tide had just turned, flattening the water like slate, and krill stank up the listless air, but those kids were having a fine old time. Their laughter had the clarity of birdsong.

What was missing were any actual birds. Shep peered up through the scrim of casuarina and mohur branches. Once noticed, the absence seemed eerie. No gulls. No finches, no cormorants, no red-tails or white-tails. It must have had something to do with the ebbing monsoon.

Hurrying as he skirted the beach steps and entered the hospital, he collided with a short anvil-shaped barrier in the person of Lieutenant Gupta. "Dr. Durant, is it not your turn for rounds at Haddo?"

"On my way."

But Gupta didn't move. Shep was about to step around him when his second-in-command blurted, "I've put in for a position in Delhi. I'm bloody tired of being stuck here in no man's land."

They faced each other fully then. "I'd no idea you felt that way."

Gupta's pencil mustache twitched. "The thing is, Dr. Durant, I asked Commissioner Wilkerson to put in a word, and he suggested that you write the reference."

Someone let out a feverish yelp in the men's ward and a pair of nurses scurried. There was only one bed filled. An elderly captain recovering from appendicitis. Nobody here was exactly overworked.

Shep said, "I hate to see you go. You've done a splendid job."

There was always a chance that the lieutenant's replacement would be someone he could abide. Better yet, that Gupta wouldn't be replaced at all, in which case Shep would be viewed as "essential personnel"—off limits for military duty. Precious little word of the war made its way out to the Andamans, but he'd hear the worst of it quick enough if he got called up.

I'm a coward, Shep thought.

"Most kind of you, Doctor. Thank you." Gupta shot a grudging glance at Shep's lab across the hall. "And how are your experiments progressing?"

The note of condescension reminded Shep so viscerally of his father that he couldn't bring himself to answer. Instead he shifted his gaze through the corridor's gloom to the coral tree out front.

As if in reply, the tree gave a strange, fluid, quickening shudder. Shep felt himself being jerked forward, slammed into Gupta's chest, and they fell together as the floor rippled, then rolled back into the wall beneath a deafening roar.

Chunks of ceiling plaster rained down. Clutter from the nurse's station turned projectile. Shep made a helmet of his arms. His first thought was a bomb. But explosions were finite. This attack didn't stop. He placed his palms on the floor and felt a succession of deep peristaltic jolts, unlike any of the tremors he'd experienced in China.

A dull throbbing started in his chest where he'd collided with Gupta's stethoscope. Beside him, his lieutenant had curled into a fetal ball. Around them, the joints of the hospital were cracking like knuckles.

"We need to get everyone out of here," Shep said.

"What is happening?" Gupta pled.

"Earthquake." Shep tried to get up, but his legs had turned to chewing gum.

He steadied himself on his knees. The building was standing. He could see that the beds in the men's ward had traveled across the room, but having taken the ride, their lone patient was sitting up unhurt, the graybeard clutching his coverlet like a guilty child. Only the nurses were screaming.

They'd been inside. Claire had offered Leyo her pencil. He held it between his thumb and forefinger the way Groucho Marx plied his cigar.

Suddenly the pencil was dropping, and she was following its descent through sunshine onto the coir rug. She bent to retrieve it. Leyo caught her arm, and her first thought was that she, too, must be falling. Her second was that his touch seemed uncharacteristic, urgent and alarmingly intimate.

A needle of reflexive fear, then suddenly he was yanking her to her feet. "*Kamin!*" As the small room throbbed, Claire glanced up into the split of time and noticed the ceiling fan swaying. But Leyo had known the quake was coming before it even began.

Naila would remember Ty's hand pumping down and up, down and up. She still had the song in her throat, slowing the way Mem had taught her—*double yew, ex . . . why and—*

Suddenly the door banged open, and Leyo came flying out onto the porch, yanking Mem by the arm, then letting her go to pick up Ty. The dirty pink soles of his feet flashed like crabs, and then they were tearing across the grass with Mem chasing them.

The earth began to roar and shift, as if they were riding the back of an angry beast. Ty laughed, even though Mem held him to her, terror in her eyes. The trees around them bent and snapped. The roof of the bungalow buckled. The ride seemed to last forever. Then the world grew still.

Only then did Naila think of her parents, who had gone together to Aberdeen that morning. She watched Ty stand and test the ground. He looked as if he were dancing. As if, she told herself, he knew not to be afraid.

Leyo moved to the fence at the top of the bluff. He yelled down at the local boys who fished off the rocks.

"Thank God," Mem said as Doctor Shep came running toward them from the hospital. He picked up Ty and drew Mem into his arms. Ty reached over his father's shoulder for Naila, but the girl knew better.

She went instead to join Leyo, who was now gesturing wildly at the boys below. When Naila looked to see why, she too cried out.

In a motion at once slow and vast, the water was peeling backward. Acres of coral lay bare as the tide lifted rowboats and fishing vessels. Some of the smaller boats capsized, catching on the shoals. The local boys paid no heed to Leyo. As if enchanted, they went scampering after the receding tide, collecting stranded fish like offerings from the gods.

Leyo screamed at them in Urdu to run to the top of the steps, the water would soon return with a wave taller than the five of them. The boys looked up as if he were mad, this black man on high.

Only when Doctor Shep joined him, shouting down in English, "*You will die!*" did two of the five turn back. "*Run!*"

The tide that had pulled back lifted to form a wide black wall across the horizon. Then, in one terrible movement, the wall began to turn.

At last the other boys started to run, but they were so far out now, the mud sucked at their ankles. They fell. They pushed up. They looked over their shoulders.

Leyo and Doctor Shep had gone out of the yard to the top of the beach steps. They pulled the first two boys to safety, then stripped off their shirts and tied them together. Doctor Shep yelled, and Naila roused herself to bring her father's ropes from the orchid garden.

When her father came, she thought, he'd know what to do.

The three boys below were now swimming. Stealthy as a serpent, the water already had surged to the base of the cliff, then to the rock that jutted like a figurehead halfway up the steps. The water churned around it, and when Naila looked back out, the swimming boys were gone.

Leyo's gaze traveled far out across the sea. Mem came to stand beside Naila, Ty now quiet in her arms. "The ferry," she said.

Naila looked and saw nothing, but her teeth began to chatter.

That day was the first time she heard that terrible word: *evacuate*. Naila refused. Her parents would be back soon. They would expect to find her where they had left her. She would wait here on Ross Island. She would stay and help Leyo pack the things that Ty Babu and his parents would need on the mainland. The mainland would be safer, they said, but she would not leave until her parents returned.

She hardly noticed when Mem and Ty had gone, though she did hear Mem promise to look for Jina and Som in Aberdeen. As soon as there was any news . . .

Naila kept her head busy tearing the word: *ee-vac-you-ate*. Her parents should be here by now. She wanted to be with them, not Leyo. Not with Mem or Doctor *saab*, either, or even with Ty Babu. Not without her own ma and pa. *Evah-kyu-eht*.

Leyo didn't speak, but every now and then he took her hand and led her back outside. Then the island would tremble and jerk, and after it finished, they'd resume their silent work filling suitcases with clothing and books and objects that Naila barely noticed passing through her hands.

The hours stretched as the sun made its journey toward dusk. She thought of Doctor Shep and Mem this morning with Ty Babu sandwiched between them. Her parents should be here to hold her like that, to murmur and comfort her, too. They should have returned this morning before any of this terrible business happened. She would stay here and make time to reverse until they had never left. But no matter how many times she looked up the ridge path or down to the beach, her ma and pa did not appear.

At twilight Doctor Shep returned from hospital, which also was being evacuated. "They'll know you're with us," he said. "You can't stay here on your own, Naila. They wouldn't want you to."

She wanted to fight, but with darkness her fear swallowed her strength, so the doctor and Leyo escorted her like a prisoner onto the lumber barge that was being used as a ferry.

"Ross Island saved us!" Reverend Crisp shouted above her head. Floodlights swam like yellow eels down through the night to wreckage. The solid world had filled the sea with metal and wood and the screams of unseen animals. Naila leaned over the railing and willed herself into the fractured light beams.

"—split the wave, sending the brunt of the tsunami up and down the coast. Few grounded boats and downed trees. The jail's watchtower collapsed, but the port escaped the worst, except for those poor souls on the *Sapphire*, God help them—"

The old priest stopped mid-sentence, but Naila's skin already was turning in on itself. Doctor Shep's hands pressed her shoulders and drew her back from the rail. She turned her head and saw the coral of Leyo's sarong, the white of his singlet, two shapes floating among the deepest shadows. Like stones under water.

The crisis of the earthquake was compounded by torrential rains that began within seconds of Shep and Naila's arrival at the Browning Club, where evacuees were being housed on the mainland. Claire hoped the girl would be too exhausted to notice, or too glad to be reunited with Ty, or both.

She'd been asking people all afternoon for news of Jina and Som, but only the shopkeeper Farzand Ali had seen them. They'd bought a necklace from him for Naila's birthday and were rushing for the ferry, he said, just minutes before the quake struck. That ferry, the *Sapphire*, was the only one not accounted for. And Som could not swim. Now this downpour and darkness.

Claire was searching for a way to distract Naila when Shep signaled with his eyes for her to leave the girl be. Ty was the best medicine for her, and nothing would distract their son from the gusts now streaming sideways against the windows. As mystifyingly difficult as Ty could be, true crisis seemed to relax him. He'd been cooperative all day, too interested in the chaos and disruption around him perhaps to be upset by it.

Still clutching Naila's hand, Ty pulled her across the room and pressed both their palms against the pane. The window overlooked Dilthamon Tank, a view dissolving in froth that made a sound like scratching fingernails. Afraid the glass might shatter, Claire tried to tempt Ty with a banana, but he ate without budging, and Naila stood with her arms around him, so stoic and silent and frozen that Claire flinched at the memory of her own mother standing just so, arms wrapped dutifully around her daughter in a pretext of comfort, their reflection captured in the hall mirror hours after Robin died.

The whole port was in shambles, trees snapped in half, electrical lines down, shanty roofs caved in, and pavement cracked in gaping zigzags, but the shoreline was the worst. Fishing boats sat on toppled palms. Shards of dead gray coral and carcasses of fish littered eroded sand. Broken timbers, bloated animal corpses, and swaths of faded cloth formed ghostly apparitions in the mist. As the rain continued and the tides came and went, some of this would wash away, but much would take months to remove or salvage. All of it was an ominous reminder of the force that had seized those unlucky enough to be out on the water.

Shep had heard stories from patients at Haddo of whirlpools that made dinghies look as if they were going down the drain, of a sailboat turning somersaults, a shark stranded in a mango tree, and an octopus clinging to the lightning rod atop a submerged bungalow. Everyone knew someone who still was missing.

"Dr. Durant."

He turned to find Alfred Baird, the Assistant Commissioner, picking his way through the foreshore debris. Shep held out his umbrella, but the major waved it aside; he wore a military mackintosh, and the rain had lightened to drizzle.

"You're all right, then?" Baird asked.

"Not all. Our servants—"

"Ah, yes. I heard." The gray light made Baird look jaundiced and gaunt, too frail for his sympathetic voice.

"Any news?"

"Well, we found the *Sapphire's* smokestack on the beach below my house at Rangachang."

Shep lowered the pointless umbrella. "What else?"

"That's all we could identify."

Shep followed Baird's gaze to the swollen flesh of animal limbs and organs strewn down the beach. Despite the rain the stench was rising. A few yards away, a pack of wild dogs nosed the carcass of a goat. Other remains were unrecognizable for the crabs encrusting them.

His voice caught in his throat. "They were like family, Alfred. And their daughter's barely thirteen."

"Has she relatives?"

"Not here. I don't think so." He hesitated. "I don't actually know."

Baird pushed back the hood of his slicker and rubbed the mist through his thinning hair. He lifted his face to the sky and moved his lips silently.

At length he said, "I've heard some of the Ross evacuees talking about leaving. The ladies, in particular. Now the Blitz seems to have ebbed, home's looking a tad more inviting."

Shep had heard this talk himself. *Even if the war is closer,* the homeward logic went, *at least we'll be among our own.* But neither he nor Claire really had any "own" apart from each other and Ty. And there were so many reasons for them not to leave. Foremost now, Naila.

"I'm afraid we've the opposite problem," he said. "It'll take me months to replace my specimens. And Claire wants to get up to Behalla to see how the Biya have fared. But first we need to find somewhere to live. Ross, I gather, is permanently off limits."

Baird considered him briefly. "In that case, maybe I can help. There's a house available up Marine Hill, just below the Commissioner's new compound."

The girl refused to talk about her parents. Claire and Shep both had tried, though neither of them could find the right words. For now, they decided the best course was to play along with her hopes. Fortunately, Ty seemed immune to her grief, though Claire wished more than ever that he would start talking. Some days the silence threatened to swallow them all.

Moving at least kept them busy. The house that Baird had recommended was strange and beautiful, whitewashed and terraced down the hill. It reminded Claire of the Greek villages they'd sailed past during their Mediterranean crossing, and she learned it actually had been built by a Greek sea captain—before he decided not to retire to the Andamans after all.

Shep hired a van to carry Claire and the children up and over the hill on moving day. Leyo would meet them there, along with Abraham, the new cook referred by Shep's driver Narinder.

"Sure you don't need me?" Shep asked as he opened the passenger door for his wife. Narinder waited across the road to drive him around the point to the hospital at Haddo.

"Not a bit." She kissed his cheek. "When you come home tonight we'll be almost all settled."

It confounded her how different life was already. Shep had had this gleaming red Morris and the services of Narinder here on the mainland from the beginning, but as long as they lived on Ross she'd rarely laid eyes on either car or driver. Now she was touched each morning by the sight of a fresh orchid in the vase that Narinder had wired to the dashboard. The tall stately Gujarati ex-convict might have a political past, but he showed a zest for grace.

In the van, Ty sat beside her, while Naila squeezed into the back among the cartons and suitcases. The girl still wasn't speaking in more than monosyllables, but the motion of the vehicle and the whipping of hot air loosened Claire's tongue. "Can we see your school from up here?"

Naila pointed without interest down through the damp sunshine toward an island of red-roofed buildings surrounded by flooding from the cricket field. There would be no school for the foreseeable future.

A dog started barking when the van passed the massive gates of Commissioner Wilkerson's new Government House. Ty's face brightened, and Claire could almost hear him shouting, "Wilkie!"—Ty's canine friend from Ross. But the boy's outburst sounded only in her imagination, and the next stretch grew quiet as the outer slope thickened with mangosteen, kapok, and banyans.

At the end of the road, they drove over a gully and through a pair of open gates to stop under a trellis of white bougainvillea. Claire took Ty by the hand, and they entered the house's breezeway vestibule.

The red padauk wood floor led to an open-air sitting room with cushioned bamboo seats and a view of Mount Harriet beyond the fretwork railing. Naila craned her head to look east, but the property was angled so that Ross was out of sight.

"It's not easy to get your bearings," Claire said. "But eventually we'll get used to it."

Straight downhill, a red clay path switchbacked through a nearly vertical garden. Ginger and jasmine bushes screened the servant quarters, a glass greenhouse, and several sheds. At the bottom of the path a gate opened onto the wreckage of the foreshore road. What was left of Aberdeen Jetty lay around the bend. Incredibly, this house had sustained no damage in the quake. The captain had built on bedrock.

Leyo and the new cook had not yet arrived, so while the van driver unloaded their bags, Claire showed the children the rest of the house. An open-air staircase led one flight down to a dining room and kitchen, another flight to two bedrooms and a bath. The rooms were white and square and equipped with simple bamboo furnishings like those on the terrace. Dirty clouds of netting hung above the beds. A third flight led down to two more large rooms, which would serve as playroom and study.

Ty pulled Naila into his room. They pushed back the shutters, and sunshine puddled hotly on the floor among shadows of giant palm fronds. Ty crouched like a frog and, silent as ever, hopped from one dark pad to the next. After each jump he turned his head and blinked expectantly at the girl, who watched him without moving.

Hop. Turn. Blink. Hop. Turn. Hop. Blink.

Finally, Naila gave in. She cupped her chin with her palms and began to flutter her fingers. She made a buzzing noise and pretended to fly. Circling closer, closer above Ty, she veered until, at last, she lost her balance.

As the gold light lapped over them, Claire saw the girl almost starting to laugh, but in that instant the little frog leapt. Their two small bodies converged, and the room seemed to hold its breath.

July 1941

From her first day at the white house, Naila sensed she had been to this place before. Or near here. She knew the dusty sweet smell of this hill, that jungle of brush across the gully, the steep angle of the slope below the road. Or, she thought she did.

The memory was dim and distant: her father taking her by the hand. She'd been younger than Ty Babu. The yellow-walled compound where her family lived then lay at the base of this hill, on the water. Her father had led her through the jungle up up up what had seemed a mountain. *Never tell anyone. Our secret place.*

The chance to test her memory came several days after their arrival, while Mem and Ty both were napping and everyone else had gone out. Naila slipped out of the house and across the gully, then skirted a thicket of leafy brambles and turned to get her bearings.

The banyans form their own citadel. Aerial roots had dangled like Shiva's arms, while the base roots snaked into the earth. She pressed on. Forward. This way. That. The grass rose above her head. She was well out of sight of the white house when she spotted the grove. Dozens of trunks, each as big around as five men. They pressed so close against each other that it seemed there was no way in, but her father had shown her the hidden passage, behind one trunk and between two others. When she located the swirling root with the knot like a raised fist, she felt him urging her on.

Gripping a stick to fend off snakes, she inched inside the maze. The air stiffened with heat, dusky as dreamlight. The soles of her chappals caught, slapping her heel each time she pulled free, but the passage widened gradually until she could stretch her arms and brace herself. Lizards skittered into crevices. Butterflies darted high above her, bright as little kites. A mongoose giggled from a middle branch. *Better, daughter?*

Better, she answered, silent as Ty and clutching the truth of the word.

Her foot found the clay floor before she could see it, buried under fallen leaves but still solid and level. When she came with her father, they'd used nets to collect the leaves and a broom to sweep the hidden platform. Above and around them, the branches reached for the sky, and the sun had shimmered among the leaves as through bottle glass.

The branches reached higher today. The sun trembled more darkly. She used her stick to clear a path, and dust whirled like smoke. She sneezed and covered her nose until it settled. No rush. The sanctuary still was a secret, hers alone to reclaim.

She examined the trunks that surrounded the floor until she came to the flat expanse, smaller than she remembered. The marks lined up in rows so carefully contained that it seemed as if the gods had designated this and only this small tablet for the record of hope, and even a single mark outside its borders would be a desecration.

Silence is a form of strength, her father had insisted when he brought her to this place. So many years ago. He called this labyrinth of trunks the Freedom Tree. *The firenghi have their churches, the Hindus their temples and the Mohammedans their mosques, but I have never known a shrine more sacred than this one.*

In the trunk's flat expanse, smooth as a man's back, a series of letters and dates had been carved. The faintest still read *R.M. Dass 1872*, beside ten cuts that numbered the convict's days in hiding. *A.J. Prakash* stayed here five days in 1899, *B.R. Agarwhal* almost one month in 1900. The last was *V.H. Choudhry*, here just three days in 1911. It was to him that Naila's father as a boy had brought food and water to sustain the freedom fighter until he fled into the forest.

She looked to the right of the markings for a cleft between two trunks. *Make a wish*, he had said. *Write it down.* He handed her a slip of white paper and a pencil, and in her childish hand she had scribbled the wish, which he wouldn't let her tell him. *Fold it and give it to the tree, and the gods will kiss it for you.*

The cleft had filled in, grown together. Ants streamed from a bore hole. There was nothing now left of her wish, which she couldn't recall.

She became dimly aware of her elbow, a scratchy sensation against the skin. *But they have given you another.* She glanced down at the wood beneath her arm and drew a quick breath, yanked back.

The black scorpion raised its tail, glaring at her, pincers snapping like a crab's. It was almost the size of her palm. Her father had told her these black ones were poisonous when young, but they gentled with age.

"Are you young or old?" she asked.

The scorpion skittered sideways. She took another step back and rubbed her arm.

Wilkerson had turned his reception hall into a war room. He wore his whites starched and pressed, mosquito boots spit and polished. This morning even his muttonchops seemed crisp. His wife had left, the war was raging on three continents, his empire under attack, and his colonial outpost had been shaken to its foundations, but by God, Wilkerson would show that he was still in charge of Port Blair.

Police superintendent Denis Ward and his sub-inspector Rao; Tom Lutty; Small of the transport division; Reverend Crisp; and the superintendent of schools Dr. Dirwan Singh joined Shep and Baird around a massive dining table spread with a wall map of the Andaman archipelago. The Commissioner had armed Baird with an array of colored crayons. When Chief Forest Officer Mukerjee arrived to report damage in the western coastal areas, Baird marked said zones on the map with small green circles. The schools most in need of repair were noted in red, Small's list of impassable roads in blue, Shep's survey of compromised hospitals and dispensaries in orange.

The whole exercise reminded Shep of the map his father had stretched across his library wall during the Chinese Civil War, with colored pins to track the winning and losing "teams."

"Casualty report, Durant?" The Commissioner swung his pallid gaze, and Shep handed him a list compiled from interviews with the injured, Ward's records, and Lieutenant Reynold's list of vessels and crews that remained unaccounted for.

"We've been able to confirm only ten deaths, sir, but treated one hundred fifty-four injuries. Several dozen individuals have been reported missing. Considering the magnitude, I suppose we're lucky, but that's little comfort to the families of the disappeared."

"Agreed." Reverend Crisp raised one desiccated palm. "Only the Lord can supply true comfort."

Denis Ward talked over the piety. "I heard you're missing a couple of servants, Durant." The young police chief's reptilian eyes flickered under the ledge of his brow. After the business with the Jarawa captives, Shep and Claire had steered clear of Ward, but resentment on both sides still simmered. Ward looked as if he meant to turn Jina and Som's death into some kind of sinister joke.

"Ah yes," piped up Dr. Singh. "One of my faculty asked me to convey his concern to you regarding their daughter. I gather the girl was his student. He was wondering, what's to be done with her?" Despite his avuncular manner and wire-rimmed glasses, Singh seemed to Shep to be shading his meaning.

"How old is she now?" Ward asked, and the chain of twitching brows around the table tipped Shep at last. The local gender imbalance being what it was, every male in Port Blair had noticed Naila growing up as she marched to and from the ferry.

Only Lloyd Crisp appeared to have any interest in praying for this poor child's soul, much less protecting her body—only Crisp and Alfred Baird, who cast Shep a look of genuine compassion.

Shep said a bit too emphatically, "She's still a *child*. And grieving."

"Is she registered?"

"Sir?"

Wilkerson thumbed the table. "Registered as an orphan for the census. Which reminds me, are there others orphaned by the quake?"

Shep felt run over. "Doubtless, Commissioner, but I can't very well declare a child an orphan without verifying the parents are dead. Why on earth do you ask?"

The Commissioner's erect white hair gave him the look of a cockatoo. "I am ultimately responsible for those who abide in this settlement. Including your little brown girl."

We are their mothers and their fathers. The colonial lament.

Ward stifled a guffaw as Lutty and the Indians fixed their collective attention on a point at the center of the map in front of them.

Shep snapped to. "Well, sir, in the case of this particular little girl, you needn't trouble yourself. Claire and I are her guardians."

"Are you?" Wilkerson sounded genuinely appalled.

"That's the Christian spirit!" Reverend Crisp exclaimed. "I'm surprised I don't see you and Claire in church more often."

Baird looked up from his disaster checklist and said quietly, "You might want to formalize that arrangement, Doctor."

"I intend to." The thought hadn't crossed his mind. "We've been trying to locate her relatives. If we can't, we're prepared to adopt her."

Wilkerson snorted his disapproval, but all he said was "Better declare her parents dead first," and returned to more important business.

Shep had caught himself off guard with his semi-public declaration of custody. The chaos, the move, the work, the uncertainty that hovered over all future plans left him little energy for his wife and son, let alone for Naila. Of course, he pitied the girl and intended to safeguard her until other provisions could be made, but the true gravity of her plight only now dawned on him. Men in the Andamans were like hyenas poised to pounce. Before he broached the subject with Claire, however, he solicited Leyo's advice.

Leyo, too, had been watching Naila grow up, and his fondness for her was transparent, but Leyo hadn't a predatory nerve in his body. "Naila is excellent girl," he assured Shep. "Most intelligent."

It was late afternoon. They stood together in the new greenhouse surrounded by orchids that Leyo had transported from the Ross garden. On his way down, Shep had paused to watch Naila and Ty on the lower terrace. *VANDA, VANILLA, ELEPHANT, SPIDER.* Ty drew on the pavement with chalk while Naila watched, absently rubbing her earlobe. The words blossomed over crude sketches of the flowers they named, the children so engrossed they barely noticed Shep passing. Som had taught them well.

"But you don't think she might be a bit *too* attached to Ty?"

The affection in Leyo's smile made Shep instantly regret the question. And when he broached the subject with Claire that night, after the children were in bed, he wondered if he'd only imagined her original jealousy of Naila's closeness with Ty. Certainly, it had since been replaced by deep sympathy for the girl.

They sat in the dark, on the loveseat in the breezeway. Claire said she'd tried every way she could think of to identify other family members, but Naila truly seemed to have no one. "Jina's parents came from somewhere in Bengal, but she has no idea where, no names or even a town."

"What about Som?" Shep asked.

She shook her head.

Across the water, heat lightning danced off North Point. Incense filled the air, but the mosquitoes still sounded as if they were doing a mating dance overhead.

"We're all she has," Claire said, but her reading of this line missed its mark. It came out more question than statement.

Shep slapped a biter that had found his elbow and began filling his pipe. Latakia tobacco worked better than bugspray.

"That teacher at school," he said. "Singh said he asked after her." It was an exploratory gambit, but Claire went on as if he hadn't spoken.

"She needs Ty. He's become her . . . her security blanket." Her voice had a troublingly sacrificial quaver.

Shep lit the pipe and wreathed them in the strong smoke. Normally Claire hated this smell as much as the bugs did. Tonight, she said nothing.

Perhaps the guilt was eating her. They should at least have an answer for Naila—what *had* happened to Jina and Som? They had an educated guess, but that wouldn't satisfy the child, and for her the not knowing might almost be the worst of all. It surely didn't help that he, as Civil Surgeon, was the one responsible *for* knowing.

He'd been about to test the notion of adopting the girl but was stopped by the undercurrent of ambivalence in Claire's tone—as well as his own misgivings. It was still too soon for any of them. Until they had some proof of death, or more time had passed, it would be a mistake even to raise the possibility.

And then there was Ty. Relying on Naila as a servant was one thing but bringing her into the family forever was quite another. Shep believed Ty would soon start to speak. He did not think the exclusivity of the children's bond was anything to worry about. But what if he was wrong? What if Naila's continued presence drove a permanent wedge between them and their son? He wasn't only concerned about the potential effect of this on Claire, but also on their marriage.

"What about you?" he asked Claire.

"Me?"

"What's *your* security blanket?"

Shep wanted her to say, *You,* or maybe, *You and Ty,* but she merely put her arms around his neck and pressed her face to his chest. He stroked her hair, though the erotic charge of this gesture was missing. The strands felt chopped and stringy, like a child's, and this sensation fired a mixture of sadness and paternalism. He countermanded it by nibbling the lip of her ear.

When she didn't react, he released her. "I stopped in at the Browning Club this afternoon. A new batch of papers have come in. The Japs have bloody well overrun China."

"You think we should leave too." Neither statement nor question, the words seemed to float in the darkness.

"Sometimes I think we're living in a dream world, Claire. Maybe the quake was God's wake-up call."

But he could see she didn't want to wake up, didn't even want to lift her head, much less return to reality. "We've been interrupted," she said at last. "That's all. Bad as the quake was, the war is surely worse. At least here we're safely out of it."

"*Accha.*" Relieved in spite of his tough talk, he rose to pour them two good stiff drinks. "That's my girl, then. We carry on."

And so a new routine established itself, with the notion of adoption eclipsed by Claire's decision to "promote" Naila to "official" ayah. This formalized the girl's right to sleep in Ty's bedroom while freezing her status at arm's length. Meanwhile, the failure of the schools to reopen allowed them all to sidestep other pressing concerns about her future.

Narinder and his cousin Abraham occupied the servant quarters, along with Leyo, and gradually the household found a new, awkward rhythm and tentative balance. Unfortunately, Shep wasn't doing much to help right the balance, since his new routine left him less free time than he'd ever had on Ross.

Gupta used to handle the bulk of his mainland cases. Now Shep split each day between the hospitals at Haddo and Atlanta Point, and despite an increased patient load after the disaster, when Gupta left at the end of September no replacement was even mentioned. As expected, this secured Shep's non-combat status, but it also left him strapped. So, while Leyo had transplanted most of his orchids here at the house, Shep hadn't even begun to resurrect his lab, and Ty was often sound asleep before his father kissed him goodnight.

Claire was right. It could be much, much worse. Yet a persistent disquiet continued to dog Shep, and he couldn't figure out why. Then one cloudy morning when he was up early and alone on the terrace, as Abraham deposited a boiled egg, a couple of slices of toast, and a cup of tea in front of him, Shep was struck by the surliness of the cook's attitude. It was not uncommon in Port Blair, this air of a former convict, resentful subject and rebellious soul, and intellectually Shep couldn't blame him. Narinder had told him that he and Abraham both had been swept up by the British when they were hot-headed students in their teens and shipped into exile before they were men. They were released from the Cellular Jail within months of their arrival, and because of their low caste, their prospects were actually better here than they'd been at home. But still their treatment smarted.

Left alone to eat, Shep watched the eastern clouds turn yellow. Narinder had a quiet cheer about him. Shep liked and trusted his driver almost as much as he did Leyo—as he had Jina and Som. Because of this, he'd accepted Narinder's recommendation and brought his cousin into the household without a qualm. A little older than Narinder and bonier than Som, Abraham wore a thick broom of a mustache and his graying hair oiled and parted to one side. His eyes were large and dark-rimmed, smoldering. There was never a mark on his white serving jacket or trousers, but he radiated the garlicky smell of neem oil, which Shep suspected he used on his eczema. He also had a limp, which worsened in the course of most days until he was forced to use a stick by evening. Probably arthritis, though the man refused his offers of treatment. Abraham lacked Narinder's strength and vigor, but that was no cause for concern.

What, then? It was so subtle, this new edge of defiance, that Shep would have dismissed it outright, were it not for the new wave of Indian nationalism unleashed across the port by the latest rumors of war. Among the nationalists it was an article of faith—and underground propaganda— that the Japanese were fighting the British on behalf of all Asians for their "greater prosperity." Many here not so secretly hailed the recent enemy advances in Indochina and would welcome Japanese occupation. No Asian could be worse at the helm than the British—such was the thinking among the firebrands. Well, the Chinese could tell the Indians a thing or two; try asking the survivors of Nanking about the yellow brotherhood. Or his childhood classmates, now men in their thirties who, staking everything on Shanghai, had wound up trapped behind the wall of war.

That said, he could hardly blame men like Abraham for wanting a taste of freedom. And Narinder wasn't the only one who'd vouched for him. Wilkerson said he'd cooked for a French plantation owner, as well as for the family of a dreaded guard at the Cellular Jail. No harm had come to any of them.

He wiped his mouth. Abraham likely was the least of their worries. They were living in a penal colony after an earthquake in the middle of a world war with their household spiraling around one child who refused to speak and another who'd just lost her parents. No wonder things seemed bleak.

November 1941

"Was anyone hurt?" Claire asked.

Leyo had just come from Behalla, his first visit since *gumul*, the end of the rainy season, when the Biya returned from monsoon camp. Though the quake had been stronger up north, it seemed that Kuli warned everyone in time.

"He can feel the spirit dance," Leyo said.

"As you did," Claire said, though in several discussions about this, Leyo had never been able to articulate *how* he'd sensed this "dancing" before the quake even began.

She longed to return to Behalla to have this conversation with Kuli directly, but the loss of Jina made it impossible to leave Ty now. Abraham had demonstrated neither the aptitude nor the inclination for childcare, and Naila was still too young for such responsibility. At the same time, the girl was so possessive of Ty that it would be risky to bring in a proper ayah—even if such a woman could be found here. When they first arrived in Port Blair, Claire hadn't appreciated what a rarity Jina was, given the gender imbalance of the convict population. She told herself that once the port recovered and Naila was back in school, Shep's duties would subside again and they'd find a way, but for now her field work remained on hiatus.

Leyo smiled, lifting one palm high above Kuli's phantom head and lowering the other to his own knees. "Kuli can hear Biliku dance more than one hour before the ground will shake." As compared to his own few-seconds alert.

Sixth sense, Claire wrote in her field book. *Magnetic fields? Natural attunement (magic!) Some deep vibration.*

"So the others depend on Kuli to warn them?"

"All except Artam," Leyo said. "But she is learning."

"How?"

Leyo explained that Kuli had instructed his people to move to higher ground and into the open. Artam, ever mischievous, decided that the climb was too arduous, and she felt sleepy, so she snuck away from the group and marched back home. Claire could just see the little imp trudging through the forest. So stubborn. So independent. She had these qualities, at least, in common with Ty.

Leyo continued, "You ask if anyone injured. Only the little one. She will not follow Kuli out. So! House beam is fall on her."

"No!"

Leyo grinned at Claire's alarm and made a slicing movement with his hand across one shoulder, spread a wide gap between forefingers and thumb.

Claire couldn't understand his glee at what sounded like a serious wound. "It might have killed her!"

Leyo straightened on his haunches. His expression grew sober. "If then, God must be angry."

Weeks passed. Months. Still, as far as Naila was concerned, nothing made any sense. How many times had she ridden the ferry back and forth between Aberdeen and Ross Island? The boats might look identical to others, but she could tell the *Sapphire* from the *Benbow* from the *Dundee* with her eyes closed. She knew the *Benbow*'s roll, the growl of the *Dundee*'s engine, the stink of rancid ghee from a spill that had seeped into the *Sapphire*'s splintered deck. Ranjit, the old pilot of the *Benbow*, kept torn chappatis in his pocket to throw for the fish, and he loved to tell about spearing barracuda when he was growing up in Haddo. Akash, one of the crewmen on the *Sapphire*, sketched passengers in his drawing pad, and his likenesses were as accurate as they were fast. In the back of his pad he had pictures of some Jarawa that he'd encountered when his group was set upon during a trek to Mount Koyob. They looked a little like Leyo, but the Jarawa carried white and black spears, and Akash said they wore only red breechcloths and bracelets. He'd shyly covered the naked breasts in one drawing as he told Naila that their attackers took some metal things—camping cups and pans—then vanished back into the forest as suddenly as they'd appeared. *Like a living dream.*

How could he and her parents be gone? *Where* had they gone? *She* was living a nightmare.

Aside from Ty Babu, only Leyo now had the power to lift her mood. Before, Leyo had come and gone, but now he lived at the white house and was always sweeping and scrubbing and helping Mem or tending to the plants he'd brought from Ross Island for Doctor *saab*. He seemed to think his duties also included playing with her and Ty Babu. They'd take Ty's hands and dance him in circles. Or when Doctor Shep was home sometimes he'd yell to Leyo, "Want a coconut?" and the two of them would toss Ty back and forth until he melted in giggles. Leyo would ride Ty on his shoulders and trumpet his arm like an elephant's trunk, waving for her to join in until she heard herself hooting and tooting. Sometimes Ty Babu sneaked up behind him and pretended to be a snake or spider biting his leg, and the crazy way Leyo hopped around the garden actually made Naila laugh.

Once he caught her looking out over the harbor while Ty was chasing a lizard down the steps, and he took her hand between both of his and blew on her fingertips as if to warm them. Instead the sensation cooled and calmed her, and when he raised his eyes she was startled by his tears and by the strange sense that he was crying for her—as if to lighten the burden of tears that she herself needed to shed. But she didn't ask or even want him to take these tears from her.

Though she could no longer picture their homecoming, she still told herself that tears *could* be shed for joy, so she should stopper these feelings—all feelings—until she found her parents. She mustn't even be angry with Leyo, for that was a feeling, too.

She withdrew her hand, tucked it under her arm, and turned away.

On the last morning in November, a swarm of military police vehicles descended on Aberdeen Market. Shep was passing the clock tower when he saw the commotion below, and the arrests were conducted so swiftly that, by the time he reached the bottom of the hill, the Kobayashis' photo shop had been barricaded and the Japanese couple already were being marched, manacled, onto the jetty where tenders were waiting to take them, along with the port's other Japanese resident, a dentist, out to a troop ship bound for Calcutta.

Shep approached Wilkerson's parked yellow and black Standard, where the Commissioner sat monitoring the roundup. "What's this all about?"

"Spies," came the terse reply.

Shep suppressed a laugh. The Japanese had been an innocuous presence in Port Blair long before he or Wilkerson ever set foot on these islands. The notion of them as war criminals was farcical.

By the time he was describing the scene to Claire that evening, however, he'd begun to rethink his initial reaction. Due to enemy submarine threats, the formerly semi-monthly sailings of the *SS Maharaja* had become increasingly erratic. Many vital earthquake repairs were on permanent hold for lack of supplies. There were shortages in dry goods, rice, and tinned foods. All over town, merchants complained. Administrators missed their bangers and mash, and transport drivers jury-rigged their vehicles for lack of parts. Those deliveries of mainland and foreign papers that did get through carried worsening news from Europe and Africa, and though months old by the time they arrived, the *Times*'s photographs of the Blitz had brought the plight of Britain into chilling focus. Then, in September, Japan, Italy, and Germany had signed the Tripartite Pact.

"So I suppose we ought to be surprised it took this long," Shep said. "If there were any German or Italian nationals here, they'd be carted off too."

Below them in the garden, fireflies had begun to blink. Naila and Ty were competing with Leyo to catch them. Ty's laughter burst like hiccups.

"Thinking about your parents?" Claire asked.

"Not much point, is there?"

"If mine were in England, I'd be worried sick."

"I know it's difficult for you to understand, Claire, but my parents despise me, and over time the feeling's become mutual."

"They're still your parents."

"I don't wish them dead."

"Well, bully for you!" She started to lean away from him, then found his hand and squeezed. "Those poor people in London and France."

"And Poland and Holland and Belgium. Not to mention China. I know."

"Focus on the currents, and you'll be swept away."

"What's that?"

"Something my father taught me out in the woods to get me across a deep stream. He said, before I stepped onto each boulder, to focus on it as if it were the whole world, but on no account to let my fear pull my thoughts into the water around it."

Shep kissed her. "Don't you want to be swept away?"

December 1941

They were having drinks at the club when a late-breaking bulletin filled with static came over the radio. Everyone leaned in as Baird labored the knob until the announcer came clear:

"Early yesterday morning, local time, Japan launched a surprise air attack on the American naval base at Pearl Harbor in Hawaii and declared war on Britain and the United States. The US President, Franklin D. Roosevelt, has mobilised all his forces and is poised to declare war on Japan."

Wilkerson let out a strangled cough. Everyone else froze in charged silence as the radio continued to pulse shock waves of details across the room, but Shep had stalled on a single word: *yesterday*. Even this galvanizing news had the faded quality, in Port Blair, of a print left too long in the sun.

He touched Claire's elbow. She was staring at the recently installed blackout drapes.

"I'm so sorry," Alfred Baird said, coming over.

"Part of me thinks it must be a hoax," she said.

"And the other part?"

She sighed almost apologetically and raised her glass in a toast. "That part thinks, now America's in, it'll soon be over."

Across the room Commissioner Wilkerson stopped tugging his mustache. He lifted those glacial blue eyes and said with alarmingly uncharacteristic humility, "From your lips to God's ears, my dear."

March 1942

Notices were posted on March 7, the day Rangoon fell. Civilians and civil officials were to leave Port Blair as soon as the *SS Norilla* could get there to collect them. A second ship would follow for military personnel.

No local-borns or natives.

And so, at last Shep and Claire were forced to confront the reality they'd been avoiding ever since the war started. In peacetime, they agreed, they surely would have gone on as they were, perhaps for years. Now it was out of their hands. They had all they could do to secure berths for themselves, and no one could say what would happen once they reached Calcutta. It was a brutal situation for Naila, but they had no choice.

That afternoon, while Claire kept the children busy downstairs, Shep summoned Abraham, Narinder, and Leyo to the breezeway. Since they'd have to spring for the ship as soon as it dropped anchor, and no one could be certain when it might arrive, he wanted to settle up now.

Narinder said he would stay on until the doctor and his family left, but Abraham quit on the spot. He said he needed to go to his village, though he'd never before mentioned having ties outside the port.

Shep wasn't sorry to see the cook's back. A few days of foraging for themselves in the kitchen was a small price to pay for one less worry at this point. So, he paid and thanked both men for their service.

Leyo stood back, still as a hat rack until the other two had gone out. "So," Shep said. "You tell me, Leyo. What shall we do?"

Leyo told him then, and after agreeing, Shep went directly to Claire's study. From the window he watched Leyo lead Naila and Ty down to the greenhouse. They would spend the next hour crating and labeling his most valuable specimens.

As he explained the plan, Claire pressed her fists together. When her knuckles turned white, he attempted a joke. "Fortunately, Leyo's gaga over the girl. And at least the dowry's within our means."

"She's *thirteen*," she snapped. "You didn't—"

"No, Claire." He patted the air for her to calm down. He wasn't lying. Leyo's offer to stay with Naila and, if necessary, to take her into the forest for safety seemed purely protective. Then again, Shep couldn't speak for the boy's desires and, by local custom, both he and Naila were plenty old enough to marry. Claire herself had told him the Biya traditionally married around fifteen, and child brides were common throughout Asia—not that he'd wish that on Naila.

"I'm just trying to make the best of a bad situation," he said.

"Your best isn't making a dent."

Neither they nor Leyo breathed a word of the plan to Naila. It would be best for her and for Ty, they agreed, if both thought she was coming with them. Claire gave her a suitcase and a rucksack to fill with her belongings. Together they packed boxes with the same possessions that, just eight months ago, Naila and Leyo had retrieved from the wreckage of Ross Island. Anything they couldn't take now, Claire stressed, would be sent on the second sailing. "Or we can just put it into storage until we come back."

Listening to herself, she thought she sounded like a nitwit, but the reassuring stream seemed to have its intended impact on the girl, whose diligent attentiveness so resembled Jina's that it made Claire ache to watch her.

On March 12, the word went out that the *Norilla* was approaching Landfall Island and would be in port by morning. Evacuees would have until two o'clock to board. No exceptions.

Supper that night consisted of mangoes and curd, some McVitie's, and the last of their gin and tonic. Then, promising a busy day tomorrow, Claire put Ty to bed early. She read him a chapter of *Winnie-the-Pooh* in as close to a monotone as she could manage. When she was sure he was asleep, she asked Naila down to her study, where Shep and Leyo were waiting.

The empty shelves glared at them through the faltering lamplight as they sat in a circle on stiff cane chairs surrounded by packing boxes. The curtains were drawn. They'd chosen this room for privacy. Leyo thought it best if not even Narinder knew their plan. But Shep had decided the time had come to tell Naila.

Claire watched the girl as he explained the what and the why and the details. Surprise never visibly registered. Naila sat with her hands clasped between her knees and stared at the pale squares on the wall where pictures had been removed. In the new pink blouse and green skirt that they had given her just last week, her black ringlets circling her face, she looked every bit the schoolgirl she should have been.

Of the four of them only Leyo seemed at ease. He stood to one side, arms akimbo, and Claire felt his gaze wash over each of them in turn. In five years, this young man had never given her a single reason to doubt or distrust him, and over these same years he'd shown unfailing affection for Naila, as he would a younger sister. Still . . .

"We're not leaving you here." Claire turned to Naila. "As soon as we get to Calcutta, we'll see Shep's friend in the Foreign Office and apply to bring you and Leyo both over on the next ship." But the impulsiveness of this reassurance immediately deflated it, and Shep's barely stifled groan warned her not to continue.

The girl shifted in her seat and turned her gaze hard to the window, but the blackout drapes blocked any hint of the world outside.

IV

March 13, 1942

Daylight is fading when they emerge. Naila leads Ty down a shortcut across the gully, but the boy is still yawning from his second nap, and she has to help him from stone to stone. Her movements feel as mechanical and disconnected as the thoughts she is trying to push out of reach.

She didn't intend to fall asleep herself.

What *did* she intend?

Just ten minutes, Mem had said. How much time has passed since then?

The ship . . .

Naila gives her head a shake and stretches an arm back for Ty to grab. She meant to show Mem, to make her grateful enough—

But Ty claps his hands and reaches up past her, and when she turns, Leyo is standing above them on the gully's rim. His coral sarong blazes in the slanting light, and the hard set of his jaw gives his face an unfamiliar severity.

Naila expects him to offer his hand. Instead he jumps down and, with one strong fist cuffs her arm while lifting Ty with the other up onto the grass. She starts to protest, but he stops her with a jerk.

"Mem has gone." He pushes her up.

Ty laughs when she stumbles into him.

"Gone where?"

"On the ship." And it is as if he's fed her a sweet in which she can taste poison.

Then Ty is on Leyo's shoulders, Naila again in his grip, and they walk up the garden path so quickly, she has to trot to keep from stumbling. "And Doctor *saab*?"

"He made Mem to go alone."

"*TY!*" Doctor Shep's voice roars ahead of him as he charges down from the terrace, nearly toppling Naila in his haste to seize his son. He hugs the boy as if he means to open his heart and stuff the wriggling child inside, and he only stops when Ty gives a shriek and pushes him away.

Then, for the first time, the doctor looks at Naila. "You stupid, stupid girl."

That night is ungodly. The two of them, father and son, battle like life-long enemies. Tears. Fists. Wails. Teeth. Inarticulate screams. Ty refuses to surrender Naila. Shep refuses to let the girl anywhere near him. Rage eviscerates his compassion.

Rage and dread.

There is no way to convey to his son what danger his beloved has visited upon them. He chases the child around the locked room like an animal in a cage, lifting him kicking into his arms, and clasps him against his chest.

Eventually, as the boy's tantrum winds down, Shep sings to him. "Toot, Toot, Tootsie! (Goo' Bye!)." "Pennies from Heaven." "The Way You Look Tonight." Songs that float back to him from those first weeks with Claire in New York, when he sang to her as they walked across the Brooklyn Bridge, or waited for the train to meet her parents, or stargazed from the top of the Empire State Building. When he saw her as his salvation.

At last Ty sleeps, and Shep lies down beside him, but his own mind refuses. It was worse with Claire. She pled with him. She wailed and beat him with her fists. She screamed. He had to call the MPs to help him restrain her after Wilkerson ordered her onto the ship.

Then Shep drugged his own wife. To get her away from him. To save her? It won't come to that, he tells himself. It can't. But if not, will she ever forgive him?

She will, he decides. She must. What else could he do?

Right now, he reminds himself, the more urgent question is Naila. Naila and Ty.

What she had heard of magic she distrusted.

The line is from *Kim*, the "she" in question the half-caste woman who cared for poor little Kimball O'Hara. After Kim was orphaned, this woman's distrust of the white man's magic convinced her that keeping the boy with her was the only way to keep him safe. But there, *after Kim was orphaned* was the crucial condition.

Though Shep's childhood China was a different Orient than Kipling's India, he always identified with the risk of being left, lost, reclaimed, and refashioned on the other side of the racial divide. Some of his own amahs were dearer to him than his mother ever could be, but others would have sold him to the highest bidder if given half a chance. And even the blend of solicitude, duty, and possessive delight that the very best servants displayed around their white charges could be unsettling. As a child, Shep never quite believed his mother's *That could never happen to you*. Flung with an air of exasperation, it always suggested to Shep that "that" likely would.

Kipling's line had first returned to him one night when Ty was nearing two. Claire was off in the forest, and Shep and his son had come home for supper after an evening swim at the club. At the table, Ty got lost in his spoon.

"What do you see in there, old boy?" Shep had leaned closer. The light outside was nearly gone, but the bulb overhead burned bright enough that the child's round face shone in the polished surface.

"Why, what happened!" Shep gasped. "You're upside down!"

Ty frowned, glancing up at him and back, rotating the spoon like a wheel. Shep smiled at his confusion.

"It's a trick of optics," he said. "Reflection on a concave surface is inverted."

Naila brought their supper to the table, setting fish and rice beside Shep, curd and mashed plantain by Ty. She hovered.

"It's all right," Shep said. "I can handle him."

The girl stepped back but didn't leave the room.

He ignored her, addressing his son, who was still examining his spoon. "Did you catch Evelyn Crisp's face at the pool tonight?" Shep asked. "She looked like she'd just given birth to an aardvark."

He dipped his own spoon into the plantains and raised it to Ty's mouth. The boy ate without seeming to notice either the food or his father.

"Fascinating phenomenon. Englishmen take such pride in producing sons, but apparently, it's against the rules to have anything to do with them if their mummies aren't around. I thought Wilkerson was going to need smelling salts to get him to the bar. Nice of Major Baird to give us an attaboy, though. He almost seemed to mean it."

In the back of Ty's spoon Shep's own face danced like a whitefly.

The child took another bite, still absorbed in his reflection. Light fascinated Ty. Music and sound and water, as well. Now he'd discovered that the same bright ball in his spoon was reflected in the lip of his silver cup, and he was trying to bring the two balls together.

Shep picked up his knife. "Listen to this, Ty." He tapped the blade against his water glass, filling the room with a resonant low note.

Ty looked up at his father, eyes widening, mouth forming a silent, perfect circle. He dropped his spoon and reached for the knife.

"No, don't do that." Shep put the spoon back in his son's hand and guided it to the cup. "Tap it." He showed him, and a mid-scale note rang out.

They listened to it quaver and fade, then Ty banged the metal too hard.

"Gently." Better. "Watch this." Shep sipped his water and brought the knife to his glass again.

Ty stared, mesmerized.

"You noticed the change?" Shep tapped again, then took another two sips, nearly emptying the glass.

The next time he tapped, it rang high. Then he held the cup to his son's mouth to drink and helped him guide his spoon.

Naila and Jina and Som all stood gawking from the doorway as Shep filled and emptied the cup and glass.

It must have taken ten rounds before the child's interest waned, at which point he yawned and reached for his father to carry him upstairs. As they passed the dumbstruck servants, his son's soft weight at his neck, a defiant thrill swept through Shep.

He thought, *Distrust* this!

In the morning, he tells Leyo to make a place at breakfast for himself and Naila. Yes, at the same table.

The sun pushes through the cloudcover, and the side of the house casts a hard, diagonal shadow across the terrace. Shep seats Ty beside him in the shade. Then they all watch the boy watch the yellow and green dotted finches sail above the garden.

Ty's eyes are as swollen as Shep's, but in Naila's presence the child willingly stuffs his mouth with bread.

Leyo and Naila continue to wait, their toast and tea untouched.

"You may as well eat," Shep says finally. "We're in this together now, and you'll both need your strength, whatever comes next."

He says nothing of Claire but looks severely at Naila. "The Japanese—I know you've heard talk in town about Asian brotherhood and all that. But Ty and I are not Asian. We cannot afford any further confusion. You're a bright girl, Naila—"

A spasm of anger overcomes him. He swallows hard and forces himself to continue.

"I know you love Ty. You—you'd do anything for him."

The girl pinches her lips together and nods. Her small frame contracts like a moth. She looks as if she might cry.

Fine. He'll drive that pain home. "If the Japanese come before the next evacuation ship, they will take us both prisoners. I don't think Ty would survive that. Do you understand me?"

At the mention of his name Ty stops chewing. To him *prisoner* is a game he plays with Naila on the beach. But the girl's eyes widen. She's a child, too, Shep reminds himself. An orphan, God help her.

She whispers, "Yes, Saab."

He cups his hand over Ty's head, then looks back along the slope of scrub toward the ridge road. Not a sound. He thinks of the commissioner's dead dog.

He passed the poor creature yesterday morning, on his way to the ship. The shepherd lay by the road with his throat slashed wide as a scream. On Ross, Ty used to ride Wilkie like a pony. The two would have long silent conversations. Yesterday Shep had Narinder stop the car. He carried the corpse into Wilkerson's compound himself. Then he put the whole matter out of his mind until he learned his son was missing.

How could he and Claire have been such fools?

Ty climbs down from his chair and tugs at Naila's skirt. When she doesn't move, he tugs harder.

Shep watches until his son's tear-streaked face reddens. "Go ahead."

Naila hoists the boy to her lap and breathes into his neck. Ty rubs her ear.

Shep says, "That tree where you were hiding. Is it true that no full-grown person can get in there?"

Naila opens her mouth but says nothing.

"Leyo saw you come from that direction." He feels rather than sees the exchange of accusation between his two servants. "Answer me."

"Yes, Saab. The way in, it is small."

A plan is coalescing—contingency plan, he corrects himself—but before he can complete it he notices dust rising along the road.

"Quick," he tells Naila. "Take Ty downstairs and give him a bath. And be *quiet* about it. Someone's coming, and they mustn't hear you. Don't show yourselves, either, not to anyone except me and Leyo—" He thinks of his driver, dispatched after the scene at the ship to search for the children up and down the coast. Shep decides to dismiss him when he returns. Better to drive himself now. "Not even Narinder."

He goes up to the forecourt to intercept the visitor and finds Alfred Baird climbing out of his Willys.

Without preamble, Baird says, "Found your boy?"

Shep crumples his expression and drops his gaze, acting never his forte. When he phoned North Station last night to wire Claire, he explained to Lutty that the message was a necessary ruse, so his wife wouldn't worry. He made sure the telegraph officer understood that the boy was "actually still missing."

To Baird now he says, "I thought you might have news."

"Ah. I see. I wish—No."

But then Baird's expression toughens. "I came to warn you. There's been trouble at the jail."

As the major details this trouble, Shep again pictures Wilkie, feels the slaughtered animal's weight in his arms, the vengeful message directed at Wilkerson and, through him, at them all.

"We'll keep searching as best we can," Baird is saying. "You did the right thing sending Claire off safe."

And the whole port must know by now how he did it. Shep slides his fists into his pockets.

Once Baird's gone, he calls for Leyo to bring the children down to Claire's study.

He closes the blackouts. Naila perches on a stool while Ty, still damp from his bath, draws flowers with a stray pencil and paper. Leyo squats beside him. The room is suffocating.

Shep leans against Claire's vacant desk. "You understand that the freedom fighters up at the jail were all sent away." This is true. Shortly after he and Claire arrived in Port Blair, a series of hunger strikes at the jail made their point, and most of the recent political prisoners were sent back to appeal their cases in their home states, leaving the Cellular Jail largely, but not entirely, empty.

"The convicts left inside are *real* criminals—murderers, thieves. They're as dangerous to you, Naila, as to me."

Leyo surely knows this, and Leyo has no more use for these local goons than Shep has, but though Naila nods, he doubts her comprehension.

"Major Baird just told me a gang of men from town went up there this morning and threatened the guards. The Commissioner was able to stop it, but not before several inmates escaped."

He pauses, looks up at the ceiling. "Abraham," he says, and his voice leans sideways. He was wrong not to trust his instincts. "Abraham was one of the ringleaders."

Leyo draws a breath and nods.

"Come here, *mitai*," Naila whispers, but Ty ignores her, busy as ever, and when Shep pushes away from the desk and discovers the boy has unbuckled his mosquito boot, he kicks it across the room.

Naila pulls the startled child out of the way.

"I have to trust you," Shep says to her. "You haven't earned that trust, but I've no choice. For Ty's sake, Naila, you must do as I ask."

March 17, 1942

Just keep him out of the way.

Claire stares into the stifling darkness and girds herself for another day of waiting. She can't afford to keep turning back. She can't stop. Her only defense is to focus on her immediate surroundings: morning at the Fairhaven. It stinks. It clatters. It blooms with the sour reek of dread. Beyond these walls she can feel Calcutta opening like a boil.

She pushes herself up and out from under the mosquito net. Through the blackout curtains comes the pump squeak from the courtyard behind the hotel. Boys below her window shout and splash. Temple music whines in the distance.

She shoves the drapes aside and stands before a spire and a dome, their black silhouettes hard against gunmetal sky. Dung smoke and lead, the rev of two-stroke engines. Only the morning's liquid texture hints at the nearness of water—and that only the river. For all the city's turbulence, it's the missing pulse of ocean that disorients her, almost as much as her missing family. Phantom limb, Shep would call it.

But then she catches the reassuring smells of boiled milk and toast. The low murmur of kitchen staff drifts, along with intermittent harangues. *Carry on. Carry on.*

Claire's room is so small that to dress she has to climb over luggage and bang into boxes of ethnographic field notes and artifacts. Serves her right. All that effort, that study. Five years. The nerve of her. As if words could save her own family, let alone a whole doomed tribe.

She catches herself on the end of the bed and reels back into the vortex of waking on the ship four days ago, the cabin whirling, a smell of machine oil and disinfectant and a small, swarthy man in uniform peering down at her, as if into a cage.

She was still drugged. The wire he handed her didn't compute:
TY FOUND AOK STOP NAILA TOO.

Even now the relief Shep was sending feels dubious and painful. She rubs the bruises on her forearms where the MPs had to restrain her. But, she tells herself, this will all be over by the time the bruises heal. A few more days, just as soon as the next ship brings them across, life can resume. She'll fumble for redemption then.

If only those last unforgivable moments would stop repeating. The children blinking, those quizzical frowns. Naila's blouse, the color of love.

They were only doing as Claire asked: *Just keep him out of the way.*

I didn't mean it the way it sounded. I wasn't myself, so much to do and no more time—I wasn't thinking, I meant for Naila to keep Ty safe, so he wouldn't be stepped on, wouldn't fall or hurt himself.

The excuses stream, but the words she actually uttered hang her.

Just keep him out of the way.

The two of them stepped with such excruciating obedience over the maze of objects on her floor. Objects that spoke to a devotion and people she prized over her own son.

Is that true? Or is it simply a story she's telling to punish herself?

Her memories grow more treacherous. She can still feel the gouge in her chest where Ty punched her with the arrowhead.

When she glanced up and the children were gone—did she give them a second thought? Worse, did she breathe relief?

Inside the Freedom Tree, Naila and Ty play a game called "camping." Part of this game is to sort the medicines that Doctor Shep has sent with them. "Fever," she'll say, and Ty will hand her the glass tube with the green label. "Cut," she slices a finger across her arm, and he points to the red. "Spider!" she cries softly, splaying her hand in the air, and Ty Babu reaches for the salve.

He remembers everything, her boy. He amazes her. And, so long as she keeps his mind occupied, he is fearless and content. But at night, under their doubled mosquito net, she holds him to comfort herself. Can she do what she must to protect him? Doctor *saab* has shown her, painstakingly, how to use the snake bite kit. *I trust you to do this, Naila. When you're alone with him, you are his mother, his father, his doctor, his sister. If he's in danger, you must do everything in your power to protect him. This is what it means to love someone.*

Better to kill the snake *before* it bites, she thinks. And then she steels herself. She will. She must.

Leyo comes to the entrance of the tree before dawn, when the birds begin to sing, and again at nightfall with food and water, toys and crayons. He trades a clean chamber pot for their used one and takes away any rubbish that might smell or attract pests. In the low light, Leyo's dark face is difficult to read, but his hands are gentle now.

"Are you still angry?" she asks.

He takes a wet cloth from his supplies and motions for Ty to wash his face, which the boy does without complaint. Leyo says to Naila, "Why ask me this? You have eyes, ears." He taps lightly on the crown of her head, but he will not smile, and she doesn't know if he means to chide, or to reassure.

"Ask this one." Leyo motions for Ty to scrub the back of his neck. "Ask Doctor Shep. Ask Mem." And his meaning finally takes hold.

"*Mujhe maaf kar dain*," she says, as if she might apologize to all of them through him. "*I* was angry."

"Yes." He sighs. "Look. It is done. Doctor Shep, Police Chief Ward and the Commissioner and Major Baird are the only Europeans left now."

"In all of Port Blair?"

"In all of the islands."

We cannot afford any further confusion. She combs her fingers through Ty's damp waves, and he arches for her to continue down and scratch his back.

"He will go on the next ship," she says. "I promise."

That afternoon Naila and Ty find some hardy aerial roots and climb them like rope ladders up to a height from which they can see the beach. Red and green fishing dhows slide across the water, and beyond them Mount Harriet rises as proud and haughty as ever.

In midday heat like this the waterfront typically is deserted, but today Naila senses a new emptiness. The shacks of the pariahs at the end of the beach look vacant. She can hear no engines, no voices, no whistles, few barks. She spots only one human figure, tall and alone in the long khaki trousers and mosquito boots of a *firangi*, moving along the shore.

Though she cannot make out Doctor *saab*'s face beneath the white topi, she can see the sadness in his body's turning, to and fro, like a lighthouse missing its beacon.

March 20, 1942

Make work. Claire spends the morning at the front desk, copying the hotel register so it can be vetted by the War Office. It's a mindless chore, but it helps stave off worries and gives her a tangible function. There might, after all, be an enemy agent hiding in the list.

She has Roger Matthews to thank for this task, as well as for her general equilibrium. Four nights ago, as the *Norilla* crawled up the delta toward its berth, she felt as if she hadn't a friend in the world. Four million souls were said to inhabit Calcutta, but thanks to the blackout, the only visible lights might have been glow worms. A half moon had risen and with it the noises and smells of industry. The ghostly shapes of stevedores swarmed the wharves. Taxi and rickshaw wallahs brayed for fares. As Claire inched down the gangplank, she had only the vaguest notion of where she would go next. Then a waving boater caught her eye, followed by the advancing glow of a tall figure in white. Roger called her name.

Matthews, a childhood friend of Shep's from Shanghai, is with the Foreign Office, stationed in Calcutta. Claire smiles, remembering their first introduction during their stopover here in '36. Shep had urged her to dress up for the occasion: dinner with Roger at the Grand Hotel, which he described as "palatial and then some." He was so eager to show her off; she put on a yellow beaded evening dress that he said she looked a vision in, and even applied a bit of kohl and rouge.

The Grand was just as he promised. A tuxedoed Sikh played a Steinway, and waiters in starched uniforms with plumed turbans glided across the white lobby. After the heat and dirt of the street, the high ceilings and marble floors seemed as cool as the walls of an igloo, though infinitely more decorative.

The two men zeroed in on each other as hale fellows well met. "What's a lout like you doing in a place like this?" Roger clapped Shep on the shoulder and gave him the once-over. "You're looking fit." Then he spun to Claire. "But hardly worthy of a g-goddess like this!"

She dropped her head, smiling, and Shep beamed as Roger took her gloved hand.

The last time he and Roger had seen each other, Shep said, they'd been sixteen and drilling along the Bund as part of the Shanghai Volunteer Corps. Young Roger had been famous for his ability to crack jokes in seven languages, plus three separate dialects of Chinese. Despite a nervous stutter, linguistic fluency came as naturally to him as breathing, and although he was treated as something of a freak by the other boys, Shep always admired him.

So did Claire. Intellect aside, he had a scarecrow's build and a wide, somewhat horsey face framed by unruly brown hair, but he wore his homeliness with aplomb. He still had a boyish quality, perhaps because he'd never married, or because his intellectual gifts greased the wheels for him so he could sidestep human foibles. That stutter, for instance. It endeared him to Claire, especially when he told them he'd become a lecturer in Sydney straight out of school and had translated several ancient Chinese tomes. Within minutes they were chattering about arcane grammar, diphthongs, umlauts, and all manner of linguistic intricacies—and his stutter vanished.

Two years later, when Ty's silence became a concern, Shep would remind Claire that Roger had overcome his impediment, as if that should encourage her. It didn't much, but she still has fond feelings for Roger. The more so now that he's put her to work for the war effort.

He's also promised to meet her today for lunch, but he's made that promise every day since she arrived in Calcutta, and every day official duties intervene, so she pays scant attention to the ebb and flow of traffic through the Fairhaven's lobby.

What she can't tune out is the passing commentary.

"The Japs call it the Greater East Asia Co-Prosperity Sphere."

"Prosperity my ass, slavery's more like it."

"The better to raise a Fifth Column."

"Wavell and Alexander ought to be court-martialed. Talk about appeasement! They directed British citizens to stay in Rangoon while the high commissioners were flying their *pets* out on military transport. I shudder to think what'll happen to all those families left behind."

"I shudder to think what'll happen here. Don't look now, ladies and gents, but the Barbarian's at the gate!"

"I hear the Wireless Centre up at Barrackpore's recruiting every Twing, Dot, and Shirley for the Women Assistants Corps. Even the COs' wives!"

Outrage, derision, alarm, and analysis of the war now accompany every cup of tea, every chance encounter, every meal or drink. Through these riptides, Claire clings to Shep's telegram like a life buoy. In six—eight more days at the most—he and Ty will be here. *NAILA TOO*, she tells herself. Well, whatever happens, they'll figure it out together.

Shep always claimed the British were experts at making light of bad situations. That's just what she needs to do now. Step back and treat the war as if it's a game whose primary purpose is to shut off all other thought. A game, as Naila might say, of map mastery.

Germany played its hand by keeping Holland, France, and Britain too busy close to home to defend their colonies in the Far East. In return, Japan swooped across Asia claiming eastern China, Indo-china, Singapore, and Burma as Axis trophies. Thus, Port Blair, closer to Rangoon than to either Calcutta or Madras, became a strategic trinket now up for grabs.

So much for games. She tries to concentrate on the task in front of her, but her mind keeps slipping. This morning she found a temporary home for Shep's plant specimens at Agri Gardens. This afternoon she'll sift through listings of possible homes for Shep and Ty and herself. Many of the British soldiers have wives coming out and no billets provided, so lodging options are shrinking fast. On top of that, she's no idea where Shep might be stationed next, or if he'll even want her and Ty to stay on. Yesterday she wired her parents to let them know she's safe—saying nothing of Shep and Ty—and her father replied with an offer to pay whatever it costs to bring them back to America. If only it were that simple.

"Military Intelligence."

The phrase tugs her out of her reverie. Two women stand before her in the foyer, one in a snugly fitting uniform and the other, older, in a shapeless floral housedress. The young Wren has an Irish accent. "You're brilliant with puzzles, Mum. They'd hire you in a minute, and you might even enjoy it. Barrackpore's cooler, greener, more spacious—heaven compared to Calcutta, and the code girls are jolly enough. It'd beat your pining away here for Dad, any day."

"Ah, Jenny . . ."

The mother's voice fades as she hitches an old white pocketbook under her arm and pushes out through the front door, but Claire considers young Jenny's proposition from her own point of view. She's heard they're hiring women as temporary assistants up at the Signal Centre. Many, like Jenny's mother, have husbands off God knows where, and this gives the wives a place to wait and a way to contribute to the war effort safely out of harm's way. To the astonishment of their male cohorts, some of these women reputedly make stellar codebreakers. But what of the women with children?

Roger appears in the doorway. Beaming. "C-Claire, I've b-brought you a surprise."

The delight in his voice, alas, raises an expectation that's dashed the instant she looks past him. He's followed not by Shep and Ty, but by a short, sturdy, plain-faced woman with a light brown bob shoved behind her ears.

Claire catches her breath and looks away to conceal her disappointment, but Roger is too pleased with himself to even notice. He nudges the stranger forward and beckons Claire out from behind the desk.

The woman looks to be in her midthirties. She wears a long khaki skirt, white Oxford shirt with the sleeves rolled up, white socks and dirty white plimsoles. A leather camera case is slung over her shoulder. Roger towers behind her.

His delivery turns clear and bright. "Claire, meet your sister-in-law, Vivian, though you'd best call her Viv if you know what's good for you."

Claire blinks in bewilderment. This must be some sort of stunt. When last heard from, Shep's sister was in Sydney. The one picture Shep possessed of her was taken when Vivian was a skinny fifteen-year-old, throwing a snowball during one of their winters at boarding school in China, and the sole resemblance between this woman and that image are the thick straight-across bangs.

This Vivian grips Claire's elbow and yanks her into an implosive hug. Only when Claire steps back does she notice that the stranger's eyes are the same sea-glass green as Shep's.

"There, now." A hand cups Claire's wet cheek. Late morning heat ripples through the front window. Vivian says, "I know just how you feel."

In a daze of confusion, Claire follows the two to seats in the coolest corner of the shabby dining room. Roger practically dances. He looks like a boy who's just thrown the switch on his model train and is more than a little surprised to see the tracks align.

Vivian is saying, "I was in Singapore when Hong Kong fell. Be there still if my editor hadn't recalled me. He always said running a newspaper gave him a god's-eye view while his foot soldiers got lost in the mud. Predicted the fall of the Peninsula weeks before any of the rest of us saw it coming. You know, the Japs took Malaya by bicycle. No motors to give them away."

But how did she *get* here? Her ship must have sailed right past the Andamans.

"And Burma?" Roger asks.

"No, not even he got that one right. I came to cover the Burma Road. So much for that now."

It has the ring of small talk. Their hands lift and drop, the perpetual dimness of the room obscuring the perpetual stains on the tablecloth. The listless fans rotate overhead. Her ship could have stopped in Port Blair. Couldn't she have brought Ty and Shep *with* her?

Well, clearly, she didn't. Claire tries to refocus. At the other tables, soldiers eat and drink and laugh, and the smell of curry and beer is infused with their masculinity. Vivian swigs a Lion Ale. With her frank, unyielding gaze and bulldog carriage, she fits right in with the boys. Shep never told her this about his sister, though perhaps she hasn't always been so mannish. Femininity might be a handicap in her line of work.

"I sent Shep a letter before I left Singapore. Don't imagine it reached you?"

"No." Claire wrestles with the banality of the question. "I don't know."

"At the best of times," Roger says, "only two mail deliveries a month made it down to Port Blair."

"What did it say?"

"What?"

"The letter."

"Just that I was coming and hoped to have a chance to see you both." Vivian leans across the table, slides her arm between the dishes to touch Claire's wrist. "And meet your glorious boy."

Claire feels herself caving in at this. She draws back and struggles to catch herself, turn this around. Vivian's presence is not the outlandish miracle it seems. It's simply evidence of normalcy. A good omen.

Roger is called to the phone, and Claire remembers her manners. Reaching for Vivian's broad hand, she says, "Shep will be elated to see you."

Viv grins. "Oh, we must do something *wicked* to celebrate! Roger tells me he should be here in another few days. I cannot wait! My big little brother. I used to hate the way he dwarfed me. By the time he was six he was growing right past me, but the dear boy tried to make up for it by letting me boss him mercilessly. Now, Claire, tell me about—"

She glances sideways and falls silent. Roger is returning, but he's moving as if he's not quite sure how. His face has drained of all color. When he reaches them his syllables fracture.

"The *Norilla* was su-sunk midway ba-ack to P-P-Port Blair."

Claire sees it in a flash. The torpedo racing black through bright water. A blast like a geyser. The ship's Lebanese Captain flying over the bridge. Flames lick the shirts off his screaming men. A floating severed hand. The *Norilla's* great steel hull tips lengthwise, driving into the deep.

A phantom chill curls up her spine, and her teeth begin to chatter.

Wind whips up the grayed shoreline, high tide crashing and sucking at the rocks, dawn a muted blur as Shep watches his son teeter out of the brush between Leyo and Naila, the three of them picking their way toward him down the dry stream bed. Locals burn garbage along this stretch, leaving the cove's beach scorched, and despite the wind, it reeks. It's a dangerous place to launch, but with no dwellings in sight, they'll be undetected at this hour, and that's what matters most.

As Ty gets closer, he pinches his nostrils, draws back when Leyo motions him toward the mangroves where his father waits in a borrowed skiff. The boy whimpers when Naila pulls him to her but otherwise holds quiet. A speaking child, Shep thinks, would make this unbearable. A tantrum right now would make their escape impossible. But Ty does not throw tantrums when Naila is in charge. Would that he did, they might be safe in Calcutta now.

And in that instant, Shep knows it's true: Without his human pacifier, Ty would have made their life here impossible long ago. They'd have had to leave, to seek help for him, and none of this *would* have happened. Naila was their blessing and their curse.

"Where are we going, Doctor *saab*?" the girl asks when they reach him. As instructed, then, Leyo has told her nothing. Shep shakes his head in reply.

Leyo tosses in the rucksack, then struggles to hold the skiff steady as Naila detaches Ty from her neck and passes him to his father. When all are aboard, Shep yanks the outboard to life, and Leyo steers them into the waves.

Ty is sick almost immediately, and Naila holds him as he heaves over the gunwale. His vomit draws sharks, which bump against the hull. Shep uses his oar to bat them away, venting his rage on the black-finned beasts for his own stupidity and cowardice.

Shortly after hearing yesterday's grim news about the *Norilla*, he caught Denis Ward in Phoenix Bay with the harbor master and two Indian drivers boarding a motorboat aimed for Madras. Seven hundred forty nautical miles, sharks and torpedoes be damned. If Shep had a fraction of the police chief's loathsome nerve, he and Ty would be with them now. Instead, he folded a hastily scribbled note for Claire into Ward's hand and said he hoped they'd make it. Alfred Baird appeared on scene and bet Ward he wouldn't. Ward, with a parting salute, said he'd take his chances over Baird's. *We can settle up after the war.*

Half measures, Shep thinks bitterly. My specialty. So here we are.

Finally, Ty has nothing left to give back and sinks into Naila's lap. They pass the outer shore of Ross, the broken crown of the hill, the shape of their old house black against scarlet sky. They'd be visible to anyone left on Ross to watch them, but there is no one.

Shep leans closer to Naila and tries to explain his plan without frightening the girl. The final evacuation has become uncertain, so he needs to take precautions. Leyo's people will keep her and Ty safe until the next ship comes. This is only an interim measure, but he has to consider all contingencies, and this now seems the lesser of evils.

The wind snatches at his voice. He thinks aloud. It's impossible to tell how much she grasps—how much any of them can.

He starts again. "I'm going to stay in Port Blair, and just as soon as I'm sure when the next ship will be here, I'll bring you back and we'll sail for Calcutta." He strokes Ty's listless back and glances at Leyo. "Shouldn't be longer than a few days."

Naila's dark eyes study him as if he's just handed her a death sentence. "I'll get you aboard," he promises. And he knows this time he must.

Eventually, they turn into the inlet that marks the start of the trail to Behalla. Ty rubs his eyes and rallies, and in minutes Shep is standing in the surf, his son in his arms and his face crushed into those sweet, salty curls.

The boy pulls his ears as they make their way to the beach, and reluctantly Shep sets him down. From his pocket he pulls a necklace that Claire gave to Naila last Christmas, which he found in the debris of the house last night.

"I fixed the clasp for you," he tells the girl. "And this one's for you, Ty." He's added his old Shanghai Volunteer Corps medallion to Naila's gold chain.

Ty cranes closer to see. The charm is a brass circle embossed with an eight-pointed star decorated with the flags of Europe and America.

"I received this when I was a boy, just a bit older than you."

His son ignores the star for the necklace's eucalyptus green moonstone globe, which he holds up to the light.

"It's magic to keep you safe." Shep turns to Naila, then to Leyo, who stands in the water, steadying the boat. "All of you."

Ty sighs heavily and passes the necklace back for his father to fasten around Naila's neck. The girl does not respond except to close her eyes at his approach.

"For safekeeping," Shep says.

They wait without talking for several minutes as Ty runs after the waves. Leyo throws his head back, a trance-like smile on his wide, easy face. Though he's doubtless just glad to be going home, Shep finds his serenity consoling. Leyo's people have welcomed Claire and been generous with her. Kuli especially, she's said. Like a second family, she's said. Between Kuli and Leyo, they'll keep Ty safe.

He tells himself again that this is only for a couple of days, that the next ship is bound to get through, but then he catches sight of the medallion at Naila's throat, and his whole bloody life seems to circle it.

Go, it warns him in his father's voice, *before you make an even bigger ass of yourself.*

He steps forward so Naila and Leyo won't see the tears welling or hear the claw in his throat. He picks up his son and hugs him tight.

"Give us a kiss, old boy. Just a few more days of camping for you, and we'll finally be off to see Mem!"

Ty accepts the kiss but gives no sign of listening. He's too busy watching a school of dolphins leap.

March 21, 1942

Ty Babu adapts quickly, every bit as delighted by his new surroundings as Naila is miserable. He takes to Artam and the two yellow dogs and soon runs naked with them around camp, splashing and hunting for frogs and turtles in the nearby stream. Without complaint, he lets Leyo rub him with oil to keep the insects from biting. Not even the lack of a toilet bothers him, as he's always hated the confinement and interruption of using the WC.

Naila, however, thinks only of escape. It is better, she tells herself, that her boy is happy. When the time comes, the less Ty wants to leave, the more Doctor Shep will need her help to pull him away. He will see for himself that he cannot take his son without her. And, she assures herself, so many already have left Port Blair that surely there will be space for her on the next ship. Just as the doctor promised.

Leyo tries to keep her company, to jolly her into smiling at the others, but it is clear that not all the Biya welcome her and Ty. She sometimes catches that girl Ekko and the wide-mouthed boy Tika pointing and snickering when Naila tries to stop Ty from tasting one of the disgusting grubs that Mam Golat roasts on the fire, or when she leads him down alone to the stream to bathe.

"Your ways are strange to them," Leyo says, and she knows he is trying to help, but the naked people are the strange ones.

"Why does she wear that skull?" Naila whispers, motioning with her head at the woman Obeyo, who spends her days alone weaving mats and baskets and rope. Obeyo has buck teeth and a shaved head, scars like a valley of rain on her belly, and she speaks little to anyone except her son

Tika. The truly disturbing thing about Obeyo, though, is that little skull, like one of the goddess Kali's trophies, dangling from a string on her back.

"It helps to keep the spirit of her youngest child close," Leyo says. "He died before the age of Ty Babu." He shakes his head. "Her husband also is dead."

So are my parents, Naila thinks spitefully. She's lucky to *have* that skull.

Leyo meets her eyes, and nods.

If only she could take Ty somewhere else to wait for his father. Somewhere the fire didn't stink of pig fat and there was no midden with moldering garbage to attract whatever creatures rustle and roll there all night long. Where they could eat rice and roti and dhal like normal people, instead of the boiled meat of animals she can't even name. Some place, too, where her own voice would make sense.

It is this that surprises her most of all. The gibberish of the clan sounds nothing like the phrases that Mem and Leyo used to practice. To communicate even the simplest question, she must rely on sign language. She and Ty now have this in common.

PART TWO

V

March 22, 1942

A single salvo across the black harbor. No return fire. Silence.

Alone in the empty house, Shep lies sweating through seconds, then minutes, peering into darkness. Finally, he rises from bed and fumbles for the blackout cord, nearly persuades himself the shots were products of a fishermen's tiff, a drunken brawl at the Hopetown landing, his own frayed synapses—

North Point erupts.

He lifts the blinds as the midnight sky flashes orange and crimson, sulphuric yellow. Tom Lutty. Dynamite. The wireless station. A pyrotechnic code for *Time's up.*

He stares until his eyes burn, then drops the blinds and slowly, painstakingly dresses. By the time he stands up from tying his boots, the night is holding its breath again. He packs his medical kit, folds his lab coat, carries these insignia up through the empty house to the breezeway . . . and there, stalls in the moonlight.

In his kit he's hidden the map that Leyo drew for him, the overland path to the Biya. More contingency plans. He pulls out the sketch now and squints, the dark stillness a drug.

The route forms a vertical Big Dipper. In 1859 the Great Andamanese followed more or less this same path when they stole through the jungle to attack the fledgling colony. Had it not been for an escaped convict who'd joined the tribals but had a change of heart—a double agent, in effect, who warned the British—"The Battle of Aberdeen" might have terminated the colony, altering history for all of them. Whenever Claire spoke of that battle, her voice thickened with contempt. *That stupid, stupid man.*

He lowers himself onto the loveseat where she used to lie mouthing the impossible syllables of a language already dead. The cushions still hold her scent. Geranium oil. That warm floral darkness. He presses it to his face and retraces the angles of her hipbones, the hollow at the base of her throat, one hand gliding through her brown hair as she presses the other into his chest. The timbre of her voice as she dares him.

He saved her by knocking her out, his intentions desperate as a boy on the end of a bayonet. But at least he saved her.

Saved her and lost her with one clean jab. Would she forgive him now?

Never. Of that he's certain. Before she lost consciousness, she knew even less than he did how dire their circumstances truly were, but even if it meant certain death, she'd never agree to leave Ty to face *this* without her.

Shep hopes for her sake that she is railing against him. That would mean the worst for her is still an abstraction.

An abstraction. His mind staggers, uncertainty and indecision crippling him. Ty could be dead—of fear, of venom, of a fall or fever. He could have been killed with Leyo's people by Japanese advance scouts or by an enemy tribe.

But not—Shep rallies himself. Not as far as he knows. Not as he wills himself to *believe*. His son's circumstances are now as unfathomable to Shep as his own are to Claire, and for this reason, and perhaps this reason alone, he can still retain his faith that Ty and Naila will survive.

Naila—

He stops himself. What purpose will blame serve now? It was the selfish, mindless act of a child. For which she is paying more than she ever could have bargained for . . .

And suddenly Shep is back with Ty in his arms, the sticky smell of sea spray, the catch of his son's breath as Shep carried him through the surf. Magic, he promised his son.

Magic. What in the name of God was he thinking?

He should be running. No matter how futile. Even if it gets him killed. But first he has to think. Which way? Spotters will have the coast and waters around the port covered, and this forest route requires a tracker—an impossibility now.

Gunboats in the moonlight. Shep puts the pillow down.

He's responsible for all of this. The thought paralyzes him.

On the wicker table his pipe lies in a pottery bowl beside a tin of Latakia and a box of safety matches. The blackout blinds are up, but he doesn't bother lowering them. He takes a stick from the box and ignites it, then holds the map with his escape route to its bluing flame.

March 23, 1942

As soon as she reaches the top of the stairs, she knows. Their voices ricochet up from the lobby. *The bloody fucks . . . We're next, y'know . . . Gave it up without a shot . . . Trust them Nips to creep in like thieves in the night . . . Nothin' but water between us 'n them now.*

And then, *What do we say to—?*

In the mirror on the landing a pair of bespectacled eyes turns up and collides with Claire's own shattered gaze, but the stairwell is going white. She clutches the balustrade, slides to the floor. Her blood pounds so loud in her ears that she can no longer hear the soldiers.

When they climb to her aid, she motions them away. The lobby is spinning, Ty's and Shep's faces popping like flash bulbs, but she makes herself stand and somehow descends. The foyer falls dead. They make her sit down. And then, it's all for nothing.

She's heard everything there is to know. A single bulletin on the radio. The Andaman Islands, taken. Sneak attack. The British authorities in Port Blair surrendered without defense.

Shep and Ty. Shep and Ty. Shep and Ty. Their names repeat like a mantra, filling her simultaneously with longing and with terror.

The phone on the front desk erupts, and a receiver is thrust into her hands. Roger on the other end: "I'm t-trying to find out everything I can. Hold tight. Vivian will be there in a minute . . ."

He hears her silence. "Claire," he says, "the Japanese are bound by the Geneva Convention to protect civilians and keep children with their families and—"

She hangs up without speaking. Her surroundings have straightened, but the masks of concern and speculation on the faces of her fellow boarders make her feel as if she's disintegrating. *Shep and Ty.*

She walks through the door and across the garden, out the forecourt to Sudder Street, then Free School, and keeps going. No hat, no parasol, no purse, no idea where or why, only that she must move.

Outside the hotel, men and women and children go about their mornings, the fate of her family nothing to them. And yet . . . every small Indian boy appears a dead ringer for Ty, every attentive big sister, Naila. Every tall bony Englishman, Shep. They trudge past shops. Pull hand carts. Squat beside sidewalk charpoys. They wear khaki, white, and pale blue uniforms, carry buckets, scream at each other. Weep.

Claire holds herself very still as the hallucinations well, permitting only her legs to move. Now the spectres stand in the sleeve of a terrace or the frame of a doorway, off in the distance waving, but always, all of them present their backs to her.

"Madam?" A bearded man in a maroon turban and white jacket approaches. "May I help?"

Please. Her arms ache. Her eyes throb. She can't breathe.

The Samaritan takes her elbow to steady her, and his touch halts the falling sensation. She looks around.

College Street. A campus gate. Indian students smile up at her, laughing.

These are not all students, though. Patients also lie on the grass, an outdoor waiting room filled with deathly still infants, keening mothers, hollow-eyed men and rickety boys. Faces ravaged by pain and madness and loss.

The young Sikh waits. "Are you a doctor?" she asks him.

"Not yet, Madam. Only an intern. Are you ill?"

She ignores the question. "But you help them." She starts to gesture at the patients, then, without knowing why, redirects her question. "The doctors."

"I assist." A look of bewilderment clouds his concern.

"Yes. Yes, that's it. You assist. And that makes it easier to bear—" She glances back at the people waiting.

The man—clear, dark eyes, neatly rolled and tucked beard, a whiff of cardamom and clove—nods uncertainly. "One does what one can."

"One does what one can," she repeats.

Then she lifts her face and salaams. "Thank you, Doctor. Thank you."

"The thing is," she tells Roger and Viv when she finds them back at the hotel, "I have to do something. And I must know. Can *you* tell me?"

Roger looks at his hands.

To Vivian: "Can *you*?"

"Claire," Viv says, "I'm a reporter. I'm going to try—"

"And so am I! That's exactly my point. I've got to *do what I can*. Look, you've got your press briefings and investigative know-how. Roger's got his Government channels. But neither of you is privy to Military Intelligence. If I go up to Barrackpore, I could be. At least I'd stand a chance of hearing if anything came across."

They both look at her as if she were raving. Less than three hours have passed since Calcutta learned of the invasion. All of them are in shock.

But their shock is no good to Shep and Ty, and the longer it takes to find out what's actually happening in Port Blair, the greater the chance that her husband and son will be taken away, moved to an internment camp, or—

"You can help me, Roger. You know who to talk to up at the Signal Centre. Tell them I know the Andamans. I know Morse. I know the terrain and the local tribes. They'll need all that for reconnaissance."

Roger frowns, but Claire persists. "Unless the Japanese are stopped in the Andamans, they'll be in Calcutta next. And if I can *help* stop them, then maybe—"

But the force of her own determination rolls back on her like an undertow. A gust of laughter rises from the hotel bar, and she pictures Ty being ripped from Shep's arms at gunpoint.

"You are British, Dr. Durant." In Lieutenant Shimura's mouth, Shep's surname breaks like glass.

"Born in Shanghai."

"Ah. Missionary parents." Every question a statement.

"My father was a doctor."

The edge of a smile. "Family business."

"Something like that."

"You are surgeon." Shimura, beads of moisture across his brow, makes a show of surveying the titles in the Browning Club library, which the occupying force is using as an interrogation room for European and Eurasian prisoners. He turns on his captive, who sits on a cane chair beside the library globe.

Shep was just shy of Corbyn's Cove when they caught him, at sunrise, and he surrendered without protest. The gambit had been little more than a gesture toward escape. Even if he'd managed to reach the skiff, the chances of getting up the coast undetected were virtually nil and only fractionally less suicidal than attempting to go it alone overland. The gesture allowed him to deny his own paralysis, but it changed nothing.

"Civil Surgeon is a misleading title," Shep says. He considers how best to position his status and opts to aim low. "I'm really just a public health officer."

"You have wife and son."

He blanches. This is all a charade, then. Wilkerson warned them that, thanks to the Kobayashis, the Japanese would likely have dossiers on everyone in Port Blair. Yet the warning failed to prepare him for this jab. "They—"

Shimura, a tall, slender figure in tropical kit, rolls one immaculate hand in the air.

"My wife was evacuated to Calcutta on March 13."

"And son."

The vise tightens around his rib cage. "Yes."

"Yes?" This, at last, is the question. "Answer."

"My son disappeared."

"You find him."

"No."

"Doctor, we intercept. You telegram to your wife."

"That was a lie." He pushes the breath from his lungs. "So she wouldn't worry."

Shimura shakes his head as if disappointed in a promising student.

"You can ask; I've searched everywhere. No one has seen them."

"Them."

"His ayah also disappeared. She was young, and very jealous." He squeezes his eyes against a spasm of nausea. "I think she would rather die and take the boy with her than surrender him—even to me."

"That is sad story," the lieutenant says without a trace of emotion. "If we find this ayah, we must punish her."

Following interrogation, Shep and Major Baird and the Commissioner are fed a meal of hardtack and weak tea, then marched to Aberdeen Jetty and shoved aboard the ferry *Benbow* under armed escort. Old Ranjit drops his eyes as he casts off, then hurries up to the wheelhouse to pilot them across the harbor. It's the first time Shep has made this trip in the eight months since the earthquake. They're being placed under house arrest while their captors decide what use they can put them to. Hostages. Forced labor. Prisoner of war trading pawns. For the time being, it's easier to secure them in a house on an abandoned island than in the restless port.

Heat and humidity glaze the surface of the water. Japanese cruisers roll at anchor, and the traffic of military patrol boats produces more activity than the harbor has seen in weeks.

Wilkerson sits across from Shep, erect and gray and closed. Baird turns his face to the crossing's false breeze. All three surrendered without protest, but being forced to trample the Union Jack drained something vital from the Commissioner, while Baird wears the situation with surprising serenity. As for himself, Shep studies his companions to stop his gaze from straying to the forest.

Dusk is falling when the ferry docks, as it was when he and Claire first set foot here an eternity ago. But the parade ground now is overgrown. Much of Ross bazaar has fallen into ruin, and the spire of the Anglican Church lies in pieces. Coconuts litter the island like cannonballs. Nothing is the same.

Ranjit's boy scurries to secure the boat. He eyes the Japanese with fascination, but they elbow him aside and prod Wilkerson out first. Shep has a fleeting notion that they might be left here alone. Why not? The island is deserted. The surrounding waters seethe with sharks. The prisoners have no boat, but even if they did, the coast will be crawling with spotters for miles in every direction.

And—he reminds himself—to be caught while making for Behalla now could destroy Ty's only chance for survival.

The men push through the debris up the crosswalk to the Assistant Commissioner's residence. The tats have fallen off the front veranda, and the steps leading up to the portico are wrenched sideways. One gable has collapsed. When the soldiers gesture for them to enter, Wilkerson stiffens, coming to his rank.

"The Commissioner's residence is there." He points up the hill.

The young warrant officer leading the escort looks momentarily confused. "You here."

The Commissioner persists, still pointing. "*My* house is not broken."

The officer pulls a sheet from his pocket, studies it briefly, and barks an order. The man closest to Wilkerson raises his bayonet.

"You here," the officer repeats, even as a soldier from the rear trots off in the direction the Commissioner indicated.

Baird leads the way into his old quarters, which have been stripped of all but skeletal furnishings. The guards remain outside. As Shep and Baird move toward the interior, a rat streaks across the floor. Shep joins Wilkerson in the front room and watches through the filthy window as the scout returns from his mission up the hill and reports to the warrant officer. Then the two hurry down to the jetty, shadows in the gloaming.

"I don't suppose you've got any lights."

Wilkerson addresses them rhetorically. The island's generator died in the earthquake, but Baird manages to find a couple of candle stubs and matches in a dining room drawer. When he strikes a flame, however, a palm slams against the window and a face appears like a Noh mask through the pane.

Baird quickly extinguishes the candle before the square-headed guard, who seems to be in charge, enters and seizes the matches and stubs.

"No blackout drapes," Shep says.

Wilkerson, wordless now, moves through the darkening vestibule to the bottom of the stairs.

"Take the master, Sir," Baird offers. "Directly at the top. If the charpoy's still there, it's passably comfortable."

They hear slow steps and the shut of a door overhead.

"Dunno about you," Baird says in a conspiratorial whisper, "but if I don't do something, I think I'll go off."

"What d'you have in mind?"

"A run around the island would be nice." His shadow opens a closet beneath the staircase. More skittering, and Shep feels something bump against his mosquito boot. "But cleaning up will have to do."

Shep's hand closes around an outstretched pole, and he finds himself holding a short grass broom of the sort that the lowest caste of servants use to tidy the households of India. Baird slaps a second broom against his own palm.

"Follow me." He leads Shep upstairs to a bedroom at the back of the house, well away from the Commissioner. "If nothing else, it gets rid of the cobwebs and puts the rats on notice."

The two men lower themselves and begin to sweep.

That night the sky explodes. Shep watches with dread and exhilaration through the open window as Allied bombers make the clouds dance. Flares of yellow, red, and orange burst above the port. Sirens wail and Japanese antiaircraft sputter in reply. Boots thud outside the house and across the veranda.

Shep expects to be dragged out and accused of signaling the planes, but the guards never enter. The attack sounds like a prayer and is no more effective than one.

At least the Brits aren't bombing to the north. Behalla will escape, for the moment.

"Calcutta knows the port's been taken," Shep says.

Baird nods toward North Point. "Lutty. Before he blew up the station."

March 24, 1942

Next morning after *tenko*—roll call with the ritual bow to the glory of the Emperor of Japan—the three prisoners are herded back on the ferry to Aberdeen, then marched through blistering heat to stand at attenion in front of the clock tower.

A few minutes later Shimura and a shorter, bulkier man wearing army insignia arrive in Wilkerson's Standard saloon, a red sun now fluttering at the prow of its yellow hood. A ring of Japanese soldiers surrounds the prisoners, but at a signal from Shimura their ranks part to reveal the residents of Port Blair, quiet and unfettered and gathered lower down the hill. They include the last of the inmates from the Cellular Jail.

Shep scans for the darkest faces, skipping over the oldest and youngest, just barely registering the grinning fervor of the boys who press closest. He drops his chin to make his search less obvious, but he saw no sign of his would-be guide yesterday during the surrender, and if the tracker is here now among the spectators, he's making himself invisible.

Just as well, Shep warns himself.

Standing on the saloon's running board and speaking through a local interpreter, Shimura introduces himself as the Commanding Officer of Japanese Naval landing forces and his companion, Colonel Buco, as Port Blair's new Civil Governor.

Shep stares at the translator: Nabi Bux is the one-eyed *durzi* from Ross Bazaar who used to set up his sewing machine on their veranda and, at Claire's direction, stitch sunsuits for Ty. The very shirt he's wearing was sewn by the man now translating the Japanese order to bow.

Then, looking away, Shep finds himself in the familiar crosshairs of Abraham's scowl. The former cook is positioned just to the left of Nabi

Bux—suspiciously close to their new Japanese overlords. Ingratiatingly close.

Buco pumps his fist in a violent gesture at the three *"Ingrish."* He has a raw, wide, belligerent voice. If the restrained Shimura's task is to cool the crowd, the Civil Governor's must be to whip it up. He wears a sword and draws it with a jab toward Wilkerson, whose old blue eyes wither in reply.

Buco seems to consider last night's air raid a personal affront. He announces with relish that the Chief Commissioner, as highest ranking British military officer, will be leaving Port Blair on the next outgoing vessel for a prisoner-of-war camp in Singapore.

Wilkerson doesn't move, and Buco makes no mention of the other British captives. Instead, he waves his arm toward the bottom of the square, and his troops push the townspeople to make way for the four hundred Indian soldiers and police who were to have been evacuated, with Wilkerson and Baird, on the doomed *S. S. Norilla.*

Now Buco speaks in English for the benefit of all British India: "Today is liberation for our Asian brothers."

Abraham trips forward in his haste to seize the moment. Buco lifts his chin, and Shep's erstwhile servant raises a small red flag adorned with the leaping tiger of the All India Forward Bloc. Triumph burns in Abraham's eyes as he leads the chant. *"Inquilab Zindabad!* Asia for Asians!"

Buco signals the Indian service members to join in shouting the slogans. All eyes are on their Commissioner as the troops comply, hesitant at first but then with more vigor as local youths and former convicts add their voices. Like a conductor with a baton, Buco waves his sword for more, and soon the cries blur into a victory roar.

"Inquilab Zindabad! Free India! *Inquilab Zindabad! Azad Hind! Inquilab Zindabad!* Asia for Asians!"

Only when the noise has reached a pitch that verges on hysteria, and Wilkerson's expression has emptied of its last vestige of pride, does Buco slice his blade to the ground, silencing the breathless celebrants.

The local community now regard the Japanese with ardor. Their bodies sway forward, palms pressed in reverence, and tears streak the most aged faces. Children are hoisted on shoulders. The Indian forces have

capitulated. Buco and Shimura gravely return their bows. It is a staggering performance.

Lt. Shimura steps up and, without acknowledging the slightest irony,
addresses the troops in English—now Port Blair's only common language.

"Japan is friend of India. All Asian brothers fight together. We are
brotherly people. European rule no more! Indian brothers, welcome. Together, we build co-prosperity."

He salutes, and a garbled rumor snakes through the ranks, but before
anyone can move, Shimura lapses back into Japanese, signaling his own
soldiers to form cordons. Nabi Bux relays the instruction for Asians to
move to one side, Eurasians to the other.

The lieutenant offers a benevolent wave as the uniformed Asians fall
back among the convicts and their families. Nabi Bux translates that
those whose parents were Bengali, Tamil, Agri, Burmese, Malay, Sikh,
Muslim, Parsi, Hindu, or aboriginal will be free to live in peace as citizens
of the Greater East Asia Co-Prosperity Sphere. "Asia for the Asians!" he
concludes, and the happy majority cheer on cue.

Then Shimura points for the Eurasians to line up in front of Wilkerson and Baird. His command reminds Shep, standing behind the two
officers, of a typhus quarantine when he was a boy at school. Three of
his classmates who seemed perfectly well were made to line up and go
off with the sick children. None of them returned. His memory of the
boys' stunned faces fuses with those of the two dozen men now shuffling
reluctantly toward him. Many could pass for Asians if looks were the only
criteria, but the occupiers doubtless have gathered as much information
about the soldiers as his school doctor had on the boys.

The thought reminds Shep of Baird's remark last night about Tom
Lutty. Tom was not one who could pass, and between his pedigreed lin-
eage and his signal skills, he'd be a prize catch for the enemy. As Shimura drones on, Shep scans the downcast segregants and tries to view his
friend's absence with hope.

He comes back to attenion as Nabi Bux announces that anyone with
English, French, Danish, Dutch, or Portuguese paternity will be pun-

ished as an infidel. Yet another set of sons, Shep thinks, to be cursed for the blight of their fathers.

The clouds let loose as they're ferried back to Ross, rain cascading off the *Benbow*'s tin roof. Shep relishes the downpour. At least this will stop them probing the jungle.

Across the harbor, invisible through the storm, Wilkerson is being taken onto one of the cruisers. His only goodbye was a slight inclination of the head and a mournful glance at Baird, who's served him ever since his arrival in Port Blair nearly a decade ago.

Shep never had much use for the Commissioner, Claire even less, as he defended the right, might, and presumed invincibility of British rule. Still, arrogance ordinarily dies hard, and Shep would not have anticipated that, of the two, Baird's the one with backbone.

False promise, the tempest ends as capriciously as it began, and sunshine gashes the clouds as the men trudge back to the house. Upstairs, the room Wilkerson vacated offers a view of the mainland, where Aberdeen glitters with fresh activity.

Shep curls his hands into binoculars. It's like trying to read the current through waves, but he can make out bulges of khaki moving store to store, clustering around toddy shops. More brightly colored knots of locals—presumably many of the same who this morning hailed their "liberators"—now hang back or surge at those looting their homes and businesses.

A barely audible murmur draws him from the window. At first, he thinks Baird must be talking with one of the guards, but the tone is all wrong. And the location.

He moves cautiously along the upper balustrade. The door to the rear bedroom is closed. The whispering comes from inside. He inches the door open.

A small man in a red-checkered shirt and white sarong squats on the floor, closely facing the kneeling Baird. At the Burman's stricken expression, Shep pats the air and steps in.

The major sits back on his heels. "This is Pati. My boy." The diminutive is spoken with such affection that it transcends servitude. Pati, a wiry man of middle age, watches Baird as if to memorize him.

"How did he get in?"

"While everyone was in town. He says the Japanese have posted sentries down the coast as far as Rangachang."

"Your house is down there, isn't it?"

Baird shrugs. "The other servants fled. I told him last week to go north to one of the settler villages." His voice dips, and Pati looks down at his clasped hands. A bundle, unopened, lies on the charpoy behind him.

"He's not thinking to stay here?" Shep is aware that the man doubtless understands everything they whisper, yet it seems less intrusive to speak as if he didn't.

"He'll have to, for the moment."

Shep weighs his options. Barely a week ago he drove to Rangachang and asked everyone he met along the way for information about Naila and Ty. He conspicuously "found" one of Ty's sandals on the point below Baird's bungalow, but he didn't see Pati there.

"Are there other landing sites?" he asks. "Are they moving to the interior?"

Baird and Pati confer. Shep lacks the major's fluency in Burmese, but he gathers that the invasion, for now, is focused on the Lambaline airstrip.

Baird unpacks the provisions Pati has brought him: pork jerky; cellophaned candy; soap; toothpaste; one toothbrush; a neatly folded pair of striped pajamas, and one small blue towel. Shep winces at the intimacy of these last items and averts his eyes.

"Mind if I take the front room?"

The major's arm grazes his boy's shoulder as he gestures. "Take some of this with you. There's a loose plank in the floor of the closet."

Alone, Shep gnaws a sliver of jerky. Out front the rickshaw buggies are back in use, laboring up the crosswalk with Japanese officers as passengers. Behind them follows a train of porters lugging crates, jars, bottles, and trunks. It looks as if the Chief Commissioner's residence is about to be reopened—for Buco's occupation.

Shep leans on the shadowed wall back from the windows. With luck Pati could still slip away tonight after dark. He probably has a canoe tucked in one of the ocean-facing coves.

He risked his life for Baird, but he won't come again. Baird won't allow it.

Naila wakes to the low patter of talk while Ty is still asleep. Impossible to make sense of the Biya language, but after a minute she recognizes the rasping voice of the elder, Kuli, and then the low, swaying chords of a second speaker. She leans out the flap of the tent that Doctor *saab* sent for her and Ty to share.

She must be mistaken. What would the town layabout be doing here?

In Port Blair, Porubi often sings as he stumbles down the alley behind the Browning Club or urinates on the clock tower. Sometimes his garbled songs sound dirty and he'll waggle his tongue at passing schoolgirls. From across the street you can smell the filth of his clothes, the fumes of toddy on his breath. What could this fool have to say to Kuli?

As soon as I'm sure when the next ship will be here, I'll bring you back . . . A thousand times in these last days she has pictured Doctor Shep striding into camp and swinging Ty Babu onto his hip. But how would he get here? It never occurred to her that, with Leyo here, Ty's father might need another guide to lead him, or to come as his messenger. Of all people, Porubi—and yet, who else?

She can hear the headman grunting softly in response to whatever Porubi is telling him. Then a third voice joins in. Leyo.

"Come," she rouses Ty, pulls him yawning into her arms, then steers him outside and across the clearing.

Leyo's attention is fixed so intently on Porubi that he hardly seems to notice as Naila enters Kuli's lean-to and slides down with Ty beside him. Her boy lays his head in her lap, watching Mam Golat stoke the fire. The others are just emerging from their huts and pay scant attention to the conference at Kuli's. No one else seems surprised by Porubi's presence, but Naila cannot get over how changed this man is.

His body is still and sober, none of the loose-limbed flailings he displays in town. And although she can't decipher the conversation, she can see that Porubi's message is grave. He talks steadily for several minutes, and Leyo and Kuli do not interrupt.

At last he falls silent. Kuli nods, and Leyo turns to place his hand on Ty Babu's chest. But his words are meant for her.

Leyo says, "We must leave here."

March 25-30, 1942

And almost in the next breath, it seemed, they were marching north—all of them—away from Behalla to a place called Buruin, the Biya's monsoon camp, where Kuli said they must go to be safe. They packed up everything but the huts, and the women, under their burdens of pots and baskets hanging from forehead straps, grumbled at Naila and scowled as if it were *her* fault they were making this trek in such haste, in the worst heat, before the early rains arrived to cool the journey.

Leyo and Kuli both insisted that she and Ty were now in danger if they remained in the south. But how did they know this? They had only crazy Porubi's word.

She staggers along, head swarming with questions, protests, complaints. Doctor Shep, a prisoner? *If the Japanese come and find the boy here, they will take us all prisoner.* Of course, Leyo said this, but that did not make it possible. The Japanese won't take Asians prisoner. *Asia for Asians,* Abraham said. But how to make sense of this, when her own ma told her, *The English will never leave.*

If Ty's father truly was taken prisoner, then he had not left. And prisoners could escape. So many freedom fighters fled into the forest. Surely Doctor Shep, too, would escape and come to find his son. And when he reached Behalla now he would find only rubbish. Then what?

"Why are we trekking to a place where Doctor Shep cannot find us?" she asks Leyo when they stop to rest.

"Porubi will guide him."

"Porubi! He is a nothing. A no one! What does Porubi know? And where has that crazy man gone, anyway?" He had left Behalla even before the rest of them.

Leyo folds his arms and turns away from the girl Ekko, who is stretching her nakedness, fingertips to toes, directly in front of him. He says to Naila, "Porubi has gone back. He will see what the Japanese do. He can find Doctor Shep and if he will escape, Porubi can bring him to Buruin."

This does little to calm Naila. Ty is no help, either. He seems to enjoy this misery.

He is changed. Gone is her Ty Babu, his white ways shed like the skin of a snake—quickly and utterly. He rides Leyo's back as Artam rides her father's, and as they ride, these little ones send each other signals the way she herself and Ty used to. Spotting owls and butterflies, orchids and spiderwebs. Dancing with their arms. Ty, the boy who would seize upon a single pebble and not budge for an hour seems now *eager* to look here, there, everywhere, as if his habit of concentration also has been shed.

But no. The longer Naila studies this new Ty—which she does as much to keep her mind off her blistering toes and choking lungs and looming fears as to make sense of her boy's cruel contentment—the more she realizes that he has not lost his concentration but only trained it on his new friend.

Artam is his fascination now. And his personal guide and companion. When Artam smacks her lips over a snack of dried grubs, Ty does the same. When Artam lets her mother inspect her for ticks and leeches, Ty waits his turn, and when Imulu removes the blood suckers—with the same glass blades that she uses to cut hair, both children hold as still at the resulting streams of blood as if watching a moving picture. Repulsive as Naila finds all of this, she tells herself she had better do at least as well—unless she is willing to leave him to these people.

At that, with darkness falling and no end in sight to their journey, she lets her thoughts sink into quicksand. *Asia for the Asians!* Why not? If the boy is so happy, let him stay in the forest, but nothing keeps her here. Doctor Shep said that danger from the Japanese is only to Ty and himself, *not* to local-borns. Not to fellow Asians. She doesn't really know what this means—"fellow Asians." She doesn't even know why the Japanese are at war with the British and Americans. She once had a tooth pulled by the Japanese dentist in Aberdeen, and all she can remember of him is the smell of ether and the white cap his attendant wore, like an island floating in darkness, and the way their eyes stretched, long and narrow, so that she wondered if they saw the world differently than she did, but no matter, because they cured her of her pain. Her ma said they had taken good care of her, so maybe she could go back and ask the dentist and his assistant to take care of her again. She could find her way back to the ocean, then follow the coast to town. She doesn't know if the dentist is still there, but at least in Port Blair she would find normal food and air she could breathe and people who spoke her—

Leyo, at her back, touches her shoulder and says they are stopping for the night. Around them the forest closes like a seething black storm. She looks up into this cauldron of darkness and snaps back to her senses. She could no more find her way to the ocean than she could find the moon tonight.

She meets Leyo's troubled gaze and nods to let him know that she understands. She has no choice. She will not run. She will not leave Ty Babu or pretend that anyone else in the world would choose to save her.

"Ty Babu is ours now," Leyo says as he sinks beside her, "and we are Biya." He smiles as the boy joins Artam and Sempe in digging a fire pit. Camp consists of mats beneath a giant elephant plant and a pit to contain the flame that Kuli carries with them in a clay pot. Artam helps Mam Golat mash the taro root with honey for their meal.

Leyo adds, "The neem oil makes him anyway dark as you."

It is true. But for the green of his eyes, Ty could almost pass for an Indian boy. She fingers the globe and the star at her throat.

"But what about Mem? *She* is not taken prisoner, and Mem visited many times to Behalla. She will come looking."

"No." Leyo motions for her to drink from the canteen that Ty has passed back to them. "Only British soldiers maybe will come."

"So, the British fight Japanese, then the Japanese will go and Doctor and Mem can come."

Naila finds a stone and kills a yellow centipede that's making for Ty's foot. Leyo says, "You want now, Mem to come for Ty."

The way he says this makes her feel for that centipede. She leans forward, chin to knees, tightening her body into a ball. Poisonous, in plain sight.

Leyo's hand touches her spine. "Soon we reach Buruin. It is beautiful. You will see."

The next day they skirt two deserted rubber plantations, and the even rows of upright trunks remind Naila of drilling soldiers. There is something ghostly about such careful planting deep in the forest, with no human presence. Where are the laborers? Their villages?

These questions make her think of the maps in Teacher Sen's classroom. *Master the map and you master the world. That is how the British did it.* But where are Teacher Sen and his masterful British now? The farther she travels with the Biya, the less use she sees for anything she learned in school.

Her weakness shames her. Whenever she asks to rest, Ekko rolls her eyes. Whenever she or Ty gestures for water, Obeyo speeds up and the little skull bouncing on her back seems to taunt them. Even Kuli and Mam Golat, who are old and wizened, far outpace her.

It isn't only a matter of strength. The Biya seem also to possess second sight. The men especially can spot a monitor lizard dozens of feet away and spear it almost as soon as they see it. Obeyo and Ekko know exactly which dead tree trunks hold black honeycombs, which thorn bushes hide ripe clusters of edible berries. All of them seem able to sleep in places and positions that leave Naila crippled, yet they wake from deep sleep at the first hint of danger, as the boy Tika did the third night out when he plunged his knife through a giant python that Naila didn't see until she woke, hours later.

Just get us through this march alive, she pleads to her parents' spirits.

Finally, on the fifth day, Leyo pauses and says, "There."

But he seems to be pointing at a wall of stone. "Do we climb it?" Naila asks.

He just smiles and motions her and Ty closer. The rock has a flat face, with diagonal stripes of red and black. Now, here is something Teacher Sen did teach her: geological stripes like these show the age of stone, millions of years thrusting up from the earth. The thought makes her feel so insignificant that it is almost a comfort.

Ty runs around a corner at the base and disappears behind a stripe that juts in front of the others. When Naila catches up she sees that time has etched a hidden corridor to the top. Generations of Biya must have carved the rough steps inside. They are layered with leaves and mud, but Kuli uses his walking stick to stab out a path.

The climb leaves Naila breathless. At the top she bends forward, unable to focus. The others stream past her to a tall protective overhang, a stockade of trees, and Leyo peels Ty off his back so the boy can run after Artam.

"Look." He takes Naila's hand and pulls her to the front of the ledge.

As they face south, a slim blue lip of sea appears beneath the eastern clouds. Below the sea, however, another kind of ocean rolls, its green swells rooted to the earth. Here and there, golden threads mark rivers snaking through it, and the sky above them seems alive with a pure, sweet light.

Leyo places his palms on Naila's shoulders. "Here," he says, "we are safe."

For the first three days Shep and Baird were left more or less to themselves, with water from the tap, a meager supply of rice, some scraps of coal in the kitchen stove. Apart from *tenko* morning and night, their captors seemed to have no further plans for them.

Now, on day four, Shep wakes to a fragrance wafting up from the kitchen. Toast . . . and coffee?

The reflexive wave of pleasure quickly turns to concern when he hears Baird's voice below. Someone has come.

He eases down the stairs and peers through the interior dusk.

"But you say no one was hurt." Alfred leans a hand against the dining room wall and talks into the kitchen where a male figure wearing local garb—far too broad-shouldered to be Pati—stands with his back to them. Beyond, a normally shut door yawns into the little valet's room off the kitchen.

The man in the kitchen turns and limps forward, hands Baird a cup, and looks past him to Shep.

"Doctor *saab*." Abraham slaps his palms and heels together in a caricature of respect.

"Our hosts have taken pity on us." Baird gestures with his cup, which drips from a hairline crack. "Abraham has come with provisions. And news. Apparently, there was quite a kerfuffle in Aberdeen yesterday afternoon."

Abraham's hangdog eyes regard his former employer. Without the old white jacket, his striped blue shirt belongs to no uniform but still smacks vaguely of a convict's. He watches Shep with unnerving calm.

"However did you draw this duty, Abraham?"

The scruffy chin slides left, right.

"Is there by chance a saucer in there?" Baird indicates the drip, and Abraham shambles back into the kitchen. Baird drops his voice. "Let's not look a gift horse in the mouth, shall we? I'm sure it wasn't too difficult for Buco to locate your bearer."

Or, by extension, Baird's own. Pati has gotten away, then.

The dining room's furnishings consist of two straight-backed chairs missing cane in the seats. They pull these together and perch on the frames. Abraham reappears with a mismatched cup for Shep, two slices of burnt toast on one tin plate and another for Baird to use as a saucer. The pretense strikes Shep as ludicrous, but their eating, it seems, is to be conditional on Abraham's presence.

"Go on with your story, then," Baird says, too lightly. "Some Japanese soldiers cut loose and ruffled young Sunny Ali's feathers."

"The sawmill clerk's son?"

Abraham snorts. "Ruffled his feathers! Funny one, Saar."

"Didn't mean to steal your thunder, Abraham. Go ahead."

The man stands with his fists on his hips as if experimenting with a new pose. "They were some mad caps, these soldiers. Very naughty boys, they are catching chickens, entering houses. Some are being very dirty with the ladies, you know, and Sunny has three unwed sisters. When the soldiers come to his father's house, Sunny tells to those soldiers, go away from here! But the soldiers, they laugh and cut nasty jokes. The women folk are hiding in the back of the house. Poor Sunny, he was most perturbed. He got a gun."

Baird groans. Abraham nods emphatically. "He is shooting this gun up into the air to make the soldiers go away." He tugs on his mustache. "But in no time those soldiers are returning with many more. Then Sunny can see the errors of his ways. Out the back of the house he is going."

Shep wouldn't have thought Abraham capable of such a volume of English spoken with such energy. But surely this story has nowhere good to go. Sunny Ali is still just a boy, a good batsman, a loyal brother whose disposition lives up to his name. After Shep took his appendix out two years back, the family made him a thank-you gift of a rare albino *Malleola*, with blooms like ladders of pearls.

"The soldiers are bringing hand grenades. To Akbar Ali they say, 'Give us your son, or we destroy everything.' Ay, the womenfolk are shrieking, and other soldiers are setting fire to the house where they think Sunny Ali is hiding, and soon this fire is spreading to other houses. All the town is in danger."

"That poor boy," Baird murmurs.

"Poor boy!" Abraham raises his voice so suddenly that the back-door swings open. He sucks his teeth and raises his hands. "Sorry. Sorry."

The soldiers glare at the two frozen prisoners, the abject servant. One uses the tip of his bayonet to fling Baird's empty cup against the wall, but eventually they withdraw.

"Fortunately," Abraham murmurs, "Narayan Rao has a good head."

"The police deputy."

"Ha. Before, and again, I think so. He is going to the authorities, and he is persuading them to give time for the people to douse the fires. Then he is coming back to say to Akbar Ali, 'Sunny has gotten us into this mess. Sunny must surrender himself for the greater good.' And he will, I think, yes he will."

"How old is this Sunny?" Baird asks.

"Just twenty." Shep's reply surprises the other two. "I treated him a couple of years ago. He's a good boy."

That afternoon, they are taken back across the harbor, back with the rest of the town to the clock tower square, only this time their wrists are cuffed, and a numbness threatens, like sleeping sickness. The heat makes the air taste of tar.

Two soldiers bring Sunny Ali through the silent crowd. Colonel Buco is in charge, no sign of Shimura. The prisoner is tied to one of the hitching posts that encircle the clock tower.

The tower is a tribute to the million-plus Indians who died fighting for the British in the "war to end war." Shep catches Baird looking down at the commemorative plaque and suspects he's thinking the same thing.

Sunny has the same round, trusting face that Shep reassured before delivering him to ether. The boy smiles now at his father, who stands wringing his hands, and at his weeping mother. He wiggles his ears at his mates from school, who grin at his defiance. Even here and now, for Sunny the occupation is an abstraction. Asia for the Asians.

"Treason!" Buco thunders without preliminaries. The Japanese soldiers tighten ranks. An outer ring stands shoulder to shoulder to prevent any interference from the locals. Between the khaki shoulders and booted feet, Shep can see the inner ring closing. "*Jujutsu!*" Buco cries.

The boy trapped inside lets out a scream as the huddle yelps forward. Then come the audible snaps of tendons, the slam of boots into bone.

The bindings cut into Shep's wrists as he strains against them. Across the square the jewel merchant Farzand Ali crouches with his palms together, eyes wide and pleading. *Dr. Durant.*

The title, the training, a travesty.

Sunny's mother collapses as the boy's screams turn into the squeals of a dying animal, then cease abruptly.

"Look you!" Buco points.

The heaving, bloodied attackers draw away from their victim, now folded around the post. One arm hangs dislocated from its socket. The boy's skin, underneath a slick of red, has turned the blue of Waterman ink. His eyes have swollen shut, his nose collapsed, and one side of his skull sinks into a concavity the size of an orange. His head lies at an unnatural angle, and when his chest lifts, the sound that issues forth is a shattering.

One of the soldiers throws a bucket of water, and the puddled torso jerks. Buco barks an order, and three unsullied recruits from the outer ring move into position around Sunny's quivering body.

After the rifles fire, the crowd does not make a sound.

VI

April 1942

Claire has been training in Barrackpore for a week when Roger summons her back to Calcutta "for a chat." She prays this means that he and Viv have turned up more useful information than she has. Maybe they were right. The pulsing constancy of Ty and Shep's absence, combined with the sudden intermittent blindingness of their spectral appearances, wrenches her out of sleep and hounds her with guilt. She longs to lose herself in concentrated purpose. *To do what one can.* God knows she tries. But the futility of the effort comes at her from all sides.

Despite the impressive sound of Eastern Wireless Signal Centre Intelligence School "C," her induction into the Temporary Women Assistants has effectively buried her in the arcane rules of cipher and call signs and operational codes. Practice and policy. School. On the plus side, the Signal Corps's functional hieroglyphics tend to blunt memory almost as effectively as they do imagination, but she's starting to despair of ever being allowed to do more than collate data. And even if she were assigned to an intercept room, she'd as likely be sorting through messages from Burma or Malaya as from Port Blair.

During the eighteen-mile gharry ride, as the rig clops and creaks along the river, the apparitions taunt her. Shep stands hand in hand with Ty and paces along the embankment. Naila wades into the water. Who does Claire think she is? All three of them ignore her. She failed her family, then left them to die. Now, in Barrackpore she's even removed her wedding ring. No one here knows about Shep and Ty. She can't bear to speak of them. Her four roommates in the Nissen hut have husbands and fathers in the Navy, and more than a few of her fellow trainees have husbands fighting in Burma, but she has no common ground with any of them when it comes to Ty. At the very thought of admitting to strangers that she left her child in enemy territory, her throat turns to stone.

"Shukriya." She pays the driver and steps down into the bustle of Dalhousie Square. She's never been to Roger's office before. Aside from his having some sort of bureaucratic authority, she really has no idea what he does. Welcome to the war effort, she thinks.

Roger's secretary, a well-starched blonde, takes one look at Claire's road grime and asks if she doesn't want to "freshen up." Of all the pointless things to want, Claire thinks.

"If you don't mind—" She motions toward the inner office.

"But, they . . ."

Only then does Claire notice the flush behind the secretary's freckles, the lightness of her primped curls, her nervous glance at the mahogany door, behind which conversation mutters. Someone else is in there with Roger and Vivian.

Though she knows better, hope propels her. She thrusts open the door. And all conversation inside stops as Claire finds herself face to face with Port Blair's Police Chief.

Denis Ward. Sunburned, in tropical mufti, perched in an overstuffed club chair.

Claire's gaze races around the room: Vivian to Ward's left, then three empty seats, and Roger, advancing. No one. No one else.

The drawn white curtains behind Ward move like liquid air.

Roger comes, puts an arm around her and steers her to a seat across from Ward. "You know each other . . ."

It really is him. Only him. "You escaped," Claire manages.

"By the skin of our teeth."

Closer now, Ward looks diseased. And that chair is much too big for him. Beneath the peeling boiled-shrimp skin lurks the frame of a cadaver. The ghoulish grin of one, too.

"They d-didn't even have a proper compass," Roger says. "Had to navigate with a hydrographic sextant. Nobody's ever made it across before in a boat that size. Sharks, mines, squalls, G-G-God knows what—"

"Oh, for heaven's sake," Viv jumps in. "What you need to know, Claire, is that Major Ward left Port Blair with three others in a small fishing boat four days before the invasion. And he saw Shep just as they were leaving. Right, Major?"

Ward nods slowly, his opaque eyes trained on Claire's.

Roger hands her a glass of lukewarm lemon water, which she empties without tasting.

An electric fan alternately purrs and hiccups in the corner. Traffic dins outside. The dulled light trembles.

"Go on," she says.

Ward reaches to the low copper table between them and dislodges a small envelope from beneath the lacquer box that was securing it from the fan's slipstream. "Shep gave this to me on the jetty."

"He really didn't think they'd m-make it," Roger says.

"Frankly," Ward agrees, "no one did. But then they were all still betting on another ship."

Claire receives the envelope. She stares at its grimy vellum, the water stains and wrinkles. She pictures Shep on the Phoenix Bay jetty, thrusting this paper at Ward, of all people. She watches him reach with his other palm to cradle Ty's dark crown and prevent his wandering off. She imagines the bustle on the landing around them, the blaze of sun on stone, the eyes of all those left behind, watching and wondering, still expecting safe passage.

"Tell me what you know," she says. "That day. My son, how did he look?"

Ward sets down his empty glass. "Your son?"

"Why do you say it like that?"

"I'm sorry. I assumed . . . With everything else going on, it was every man for himself, but word still got round."

Vivian leans forward. "What word?"

"Far's I was concerned it was only a rumor, but . . ." Ward presses the heels of his hands into his knees. "I heard Shep spent days searching all the way down to Rangachang. They said he found a sandal on the beach there, but that was it. I'm sorry, Claire."

Her thoughts accordion, pressing and pulling what passes for facts and information. Even if she could trust Ward, even he admits this is nothing but hearsay. Shep's wire came through that very first night: Ty and Naila both safe.

He must have been searching for something else. A way out.

But then, why wasn't Ty with him at the dock? Surely, once Shep found him, he'd never let their boy out of his sight.

Then the bellows stop. Ward got out before the Japanese landed. Shep and Ty did not.

"Read," Vivian urges.

The envelope lies in the pleat of her skirt. She turns it over, and the sight of her name in Shep's hurried scrawl nearly blacks her out. She lowers her head, gets her bearings, and starts again.

The unfolded note consists of just four blurry pencil lines:

> My darling, if this reaches you, know that I love you.
> Eria —

And here a grease stain obscures a couple of letters. Then:

> — Kurzii
> God save us all,
> Shep

"What do you make of it?"

She looks up to find her sister-in-law staring expectantly.

"It's some kind of code, no?" Roger says. "Latin, surely, but nothing that seems to make sense."

Of course, they've already read it. Now they're treating it as a game— an occupational hazard she's become familiar with at Barrackpore. The codebreakers celebrate their breakthroughs with cheers that echo through the plaster walls. Claire never knows precisely what constitutes a victory in the enemy tracking rooms, but she marvels at the capacity for pleasure among people who, presumably, have just divined the coordinates of a bombing raid or a new aerial target.

"Shep told me once," Claire looks at Vivian as she says this, "that your father used to take you all up to the roof of the Peace Hotel to watch the Chinese armies fight it out in Shanghai. He said your parents never even recognized the irony. They'd sip gin and tonics and watch as if the war were a football match, except the losers got shot." *They made me ashamed to be British*, Shep would say, *and even more ashamed of my father.* He couldn't comprehend how a man who called himself a doctor could be so callously indifferent to human suffering.

Vivian gets up without answering and pushes back the curtains. The room floods with turmeric light and the tinny oompah of a wedding band. A flock of pigeons careens through the sky, drawing circles over the rooftops before pulling south toward the sea.

"No," Claire agrees with Roger. "Nothing about this makes sense."

An hour later, it makes even less. Ward, it turns out, is related to Roger, a cousin of some sort, and though he was raised in the Punjab and never set foot in Shanghai, he seems inclined to milk the familial connection. Roger gives no sign of resistance. If anything, he invites Ward's full-throated support for their "retaining" Shep's note as "intelligence."

Roger, of all people. Claire quits them both in hurt and disgust.

Vivian, having held her tongue during this final dispute, follows Claire outside and points her toward the Grand. "Let's go have a drink."

The hotel today bears little resemblance to the sumptuous palace of five years ago. The elegant salon where she and Shep and Roger first dined together has become a mess hall, the bar a canteen, brimming with soldiers from every part of the Allied world. The marble floors and high ceilings still make the Grand's lobby the coolest room in Calcutta, though, and the beer and gin flow harder than ever. The two women arm themselves with one of each.

"Roger's signed the same secrecy oath you have," Vivian says. "I don't know how long he's had possession of Shep's note or why he won't turn it over to us now, but here are my suspicions. That one line of Latin suggests that Shep was afraid of the note falling into enemy hands. And that makes the message more than private correspondence—at least as far as the War Department's concerned. Do you have *any* idea what he was trying to tell you? If we can prove it has no bearing on the war, they'll release it."

"*We?*"

Vivian takes her hand. "Roger may be compromised, but I'm not."

Claire stares at their locked fingers. "I feel like I'm fighting shadows."

Vivian gives her a squeeze and leans back, seeking the current from the nearest ceiling fan. At length she says, "Tell me about Ty."

The question catches Claire off guard. "Denis Ward doesn't know what he's talking about."

"Of course, he doesn't. If Shep said he has Ty, then he has him. But sometimes if you talk about people, it brings them closer. Besides, he's my only nephew and I still know next to nothing about him."

Claire pulls a glass ashtray from the center of the table and stares through it as through a camera lens. "He's beautiful. Wiry like Shep, but with hair as curly and dark as my father's when he was young. Black Irish, Dad said they used to call him. But Dad had brown eyes, and Ty's are this deep mossy green. He has the longest feathery lashes. I used to love to hold him so close I could feel them fluttering against my throat." She looks up as someone begins to play "Clair de Lune" on the piano in the far corner. "He has perfect pitch."

"He sounds perfect all over."

Claire sips her gin and tonic. "Not exactly."

Vivian waits.

"If he were perfect—or if I were more so—we'd all be together now."

"Claire—" Viv starts to protest, but Claire cuts her off.

"Ty didn't talk. At least, not in words. And not to me." She describes her son's obsessions, with plants and water and light and music—*humming* in perfect pitch but never singing, his tantrums and remarkable memory. "I could see what he loved. Sometimes I felt as if I could see his brain working. Shep said the same thing. But around the time Ty should have started talking, something went wrong. I can't explain it—" Her voice cracks. "The girl who looked after him, though. She understood him as I never could seem to."

Two pie-faced lieutenants across the lobby begin to sing, "For He's a Jolly Good Fellow." As Vivian waits for them to subside, she seems to be measuring her thoughts.

Finally, she says, "I was four years old before I uttered my first word, Claire. Shep wasn't nearly that late, but when he still wasn't speaking at two, I remember Father dismissing us both as 'retarded.' Shep could not, however, hold a candle to my earliest tantrums." She grins. "Sounds like your boy's a chip off the old block."

Claire shuts her eyes to stop the sudden waffling motion that comes over her. This must be how car crash survivors feel when presented with evidence that they could have prevented their family's death if they'd just consulted the right mechanic.

She can't have heard right. "Shep never so much as *hinted* that Ty's condition might be inherited. As far as I could tell, it mystified him."

Vivian sighs. "It would have. Remember, I'm nearly four years older. By the time Shep was three, we both were talking just fine. And in any case, we were raised to be neither seen nor heard, so other than that crack about retardation, the issue was never mentioned. In our family, admitting flaws or weakness was almost as inexcusable as expressing love."

That abyss between Shep and his parents. Was it conceivable that Shep himself—?

"You know who else was a late talker?"

Claire looks at her.

"Einstein!"

"Einstein. Vivian, if Ty could talk, he and Shep would be here now."

"How?"

She shakes her head. How can she explain the role that silence played in Ty's devotion to Naila? How can she even be sure that she *would* have acted differently that last morning if she had a normal bond with her son?

She would have. She would have prized him above all else. Above her work, those damned artifacts. Above even the Biya themselves. If she had a normal bond with her son, maybe she wouldn't have tried to shift her affections to her subjects in the first place.

"I don't mean to be insensitive," Viv says. "But maybe Ty is less helpless, more resilient than he seems."

"Ty is *four years old*."

"I know." Vivian bites her lip. "I know that."

Claire stares at the fans circling overhead. "How do you know? About Einstein."

They fortify themselves with another round of drinks, and Vivian explains that she was once assigned to write about Einstein's midlife travels in the Far East. "I knew next to nothing about the man, so I read everything I could get my hands on, including some fascinating descriptions of him as a young child that made me feel as if I were reading about myself: easily bored by the demands of others, perceived as rude and incorrigible, obsessively interested in mysteries that no one else seemed to notice, willfully stubborn and self-contained and frequently written off as stupid. He nearly brained his sister with a bowling ball during one tantrum, and he didn't say his first words until he was three."

"But Einstein's a *genius*, Viv."

"Everyone says so now, but his parents and teachers never thought so, any more than mine did. I'm not saying I'm in Einstein's league!" She snorts at the thought. "But I could read and play the piano before I uttered my first word, and I do recall that when I finally started talking, it seemed rather pointless, since no one was interested in the things I wanted to talk about. That was Einstein's burden, of course, to the nth degree!"

"But what explains it?"

"I couldn't find a medical reason. However, I did find a number of other childhood mutes who also turned out all right. The pianists Clara Schumann and Arthur Rubinstein—"

"You dug all this up and never told Shep?"

Viv rolls her bottle of Lion Ale between her palms. "I'm sure I meant to send him the article, but then, Shep never mentioned any concern about his glorious boy. This is the first I've thought of Einstein in years."

She looks up. "I'm so sorry, Claire. It might have spared you needless heartache. At least offered a possible explanation."

The singing lieutenants break into a jig. A chip off the old block, Claire thinks. Different, but normal. Maybe even better than normal. She wants to get up and scream at those stupid soldiers. Whether or not she dares to believe Vivian's theory is irrelevant now. *Needless heartache?* Her four-year-old son and her husband are prisoners of war—or worse. Could any of this foreknowledge possibly have changed their fate?

"I can't go backwards," Claire says, staring at their rowdy neighbors but no longer hearing them. The words feel like gravel in her mouth. "I can't change what's past. I have to concentrate on what's possible now." She turns back to Viv. "How could Denis have escaped and left Shep and Ty behind?"

Vivian leans back in her chair and for a moment the breath seems to go out of her. The singers retreat to the bar, and the stillness that replaces them settles like a pall.

"I don't know," Vivian says in a lowered voice. "But I think there's more to it than either he or Roger are letting on."

"Why they kept Shep's note?" At Viv's nod, Claire slides closer.

Vivian drops her voice to a whisper. "While we were waiting for you and Denis to arrive today, Roger told me that Ward spent his last few months in the Andamans scouting landing sites, elevations, tributaries. And cultivating informants."

"*Landing* sites?"

"It's pure speculation, of course."

"You're not suggesting that Denis Ward *himself*—"

Viv shushes her. "God knows how long it would take to mount a mission like this, but I'm told that Special Operations has a training camp for commandos in Ceylon. There are rumors of a reconnaissance team heading for Sumatra . . ."

Claire's head is pounding with the magnitude of Vivian's suggestion, but she picks up the thread. "And the Andamans are so much closer."

❧❦❧

Naila stands by herself at the front of the ledge and looks out as far as she can see. Morning mist roils over the forest to the southwest, but Port Blair is too distant to locate even on the clearest day. She's cut off from any terrain that's familiar.

Because they've arrived before the rains, they are sleeping in the open for their first few nights in Buruin, but the Biya are building a shelter they call the round house. The women weave thatch, and the men cut lengths of cane and saplings for the frame. Naila, Artam, and Ty twist vines into rope. During the monsoon, Leyo has explained, the round house will be strong enough to withstand the heaviest rains. Everyone will sleep inside it together. "I like this."

Naila knows he means that he likes it better than living in the bachelor house that he and Tika shared in Behalla. He likes having everyone close to him.

She is not so sure. She fears waking in the night to find that Ty has gone to sleep with Artam and her parents, and the boy's desertion seems a greater danger with everyone under one roof.

But Ty has eagerly joined in the construction. Behind her even now he sits, screwing his mouth in concentration as that boy Tika teaches him to lash the crossbeams with rope, to fasten the mats to their upright poles. Building for Ty Babu is like a puzzle, and he quickly masters the basics.

Away from Port Blair, Ty seems less of a baby, more of a little man, with newly muscled limbs and a new set to his jaw—a look of determination that resembles both Doctor Shep and Mem. He has always been stubborn, fixed in his attentions, but now he'll pat her hand like a condescending uncle and double stomp his foot for Leyo to come and show him the special knot that secures the pandan walls. Even that foot stomping is a gesture that Leyo has taught him, part of the full moon dance that preceded their trek north. Soon he won't need her at all.

Leyo moves toward her. "Look," he says, and turns her to face the round house.

The half-finished structure abuts the rock overhang, tall enough for the Biya to stretch their arms overhead inside. It looks not round but like some fancy bird with all its flaps and wings of matting.

"So small," Leyo says. "Every monsoon, this house grows smaller."

Not so long ago, he says, the camp held twenty or thirty people. In his grandfather's time, each couple had several children. "Then the British are coming, and the children begin to die."

He tells her that Kuli's father, named John by the British, was held for some years as a boy in the Andaman Home on Ross Island, and there he learned English and Hindi and the story of Jesus Christ. He learned to operate a camera and pilot small ships. He also saw the guards and foreign seamen give his people alcohol and paan and force the girls and women in the Home to lie with them.

"To lie with them?" Naila asks. She knows from Leyo's serious face that this business is bad, but the words sound no worse than her own parents lying together, as they used to when they thought she was asleep, murmuring and nuzzling each other in the dark.

Leyo says, "The men were sick, and they pushed this sickness inside the girls." After watching the girls develop fevers and sores, after their babies began to die, Kuli's father decided that the *firenghi* were full of disease, and he ran back to his tribe and warned everyone to stay far from Port Blair. Those who ignored him continued to die. Then there were not enough boys and girls to form families, and the sickness spread to other tribes.

"What happened to your mother and father?" Naila doesn't want to hear any more about sickness or bad men. She is suddenly ashamed that she never before thought to ask about Leyo's parents. Not even after she lost her own.

He takes her hand and squats, pulling her beside him. "We were fishing. I was small, like Ty Babu. A big boat came and there was a loud noise, then my father was in the water, my mother also. A white man used a long hook to pull me to his boat. He wore a black dress, white hat. Later I knew he was a priest. He took me to mission school. I tried to run away, but where to go? This school was far from my people. I stayed with that priest a long time."

"Your parents?"

He pushes his palm through the air. "One day, policemen came to school. They liked that I speak English, so I go to Port Blair, different school. And some Biya boys there I knew. This time we escape, one boy knows the way." He smiles. "I think my mother and father will be here, but no one has seen them since the day I disappear."

"But you didn't disappear."

He pulls a blade of grass from a crack at his feet and twists it between his fingers. "Kuli already was chief, Porubi already his eyes and ears in Aberdeen. Mam Golat say she is my auntie. I did not remember her or the others, but she want me to stay. Only Kuli said I must do as Porubi, but on Ross Island where the British officials live. So, I return, and the British make me *chowkidar*."

"You were *spying* on Mem and Doctor Shep?"

He shrugs. "Only at first."

His expression brightens. "Then I was spying on you!"

She rocks back on her heels, too stunned to react, but Leyo can't contain himself. The laughter rolls out of him. He falls onto his side and stretches his legs, tears drenching his cheeks. She can't tell if he is happy, or crazy.

She remembers being small and having the uncomfortable feeling that Leyo was watching her with thoughts she could not make sense of. She remembers two boys coming up to her at school one day after she rode the ferry across from Ross Island in Leyo's company. *You like them naked and black, do you?*

She stands up quickly and leaves him to his laughter.

"Trouble," Baird says.

They're sitting across from each other in the Assistant Commissioner's former bedroom, which the two of them now share. It's preferable to waking, as each has done, to find one or another of the guards hovering above them in the dark. The reason for these nocturnal inspections remains a mystery. Baird guesses the men are just satisfying their curiosity, but the visits do cease after they move in together. Privacy, under the circumstances, assumes a negative dimension. Now they rarely leave this room except for *tenko* morning and night and their daily ration of rice and tea. Their sole diversion is the *Andaman Shumbun*, the local paper turned Japanese propaganda sheet, which is delivered as an irritant. The major reads it cover to cover.

Shep has been staring at the front page. Today is April 15, 1942. A prominent photograph of His Excellency Emperor of Japan announces Hirohito's approaching birthday.

He looks up. "What is it?"

Baird stabs at a lesser article. "This fellow, Dipak Patel. They've given him a bloody medal and made him Chief Naval Intelligence Officer." He shakes his head, and Shep sees the weight of exhaustion beneath the gray eyes, the strain around Baird's mouth.

"I don't think I know him."

"You're lucky." Patel, Baird explains, managed a cinema hall in Bengal before he was convicted of murder and sent to the Cellular Jail in the early twenties. After a few years, he talked himself out on work release, married one of the female convicts and had a son. Later Baird made the mistake of employing him as a groundsman at his house in Rangachang. "A couple of years ago we caught him thieving, and it turned out he was smuggling knives and razors to his cronies in the prison. I testified against him. He's a snake, that one, but a snake with a silver tongue. Just Buco's type."

"Baird."

He looks up, and Shep notices a crack whiskering across one of his lenses.

"What were you doing down the hall this morning?"

Shep had awakened before dawn to find himself alone. There wasn't a sound downstairs, and for one blinding moment he thought Baird had made a run for it. When he went out to investigate, he noticed the rear bedroom door, which normally hung open a crack, was shut tight. He didn't dare open it, then didn't dare ask the question, but couldn't leave it alone.

His companion regards him with a steady, thoughtful gaze. "What did you see?"

Shep watches his voice. "I'm hardly likely to squeal on you."

Baird removes his glasses and presses the heels of his hands against his eyes. "It's no use, you know. All the careful plotting and planning. Reality's overruled us. We can SOS till our hearts explode."

Shep checks the hall, then looks out the window. Izumi, the only one of their guards who speaks any English, stands smoking with Buco's aide de camp in the shade of the traveller's palms out front. The morning heat is taking hold and the other guards are bound to be slumped half asleep in their sentry positions.

He presses the door shut. "What are you talking about?"

"I've a wireless hidden behind the baseboard in the back bedroom. Pati."

"Where'd Pati get it?"

"Lutty. He managed to get down the coast to Rangachang after he blew up the telegraph office. That part of the plan went off without a hitch."

"Plan?"

Baird's palms fall open. "I was to have met him there. If I had, we'd have been on the other side of the island before they sealed off the port. When he found me gone, Lutty took off into the jungle. Panicked, I suppose. He should have taken the bloody transmitter with him."

"Where were you that night?"

Baird slides his chin toward one shoulder, a seemingly unconscious variation of the Indian gesture of evasion. He'd spent his last free evening with the Commissioner and Prasad, the Forest Officer. "Wilkerson wanted to blow up the sawmill in the event of occupation. Prasad was arguing for the livelihood of the mill workers. All purely theoretical, you understand. And then it wasn't. Prasad had just left when we heard the shot across the harbor. Wilkerson looked at me and said, *Well, that settles that.*"

"Did he authorize your plan with Lutty?"

"He'd authorized Lutty to destroy everything and surrender." The major's gaunt face tightens as he registers Shep's surprise. "You saw how Wilkerson dealt with reality. Between the wars he romanced the daughter of a German general. He believed in the code of officers and gentlemen."

His candor is bracing but also unnerving. Shep gets up to check the hall again. Down in the kitchen Abraham begins to hum "Falling in Love Again," the Marlene Dietrich song that seized Port Blair's imagination some years back when *The Blue Angel* reached the local cinema. Abraham hasn't cooked for them since the first morning's toast, other than tea and rice—of which he takes the lion's share for himself. His principal interest seems to be cozying up to the guards. Now the front door squeals open and Izumi's low-throated bass chimes in. The duet climbs in volume. Over the banister and through the morning dusk Shep can just make out the two men's feet, one set mosquito-booted, the other bare, shuffling in a dance. He withdraws and re-closes the door.

"Pati thought he was doing me a favor," Baird says.

"You reassembled it."

Alfred shoots him a warning look. "There's no guarantee anyone but the Japanese would pick up the signal, and they'd likely trace it."

Shep nods. "Last resort."

"No. Suicide."

All Shep knows about wireless technology is what he learned with Claire during those brief precautionary lessons at the telegraph station. The set she took into the field was a simple key transmitter, but Lutty insisted on introducing them to state-of-the-art telegraphy, as well. One day he showed Shep a miniature transceiver packed into two gray metal boxes the length of his forearm: some wires and keys, a battery pack. Lutty described it as a "biscuit tin radio." *Size is its main advantage, but in a pinch size could count for a lot.*

The possibilities now jam Shep's thoughts. What would they telegraph if they could? An SOS for themselves? Wilkerson's supposed destination? The size of the occupying force? Even if they had any true military intelligence, it would be suicidal to attempt it without a code. But the truth is, for Shep there's only one message worth such a risk, and that's his son's location.

He needs to be sure of himself before he broaches the idea with Baird, though. Even if they could get a signal out, and even if by some miracle it were picked up by a British ship without the Japanese tracing it—already a crippling number of *ifs*—what is his expectation? Can he really imagine the War Office mounting a rescue mission for a four-year-old in enemy territory? That King and country would risk heaven and earth to do what the boy's own father was too much of a bloody coward to try?

The illusion of choice that paralyzed him the night of the invasion now assails him again. If Lutty could escape into the interior, then he—Shep—could have done, too. He should have known—he did know—that he'd never get away by boat, but if he'd headed inland, if he'd *run*, he might have gained enough distance to have a chance. He might have been killed, but if so, would Ty be any worse off than he is now?

The next days pass in a welter of self-recrimination, yet, over and over again, Shep comes up deadlocked. Ty's protectors know how to survive in the forest, and since he made sure the boy is officially dead to the locals, none of them will point the Japanese toward him.

On the other hand, in Calcutta, Claire must be telling everyone that Ty is alive—and if they *were* to come looking, they'd expect to find him in Port Blair. If she knew her son's true location, she'd at least be able to provide the right coordinates to any would-be rescuers, and she'd have reason to hope.

There will be a landing. Shep feels sure of it. However belatedly, the generals must now recognize the strategic importance of these islands. It's only a matter of how and when they come to re-take Port Blair. Ty is such a small part of the puzzle, but he's not insignificant . . .

Is he mad to think this? Mad in the midst of war to think an innocent child—any one child—could possibly matter? Let alone one whose own parents abandoned him.

No, not *parents*. Father.

They were called the Choctaw Code Talkers. Dr. Benedict called them "a case of anthropology's obscurity benefitting the national cause," of supposed primitives "redeeming" themselves in the eyes of their conquerors. "A new twist on the old saw of ignorance begetting bliss."

In 1917, members of the Choctaw nation were not considered U.S. citizens, but eight of them nevertheless wound up on the front lines in Europe speaking among themselves a language unintelligible to Americans and Germans alike. At the time, no German linguist or even garden variety ethnographer had ever set foot in Indian Country (a circumstance, Dr. Benedict informed her students, which the Germans remedied in the Great War's aftermath). The Choctaw foot soldiers, as a result, could speak freely over field telephones and radios, which were almost universally tapped. When the Choctaws called in fire on an enemy position, the attack invariably caught the Germans by surprise. When they requested supplies or back-up, the materiel was never intercepted. And the more their companies relied on the Choctaws to communicate, the fewer men the Allies lost near enemy lines. Eventually, their commanding officers noticed. Another dozen Choctaw code talkers were summoned from home, and field telephones and radios, which had been rendered virtually useless by German interception of other codes, were reinstated on the front. The Allies won the war, and not a single one of these so-called heathens was killed or captured in the process.

If Denis Ward—or anyone—is going to return to the Andamans undercover, he'll need an unbreakable talking code, just as the Allies had in the last war. And if Claire can somehow supply that code, she'll dial herself into the heart of the mission that could rescue Shep and Ty.

But it mustn't be as obscure or idiosyncratic as whatever Shep was attempting. *Eria kurzii*, in the texts she's found, is a rare but poorly documented orchid whose blossoms resemble an explosion of small white stars. It must have meant something to him, but what, she cannot fathom.

A successful code has to have enough logic that the intended recipient
can decipher it quickly, yet also be impenetrable to anyone else. The

magic of the Choctaw language was that it was unwritten and arcane, with no standard alphabet or symbols, and also that it was used exclusively by a small and highly localized tribe. *In other words, it's like Biya, except that Biya has the added advantage of virtual obsolescence.*

Claire stares at her journal for several minutes, then looks to make sure none of her roommates came in while she was writing. She runs through the idea again, checking with her phantom family. Shep nods. Ty smirks and looks for Naila's assent. The girl waggles her head noncommitally.

But it actually could add up. Claire tears the page from her journal and feeds it to the hurricane lamp.

That afternoon she retrieves her Andaman manuscript and notebooks from the trunk she's stored in the Fairhaven attic. On her next free days, she returns to Calcutta to swelter in the stacks of the Asiatic Society. Radcliffe-Brown, E. H. Man, and M.V. Portman all published studies of the Biya language, but except for R-B, they wrote these treatises back in the 1800s, and there's virtually no consistency among their systems of translation. As for distribution, she seriously doubts that anyone outside of the British Civil Service, R-B, and herself have laid eyes on the works of Man and Portman, let alone studied them in the past fifty years. Even here at the epicenter of the Raj, Portman's *Manual of the Andamanese Languages* still has uncut pages. And Radcliffe-Brown concentrated far more on culture and lore than on linguistics, which he made a hash of when he did give them a go. Her own work, quixotic as it now seems, appears to be the most direct and comprehensive survey of the Biya language in existence. With one possible exception.

"Roger, what's become of the Japanese arrested in Port Blair?"

"Delhi internment camp, I think. Why?"

"I knew them. I mean, I knew two of them in passing. They had a photo shop where I took my film—until I dropped my camera in the surf."

Roger narrows his eyes. "When was that?"

"Early on, thank God. Ty was a newborn. I got one snapshot of him off to my parents, and that was it. At the time, it seemed a crisis."

He paces the length of his office. When he turns, his long, normally placid features seem askew. "What else did you ph-photograph?"

"I tried to conserve my film for field work, but the camera only made the first trip to Behalla. Not that any of the pictures were worth a damn—fuzzy black shadows by fuzzy white fires or wading in fuzzy gray streams." She watches him go to the sideboard where a tray of bottles with metal tags wink in the morning light. "I mailed off for a new Kodak, but it probably was stolen somewhere in transit. So, I spent more time with the Kobayashis over the broken camera than anything else. They tried desperately to fix it. Now I understand why."

She watches his shoulders relax and returns to the reason she's come. "They and the others must have been interrogated."

"I'm sure. Pink gin?"

She shakes her head, but he proceeds to fill two glasses with Plymouth and bitters. He hands her a tumbler.

"This is an official call, Roger. Do you always ply your visitors with drink at eleven in the morning?"

"Only visitors who raise my b-b-blood pressure with questions of interrogation. What's this ab-bout, Claire?"

She takes a swallow and grimaces. "I have an idea for an encoding device that could be used in the field. You know this is what I'm being trained to do up in Barrackpore, translating code from the fellows in Burma and Ledo. Half of it's indecipherable—"

He holds up his palm in warning. "Loose lips."

But Roger is a linguist and a quick study. She reads his expression and continues, "I need to confirm something about the Japanese in Port Blair. I've got to know whether their reports would compromise my idea."

He reaches up and tugs on his forelock. Like Ty used to.

The floor swerves, and she shifts her focus to the shuttered light that stripes Roger's white shirt. He says, "You can't expect me to tell you what's in their f-files. Even if I did have access to them."

"I only need to know what's not in them."

"You expect me to prove a negative."

"Proof is a luxury of peace. I'm prepared to make do with a firm suspicion."

May 1942

"Doctor *saab*!" A hand lands roughly, yanking Shep out of a river choked with dead fish. "Please, doctor."

Rain drums on the tin roof. In the navy light he can barely identify the figure crowding his bed.

Across the room Baird sits up. "What's happened?"

"Bad, I think." Abraham. Breathing in short, uneven bursts, he tugs at his sarong and extends a leg. Shep can smell what he can't quite see: blood running from puncture wounds that extend down the man's calf. Sour saliva. Cold sweat. Something large and angry tried to eat Abraham for breakfast.

"A dog, Saab."

Saab, is it? Shep gets up. "Why come to me? I've no way of treating this." Shimura's men relieved him of his medical bag on day one.

"There is no one else."

"Surely the Japanese have infirmaries."

"For s-s-soldiers only." Abraham doesn't normally stutter. It could signal the beginning of septic shock, but he also seems genuinely frightened.

"What dog?"

The man stifles a moan as Shep lifts his foot. "The dog of Commissioner Buco, Saab."

"Good God, man." Baird strips off his pajama top for Shep to use as a tourniquet. "What were you doing with Buco's dog?"

Shep holds up a hand. Abraham is an opportunist, but not an especially smart one. He doubtless has plenty of co-conspirators among the servants now working for the officials, and plenty of customers among the townspeople who've been shoved aside during the occupation. Even poor Sunny's relatives need to eat. Abraham's cozied up to the soldiers, too. But dogs are another story. Especially dogs that catch you stealing from their master's kitchen.

"You're certain no one saw you? What about the sentries downstairs?"

"The rain is very loud. I am anyway lame." Abraham winces as Shep tightens the tourniquet. The lesions are practically to the bone, and in this heat and humidity, infection's a certainty unless the wounds are debrided and sterilized.

"You could lose this leg altogether."

"Doctor, no!"

"I don't know what you expect me to do. The Japanese have—"

"I cannot." Abraham's grayish pallor deepens. "Buco will have me killed."

"I daresay." Baird steps back and glances out into the lessening rain. Patches of light flare in the east. "But you, my man, at least are Asian. We, it appears, are not. So, why should the good doctor here risk his neck to save your life?"

Still on his back with his leg in the air, Abraham gulps like the fish in Shep's dream. Much as he distrusts this man, leverage is leverage. Dead or vengeful, Abraham is no use to them, but if pasted back together, he'd owe them his life.

"Abraham," he says. "Listen to me. You know the Civil Surgeon's bungalow here on Ross—before the earthquake, yes? In the backyard there used to be an orchid garden." Shep throws Baird an apologetic glance before ripping off a pajama sleeve to wrap around the wound, then he lowers the leg and helps Abraham to sit. "You're going to have to manage to get there and back on your own. There are three plants that should still be growing in the garden. Listen very carefully, then collect the leaves and seeds that I describe and bring them here." He draws verbal pictures of the *Spathoglottis plicata*, *Rhynchostilus retusa*, and *Aerides odorata*, then rearranges the sarong to conceal the damage.

"We've got *tenko* in less than an hour," Baird says when Abraham is gone.

Shep stands at the silvering window and watches his patient's black umbrella inch its way up the crosswalk. His mind fills with images of Claire looking up at him through the lamplight of their old bedroom, of Naila and Ty sitting cross-legged on the veranda, of Claire reading aloud to Ty as the sun kissed the horizon.

Twenty minutes later Abraham struggles back upstairs. His skin looks bleached—he was stopped by the guards, claimed a hangover so as not to arouse suspicion—but somehow, he managed to find the right plants. Shep strips the Spathoglottis leaves and grinds the Aerides seeds with a spoon in the wash basin, then unwraps the bandage and squeezes the juice of the Rhynchostilus directly onto the wound as Abraham bites down on the broom handle Baird has given him. Shep layers the Spatho-glottis and the Aerides paste to form a compress, but for all the faith he has in these remedies, he wishes to hell he had sulfa powder.

"You'll have to rely on toddy for the pain. Those tendons and ligaments are never going to be the same. But with luck this might save your leg. I'd come up with a good story if I were you."

Abraham has been staring at the ceiling. He grinds his teeth as he tries to sit up.

"Easy. And don't spend any more time on that leg than you absolutely must. Keep it raised above your heart."

"Doctor *saab*." Abraham catches his breath and glances at Baird, who watches steadily from his cot across the room. "Last night the Commissioner's cook is telling me about the wireless operator Lutty. Soldiers are catching him up the coast."

Lutty. The last time Shep saw him he was curled over the receiver, hair red as sorghum and disheveled as weeds after a night monitoring news of approaching vessels. No need to badger Tom for intel; thanks to his Scottish father, he was as desperate as the rest of them to get out. When he received the cable about the *Norilla's* sinking, the entire port knew within minutes.

"Saab," Abraham goes on. "Do you remember some years ago, before the freedom fighters were sent back to India, a boy is escaping from Cellular Jail, a Burmese boy named Ned Min, and when police caught him, his refusal of capture was so great that he shot himself in the head." He hesitates. "Lieutenant Lutty is your Ned Min."

The air goes out of them both.

Abraham chews on his mustache. "Something else. I am not thinking it is important, but now." He turns to the man whose skill and silence he now requires. "You know that black beggar in Aberdeen who is all the time drinking toddy and chewing paan."

Shep makes his face a blank.

"Some days ago I am passing him in clock tower square. He looks to be asleep in that doorway, but no sooner I pass than he is calling after me. Then he comes to follow, begging, all the time begging to carry my parcels for food. I am lame, so I let him carry my load to the ferry. We are talking, talking. He is a dirty drunkard and so primitive, but what can you do? Just before we reach the jetty, I am mentioning your name, and you would think I referred to Krishna himself. 'Oh,' he says. 'That Doctor *saab*. You tell him he's all right. Yah. He is all right.' And he will not let me go until I promise to tell you. So now I am telling you. What must you have done for this mad man to sing your praises?"

He's all right.

Somehow Shep manages to shake his head as if he hasn't the slightest idea. He hears himself say, "I cauterized an abscess in his toe a few years back, but he howled like a stuck pig. I can't imagine him thanking me for that. Doubtless just his usual ravings."

"Maybe," Baird offers, "old Porubi's so drunk he's failed to notice the changing of the guard and thinks there's still some good to be gained from currying the British doctor's favor."

"And so there is." Abraham salaams in Shep's direction. Then, leaning heavily on the banister, he drags himself downstairs.

Shep closes the door and breathes. *He's all right!* He even dares to smile.

"It wasn't that funny," Baird says. But Shep just gives him an Indian nod.

That morning after *tenko* they're ordered uphill to begin demolishing the old Subordinates' Club. They have no tools but their bare hands. Izumi laughs and tells them Commissioner Buco decided they were getting fat. He instructs them to salvage the bricks and all metal—nails, screws, hardware. The Japanese need building materials, and the British no longer are using their clubhouses.

Between the oppressive heat, Izumi's derision, and the abrasions that quickly cover his hands, Shep should be as miserable as Baird, but he feels buoyant. And focused. If Ty is alive and well, he *must* find a way to relay the child's whereabouts to Claire.

His mind corkscrews. The Emperor's birthday might give them adequate cover, but the code will have to be failsafe. Even if by some miracle Ward made it across, even if he had the wit and decency to get that little scrap of desperation to Claire, she'd likely never make sense of it. What he needs is some implicit key, at once indecipherable by the Japanese and as transparent to *Claire* as the code of plants is to him. At the same time, he needs a tag clear enough to signal any British operator within range to pass the message on to Calcutta. The whole enterprise is a fool's errand, yet thanks to Porubi, he's now a fool with hope.

"Are you all right?"

Shep opens his eyes. After working ten hours straight, they're back in their room. Alfred stands in his boxers, arms stretched high. Perspiration coats his bony frame. He uses calisthenics to distract himself from hunger. He considers it a form of resistance.

"You've been mumbling to yourself."

A dagger of light from the setting sun slices Shep's face. Outside, Izumi is upbraiding a new recruit. The heat and pending monsoon are getting on everyone's nerves, and the celebration of the Emperor's birthday will doubtless give the soldiers a welcome opportunity to let off steam.

Shep whispers, "My son's alive."

Baird, touching his toes, looks up sideways.

"I sent him away as a precaution."

The major comes up slowly. "Away?"

"Into the interior."

"The interior!" A bead of sweat travels like a tear from the corner of one eye. Baird swats it away. "That's not a precaution. It's a death sentence. Who's looking after him?"

"His ayah."

"The girl you claimed drowned him?" Baird wipes his neck and chest with his blue towel.

"That message from Porubi. It was about Ty."

Baird sits down across from him. "It's never going to work, you know," he says when Shep finishes describing his plan. But then he leans forward and places a hand on Shep's shoulder. "'Like love, all reason is against it, and all healthy instinct for it.'"

"Who wrote that?"

"Samuel Butler. But I wish I had. Love's the only thing that's worth risking everything for." He pauses. "I consider it the noblest form of resistance."

The next day, fireworks begin to explode above the mainland before dawn. Every Diwali sparkler in the port has been requisitioned in Hirohito's honor, and at morning *tenko* Izumi informs them that, "as special gesture of generosity," the prisoners are to be excused from the day's work detail. This frees their guards to make their own celebration, well lubricated with palm toddy, on the old parade ground.

Baird can't say whether the surrounding noise will interfere with their paltry signal, but Shep clings to the hope that the Japanese operators will be too inebriated to notice a few weak lines of gibberish clicking past them out to sea.

She works alone in a small white room with a view of the garden and a sign on the door that reads, *KEEP OUT. THIS MEANS YOU!* Her only visitor, Colonel Hastings, is a leaning tower of a man, a widower whose son recently was shot down over France. Not unlike her own, the colonel's antidote to grief seems to be to work around the clock. They rarely discuss their respective losses, much less the phantom faces peering over their shoulders, but Hastings always greets her with a handshake that lasts a second longer than most and ends with his clasping her one palm between both of his. What they do discuss is the codebook and, at length, the reasons why languages such as Choctaw and Biya are so well suited to cryptography.

Standard cryptographic technique involves either codes or ciphers. Codes substitute letters or figures for phrases, words, or concepts, while ciphers replace individual letters with numbers that then correspond to a key, such as a poem the operator has memorized or a numbered one-time key that he (or she) burns after completing the transmission. Most codes and ciphers ultimately are vulnerable because of the language of the original text. Allied code breakers scan for repeating patterns that correspond to patterns in written Japanese, and their Japanese counterparts, presumably, look for patterns typical of Romance languages, such as the frequency of vowels, or H after T or S. But if the underlying language has *no* existing written version, and if its oral version is unknown to the enemy, then this language should be safe both for code talking between agents on the ground and for distance telegraphy.

The first challenge in using Biya, as it was for the Choctaw coders, is to identify the native terms best suited for the messages agents are most likely to send. The master glossary that Claire developed with Kuli and Leyo will serve only as a scaffold for the more targeted code she now has to design, per Colonel Hasting's instructions, to include the basics of navigation and geography, climate, and military formations. Unfortunately, few Biya terms are exact. *Dula thire*, for instance, means *crescent moon,* but the literal meaning is *child of the moon.*

The evening after Leyo taught her this phrase, she and Shep stood with Ty on the bluff outside the Ross bungalow. Ty, then nearing a year old, was in a rare placid mood. She pointed to the crescent moon emerging from behind a great blue satin cloud. *Dula thire. You see the child of the moon, Ty?* And he reached an arm around her neck and laid his head on her breast.

And Shep said, *Ty, you're mennot thire. Am I right, Claire? Child of ours?*

They're quicksand, these words.

There's also the problem of sound. In her original attempt to represent the exact intonations and glottal stops of the native speaker, she created an alphabet of some forty symbols, not all of which corresponded to Roman letters, much less Morse. Here the Japanese give her an assist, however, since their *kana code* is a phonetic Morse. A few of the *kana* symbols correspond to Biya articulations—and, if mixed with International Morse symbols, they'll add an extra layer of confusion for Axis interceptors.

The final challenge, the colonel reminds her, is that landing teams, especially wireless operators, need to be able to memorize her code, since codebooks are prohibited in the field. "It must be as elegantly simple as it is complex. The trick, I've found, is to nibble."

Hastings bares his front teeth and gnaws on his lower lip. "I used to tell Christopher when he had a vexing algebra assignment, 'Just pretend you're a mouse working your way through a great block of Stilton. Crumb by crumb. It may take days or even weeks but keep at it and the plate eventually will be clean—and cook fit to be tied.'"

She pictures the boy and his much younger father together in a pool of lamplight, secretly, silently laughing as they lick their shared plate clean.

"Maybe Roger told you."

"Told me what?" Viv pulls a folding fan from her bag and whips it open.

"I asked him to do some research on the Japanese arrested in Port Blair, and he found no evidence that any of them were linguists. They were gathering information on the Indians and Europeans and the islands' resources and terrain. Their only interest in the Andamans was military. If they thought of the natives at all, they thought of them as vermin."

Claire pries her wet skirt from her thighs. They're sitting in the shade of the arbor behind St. John's Church. The cemetery this late in the afternoon is reliably deserted.

"What are you up to?"

She presses a finger to her lips. "I've started developing a mobile code."

Vivian looks for several seconds as if she's performing a complex calculation, then she sits back and whistles. "That's brilliant, Claire!"

Across the yard three young boys, naked to the waist, are shooting at grackles with slingshots. The birds, perched throughout the treetops, ignore them.

Claire asks, "Denis Ward's operation is on, isn't it?"

"If it is, it's Top Secret."

"But you know."

"Trust me, I'd tell you. Last I heard, Denis was headed for Simla. That's really all I know."

"The code I'm creating could be used anywhere. Burma, Sumatra . . ."

"But that won't get you onto the Andaman mission. Is that it?"

"I can't volunteer myself. Especially not if Ward has anything to do with it. We're as good as sworn enemies."

"He did deliver Shep's message."

"Only because it gave him a chance to play hero."

A pause. "So, the problem's not exclusively on his side of the table."

Claire waves this away. "I need you to keep your eyes and ears open—especially with Roger—for any opportunities to plant the idea so it circles back to the higher echelons without my fingerprints directly attached."

Vivian studies Claire's face before answering. "I'll do that. You know I will." She clearly meant to say something else, but it's something neither of them can bear to contemplate.

"Ty's the first thing I see every morning," Claire says. "And over and over and over again every night in my dreams. He's almost always two years old, running away from me."

The slingshot boys give up and move off into the haze.

Over the days that follow the Emperor's birthday, oppressive humidity combines with rampant hangovers to lay low the entire occupying force. Even Buco, a creature of punctilious regularity, is half an hour late for *ten-*

ko the first morning, and an hour early returning to the Commissioner's residence that night. Then Abraham tells them Lt. Shimura has gone. The naval commander, a subtle force for moderation, left that morning. The martinet Buco is now wholly in charge. Moreover, Buco has announced the creation of a new Administration, to be called the Gunseisho, consisting of both Japanese military and elected local civilians.

"Home rule!" Abraham makes no effort to contain his elation. Having survived his misguided raid on Buco's larder, he now steers clear of the Commissioner himself, but as a self-styled freedom fighter, he cannot resist this political sop any more than he can see the lie within it. In his excitement, he even seems to forget that his saviors belong to the opposition.

One week later, a squad of sentries surround Shep and Baird at their demolition site, barking orders in Japanese, shackling their wrists and hauling them down the hill to meet Abraham, likewise cuffed, and teetering in bewilderment.

Izumi shouts, "Spy!" and "Arrest!" But they're given no specifics, and the unfamiliar officer in charge seems half asleep. Baird looks at Shep and shrugs as the soldiers point their bayonets and prod them toward the jetty.

In Aberdeen, Abraham is led toward the Commander's headquarters, and Shep and Baird are marched up Atlanta Point.

"A taste of our own medicine," Baird mutters as they pass a jeering crowd that includes more than a few of the Cellular Jail's former residents. On the prison flagpole, the golden tiger of Free India now sags under the protection of a blood red sun.

They're placed in separate but neighboring cells, and their guard, a baby-faced boy named Okita, seems so lonely and scared that he actually welcomes the neutered company of two noncombatant prisoners. When he brings their first few jail meals of rice and brackish water, he conveys through rudimentary sign language that pieces of a wireless set were found in the kitchen of their house on Ross.

"In the *kitchen*?" Shep tries every which way to confirm this detail—pantomiming frying, tasting, stirring, shaping the parameters of a room around an invisible stove. Then he drops his mouth in a look of exaggerated but honest bewilderment. He and Baird never took any part of the transmitter downstairs, let alone into Abraham's domain.

Okita, seizing the impromptu English lesson, nods enthusiastically as he elasticizes the translation. *"Dai-do-koro. Kit-chen."*

The thing is, Shep checked to make certain their wireless was still in its hiding place behind the baseboard just hours before their arrest. To his knowledge, the upstairs was never inspected. Also, Okita says nothing of signal interception, and no one's accusing them of actually transmitting any messages. Either the boy is mistaken about the location of the set, or something entirely different is going on.

The confusion is enough to offer hope that Abraham might sort things out, since he, too, stands accused. A mean irony, the thought of their fate resting with Abraham. But then Shep manages to decipher the code that Baird is tapping through the wall: *Dipak Patel vendetta.*

They may have converted Abraham, but Patel still bears his grudge against Baird for his past testimony. Now, as Buco's anointed chief of intelligence, Baird's prince of thieves is perfectly positioned to take his revenge by filing a false report.

Asia for the Asians. In the elaborate dance of fraternity, Buco would be only too happy to accept trumped up charges and prosecute the British officer. In exchange, Patel could help suppress the ongoing resentment over the Sunny Ali debacle. Maybe Buco even welcomed the excuse to make a spectacle of his prisoners.

But if Patel planted a dummy wireless, and *that* is the excuse for their arrest, then their actual set must still be hidden. More to the point, no one is giving any indication that their signal was detected. This slender thread sustains Shep.

The laughter begins as usual, sharp as a hiccup. Then Ty gazes up at the trees, and his breath grows liquid and loud. He points at figures of sunlight dancing above the stream. Naila claps her hands. She and Ty stand knee-deep in the water, and as the lights dance faster, higher, the children wave for them to come back. Then Ty signals something to

Naila and scrambles among the boulders. He's chasing the flashes as he used to chase fireflies, but these magic beings are only scraps of reflection off the stream. Naila calls Ty back to explain, scooping water into her hands and holding it to a sunbeam. Ty watches closely, then goes to work making spirit lights of his own. Over and over he scoops and aims reflections at rocks, trees, spiderwebs, into the girl's eyes. Each time he succeeds in making her blink, he raises a V for Victory.

Shep opens his eyes. Flat on his back at midday, he stifles a moan and tries to claw his way back into the dream, instead finds himself staring at a lizard on the ceiling.

Stuck up there like a taxidermist's sample, the small, still creature reminds him of a hummingbird he once came upon as a boy, all iridescent greens and reds, no bigger than his thumb and perfectly motionless, perched on a dwarf pomegranate branch. He remembers holding his breath as he approached, thinking the bird's sublime stillness a gift, a kind of natural benediction signifying something about him that warranted this tiny creature's trust. When the bird refused to wake for him, the pain felt visceral as a knife thrust. But minutes later it did wake, slowly on its own terms, as if from hibernation. *Torpor*, he would learn, is an imitation death state designed to conserve the bird's energy, reduce its need for warmth, and prolong its survival.

The lizard stretches its little green jaws and snaps them on a mosquito. Shep turns his head and lets the sweat run down his arm. His cell has a barred front that faces the outer loggia. From his wooden pallet, he can see a wedge of prison yard, the solid back of the next cell block. A sliver of white sky is visible above the roofline. Engines and wheels stutter, distant as the horns barking up from the harbor. He can make out regimental tramping and the occasional slap of voices, but his sense of the outer world comes mostly from gestures of light playing over that facing wall. Today the screen is obscured by a steady drizzle, which at least brings some relief from the heat and the stink of the chamberpot, if not from his dysentery. Or the mosquitoes.

He slaps one of the whining pests from his ear and knocks softly on the wall. Baird taps back, *Courage, old man.* This latest madness could yet turn out to be a test. By most standards of war, they've received benign treatment, and logic dictates that their skills will yet protect them. Medical expertise is always at a premium in war, regardless of race or nation. And Baird's twenty years in the Andamans should make him invaluable. Commodities, provisions, organization, Baird's your man, his penchant for rules and order right in line with the Japanese obsession with same.

If only this were the India of *Kim*. No matter how narrow the corner, Kipling's young hero could survive by his wits, his powers as a cultural chameleon, his linguistic versatility. But solitary confinement did not exist in Kim's India. However dire his circumstances, the boy hero always managed to access sources, confidantes, or dupes. In isolation, Shep is the dupe and hope his undoing. Waking from that glittering dream of Ty and Naila was like dying.

Now he hauls himself to the corner of his cell. The metal pot already is overflowing, so he empties the latest platoons of parasites from his bowels directly onto the floor. If the rain sharpens and the wind drives it into the cell, gravity should pull some of this revolting stench down the drain. But nothing will stop the spasms in his gut.

He is still squatting when he notices the drums. Difficult to tell their location, given the jail's configuration, but Shep guesses the beaters are in Aberdeen Bazaar. Another summons. He hauls himself up and ties the flaps of his trousers around what's left of his waist.

An hour later the drums are still going. A guard Shep has never seen before, built like a Panzer, hauls open the cell door and shackles him. Down the block a squad of soldiers wait with Baird, who stands in immaculate dress whites. The uniform, clearly fetched by order of the authorities, hangs on him and contrasts alarmingly with Alfred's jaundiced complexion. Though Shep has received no such change of clothing, he can see they are both to be put on display. The drums, then, are for them.

Outside, the drizzle has stopped, and white clouds spar with gray. They're shoved into the back of a jeep, the Panzer guard with the driver in front. Baird's skin looks like clay. His eyes stare straight ahead, but as the vehicle jerks into gear, Shep feels the touch of skin. Alfred has slid his wrists toward the center of the seat, is reaching for his hand.

That uniform is like a barrier of contagion; Shep's first instinct is to pull away from this man so visibly condemned, but they round a curve and come shoulder to shoulder, the weight of their bodies pressed, and almost without intending to, Shep finds Alfred's fingers, holds fast. The sense of connection—union—overwhelms him, and he understands that this is their pact.

Of strength. Of dignity. Of solace. Whatever is about to happen cannot, will not, break their shared human *being*. It is a kind of prayer.

Familiar vistas kaleidoscope as the jeep flies down to the harbor, then up toward the clock tower. As the drums grow louder Claire comes to Shep, laughing full-throated in the swimming pool, holding Ty as a baby outstretched and pummeling the water as if to churn it into gold. Shep closes his eyes and wills himself to drown.

The jeep halts at the top of the hill, and Baird squeezes his hand hard before letting go.

He is pulled from one side, Shep from the other. The drums at last fall silent as the Panzer shoves his prisoners toward Buco, a Japanese Napoleon in spit-shined boots on the steps of the Browning Club. A small gray-bearded man with brittle eyes hovers at Buco's right hand. Shep recognizes Dipak Patel from the newspaper story about his elevation to Chief Intelligence Officer.

Around the square the entire town stands at wary attention.

When Buco is satisfied with the placement of Shep and Baird in front of him, he flips one hand at his lieutenant, and Abraham staggers forward, shackled and downcast, to cringe beside them. Patel begins to heckle Abraham, who keeps his face to the ground and nods. And nods. And nods again as the sun burns white through the mist.

At first the testimony is given in Urdu for the benefit of the assembly, then Buco's lieutenant barks at Abraham to translate into English. He obliges as if reciting an oath he's learned by rote.

"These British have made me to hide a wireless set in their kitchen. Yes, they swear me to silence, but I am knowing my duty to tell to Dipak Patel the truth."

Abraham rubs his leg as he lies for his life and never once looks at the accused, yet even as these lies condemn them, Shep calculates and rejoices. If Abraham knew about the real wireless, surely he'd be shouting that from the rooftops to make himself a hero. Instead, he's parroting this fabrication.

Shep risks a glance at Baird, whose inscrutable half-smile confirms his suspicion. They were not intercepted. Ty's location hasn't fallen into enemy hands, and if the signal reached its intended target, there still could be reason for hope.

As Abraham falls silent, Shep scans the local faces, some of which are electric with vengeance, others trembling at the prospect of more violence. A tall boy with flat black eyes who bears a disturbing resemblance to Patel raises his fist, and the inevitable chants of *Azad Hind!* and *Inquilab Zindabad!* begin, but then Shep spots his driver Narinder and, beside him, Baird's beloved Pati. Shep hears a choking gasp as Baird, too, locates Pati, and the distance between the two men seems charged with grief and longing.

It would be like this for him and Claire, too, if she appeared before him. But no, he thinks. Because of Ty, it would be vastly, unimaginably worse.

Then Narinder signals Shep. Between his palms he holds a stem of white elephant blossoms.

And snatches of a passage or maybe a prayer now whisper through his mind. A glen with a brook. A tree possessed of magic.

A cry goes up, and Buco, his red face a mask of ecstatic menace, invokes the Emperor of Japan. Then, in English, "You are guilty of treason and according to laws, punishment is death."

But in Buco's mouth, it sounds like "debt" and, still preoccupied by the retrieval of his prayer, Shep is startled when two Japanese soldiers step forward and grab Baird by the arms, drag him to the clock tower, where another five surround him. Shep's hands throb with the memory of their contact just minutes ago, and he tries but can't quite meet Alfred's gaze before the human stockade engulfs him.

And then, as with Sunny Ali, the square explodes with the thunder of boots and blows, grunts of exertion and the compressed cries of his friend's surrender. That compression seizes Shep's own throat, his head and his heart, with a visceral, crushing sensation. None of the witnesses weep or wail, though many look on like stoics. Shep wills Pati to slip away, but even in this desperate prayer he is impotent, for Baird's beloved remains unflinching, his stillness its own silent protest.

Again, the insistent memory of words pleads for Shep's attention. He can't tell where the voice comes from, only that the lines resound, as pure and clear as if someone were reading to him. *He did not want to cry—had never felt less like crying in his life—but of a sudden easy, stupid tears trickled down his nose, and with an audible click he felt the wheels of his being lock up anew on the world without.*

When the torturers step back, breathless and spent, the white British uniform is black and red and ripped from Alfred's contorted body. One arm lies backward on the cobblestones. They have peeled the left cheek open. Alfred's crushed thorax heaves as his pleas for water bleed from the side of his face. Shep feels himself splinter as he lurches forward and is yanked back, a rifle stock slamming his jaw. When his vision returns, Buco is dribbling water along the blade of his sword.

Alfred lies still now, conscious or not, it's impossible to tell. His eyes have closed in their sockets, his breath become a death rattle. Buco tosses the emptied canteen at his feet and raises the sword with both hands.

Witness, Shep commands himself through the tears that suddenly rage out of him. *Do not look away.*

The square resounds with Buco's bellows of orgiastic fury as he drives the blade down through sinew and bone, and the long gray head that just seconds ago belonged to Alfred Baird rolls back against the monument to India's fallen heroes.

A well of silence opens within, offers to swallow Shep, too, but the words begin to spiral now, untouchable and proud. *His head lay powerless upon her breast, and his opened hands surrendered to her strength. The many-rooted tree above him, and even the dead manhandled wood beside, knew what he sought, as he himself did not know.*

The nerve. Shep squeezes his eyes against, then into the memory of Claire, her voice, her body, her *nerve*.

"Gaijin! Hannin!" Buco's shriek unleashes a frenzy of cocking and loading of rifles, a jab between Shep's shoulder blades, a voice in Japanese-English roaring for him to open his eyes, and the final spasms of his bowels empty what little they had left. The stench enrages Buco so that Shep's already floating consciousness wonders if the little man will simply whip the sword sideways and do him in right then, but no, the screams appear to be aimed at the fingers closing like vises, hoisting Shep's still technically intact body and yanking him ten feet forward to teeter beside Alfred's rent corpse.

Shep watches now from a foot or so behind himself as the eyes of his killers widen. Some are the color of yolks, others crimson with veins like yarn—hepatitis and uveitis, the physician dying in him notes—and some with pupils wide as black holes—but the thought, if that's what you'd call it, is interrupted by a wooden fist smashing into his occipital bone. A bayonet flays his right upper arm, and he stares at the wondrous infinity of layers opening to receive the scalpel—no, not a scalpel anymore. Nevermore. Never again that crippling ooze of fear.

Laughter fills the bowl that's opened in his brain, the sound of it like relief, after all, that this—*this* is all that lifetime of fear was really about. Alfred Baird's old gray eyes must be laughing, too, and the sensation of his touch is making Shep's palms itch when a boot heel in the groin propels his consciousness up to the top of the clock tower, where it hovers. The anesthesia of shock, true magic.

Death knew what he sought as he himself did not: Claire smiling from the depths of the garden, opening arms to take him in as Ty, between them, laughs. Laughs, yes, as the noise of pain and rending now peel upward, and the stillness deep inside him curls it right back down. That voice, not the laughing one but the worded one, is his own! The voice of the boy he once was, reading himself to sleep. *From the enormous pit before him*, once more, just once more forever, *white peaks lifted themselves yearning to the moonlight*. And *the rest was as the darkness of interstellar space.*

VII

June 1942

Never has Naila known rain like this. The way the treetops catch the wind, as if trapped in a great black jar. Water pours everywhere—over the thatch, through the cracks in the cave, across the lowest depression in the ledge. At the height of the storms, it roars into a broad V-shaped waterfall that threatens to sweep them away.

Standing at the front of the round house, Naila clings to Ty and yells over the thunder. "You must not go into that rushing water, do you understand, *mitai*? It is like a river, an ocean—" She thinks of her parents. "You remember that terrible day when the earth shook and the sea rose and we watched the water take those boys from the rocks?" Ty blinks at her. "This water will take you as that water took those boys, and you will never, ever come back.

"Ty Babu, this is not a game. Do you hear me?"

The boy tips his head to one side, considering the liquid and wind and noise and darkness. Several days ago, because Artam was having her head shaved, he allowed Imulu to shave him, too, and so he is barely recognizable, the dome of his head mushroom pale above his brown face and body. Afterwards Naila, too, let Imulu shear off her hair, so she knows that Ty is more comfortable, free of the sweat and insects and tangles, and she knows that hair grows back, but she misses his dark tendrils as she does the softness of his baby arms and legs. He has so quickly grown tough, strong and also defiant, like the Biya.

The big winged house creaks and moans above them, and the smells of wet stone and grass and the fire back under the overhang coat their skin. Artam lies in front of them with her head poking out. She laughs into the rain, and Naila worries more than ever what this crazy girl might lead Ty to do.

Then a memory comes from long ago, of her mother making a paper doll—and feeding it to fire. A warning that needed no explanation.

"Here." She reaches to a pile of reeds that the three of them have been pulling into strips for Obeyo and Ekko to weave into mats. Naila ties some of the shorter strips into a crude boat.

Ty grins at her handiwork and puts his hand out. Artam, too, wants to play with the toy, but Naila holds it above their heads.

Now the women clustered around their weaving and food preparations make clucking sounds, of amusement or disapproval, Naila can never tell which. It would serve them right if the flood sent Artam crashing down to the rocks below, but she is not going to let that happen to Ty Babu.

"Hold hands," she tells the little ones, extending her own free fingers to Ty. And like that they edge out into the downpour and toward the dark channel where floodwaters collect from the upper hillside before tumbling over the ledge.

"Sit down," she shouts over the wind. The rain falls in spikes but Ty and Artam seem indifferent to it as they squat at attention.

Naila shields the little boat in her hands and yells to Ty, "You are this little boat, yes? And you do just what this crazy girl wants, which is to go in the water. Yes?" Ty's expression is bright against the day's darkness. He nods. "Good. Now see what happens to you, little boat."

She takes two steps farther down the ledge and drops the boat into the floodwater. It bobbles briefly under the pummeling rain, then spins forward and disappears over the falls. "You see—"

Before she can turn around, Artam pops up and springs toward the front of the ledge. Naila leans to catch the child, but her foot slips on a patch of wet lichen. Down she goes, yelling for Artam to stop, but of course her words mean nothing to the Biya child, who now stands peering over the precipice.

A screeching whistle slices through the rain, and Artam snaps back like a hooked fish. Obeyo stands at the front of the hut with her hands on her hips and the skull of her dead child slung forward on her breast.

As Artam's mother, Imulu, saunters out wiping her palms on her thighs, Obeyo takes it upon herself to scold the little girl and order her back to the hut. Not a glance, not a sound from either of them for Naila.

Through all of this Ty Babu remains squatting where Artam left him, watching the rush of water, the other "boats" in the form of leaves, twigs, petals, snails, beetles with their feet in the air, even a bright yellow whip of snakeskin that gravity and the force of the rain have swirled into the flood. Perhaps, Naila thinks, Artam's powers over him are not as great as she feared.

But now, as the barking of dogs announces the return of the men, Ty seems to jerk from his trance. He darts back to the far side of the hut where the animals leap into his arms. These yellow mongrels he loves even more than Artam.

The men slide down one of the hunting paths that lead up and over the hill behind the ledge. Artam's father, Sempe, carries a green monitor lizard over his shoulders. Behind Leyo comes Porubi.

Naila still finds it difficult to believe the story that Leyo has told her about Porubi, but it seems to be true. Kuli first sent him as a boy to spy in Port Blair because the British were sending released convicts to build new villages in Biya forest. Although Kuli had no power to stop these settlements, by learning of the plans in advance he could move his people before the work gangs arrived. If he did not, the gangs of Indian and Burmese convicts would prey on Biya women and start fights with Biya men. Porubi found that the British and Indians would say anything around a silent drunkard, as if he were invisible, and Leyo says that perhaps the Japanese will do the same.

"Come on," she says to Ty. "Bring the Bibi dogs inside. I'm sure they want to get out of the rain, even if you don't." Ty answers by shaking himself as the dogs are doing.

Porubi goes straight to Kuli's corner, waking him from a nap, and the two sit with Leyo while the others set about draining the lizard's blood and preparing the fire.

Because so much Biya talk takes the form of gesture, a tilt of the head or shoulder, or else through one person talking story, it is strange to hear the men speak back and forth. It sounds like a normal conversation, Naila thinks, with a pang of longing.

Ty, as if sensing her sadness, licks her arm. He's taken this habit from the Bibi dogs, the more because Leyo's singlet, which she wears because it is cooler than her blouse, has no sleeves for him to tug. She bends down and pretends to take a bite from his ear. He replies by clapping his hands.

She forms a circle with Ty and Artam, then, and busies them with a hand-clapping game that Mem taught her in their other life. Naila says the words softly under her breath, but the pattern of action is what Ty likes, hands to thighs, to clap, to Artam's:

Pease porridge hot,

Pease porridge cold,

Pease porridge in the pot

Nine Days—

"Naila." Leyo beckons her to join him. His expression warns her to leave Ty with Artam.

Kuli kneels with his hands on his thighs. Porubi bows his head.

"What it is?" she asks coming toward them.

Leyo holds her gaze and waits for her to settle. "Doctor Shep, Naila. He never will come."

Never. The word teeters between them. Naila wants to pick it up and turn it, to find the secret hollow inside where hope is hidden, but the word refuses to lift. It has planted itself like one of the stones in the old Ross Island graveyard.

She knows and refuses to know what Leyo means by this word. She dares not repeat it, even to herself, and she fights the desire to turn back to Ty, to join him laughing and knowing nothing, guessing nothing, missing nothing and no one.

The fight leaves her empty, unable to speak as she pictures Doctor Shep's pale green eyes, the pain in them that final day as he placed his charms around her neck. She fingers the points of the gold star now, feels the moonstone's cool round surface against the hollow of her throat. *Magic to keep you safe*, he said. He should have kept it for himself.

Leyo cradles her cheek in his palm. "Ty Babu is ours now, Naila. You have your wish."

He catches her sudden, flailing hand and presses it to his heart.

October–December 1942

Ward appears in early October, with a perfunctory knock. There's a single wooden chair in front of Claire's desk, but instead of sitting, he stands and grips the back of it with both hands.

"You're back," she says lightly. "How was Simla?"

"Like paradise compared to this." He gestures at the open window and the mustard air outside. The rains have subsided. The smothering heat has not. His selection of the word *paradise* strikes Claire as a cruel rebuke, though Ward has no way of knowing all the shades of meaning it possessed for her and Shep.

"Brisk enough for a blanket at night, imagine that." He doesn't bother to ask how she knows he went to Simla. "So tell me about this code."

She opens to a new page in the notebook in front of her. "I'm almost done with the core of it, but I'll need a list of any terms specific to your mission."

"What exactly did you have in mind?"

"I don't know. Equipment, names of people, logistics. The idea is to mold the language so specifically to your purposes that it becomes a code within a code."

"How much do you know about this operation?"

She stiffens under his scrutiny. "Only that I need to provide you with a system that's safe for both field communication and telegraphy."

He swings the chair around and straddles it backwards. It's difficult to remember that Ward is British; he seems to be imitating Clark Gable's brash bad manners in *Gone with the Wind*. She feels another stab of longing for Shep's guilelessness.

"It's not a search-and-rescue operation," he says. "It's military reconnaissance."

The blow lands, but she will not let him see that. "My job is to help you, whatever you're doing." She hesitates. "Wherever you're going."

"It's not *your* job I'm worried about, Mrs. Durant."

He's watching her closely now, so she lifts her chin. "Major Ward." She struggles to keep the need out of her voice. "I'm sure it would make your life simpler if I were someone else. An ethnographer from Calcutta University, perhaps. Or a linguist from Oxford. But if I were, I doubt I could be as much help to you. And I am giving it my all."

"I'm sure you are." He has a scar across his left temple, which he rubs now with the back of one fist. He's filled out since his harrowing voyage to safety. He's recovered.

"I'd have taken them, you know," he says. "Your husband and Baird, anyway. Only so much room, but they were the top of the food chain. Wilkerson was such a damned fool."

She has a sudden hideous thought. "How did you know?"

He tracks her meaning without even the pretense of confusion. Give him that. "Gut," he says. "You'd have had to be daft not to figure our days were numbered, and frankly I had more faith in my noble boatmen at that point than I had in the British government. Not that I honestly believed we'd make it. The truth is, I was just too scared to stay."

"And now you're going back." The chill in her voice sets between them.

He squints at the window. A man so desperate to escape that he'd trust his luck solo against enemy submarines over the promise of his own government; so fearful that he'd volunteer to return to the same enemy territory he risked everything to flee. "I couldn't tell them."

"Tell them what?"

"After Pearl Harbor we set up a DF—direction-finding—base near Middle Strait to track radio traffic from Burma and Sumatra. A couple of my boys manned the station. After the *Norilla* was sunk, I received orders from Calcutta to dismantle and hide the equipment. That's all I knew, but I figured then our goose was cooked."

Guilt is scribbled across his face so clearly now that she might be read-ing his confession. "So, you stole some of that equipment to guarantee clear sailing."

He touches the scar again. This haggard, wretched hero liar. Trading on the myth of his crude hydrographic sextant, on the "miracle" of his safe passage.

"That's why you couldn't tell anyone what your odds really were." Without looking, she senses the air going out of him, the last of his pose dissolving. This is over, then. Why else confess to her? He means to hang her with his guilt.

"I would have taken them," he repeats, his voice faint now.

"But you didn't."

"If Wilkerson had found out, he'd have had my own men arrest me . . . You see why I have to go back."

She presses both palms against the sharp edge of her desk. "You just said this is not a rescue mission."

"That's because I want to make sure you understand the *official* terms of this operation."

She gives him another look. He appears to be pleading now, but be-neath the cliff of his brow, his eyes have darkened and watch her with care.

The quickening between them makes the afternoon shimmer with a fleeting radiance. Shep raises his palm. A wave? A warning? She struggles to read him before he is gone.

"My job," she repeats, matching Ward's caution, "is to help you see this operation through."

Ward and his team will be four altogether, and of them Sergeant Culman, a young Royal Signals operator from Brighton who escaped Rangoon, is the only stranger to the Andamans. The others at least can picture the source of the language they're learning, though none has actually heard it spoken. Hari Khan, a former MP from Dehradun, was stationed in Port

Blair in the early thirties. Luke Benegal, a forest worker, grew up on a coconut plantation north of Mount Harriet.

Several days after their initial introduction, while Ward and Culman are out of the room, Luke asks Claire if by any chance she might be related to Dr. Durant in Port Blair. Ward has explicitly told her not to reveal her personal details, so she can only nod obliquely, but her face gives her away.

Hari and Luke exchange glances, then Luke says he knew Shep. He accompanied him several years ago on an inland collecting trek. "We found a leopard orchid so enormous that one root alone nearly capsized our boat!"

His narrow, feline face widens into a grin before he catches himself. "I am sorry, Mrs. Durant."

She shakes her head, swerving. She has no recollection of that orchid or of Shep's talking about that excursion, and it would be best not to show too nakedly how grateful she is for Luke's memory, but her throat seizes up on her.

"I'm sorry," he says again. "That was the only time we spent together."

"Please," she manages, addressing both men. "Please call me Claire."

Now every day of delay is excruciating. The visitations multiply, her reckoning with Ty and Shep and Naila, too, seeming always just out of reach. But two months will pass before the operation receives final clearance, and as it turns out, the team needs every minute to learn and fine tune the code.

Luke, who can giggle like a mongoose and imitate half a dozen birds, proves the quickest study, especially in the vocal code that the team will use for mobile communication with each other. Hari can produce the sounds, but his inability to memorize the code gives her pause until she learns that he's sharing barracks with a bagpiper who delights in tormenting the "wogs" by playing when the men are asleep. His memory improves dramatically after Ward arranges for the team to be billeted together in a bungalow by Governor's Park.

Unfortunately, the slowest of her students also are the most vital. Neither George Culman nor Denis Ward, it seems, has ever before attempted to speak a foreign language. George is a genius with wires and batteries, and he was a strong contender for Britain's Olympic pentathlon team heading into the War, but while his facility with equipment extends to numeric ciphers, it seems to hit concrete when it reaches his tongue. His difficulty, she suspects, is mechanical—as she once thought Ty's might be. Even in English, George's speech is halting, and ultimately, they agree that he'll concentrate on the written and Morse versions and leave code talking to the others.

Ward has no such excuse. He simply thinks that anyone who speaks a different language should or eventually will learn English. That the current terms of battle expose this linguistic arrogance as a weakness does not sit well with the major. "Bollocks!" he'll erupt and storm out of the room, leaving the others to grin at their hands.

Claire herself hits a wall when it comes to devising the final code words for precision formations and weaponry. If Operation Balderdash is to fulfill its official mission, the team will need to relay the exact size and composition of enemy installations and troop and fleet movements. Unfortunately, the only weapons in the Biya arsenal are spears, bows, arrows, knives, and harpoons. How to translate Stone Age tools into modern implements of war?

It's Hari who suggests they work on the problem together. "If we design the terms," he says, "perhaps we will have less difficulty to remember them."

So, one day when Ward and Culman are meeting with Hastings and the higher-ups about their logistical requirements, the rest of the team pores over Claire's master glossary in search of inspiration.

"What about the animals?" Luke points at the long list under the heading *Fauna*. "Snapping turtle. Dragon fly. Beetle."

"Cockroach!" Hari cries. "That's the ticket."

"But what do they mean? We must employ logic. And the sound of the word in Biya must not give anything away." Hari frowns at the page.

"*Attangadaang*, for example. This sounds too much like an antiaircraft volley."

"What does it mean?"

Hari checks. "Turtle's ass."

"If we could come up with a simple principle," Claire says when the laughing subsides. "The sound the animal makes, perhaps, or the way it moves. Some essential trait that resembles the weapon."

"The birds should be the guns, because they shoot sound."

"The fish should be the boats because they swim."

"And the footed crawling things—lizards and turtles—those can be land vehicles!"

Hari grins. "And the Japanese are dogs!"

"You know, there were no dogs in the Andamans before the British," Luke Benegal says with a sidelong look at Claire. He wouldn't dare if Denis and Culman were present.

"All right," Hari says. "Then maybe the British should be the dogs and the Japanese become cockroaches. Look here, the small cockroach is an easy one—*taahu*."

In this fashion, the codebook is completed.

One evening she walks in on Ward and Hastings conferring over a yellow wireless form on the Colonel's desk. She starts to retreat, but Hastings beckons her in.

"Something unusual. It was taken down months ago by one of our subs, but no one could make hide nor hair of it. It didn't resemble any known code, and no one could find another like it, so they chalked it up to an error in transmission. Then one of the melders back at Bletchley was culling through the dregs when she noticed what looked like our call sign, not at the top, but at the end of the message. The major thinks the rest looks like your code. If he's right, yours is worthless and we'll have to start from scratch."

The men step back, and the Colonel offers her his chair. She lowers herself without breathing. Without the code, she'd have no access to Ward, and he'd likely shut her out of the operation entirely.

She holds the paper under the lamplight:

MNTILAKOTANOTIKOON

"It came through in Morse, no spaces or stops."

"Could be cipher."

She stuffs her heart back in its cage. The tricks with ciphered messages, she's learned, are nearly endless. There's no knowing. You might have to drop every third letter or replace each letter with its counterpart from the end of the alphabet, or strip out repeating combinations, like IN or CH, before applying the key. But that assumes you have the right key, which could be anything from a limerick to a one-time pad. Anything from anywhere. Shep winks at her and shrugs.

She searches for the numbers and preamble that normally frame these messages to help operators redirect them, but there are none. This suggests the work of an amateur.

"Where was the sub when it picked this up?"

"That's the thing." Hastings gestures to Ward, who repeats the coordinates that the operator noted when the message was received, then pinpoints the location on the Colonel's wall map. "Twenty miles south of Neil Island."

"You're saying it could have come from Port Blair?"

"Exactly what troubles us."

The date of transmission was April 29. More than seven months ago. She stares at the smudged yellow margins to steady herself, then relaxes her eyes until the letters swim.

Combinations form that could sound like Biya, but since they're dealing with a spoken language, spelling can't be certain. Ward hands her a notepad and pencil, and she begins to separate, add, and scramble letters into possible words.

MiNo/ThILiu/KOTrA/NOThI/KhuN
　Potato/clouds/belly/uncontrollable/bring
MiNe/dIchaLo/KeTtA/NO/TeI/KON
　Brain/got away/fish/make/place/rise up

Ward and Hastings peer over her shoulder. "Second one sounds like a warning," Hastings mutters.

"What place? What could *brain* mean?"

"Stop it!" Claire looks up in exasperation. "I've barely begun."

"And we could be totally off base," says Ward.

"We'll leave you to it," Hastings tells Claire. "Give a shout if anything surfaces."

When they're gone, she digs her knuckles into her eye sockets until she sees sparks, then stares at the message until the sparks clear. This has the effect of shuffling the letters.

For hours, she scribbles line after line of gibberish. Her vaunted code-book gives her nothing.

One morning a low moan breaks Naila's sleep, and she wakes to see Mam Golat kneeling beside Ekko, who lies on her mat in a ball.

"Is she sick?" Naila asks, though Mam Golat is smiling as she pats Ekko's belly, and no one else seems particularly concerned.

Leyo draws the corners of his mouth down as he often does when he can't—or won't—answer her questions. After the morning meal, he goes off to hunt with the other men.

Artam's mother signals Naila to come gathering with her and the children. When they reach the bottom of the cliff, Artam and Ty begin poking the earth for the *gumul* grubs and beetles, which the Biya relish, but Imulu clucks at them to keep walking. She draws Naila's fingers through the mist, outlining the shape of long slender leaves, and makes a pinching gesture at her nose to indicate a fragrant odor. The words she uses—*celmo* and *poramo* and *cainyo*—mean nothing to Naila until Imulu scales a nutmeg tree. Then she breaks a branch off a bulletwood tree. She directs the rest of them to collect fresh leaves from the laurels and pandan that grow along a nearby stream.

By midday the fog has cleared, and they head back with the baskets on their backs filled with foliage and twigs, two of which the children use for swordplay. Ty is drenched in sweat, and mosquitoes cloud his head, but he trudges after Artam, who circles her arms like propellers to keep the bugs from biting. Artam never expects to be carried, and so now neither does Ty.

Imulu claps her hands, a joyous sound to relieve the monotony and to warn away snakes, but Naila insists that they walk in silence.

"*Jeti ke*," she whispers, a Biya term for enemy hunters. She doesn't know the word for danger, so she says, "*Jirmu*." Beast of the forest.

"Ja-pa-nese." Imulu sounds out the foreign word and giggles. Her square hands rise to resume their clapping.

Naila grabs her wrists. She remembers a story that Kuli told some weeks ago. As best she can, she whispers it now. "'The ancestors were playing in the forest and making a great noise. Then Biliku grew angry because she could not hear the birds and cicadas. So, she sent a great storm and turned all the ancestors into turtles and fish.'"

The children stop to listen. Imulu gives a low grunt. She plucks at the straps of Naila's singlet and flicks her fingers to indicate it is time to throw this filthy rag away. But they continue in silence.

When they reach camp, a light shower starts. In their absence Mam Golat and Obeyo have erected a new lean-to outside the round house. Two can sit under the low overhang, but it is not big enough to lie down. While water drips from the sides, Ty and Artam fly to the dry spot in the center and wrestle with the dogs. Obeyo shoos them away, then helps Imulu unload and sort the leaves from the basket. As she works, her little skull's eyes seem to search Naila up and down.

Suddenly the dogs come over and lick Naila's thighs. She swats them, but they won't quit, so Imulu pushes them away. She leans down, exclaiming, and plucks at the hem of Naila's singlet, the knickers underneath. At the fabric clotted with blood.

This, then, is *aka yaba*. The two girls sit in sullen companionship, each dressed by the older women in a halter of pandan strips across the chest and a belt of pandan leaves that secure a pad of laurel. While Imulu tends to Ty and Artam, Naila and Ekko are made to kneel on a bed of nutmeg leaves, arms folded across their breasts. Tree stumps are brought for them to lean against. Chunks of roasted lizard meat are presented on bullet-wood skewers, which they must hold with their right hands. Both are forbidden to speak.

None of this makes any sense to Naila, but Obeyo firmly presses her back every time she tries to get up or lie down. She places a hand over her mouth whenever Naila makes a sound. For the first time, Obeyo seems to relish Naila's company—as a guard might her prisoner's. Leyo and everyone else stay out of sight, so she has no one to appeal to. Ekko's resentment at having to share her ceremony is Naila's only reward.

At first Ty seems amused by her predicament. He noses his face between her knees and sniffs at the new metallic smell of her. He climbs on her shoulders, tugs her ears. She tries to respond to him without violating the rules of her confinement, but he and Artam quickly lose interest when the girls don't move, and back at the round house the others are dancing.

As darkness falls, Naila becomes aware of new sensations within her body. Her breasts feel swollen. Deep in her belly a large fist squeezes. She tries to catch Ekko's attention, but the other girl stares straight ahead, her face in the same rude mask it has worn all afternoon.

She remembers her mother washing blood from rags. Naila asked if someone was hurt and her mother shooed her away, saying no, it was only women's business, but someday she'd understand. She remembers also Mem standing in the kitchen over a pot, boiling something that smelled like seaweed. This was the only thing that Mem ever insisted on cooking herself, though when Naila stole a peek, all she could see in the pot were sponges in reddish brown water.

Deep in the night the rain stops and a crescent of gold shines between the clouds. Its light skims the ledge, making a path to the hut, where Ekko lets out soft snoring spurts. Her own body aches too much to sleep, but she shuts her eyes and tries to relax. When she looks again to the path of light, Leyo's straight lean silhouette forms a bowstring on the moon.

Two evenings later, they are released. Artam's mother has washed Naila's singlet and drapes it over her before they return to the round house. Naila tries to embrace her to thank her for this kindness and for keeping Ty safe, but Imulu just spins her around and pushes. Leyo stands so close that she bumps his chest.

He laughs as his nose grazes her cheek. "Now you are Yulu." He points to a nearby cluster of trees bearing fragrant white flowers. "Yulu, your flower name."

And she blushes at a memory of his saying once, four years earlier on Ross Island: *Yulu is most beautiful.*

Turning, she sees Ekko, now to be called Chenra, standing on the far side of the ledge. Tika has slung his arm around her waist and is smiling into her ear. Ekko at first shrugs him off. She glowers at Leyo, but then grabs Tika's hand and pulls him into the forest.

Kuli kept his distance from the pandan hut, but through her long hours sitting there Naila watched him closely and realized that he does not simply stare into space all day. Rather, he stands the way old Ranjit used to stand in the wheelhouse of the ferry *Benbow*, the way Doctor Shep and her father stood as they gazed down the rows of orchids in their old shade garden, the way she herself once stood on the bluff scanning the seas for her parents.

Kuli spends his days searching. And a few days after Naila helps tear down the girls' hut, he calls the clan together to tell them what he's found.

Leyo sits beside Naila with Ty in his lap and teases her by calling her Yulu. "Tell me what Kuli is saying," she scolds. She can follow routine talk now, but tonight's is too difficult.

"Kuli says that the rains discourage the Japanese from entering the forest, but during *gumul*, the weather will be softer. Today he saw a new break in the forest far to the south. Someone is clearing trees near the coast."

Porubi has told Kuli that the Japanese are offering words of honey to the Indians and Burmans, saying that they will be allowed to live in peace. Kuli doubts that the new invaders will make war with the Biya, but he doesn't trust them any more than he trusts the settlers. His people must not cross paths with these new invaders or attract their attention. He repeats the tale about the ancestors that Naila told to Imulu in the forest.

From now through the dry season, Kuli says, there will be no chanting. The chief then turns to Ty, who is busy exchanging finger signals with Artam across the fire. He waits until the children pay attention.

Some dancing will continue, Kuli says, as it serves to warn vipers, cats, and bad spirits from troubling the camp, but each dancer must sing soundlessly. "As the sun sings," he says in Biya.

And Ty, understanding perfectly, raises one finger to the sky and, with Artam at his heels, circles the fire in silence.

They meet at the Barrackpore golf club, where, according to Vivian, forty percent of the members were Japanese before Pearl Harbor. Viv has come up from Calcutta to investigate what those erstwhile members might have been up to and where they went, but at the moment her lunchtime conversation with Claire is focused on Roger.

Viv has been staying with him for eight months now. Lately, she's noticed a change. "He'll be dozing over his papers and bolt upright. I think he has nightmares about the invasion."

"We all have nightmares," Claire manages to say without inflection as Ty splashes into her spectral sea.

Vivian hands her plate to the white-gloved waiter. Despite the war, the club still strives to maintain the airs of the Raj. "I don't remember my dreams."

The reply comes automatically. "Shep doesn't either."

"Growing up in China..." Vivian hesitates. "In ways, it was worse than India, especially during the winter and wars. I remember frozen babies—

cartloads of them. You learned to block out the horrors. You especially learned not to let your imagination run the show. That's one reason Shep fastened onto science and I went for the news. Facts and figures are safer than stories your mind makes up."

"What happens when the facts and figures *are* the horror?"

Viv stares at a rhombus of blue light cast onto the table from a mirror across the room. It threatens to suck them both in. Then, abruptly, "How's our favorite major?"

"Charming as ever."

Viv gives her a hopeful glance. "Yes?"

Claire nods, but zips a finger across her mouth. Secrecy as refuge. As conspiracy. "So, what've you learned about Tojo's golfers?"

Her sister-in-law watches her closely. "The Japanese apparently are very keen on golf. So keen you'd think they'd have preferred the Tolleygunge course, but what Barrackpore lacks in its fairways it more than makes up for in its proximity to strategic armament factories and waterworks. One month before Pearl Harbor, the Japanese members all were mysteriously called home. Those are the facts. The caddies tell me they spoke Japanese exclusively and pretended never to have heard of the concept of *baksheesh*. Apparently, their assignment did not extend to promoting the Greater Asian Co-Prosperity Sphere."

"I'm grateful," Claire says. "Thank you. I really wish I could tell you more, but even what I have to tell doesn't add up to much. Believe me." She can tell Vivian doesn't.

The waiter brings their tea, and they drink it in silence as the dining room empties around them. She needs to get back to the College, but Viv stops her getting up.

"Do you think you could get the day off next Sunday?" Her voice has an unusually sheepish quality.

"I expect so. If it's important."

"It is to Roger and me. We're getting married. Just a small ceremony at St. John's. We'd like you to be our witness."

Claire is too surprised to reply.

"We'd also like your blessing."

"Sorry. Yes! Of course. It's just so unexpected."

"Is it?" Viv grins.

And finally, she comes to her senses. "I'd be honored." She smiles despite the accompanying wrench of sadness. It's Shep who should be their witness.

His sister pats her hand and stands. "We decided it was time to stop the wagging tongues around the FO. They're a much stuffier lot than the press corps."

Claire hugs her. "I'm so happy for you both. I know—I know Shep will be too."

"Is it what you actually think, or just what you want to believe?" Ward asks the following Sunday.

Claire locks eyes with the bullock that's blocking the bridge ahead. They're riding into Calcutta together, a sensible arrangement, since Roger has asked his cousin to be the other witness at the wedding—and it's about time she and Ward talked this through without any witnesses of their own.

The ox swings around and lumbers off the road, and a jeep filled with American GIs blasts its horn and guns past them. Claire closes her eyes against the ensuing geyser of dust and sees Shep smiling, Ty pinwheeling his arms.

Child of ours, at friend's shelter in the deep forest.
MeNnot/ThIre/meLE/eKOTrA/NO/TImiuKOON

Four weeks, it took. Last night she fell asleep at her desk, then awoke and had it.

Their driver snaps his whip, and the gharry begins to move.

"Both," she says finally. "It means they're alive—almost certainly hiding at the Biya camp where I was doing my fieldwork."

"Or that the Japs—"

"—would have no way of coming up with this."

"Unless they caught Shep sending it."

"No."

A careening red sun. A racing torpedo. Shep flying, then falling. And then . . . Shep elated, holding aloft his trophy of blossoms the way a very different man would hoist a great white shark. The flowers shine like tiny stars against the blue backdrop of water. "*Eria kurzii*," she whispers. Gobsmacked.

"What?"

How could she have been so blind? "The Latin in the note you carried. *Eria kurzii* was the first orchid Shep found when we went into the field together. He found it just outside the Biya camp."

Ward's voice flattens to an ugly sheen. "And you just remembered this."

"It's only beginning to fit together. My God, of course. It was always Shep's assumption that Naila and Leyo would flee to the forest—if the Japanese came after we left." She struggles to find the right term in Ward's lexicon. "Their bolt-hole. He must have sent the wireless message on his way there."

A glance of surprise. "It's a neat theory, Claire. But plans are one thing—"

She waves him off. "Shep can't have been detected. If they caught him, there would have been other messages. They'd try to use the code to ensnare us." But then she realizes her own mistake. Shep only knows a handful of Biya words. He'd be useless if the Japanese caught him. She doesn't tell Ward this.

"You're betting a lot on a highly wishful decryption of a message that could have been sent by anyone."

His logic sideswipes her. The message is so crude that there's no way of knowing even which side sent it. Perhaps it's just the fumbling of some shipwrecked Japanese.

Ward glances up at the driver. The wheels creak and the horse's hoofs clop on the parched dirt road. Still, he lowers his voice so she can barely understand him. "If you're wrong about this, our entire operation will be exposed. There are other codes we could—"

She focuses hard on the gold Sanscrit letters crumbling along the back of the driver's seat. Ward's inflection makes it clear that "we" in his alternative won't include her.

"Any code or cipher that translates into a known language is vulnerable," she recites from the training manual. "And none is safe for mobile units on the ground."

He pulls a pair of dark glasses from his pocket and arranges them over the caves in which his eyes dwell. "It was your husband who let on that your son had died. With the girl. And they do things like that, the Orientals."

"Like what?"

"Girls here set themselves on fire after their men die or reject them, rather than carry on."

"You think Naila would *intentionally* have killed our son?"

"They'll do almost anything to escape dishonor."

"What *are* you saying?"

A muscle twitches in his jaw. The glasses aren't quite dark enough to hide the vulgarity of his thoughts.

Shep and Naila? Relief spars with revulsion. But of course, that's what he'd think. It must have gotten all over Port Blair that Dr. Durant had to knock out his wife to get rid of her. That the ayah hid the child as a hostage to ensure that her lover would stay. Stranger things happen in Asia.

"If only it were that simple."

He frowns.

"Believe me, there was nothing between Naila and my husband. But our little boy was her whole life. If anything happened to Ty, she would kill herself. I've no doubt of that. What she couldn't do was let him go."

"Why didn't you all leave months earlier then, when you could have taken her with you?" The vulgarity is gone, replaced by genuine puzzlement. He hands her a white handkerchief.

She blots her eyes and cheeks with the cloth, then refolds it, clean side out. The gharry sways as it picks up speed. "Blindness."

❧

After the brief ceremony at St. John's, Viv and Roger host their own celebration at the Great Eastern Hotel. It's just the four of them—"just family," as Roger puts it—but they treat themselves to prawn curry and a bottle of Veuve Cliquot, courtesy of Viv's boss back in Sydney.

"With a telegram saying I was hands-down the last girl in the world he ever expected to tie the knot."

"Not sure if I should drink to his health," Roger says, "or challenge him to a d-duel."

"I took it as a compliment." Viv raises her glass to her new husband. She's pinned a gardenia above her ear and traded in her broadcloth and khaki uniform for a blue silk dress.

"I expect if he could see you tonight, he'd eat his words," Claire offers. It's all she can do to play along, now that she's deciphered Shep's note. She wants to hop the next bomber, to parachute directly into Behalla. She wants to alert the War Office that she *knows* where her husband and son are hiding, to demand an immediate rescue. But she also knows that her discovery can change nothing until Ward and his men make their crossing. She longs, at the very least, to alert Shep's sister. But Ward has commanded her to hold her tongue.

"I *still* take it as a compliment." Viv tosses her head and the gardenia flies across the table, landing in front of Denis, who places it between his teeth. She laughs. "*Olé!*"

Ward pivots in his seat, leans forward, and drops the flower by Claire's hand. The petals are beginning to brown, and his teeth have cut small pale scars along the stem, but the fragrance rises, still strong. She brings it to her face and closes her eyes. The six-piece band tonight is playing "White Christmas." She and Shep married in summer, but the memory overwhelms her anyway, of dancing across her parents' parlor with her hand at the nape of his neck, the scent of the gardenia in his lapel, the still unfamiliar quiet and height of him.

A siren shrieks, rattling the tableware. The music falters, then ceases.

"Air raid!" Roger groans.

"Oh come on," Viv says. "It's not the end of the world."

"Says you."

A hand takes hold of Claire's elbow as she overturns her chair. She grabs her shawl and purse and turns, only now registering the concern in Denis Ward's eyes.

All he says is, "This way."

Calcutta takes its air raids seriously, but there has never been an actual attack, and even among the officers, plenty have yet to hear their first bomb fall. As they follow the general current toward the hotel basement, cries of *False alarm!* and *I say, watch where you're stepping!* and *You won't catch me down that rabbit hole!* pop up and down like buoys. Then the distant ack-ack-ack of antiaircraft guns penetrates, and the current flows faster.

Rumors of gas begin to percolate back through the crowd, prompting a threat of panic, as no one seems to have any idea if or where there might be gas masks. Fortunately, Denis and Roger are tall enough to sound commanding.

"This way, ladies and gents. We'll get everything sorted out downstairs."

Claire notices that now, when the pressure is really on, Roger's stutter vanishes.

In the crush, she loses sight of Vivian. Then, as she's starting down the steps, the power goes out, and utter blackness descends. The sudden hysteria in the crowd is more terrifying than the sirens and guns, and for the first time Claire understands what people mean when they talk about smelling fear.

"Claire?"

"Yes."

"Good. Hang on." Denis again, his hand on her shoulder. No one can move, yet she's surprised by his presence. What did she expect? That he'd charge out into the street and take aim at the skies to fight off the invaders himself? He does tend to invite such caricatures.

Then the first bombs hit, and the concussion throws them down the stairs. Claire breaks her fall by catching hold of the handrail, but around her the moaning and wailing quickly escalate. A flashlight beam ricocheting across the basement reveals Denis crouching several feet away, near Roger and Viv, who are comforting a slight, terrified Eurasian woman.

A few more thuds register, though none as close as those first ones. The injuries appear to be minor, more psychic than physical, but the thirty minutes of darkness feel endless as the crowd in the basement waits for the all-clear to sound.

When it does, a collective cheer goes up. Soon the electricity comes back on, but there's no resuming any celebration. Upstairs the floor is awash in broken glass and china. No one appears on scene to sweep it. Customers descend on the bar, but just one lone bartender returns to sort through the surviving bottles. And though the band gamely takes up their instruments, the few visible waiters are making for the exits.

"Do they know something we don't?" Claire asks.

Viv watches the shaken young woman she consoled downstairs return to her station at the reception desk. "They've no frame of reference."

Roger kisses the top of his bride's head. "Helluva wedding bash."

"Major?" An MP approaches Denis. "There's a man out front, been injured. Said he thought you might be in here."

They all follow him through the lobby, between the blackout drapes, to the crater that now stretches directly in front of the Great Eastern's entrance. It's difficult to see in the dark, but several uniformed men lie on the opposite sidewalk. A nurse kneels beside one of them, cradling his foot in her lap and calling for a doctor.

"Culman!" Ward bellows.

VIII

January 1943

Before the bomb shattered Sergeant Culman's ankle, Claire was told only what she absolutely needed to know. After decoding Shep's message, she fantasized that Ward would make a grand dash, speeding across to fetch Shep and Ty and immediately hightailing it back with them, but two days after the Christmas bombing, the major takes her for a stroll through Governor's Park and disabuses her of all such illusions as he proposes something even more far-fetched.

"This is a hare-brained idea," he says. "Not mine, I can assure you."

"Whose, then?"

He ignores the question. "I have to ask. But you can decline."

"No one has as much at stake in this as I do."

"Precisely what worries me. The odds are stacked against us to begin with, and what we find could be grimmer than any of us imagines—if we even make it across."

"I'm the hysterical female, is that it?" Claire spots Shep's familiar figure, striding alongside them. He salutes her through the morning haze.

"The length of the operation alone should exclude you."

"Why?"

"The chances of an emergency evacuation succeeding are nil, and the plan is to stay over there until March."

Just barely, she manages to check her dismay. "Why should that exclude me?"

His cheeks redden. Despite his bravado, it appears, there's one frontier Ward has yet to cross. "Hygiene."

It comes out sounding so much like a sneeze that, in spite of herself, she laughs. And suddenly, for a moment at least, she really isn't terrified. "Don't tell me you're embarrassed."

"There are certain—sanitary considerations."

"I grew up camping in the Adirondacks every summer. And I've probably spent as much time in the Andaman wilds as you have."

"I mean—" He blushes again and draws the word out as if instructing a slow pupil in a foreign tongue. "*Sanitary.*"

"Ah." She marvels. How have they gotten so quickly so far from the matter at hand? "You don't spend much time eavesdropping on the Wrens, do you, Major? If you did you might know that the tropics wreak hell on the average white woman's cycle. That's before you even factor in the effects of war. I've lost about twenty pounds since leaving Port Blair, and that's further complicated the situation. I'm sorry if this intimate conversation embarrasses you, but since it appears to be germane, I can assure you I haven't had a period in more than a year, and I hardly think one's on its way." She pauses. "I'm not sure if that makes me any more of a man, but it should give you less worry about my being a woman. Shall we move on to your other concerns?"

Did she really pull that off? Her heart was slamming against her ribs, but all the while her voice held strong. She can hardly believe that Colonel Hastings had a hand in this—any more than she could imagine her own father giving his blessing. But then, it was her father who taught her to camp and fish and hike and climb. After Robin died, Claire tried to become both daughter and son to her parents. This gave small comfort to her mother, but it secured her father's love and gave her a measure of confidence that she's only now beginning to appreciate. In fact, she suspects her father would understand, even if he couldn't approve of what she's about to do.

Hastings, too, knows just how little she has to lose and how much to gain. If he were in her place, he'd insist on going. Claire searches for Shep, finds him leaning against an ancient temple in the distance. He shoots her a thumbs up and reaches for Ty. They vanish.

"My primary concerns," Ward says, "are getting this operation off on schedule and ensuring its success. With Culman sidelined, these concerns seem to be somewhat at odds with each other."

"Unless you take a chance on me."

"That's not my only option." But Ward's bluffing every bit as much as she is. Culman's injury guarantees him a desk job for the rest of the war, and no one else on their team has as much cryptographic training or experience with the wireless as Claire. The time it would take to train another operator in their rarified code would set them back months. Denis's only other option is to jettison the code and take an operator who uses cipher, but he has no candidates who know the first thing about the Andamans, and this new member of the team would be useless when it came to code talking on the ground.

She says, "I will not compromise your operation."

"That's easy to say." The morning light falls flat on his face. He peers for several seconds at a white cow that has materialized through the low gauze of dung smoke.

When he returns to her, Ward sounds almost apologetic. "I need to be brutally frank with you, Claire. What the Japs are doing in Port Blair could cost us the entire subcontinent. If we were to rescue a few of our own in the process that'd be grand, but the purpose of this operation is to stop the enemy from winning this bloody war. We're going to gather intelligence, and *if* you join us, your sole purpose will be to transmit and receive information via the wireless set. That will be your sole responsibility. I'll find out whatever there is to know about Shep and your son and anyone else we've left behind, but there will be no wild goose chases. Is that clear?"

Nothing is clear. If it were, she'd never be here, never would even have considered the risks she's about to hurl herself into. If it were clear, those spectres would live and breathe.

He says, "I know you don't want to believe they're gone. But for our purposes, at least going in, they must be. As far as the rest of the team is concerned, they are. *Both* of them."

"I've told them nothing to the contrary."

"And you won't."

"No," she says. And though the word rings inside her head, she will not speak it aloud: *unless.*

Three days later she seeks out Colonel Hastings to say goodbye and to thank him.

He tips his head to one side, reminding her of Alfred Baird. "I'd give anything to go instead of you, Claire."

"I know you would." She forces a smile. "But this operation is the only thing that's keeping me alive."

He takes her hand between his fatherly palms. "God bless you," he says. "God keep you."

Next morning at six o'clock Roger and Viv see her off at Howrah Station. They stand buffeted by throngs of wallahs, beggars, travelers and hysterics, screaming babies and their distracted ayahs, sweepers and soldiers, pigeons, pye-dogs, and jerking carts of baggage. The exodus from Calcutta has become a mass migration of refugees, mirror images of Shep and Ty and Naila threading among them at will.

Claire is to travel on her own as far as Madras, where Ward will join her for the remainder of the trip to Colombo. There they'll train with Special Operations commandos for two weeks in the Sinharaja jungle before shipping out. The rest of the team is traveling separately.

Of course, they're all forbidden from telling anyone anything about their destination—or when they might return.

"There's an Indian proverb I heard," Viv says. "If you put a bag of Calcutta dust under the bed of a good woman, she'll become corrupt. So here we are, you and I. Corrupted."

"Who'd a thunk?" Claire gives her sister-in-law a kiss on the cheek and finds when she hugs her, she can't let go.

"You'll keep us p-posted," Roger says. "When and as you c-ca-can."

And suddenly she sees his pale frame amid this dingy crowd just as he appeared on the docks that awful night when she arrived from Port Blair. "You collected me," she says. "How could I not?"

Then his arms are around her, with their scent of tweed and lime and tobacco and tonic, and she envies him and Viv with a fervor she thought she'd lost forever.

She raises up and kisses Roger's clean-shaven jaw. "Take care of her, will you?"

Morning spreads a thin coat of silver over the forest, the day opening to a cool mist. Imulu was sick in the night, so Artam has come to play with Ty while Kuli and Obeyo tend to her mother's fever. The rest of the men leave to hunt, and Ekko, now to be called Chenra, signals Naila, who refuses to think of herself as Yulu, to bring the children to forage for yams.

Coming from Ekko-Chenra, the invitation startles her, but Mam Golat nods for them to go. Friends or not, the two are now considered sisters, and Chenra does seem a more engaging version of her former self. After the *aka yaba* ceremony she tied a strip of red cloth across her forehead, which makes her brown eyes snap. Above the red band her tight black frizz rises in a cloud. And she's taken to standing with her hands clasped behind her head, elbows wide as if to show off her high round breasts and the new pandan breechcloth that Mam Golat has made for her, with its teardrop leaf.

Chenra takes her time as the children race ahead, wordlessly daring Naila to match her queenly pace, but that is all right. Ty has grown as comfortable in the forest as he ever was on the beach. He can shinny up a young padauk more gracefully than Artam, and the two of them know all the nearby vines that are strong enough to serve as swings. He and Naila both long ago shed their tattered shoes, and the soles of his feet have worn tough as bamboo.

Still, as he flits among the shadows, her pride in him duels with her perpetual fear of losing him. *"Chati!"* She calls softly for the children to come back and dig. Yams are plentiful in this area.

Artam comes trailing Ty, who's found two paddle-shaped lengths of bark to use as diggers. Once they set to, Chenra draws Naila several feet away and squats.

The girl's expression has the earnest quality of a confession or plea. She draws in the air with her hands, big and little, soft and hard, round and long.

Naila watches, nonplussed. "*Ekira*," she implores. *Speak.*

Chenra pretends not to hear or understand. Her full lips part dreamily as she runs her palms along her own smooth arms, embraces herself shyly, then, without warning, reaches over to stroke Naila's cheek and neck.

The contact makes her flinch. There is nothing sincere about such exaggerated tenderness. This seems just another of the old Ekko's performances, like her impressions of Kuli's stories. But maybe this is an extension of *aka yaba*, some ritual of bonding?

Steeling herself, Naila leans back in and is rewarded with a big grin and a sigh of pleasure. Her new sister presses her own forearms tight against each other, palm to palm. Then she peers around her hands and winks with an expression that says, *Watch this.*

Very slowly one middle finger folds down and, in a thrusting motion, pushes back and forth between the fingers of the opposite hand. All the while those round dark eyes watch her target, taunting, as if to say, *You love it, you know you love it.*

A confusion of disgust and shame sends Naila sideways. She falls onto her palms as her tormentor warbles with laughter. This Biya girl can't know how the men used to taunt her as she walked through the port, and yet she does. She *senses*. And there is nowhere, nowhere now to escape.

Ty. Ty is her escape. He's immune to such meanness.

He sits on his haunches completely absorbed in the process of extracting yams. He has a pile of four or five already, and Naila picks up a wedge of bark, then drops to her knees beside him. She violently stabs the earth until her anger subsides. Then she falls to, wishing to pull herself into his spell of absolute concentration.

Forget Chenra. Chenra is nothing. This dirty girl is Ekko, will always be Ekko and never her sister.

But it is too quiet.

She looks around. "Ty, where is Artam?"

He bats her away as he always does when in one of his states. Not even for Artam will he look up. Or notice when she wandered off.

"Ekko!" She whispers over her shoulder. "Chenra! Artam is gone!"

The other girl, lying now on a pillow of leaves, stretches her arms and yawns. *"Aka doi."* The child will return.

It is true. Artam knows the forest like a second skin. But Imulu is relying on them to keep her daughter safe, and as she scans the undergrowth Naila grows anxious.

She locates the trail of Artam's footsteps and follows it as long as she can without losing sight of Ty. Then she returns, hoping the child will have circled back by another path. But there still is no sign of her.

Naila considers enlisting Ty, but he won't easily come along, nor would it help to alarm him. *"Mitai."* She squats beside him. "Stay right here with Auntie Ekko—"

"Chenra," Ekko corrects her. She has grudgingly begun to dig for yams.

Ty yips like a dog, his new signal for assent, and continues digging. Ekko might leave him here, but he won't move.

The trail of prints leads Naila through a lizard run to a stream where the Biya men often fish and go turtle hunting. Artam knows this stream. Perhaps she went splashing in search of her father. Naila follows it until the water splits around a wide hill. Beyond, it will deepen into a river. She's been gone perhaps half an hour. Too long. But just as she's about to turn back, she spots another small footprint across the stream.

She crosses the shallower of the two forks and is starting up the slope when the birds around her screech, and the hot green air rains leaves. A small voice sings on the far side of the hill.

Naila pauses, giving thanks, then resumes climbing. This way is steep but faster than circling the hill.

Suddenly Artam's song is swallowed by other, far louder noises. A thrashing and thudding, like animals forcing their way through the underbrush. Then raucous laughter. Men.

The child screams. *"Pho khotewo! Bayde—"* A strangled, unearthly sound follows.

The air seems to melt white, then red. Then, all Naila can hear is the violence of her own heart.

She drops to her belly and worms her way under the ferns. She must go to Artam. She mustn't be found. She must save the child. She doesn't know how. Her thoughts are like two strangers fighting within a fever. Sweat stings her eyes; her throat is parched; the beating of blood fills her ears.

Japanese. That must be the men's language. They are yelling. Two voices. Only two, but they have Artam. The child's song brought them, and perhaps more will come. Any second now they'll come for Naila—*You stupid, stupid girl.*

An explosion cracks the air above her. Then the two men start a new round of shouting. A parrot squawks. Hard, stabbing, careless laughter.

"Kono hentai!"

"Damare yo!"

"Kuso!"

Naila watches a livid green mantis work its jaws on a leaf insect dying in front of her nose. The spiny brown body twitches and flails, but it is no match for the larger, stronger creature. She would crush the mantis between her fingers if only she could move, but now the ground begins to shake with loud, lurching bootsteps. She closes her eyes.

Slowly the drunken shouts stumble away. Slowly the birds resume singing. Naila waits and waits and waits, then begins to crawl.

She finds the child lying on the far bank. Artam's eyes are wide and staring. The wet moss beneath her is black. In her chest a hole has replaced the pink star of her birthmark.

Naila gathers the small lifeless body into her arms.

She stumbles under the weight of her burden and her fear. The trip back seems to take years, and when she reaches the others at last, Ekko backs away from the sight of her.

Ty springs forward. Of course. Naila has turned other terrible moments into play.

All she can do now, however, is tighten her grip on Artam's body, so cold against her chest and so much heavier than in life.

Betrayal fills Ty's face. His throat shudders with incomprehension. His eyes beat darkly, and senseless sounds come out of him.

Ekko pushes his shoulder. *"Liake."* The whites of her eyes shine in warning. When Ty turns at her touch, she grabs his hand and spits at Naila's feet.

I didn't do this, she tries to say. But she has no voice.

Then Kuli is there. Wordless, he takes Artam's body from her. Did he hear the shot? Perhaps he saw or heard the men. He has powers of perception. But not even Kuli knows how to bring his granddaughter back.

Imulu's moans surround them before they reach the top of the ledge. Mam Golat rushes forward and secures Ty in her arms. Leyo takes Naila's hand and leads her out of sight of the others, to the place where the pandan hut stood. He brings a bucket and strips off her garments, washes the child's blood from her body.

Afterwards he sits beside her, Ty in his lap. He whispers that Artam's spirit has gone to live with Biliku.

Kuli, Imulu, and Sempe grieve into the night as they ready their daughter for burial. They shave her head and wash her flesh, paint her front and back with lines of white clay and red, as if preparing her to return to the womb. Only after they finish are the others called to join them.

The family stares at Naila even as they weep. She hasn't yet told anyone how she found the child. The wound in the breast tells one story. Whatever Kuli saw or heard tells another. But Imulu and Sempe's faces warn that Artam's story will never belong to any outsider.

She closes her eyes. Beyond the guilt and grief, beyond even the day's inexpressible horror, another response gnaws at her. As she watches Artam's parents caress the small body, wrap it in palm leaves and pass it back and forth, she struggles to identify what she feels.

Leyo strokes Ty's hair and face and rubs the tears from his cheeks, then stands and sets the boy beside her. When she looks up through the smoke and darkness to see Leyo moving away to the others, she recognizes her ache at last as a deep and sorrowful envy.

The burial is held by torchlight, the grave dug in a plot where enough earth covers the ledge to protect the body from animals. Above, shredded palm stems are hung from trees and shrubs to mark the site. A year from now Imulu and Sempe will return to reclaim their daughter's skull. They will carry it as Obeyo carries her son's.

No one but Ty looks at Naila. She rests her forehead against his. He trembles with questions she cannot answer, will never be able to answer, but even these questions finally surrender to his need for sleep. It is then that Kuli summons her and Leyo to speak with him alone.

She tells Kuli every detail. His old eyes watch her without blinking. After she finishes, he sits for several minutes rubbing the nail first of one thumb, then the other, still staring as if to see to her bones. He dismisses them without speaking.

When morning finally arrives Kuli calls the others to him, excluding Naila, but their voices carry like cinders across the camp. To Naila's surprise, Obeyo speaks first. Low and rasping, she begins to chant the legend about a stranger who visited Lady Turtle and so admired her son that he asked to take him away. When Lady Turtle refused, the stranger bit her young son's arm. Then the stranger left, and that son died. Obeyo believes this legend was truth and the murdered son was her own.

Naila knows the true story. The skull Obeyo wears belonged to a boy who had a bad foot, and the one time Doctor Shep came to Behalla he wanted to take him to Port Blair to fix it. Obeyo refused to let the child go. Then Obeyo's son died. Obeyo wishes to blame Doctor Shep, but Naila thinks this must be so she does not have to blame herself.

Leyo interrupts to remind the others of the legend's ending: Lady Turtle in her grief destroyed everything the stranger had touched, and this so displeased the god Puluga that he killed the entire tribe.

Naila listens for some sign from Kuli, some hint that the others will heed Leyo's warning, but she hears only rustling and clearing of throats and then Ekko's piping whine. The next familiar tale, in the girl's telling, claims new and terrible meaning.

"Lady Snake climbed a coti tree to steal its fruit for herself. Other people came and begged her to throw down fruit for them too, but Lady Snake told them to go away or she would call Jirmu, the beast of the forest, to kill them. The people would not go, so Jirmu ate them all. Only Lady Snake was spared."

Ekko points across the distance at Naila: *Lady Snake.*

Two hard days pass. Naila and Ty both are treated as pariahs by everyone except Leyo and Kuli. Even Mam Golat keeps her distance. Leyo tells her not to worry, that Kuli is fair and just, that she's done nothing wrong, but Doctor Shep's voice keeps roaring in her ears.

You stupid, stupid girl.

Everything she's done is wrong. Everything.

On the third night Kuli insists that Naila and Ty chew some *tabeno* seeds to help them sleep and forget.

She awakens late. The day already is bright and hot. At first, she thinks her acute sense of emptiness must be caused by the drug. But unless she still is asleep and dreaming, her eyes tell her something is wrong. Outside in the pit the fire burns, but the camp has been stripped of its mats, buckets, baskets, and pots. And occupants.

She sits up. Everyone is gone.

They've taken Ty Babu in exchange for Artam. They've taken him and left Naila to die.

She begins to shake then, holding herself, and lets out a wail.

"Naila!" Leyo's voice rises behind her. He grabs her by the shoulders. "Stop. Ty Babu is here. I am here."

He comes around and crouches in front of her, and for several seconds they stare at each other as strangers.

"Get up," he says finally, flipping his hands as if to shed her fear.

She stands with his help and sees Ty squatting in the far corner where Artam's family slept. Busy, the boy has his back to her. But all the others—even the dogs—truly have gone.

"It is Kuli's decision."

"To leave us?"

He blows on the embers and adds wood to keep the fire going. The others have left them one pot, which Leyo fills with water from the cistern and sets over the flame. "To heal the tribe."

"She hated me from the start, Ekko." But as soon as the name reaches her lips, she feels her mistake and braces for Leyo's rebuke.

Instead he takes her hand. "You are not the problem."

His gaze slides across the hut in Ty's direction, and he squeezes her fingers. "All our troubles began with *his* people. To Imulu and Sempe and the others, the Japanese are only the white man's *Jirmu*. Japanese, Europeans, Indians, all are one enemy here. All outsiders."

"But Porubi said the Japanese *killed* Doctor Shep." As she says the word Naila sees little Artam's body again, yet she still cannot imagine Doctor *saab* dead.

Leyo sighs. "Obeyo never would speak to Mem, all those times she came. And Ty now is the age her Jodo was when he died. Jodo and Artam both, yet Ty Babu lives."

Naila shivers. "We should never have come."

"That may be true, but where else?"

"But Ty *loved* Artam."

"That's why . . . *Jirmu* take her to keep her for Ty only."

She shakes her head. "I can't believe that Kuli—"

"Kuli chooses this way for you and Ty Babu to be safe."

"*Safe?*"

"From the others. Until they finish their grief."

His voice is so tender, his hands so sure, she wants to rest her head on his chest and weep there. Leyo would hold her and rock her like a small child, and she craves this rocking now more than she can say.

But she is not the small child. If he's right, she wasn't even the reason the others left.

Ty comes to the front of the round house holding two sticks tipped in clay. The color has dried but he drags the clay across the smooth stone, drawing as he used to with chalk on the veranda of the Ross bungalow or with sticks in the dirt at the white house and inside the freedom tree. It has been months, Naila realizes. Artam and the Bibi dogs were too restless for such quiet activities. Now that they are gone, and Ty is alone with her and Leyo again, he is starting over, back to his old self. This thought makes her ache.

The sticks are too long. Leyo breaks them to the length of a pencil, then pours a handful of water into each pot of dried color. Ty sits cross-legged and promptly immerses himself. With the same focus he gave to yam digging while Artam wandered off to her death, he now draws lines that mirror those her parents drew on her body.

"Why did you stay?" she asks Leyo. "Ekko didn't want Tika. She wanted you."

He drops his gaze, then returns to her shyly. "But I know *you*."

And the simplicity of this statement coupled with the slight quaver in his voice fills her with tenderness. It is true. He knows her better than she knows herself.

Before she can think how to answer him, he shifts. "When the monsoon comes again, Kuli will bring the others back. You will see." The water has begun to boil. He fills a bowl for her. "Then everything will be new."

February 1943

Ward comes for Claire in the General's Austin sedan. "I thought this whole thing was supposed to be low key," she chides him.

"Good evening, Claire," he replies. "You're looking well—and you smell heavenly."

"What happened to your hair?" He's been shaved clean to the scalp, which accentuates the heavy shelf of his forehead and makes his eyes look like small, feral predators. The effect isn't helped by his uniform shirt and shorts, which look as if he slept in them—

He does bring out the mean in her. Really, she ought to kiss the ground this man walks on, but if by some miracle Operation Balderdash succeeds, she, along with the entire Eastern Command, will have to, because Major Ward will demand it.

"Let it go," he says, and the sudden drop of his voice recalls the sensation of creepers and thorns, the tendrils of sticky vine catching her sleeve, the massive webs that over the last two weeks have left her feeling as if she's infested with mites. Her own shorn locks are only an inch or two longer than Ward's.

They drive in silence then. Off in the distance, the dockyards bombed last April are a blackened gash beneath the blazing red sunset, but couples and families stroll the Galle Face as ever, dodging strafe pits along the parkway in exchange for the tepid ocean breeze. Some children even carry balloons, and the yellow, green, and pink of the women's saris pop in the sidelong light. The war has tilted in the past seven months, though it's still far from turning.

"Having second thoughts?" Ward asks.

"I can't afford to give you the satisfaction."

"No skin off my teeth."

"Well, that's big of you. Considering." *Considering what's at stake.* But she won't keep this going. Not here and not now.

Bolger I (their team's SOE codename; Operation Balderdash, if successful, will bring additional Bolger landing parties to the Andamans in future) was met at Pembroke thirteen days ago by two seasoned Burmese saboteurs. They were issued camouflage trousers, shirts, and bush hats and taken into the Sinharaja jungle to learn the art of trekking without leaving a trail. They climbed vines to hidden lookouts, foraged for hidden sources of food and water, and practiced unpacking, paddling, and collapsing folboats—folding kayaks—in raging rivers. They also lay motionless in sand burrows in triple-digit heat and ran up stream beds at forty-degree angles under thirty- to fifty-pound packs.

Hari and Luke were deferential at first, offering Claire chances to rest, drink water, or reduce her pack, but Ward would have none of it. Even before she could object, he reminded them, "The last one standing has to be able to go on alone. And any of us could be the last." Claire and Hari Khan, being the smallest of the four, had the disadvantage in portage, but they'd proven far nimbler than Ward and Luke when it came to climbing and falling.

One day as they stood waiting for the others at the crest of a ridge, Hari told Claire he'd grown up watching the monkeys of Mussoorie, learning their tricks, and before he was ten he could shinny up the side of a house, raise the window, and steal inside just as the little apes did. Now he no longer stole, but he still liked to swing through the trees.

"Like Hanuman," he said.

"Like Tarzan," she countered.

"Is that a type of monkey?"

"Only in America."

"I often miss my home in Mussoorie. Do you miss America?"

She had to think very hard. "I don't remember anymore."

They climbed higher into the rain forest, based out of camp there for a week, and Claire felt for the first time in a very long while that she was back in familiar territory. The shrill plumage of the birds, the mist that draped itself high through the canopy, those heartstoppingly beautiful butterflies. Vipers the color of lemons and rubies slithered through the undergrowth. The monkeys here had purple faces, and the deer barked their alarm. And orchids bloomed seemingly on every tree trunk. She tried to picture the joy on Shep's face if he could have seen them, his ecstasy of discovery, but he kept dissolving into a mirage of Ty and Naila holding hands as they danced among the ferns.

Then the training shifted to a cove outside Colombo where the team were to be drilled in entering and exiting a surfaced submarine—and swimming down to enter the escape chamber in case enemy fire or surveillance prevented the sub from surfacing. At this point it dawned on her that she'd need either to use her underwear as swimming wear, or vice versa.

In her billet, a beachfront hotel she was sharing with a dozen Wrens, she found a *Life* magazine with a photograph of a two-piece bathing suit that, in her circumstances, could serve both functions. Fortunately, the local *durzi* needed only a couple of hours to crank out two of the suits in black jersey.

But that was the sole concession to her sex that she was willing to make. So, mud became her cosmetic, DDT her perfume, and sulfa ointment her skin crème of choice. Her only jewelry, her wedding band, was sewn into her breast pocket. She would not give Denis Ward one ounce of ammunition.

Two miles inland the car turns through the now familiar iron gates and starts up the gravel drive to Pembroke College. Mustangs, Lightnings, and P-38s careen overhead, on their way down to or up from the Racecourse Aerodrome. Under the silvering sky the greens of the requisitioned campus stretch absurdly, like cut velvet on a dowager bride. This last supper, too, is a charade, but what isn't these days? Every foreigner and most of the working locals in Colombo are codebreakers, signal operators, intercept telegraphers, cryptologists, or intelligence officers, all masquerading as secretaries.

The car stops in front of the boys' school turned intercept and codebreaking headquarters, and the Sinhalese doorman offers a white-gloved hand to help Claire down from the running board. The insult of long-sleeved uniform jackets and ridiculously plumed turbans in this climate never ceases to mortify her, but she returns the man's smile and accepts his assistance. His dark young eyes remind her of Leyo.

She follows Ward down the marble loggia and into the drawing room. Here, with blackouts pulled, and fans at maximum spin overhead, the team will wrap up their preparations before embarking tomorrow at dawn.

Claire gets to work making her final tests of the TBX-8 transceiver pack, which will be her primary responsibility, and the SCR-536 mobile Handy-Talkie that Ward will use for voice communication back to the TBX. Ward and Luke pore over maps of their intended landing site. And Hari squats over the equipment spread across the floor, ticking off items against his master list of field supplies, which include such provisions as morphine, boric acid, water purification tablets, Prontosil, Atabrine, signaling mirrors and pistols, flares, jungle knives, mess kits, a net for catching fish, vegetarian rations (including ghee, dehydrated potatoes, pumpkin, and rice enough for the first eight meals, plus chocolate D-rations), a shovel for digging and covering latrines, three pup tents, two folboats, four ponchos, mosquito nets, two Mark II stenguns, and a Welrod silenced pistol.

At nine Claire notices the clock on the wall. Its matter-of-factness stuns her. Eight hours from now they'll board a Dutch O-boat bound for Flat Island. There will be no turning back for eight weeks. That's all they know for certain.

"Last chance," Ward says to her as they stow the last of their gear for transport to the sub.

She smiles. "Still trying to get rid of me?"

"You've managed to keep to yourself through all of this, tight quarters and all."

"I can follow orders."

"The men like you." Ward gestures with his head for her to follow him out front, where the moonless night obscures them both. "It's a gutsy thing you're about to do."

"One minute you're pushing me overboard, the next you're serving up flattery. Best decide which side you're on."

"The first time we met, your short hair should have tipped me off, but somehow, I never would have pegged you for a real American dame."

"We'd better get one thing straight," Claire says. "I've made it my job to watch and listen to others, but I've absolutely no interest in other people's observations of me. Especially not now. If you're giving me an order, please get on with it. Are you, Major?"

The General's Austin is long gone, and all along the dark avenue coconut lamps on rickshaws glow like fireflies spiting the blackout. She'll need to rouse one of the pullers to run her back to her billet.

Ward steps back and snaps his fingers. A thin shadow peels itself from a nearby tree and walks to a jeep parked across from the rickshaws. The driver opens the passenger door.

"Yes," Ward gives her a gallant bow. "Go get some sleep."

He waits for the driver to step away. "See you bright and early."

The sailors who give Bolger I safe passage form a motley crew. All men, of course. Two dozen, give or take, with overbites and thick necks, wooly eyebrows and trim mustaches, biceps like Popeye's and oatmeal complexions. Despite the close quarters, Claire keeps her distance—with the aid of Captain Maikel van Dulm. "The men," van Dulm tells her, "you must forgive them, beauty is not a frequent passenger on a submarine at war."

The captain is too tall for his boat, forcibly stooped at thirty-four (the second night out they celebrate his birthday along with Claire's twenty-eighth). His most striking feature is his hair, which rolls in waves like polished brass back over his crown. A rare amalgam of gentility and virility, van Dulm has most of Bolger I's respect as soon as they learn that he safely landed another Special Operations shore party in Sumatra back in December.

Only Ward takes longer. He grouses that the captain's mother was Austrian, and that van Dulm didn't flee to Britain until Germany occupied Holland in '40. The rivalry is a familiar one of wartime distrust fueled by colonial class and circumstance. If van Dulm were an East Indian Dutchman, the major would likely feel more affinity, Ward having grown up in Lahore as the son of a jute manufacturer. But the captain knows how to buoy men's egos, even abrasive ones like Ward's. The two soon bond over the major's obsession with strategy and maps—and the bottle of Macallan single malt that the captain keeps in his wardroom.

The first couple of days, cruising at surface speeds, Claire stands on deck and watches pods of dolphins leaping—and sharks circling. The war seems metaphoric. From the third day they have to stay submerged during daylight hours, but the captain's easy manner retains a standard of calm that proves contagious.

In the wardroom their last evening, van Dulm says, "The most difficult thing is to remember that the enemy is human, but this is also the most important."

"I hope we won't have occasion to remind ourselves of this wisdom," Ward says.

"I find that I must remind myself constantly," the captain replies. "Especially when I find myself being my own worst enemy."

"Does that happen often?" Claire asks.

Van Dulm smiles and ducks his head. "It is a daily conversation."

The submarine surfaces off Flat Island that night, then eases in toward Middle Andaman under a full moon. Their target is a wild stretch of beach near a stream that needles into the forest, and just for an instant as she breathes in the darkness, Claire remembers her very first glimpse of these shores—her unexpected terror at their dark immensity, and Shep's childish quip: *No see-ums.*

She shakes the memory like water from her ears and bends to work. The sub is partially shielded by an islet thick with mangroves, and the roar of the surf swallows the noise of their loading and unloading the dinghies and dragging supplies up the sand. Within half an hour they have all their gear ashore and the Dutch crew gives them a silent salute and are gone.

Before midnight Bolger I has set up a staging camp, invisible from shore or inlet but within easy reach of fresh water. Claire knows better, but the others make cracks about claiming virgin territory.

Ward speculates that the Japanese are more interested in the eastern seaboard, from which they can monitor and defend supply lanes to Burma. "Let's just hope they don't get round the horn past Chittagong."

A short climb from camp the next morning clarifies his concern. The nearest promontory gives a clear view of the Bay of Bengal, with Calcutta beyond the northern horizon and Madras due west. From a well concealed corner of this hill they direct their long-range antenna without obstruction toward the Allied planes and vessels that still dominate this air and sea space. The strategic value of this coastline to the Japanese would increase exponentially if their mainland offensive succeeded in pushing past Burma into India.

"So our job," Ward says, "is to keep the Nips so busy to the east that they forget the west exists."

Subtlety is beyond this man. He doesn't notice the glance that passes between his Indian subordinates, but Claire does. They'll follow Ward because they—unlike many of their countrymen—distrust the Japanese even more than they do the English. They'll follow him because they respect his calculation, stamina, and skills. They might even come to like him, in a way, but they will never admire or fully trust him. Not the way, in just four days, they came to admire van Dulm. Not the way Leyo and Som and Dr. Ratna Bose admired Shep.

"How exactly do you propose we do that?" she asks, then adjusts her tone. She, too, can be her own worst enemy. "I mean, exactly."

It's a fair question, though not one the others would voice. The chain of command requires them to receive information if, as, and when their CO chooses to dole it out, so she expects pushback. Instead, Ward drops to a knee and pulls a map of the islands from his pocket.

"We're here." He points. "Four miles south of Flat Island, ten north of Andaman Strait and seventy as the crow flies from Ferrargunj."

"Ferrargunj," Luke repeats.

"Our informant's the headman there, Pandu," Ward says. "At least I hope he still is. We used to frequent the same toddy shop when I passed through."

Claire peers at the map where Ward's finger rests, northwest of Mount Harriet, about sixteen miles from Port Blair. Ferrargunj sits at the confluence of two rivers—some twenty miles southwest of Behalla. *For our purposes, your husband and son are gone.*

Ward says, "Too bad we're not crows—their seventy will be more like two hundred for us." His plan is to cross the strait by folboat, then head south overland. But there are no roads or rivers marked in the green, yellow, and brown elevations of the map's interior. Most of the measurements are guesswork, since no British surveyor has ever penetrated the central forests. The combination of miserable terrain and primitive tribes with a false but widespread reputation for headhunting has kept westerners safely confined to the coastal areas for more than two centuries. If Captain van Dulm is right, then the Japanese will be equally reluctant to confront the primitive boogie man. Which means that Bolger I's most secure route leads directly through Jarawa territory.

But Ward is focused on his destination. "Depending on what we find in *Ferrargunj*"—he aims his emphasis at Claire—"we'll establish a wireless base on the west coast, as close to our source as feasible. Most likely here along Constance Bay."

Tapping a long hook-shaped harbor on the opposite side of the island from Behalla, he might as well be saying, *I dare you.* But she doesn't dare. Not yet.

Ward folds up the map and retires to his tent. Luke approaches Claire alone.

"Ferrargunj was where I met your husband," Luke says. "There was a clinic there. First, he examined the children and treated those who were sick. Then we went into the forest to hunt for orchids. I liked him very much."

And she just can't help it. The tears come in a flood. They stream down her face and her hands and her arms, and although she doesn't make a sound, poor Luke has no idea what to do with this weeping white woman who shouldn't even be here, so she pats his arm as if he were the one who needed comforting.

"So," she manages at last, "do I."

They travel down the coast under a waning moon and against the current. From the first folboat, which has a silent outboard, Ward and Luke use fishing line to tow Claire and Hari in the second. It's slow going, with the first crew navigating, the second keeping watch. None of the men Ward's chosen wear glasses, and Claire now appreciates that. Vision is at a premium, and reflection off lenses could be lethal. The boats are black-skinned, and she and Ward use henna to darken their arms and faces. The others more naturally disappear in the night, especially Hari.

Even with a half load of rations and water, the front kayak sits so low that it's almost impossible to maintain any freeboard, so they shift the heavier elements of the load back with "the lightweights," as Ward takes to calling her and Hari.

He's at such a natural disadvantage, Ward, a large ungainly white target of a man, and yet, even in blackface, he finds these small, perhaps unconscious, ways to demean those on whom his life might depend.

She scans the pale streamers breaking on the shadowed coastline. No visible light comes from the land, but there could be a bonfire twenty feet inside the jungle, and no one would be the wiser. Ty and Shep could be standing on a bluff in that patch of darkness right there. They could be attempting to signal from the shelter of that cove, or the top of that rise. They could be lying at the feet of a Japanese search party just beyond that beach. These islands have devoured whole tribes, perhaps whole races of human beings, without leaving a trace.

But no, she gives herself a ruthless jab. The islands themselves aren't the culprit. The worst killers have always been the invaders who arrive by boat.

Around five in the morning, when the sky begins to gray, they pull up on Spike Island, at the mouth of Homfrey Strait. Ward found an abandoned hut here while exploring the Middle Andamans two years ago. The roof and walls have since been lost to the monsoons, but a square of hewn logs and a ring of stones still marks its history as a Jarawa camp. A flank of coconut palms screens the site from the main shore, which is about as far away as Aberdeen from Ross.

An image crosses Claire's mind that she's been resisting for months, of the young Jarawa mother Bathana and her daughter imprisoned in Port Blair, and behind that vision another, of their whole family diving and dying under a hail of bullets—all thanks to Ward's bullying ignorance.

To recognize the enemy's humanity is often very hard. She kneels beside the square of timbers and briefly shuts her eyes.

Before the marine layer lifts, Hari has laid a fire, made tea, and grilled a small barracuda, caught by Luke over a coral bed on the western point of the island. They extinguish the fire before eating, then, two at a time while the others keep watch, they sleep through the heat and light of the day. At six the sun sets, and they reverse the process, this time consuming an eel that Ward caught while on watch.

"Hope you like seafood," he says to Claire.

"Hari has a way with it," she says to her folboat partner, who grins as if she's awarded him a prize from Le Cordon Bleu.

"Can't cook a fish unless someone catches it," Luke teases, "and Hari here would not know a hook from a sinker."

"What I was afraid of." Ward scans a dark train of clouds pulling in from the west.

The rain begins as they paddle out of the ocean current and enter the throat of the strait. It falls in pins on their necks and backs and threatens to fill the already low-riding kayaks, but it also gives them cover. The water here is less than a mile wide, cutting between limestone palisades that rise a hundred feet or more on either side before disappearing in mist.

About twenty minutes into the strait, the water drops, sucking them into an eddy, and when they pull out of it a stiff yellow light bores through the rain. They've been driven dangerously close to an old police outpost on an island near the north shore.

The beam moves, a searchlight skimming the water.

Ward signals them to stop paddling and let the current push them ashore. Their drills would have them portage well beyond the light's radius, but the wall of mangroves to the south makes that impossible. Fortunately, a narrow channel runs between the first tier of trees and the shoreline. With wider boats it would be impassable, but they can use the roots on either side to propel themselves by hand. The problem is, they're not quite out of the light's reach, and the foliage is sparse, so they have to work from a flattened position, advancing by inches.

Minutes after the folboats enter the channel, the station guards come out to their dock. Silhouetted against the revolving beam, they toss stones into the current and grumble in Japanese. One tells a joke, and the others roar. Spirits apparently improving, they unholster their guns and shoot at something in the water. A turtle. A snake. Not fifteen feet away. One man jumps from the dock to retrieve the target. Another begins to sing.

It's a melancholy tune, and Captain Van Dulm's advice returns to Claire as she absorbs the sorrow of the clear, effeminate voice echoing down the strait's canyon. These three marooned guards have been torn from their families, too. They probably don't want to be here any more than she does.

The middle man helps the jumper back up onto the dock and slaps him on the back. They're examining their trophy when the channel runs out on Bolger I, about ten yards shy of darkness.

For the next ten minutes they hold still, besieged by mosquitoes, until the trio on the dock finally go inside. Ward signals them to let the tide carry them forward. They've barely gotten beyond the light, however, when the tide turns. They have no choice but to take up their paddles, risking both sound and the disturbance of the water's surface.

An hour later, at the junction of Homfrey and Andaman Straits, a white motor launch bobs at anchor. From here on out, the waterway will be wider, more navigable—and likely more crowded.

They lie flat as the folboats drift backward. Clouds hide the moon and stars, but the canyon's rock walls are luminous enough to reveal black threads where cascades fall from tributaries above. Claire senses more than she can actually see Ward searching for the thread that will indicate a climbable slope.

He knows bird whistles. He's told them his father used to take him out of school in Lahore to follow annual migrations over the local marahajah's hunting grounds. Luke, too, is versed in birdcalls, which he and his brother used as a secret code when they wanted to ditch their chores to go fishing. Hari and Claire have no such skills, but the other two have taught them to recognize the nasal song of the bulbul, the whoop of the hoopoe, and the signature hiccupping cry of the cuckoo. Now Ward sounds the cuckoo, their signal to get to shore.

The mud beneath the giant mangrove roots sucks them to their knees, but Claire hardly notices for the mosquitoes. The DDT they applied before leaving Spike Island has no effect here, and she and Ward make a mad dance of slapping their heads and necks while lugging the boats ashore. Luke and Hari watch their two black-faced companions swatting and swearing for several minutes before Luke takes pity on Claire. He presses into her hand a tin containing a dark, oily emulsion. The smell takes her back to the kitchen on Ross Island and the first of several intensive conversations between Shep and Jina about the contents of her cooking and medicine cabinets. Jina insisted that neem oil was guaranteed to keep mosquitoes from biting. Somewhat shame-faced, she added that, unfortunately, it also turned one's skin dark red. Now Claire and Ward greedily smear their faces and necks, rub the oil into their scalp and over their arms. It makes them smell like peanuts and garlic, but the relief is instantaneous.

For the next hour they work in silence dismantling and hiding the folding boats and redistributing the supplies among their rucksacks. Then Ward looms in front of them with a Logan Bar and his canteen.

Claire drinks just enough of the precious water to erase the taste of the unmeltable chocolate, and Hari helps her shoulder her pack. If she stood straight it would topple her backward, but his is double the size of hers, and he weighs not much more than she does. Luke and Ward carry the tents and wireless equipment. So, they begin to climb, Ward first, then Claire, with Hari and Luke bringing up the rear.

The rock is slick with mud and mist, and the plants here are not deep-rooted. After the first sapling comes away in his fist, Ward throws it backward in warning. They're to rely on handholds in the stone, test each tree before trusting it. Claire was afraid she'd be the one to hold them up, but Ward's progress is painstaking. After an hour she senses that they're less than halfway to the top, and she's glad then for the darkness. If she could see to the bottom, she'd freeze with vertigo.

When, minutes later, the sky begins to lighten, she sees the larger danger. If they keep going, they'll soon be visible from across the gorge.

Ward reaches a deep ledge overgrown with bamboo and ficus trees and stands panting as the others catch up. A natural pool has formed at this step of the falls, and an outcropping above combines with the bamboo to form a shallow grotto, a shower room of sorts.

"Rest up," Ward says.

Their rest lasts twenty-two hours, during which Ward and Luke make a reconnaissance trip to the top and decide to continue the journey by daylight. When Claire hauls herself over the lip she sees why. This section of the Andamans dwarfs any forest that she can remember around Behalla. It makes their training ground in Ceylon seem like Central Park.

The trees here grow so tall that their upper branches look like threads etched in tintype, while their lower trunks are buried in a waist-high web of vines, thorns, and nettles. Ordinarily, forest officers would use a *dha* or machete to whack their way through the undergrowth. They'd cut a trail, not only to help them move forward but also to guide them back. Here such a trail would spell certain death if found by a Japanese patrol.

Luke sets his compass to make sure they're moving due south, then inches his way into the creepers. He slices vertically into the growth, then he and Ward pry the slits open for the others to close behind them. They can see no more than two feet in any direction, and each step is unsteady, as if they were treading on a living mattress—in a steam bath. Often, they're forced to crawl.

Every now and then a distant snort signals the presence of a wild pig, and it's tempting to follow the animals' trails, but Luke vetoes that, pointing his fingers from his nose to mimic a charging boar. Ward pulls down on the corners of his eyes and crouches in caricature of a Japanese soldier.

Two hours into the forest a yelp up ahead causes Hari to pull Claire down. Before she can locate her stengun, however, Ward is gesturing frantically for them to get up. He flicks off several of what look like large dark slugs from his sleeve, then pulls up his left pant leg, which has come loose from his mosquito boot. Claire quells a surge of nausea at the streaks of blood and the sight of a dozen or more fist-sized leeches gorging on Ward's leg. She looks away only to see Luke and Hari checking their own flesh. And then she examines herself.

They cling to her boots, to her trousers, collar, and sleeves. And neck. "Like this," Luke murmurs, and uses his fingernails to detach the suckers.

"Why didn't I feel the damn things?" Ward's pulled a cigarette from his pack and is scrounging for a match.

"They express a natural anaesthetic to numb the victim. No, do not try to burn them off."

"Why the hell not?" Ward's face is livid with revulsion. Claire has never seen his guard drop so completely.

"If shocked they will regurgitate into the wound. More chance of infection, very bad." Luke squats by Ward and uses his fingernail technique to remove the leeches one by one. Before he's reached half of them Ward's leg is awash in blood, as is Claire's throat.

"No worry," Luke assures them. "It is a natural anticoagulant. It permits the blood to flow so that the creatures may feed more quickly."

In spite of her horror, Claire is fascinated. She hands Ward a sterile cloth and sulfa ointment from the first aid kit. "How do you know all this?" she asks Luke.

He ducks his head. "That day in Ferrargunj clinic, I am listening to Dr. Durant as he removes a great many leeches from one very small child. Afterward, the boy is asking to take the creatures in a bottle to his home."

"Christ," Ward says. "They're bloodsuckers, not ladybugs. Let's get out of here."

They will trek—if a hundred feet an hour can be called trekking—for more than a week down the spine of South Andaman Island. In the rare moments when Claire pauses to look up, every other tree seems to hold a fountain of orchids that Shep would give his all for. But then, she tells herself, in Behalla he has plenty, and she can ill afford to look anywhere but straight ahead. The threat of poisonous centipedes and spiders is eternal. Vipers prefer to keep their distance, but the masses of them coiled around limbs to the right, left, and above, do give one pause. So do those huge prehistoric reptiles, the monitor lizards, until Luke uses the Welrod to shoot one for supper on a day when they're all ravenous.

"The Malay say it's an aphrodisiac," Ward whispers in her ear, and the sight and smell of him repulses her even as she reaches for more of the meat. Hari has managed to grill it so that it tastes like smoked chicken.

The trick is to drink and eat enough to satisfy the leeches, which fall off on their own, once sated, but Ward can't stand the sight of them ballooning on his blood, so he insists on stopping every few hours to scrape them off. Claire makes herself a veil of mosquito netting, like a beekeeper's helmet, to keep them from dropping on her head or inside her shirt, and she checks periodically to see that they stay south of her knees. Otherwise, she lets them be. Luke's story about Shep converting the child's fear of leeches into fascination subdues her own horror. If it's possible to make peace with leeches, then there must be hope for Shep and Ty with the Japanese.

But at night there is no peace. She lies stifling in her cocoon of mosquito netting as unidentified objects thump and slither against the shell of her tent. Beneath her ground cloth the earth pulses with its ceaseless work of decay. She imagines herself and her companions as fleas on the back of a putrid dog whose skin is so raw and painful that the dog pants in protest. It's not difficult to see how the legends of the Biya arose.

Once Leyo told her that his people believe night was created as punishment. Before the creation of night, the ancestors knew only daylight.

Then one day an ancestor named Sir Lizard went into the jungle to dig for yams, and he discovered a cicada, which he brought back to camp and rubbed to death. The cicada screeched and the world went dark. Then the ancestors made torches and danced and sang to bring back the light, but daytime would not come until they engaged the bulbul and finally the ant. It required the industry and cooperation of all these creatures to restore the day after night.

As the memory of Leyo's smooth voice lulls her, she takes Ty into her arms, and they lie in the shade against Shep's chest with the waves easing over the sand. Finally, she sleeps.

The Christians, Leyo says, have the story of Adam and Eve. The Biya have a similar story of Biliku and her husband Tarai. Biliku and Tarai, like Adam and Eve, lived alone in the forest and made a family with their son Perjido, needing no one else. These first families lived as he and Naila and Ty must now, creating their own rules and rhythms. In this way Leyo shows that their situation is not so strange, not so sad or difficult as it might seem.

They agree that Ty should start hunting with Leyo, since the boy will need to know how to shoot and hold a spear. Naila will stay close to camp and forage, gather wood and tend the fire. At night, Ty lies between them.

He whimpers for Artam only at first. Soon he sleeps soundly, Leyo's presence a balm for his grief. But Naila senses that Leyo is becoming something else for her.

She truly is grateful and glad and relieved that he is here, but just as she doesn't like to stand too close to the front of the ledge, she can't trust herself to meet Leyo's gaze or sit too close to his body. Is it that she can't trust *him*? Some nights she lies awake, so alert to his nearness that she can hear him blink in the darkness. She can smell him sleep. Never before did she notice his scent, but its essence now seems to follow her even when he is gone, and this new awareness of her old friend troubles her.

She tries to push such thoughts away, because the one thing she knows for certain is that she and Ty both depend on him, but she does put back on the clothing the Biya shamed her into abandoning. She tears her old green skirt into a short sarong, and although the yellow blouse that her mother sewed is splitting at the seams, within its shell she feels closer to her true self.

And braver. For the longer she is away from the other Biya, the more likely it seems that the world outside the forest will one day welcome her home.

As if he senses this, too, Ty Babu also edges back into his old ways. Leyo has replaced his clay sticks with chalk-like stones, which are easier for Ty's small hands, and soon the floor blooms with his memories. A cluster of little elephants. The white spider that had such a beautiful scent. The striped tiger with the open snout, and the little yellow monkey that Doctor Shep made sing. Ty absorbed everything, Naila thinks. Everything that he chose to.

She searches her own memory, then one day takes a stone and writes above the elephant flower: *Aerides*—

Ty looks to see what she is doing, and she gestures for him to take over. He carefully sets down his red stone and accepts her white one. Without hesitation he completes the name: *Aerides odorata.* Just as Doctor Shep instructed Naila to write it in Port Blair.

"*Yche*," Leyo says. God.

But Naila smiles and shakes her head. "*Atota.*" Son.

And then one night when Ty is asleep, she wakes to find Leyo kneeling beside her. She raises herself in alarm, but he reassures her by running his palm lightly over her cheek and shoulder. He takes her hands and signals for her to follow.

A full moon has risen outside. He brings his sleeping mat into its light and sits down with his legs outstretched, then pulls her gently by the hips until she is seated on his lap. He presses his face against her neck and encircles her. As if they were her own, his arms cross in front of her breasts, his hands resting on her shoulders. For several minutes they sit without moving as the light of the moon and the pulse of the forest surround them. She is conscious of his skin against hers and the rise and fall of his breath, of his body beneath her, and the forest and moon and herself, and soon they all become inseparable. And this feeling of connection unlocks a sensation that no one could ever describe to her.

Leyo laughs as she slowly turns in his arms, but he stops when he feels her shaking. He takes her palm and holds it to his chest so that she can feel his own steady rhythm. This, she understands, is his promise.

A few hours into the sixth morning's march, Ward, in the lead, stops abruptly and signals everyone to freeze. Through the vines he's spotted a cluster of lean-tos.

The clearing is empty, but smoke still rises from a pit at its center. Near the fire lie cooking implements and a pile of vegetables. Near the vegetables prints of small bare feet mark the earth. Red fibers like those that Bathana and her daughter wound around their foreheads hang drying in the sun.

Claire mouths to Ward: *Jarawa.*

The wise move would be to pull back and skirt the camp, but Bolger I's food supplies are dwindling, and none of the team have sufficient familiarity with this part of the forest to know which plants are edible. All four of them turn slowly, scanning the forest wall, but the birds continue to twitter and the sweat to flow, and no one appears to menace them.

Holding his sten at the ready, Ward signals Hari to collect the food, but Claire whispers, "Stealing will make us their enemy. They're probably watching."

She moves forward. "Hari, come, but just look."

"Like yam, manioc, jackfruit, dugong eggs, taro." Hari ticks off the foods he knows to resemble those before him. "But these berries and nuts I do not know." He looks up and spots some of them in the surrounding branches. "And this cane." He looks closer to memorize the markings.

Claire reaches into her pocket and brings out a handful of Charms candies, rattles them like dice, and thinks better of it. She remembers how Bathana and her daughter refused to touch any food that was unfamiliar.

"What do you have to leave for them?" she whispers to Hari.

He roots in his pocket. "Only a charm."

"They won't want them."

"No." He opens his palm to reveal an iron arrowhead with a scroll design worked into it. "From home."

"Good. Place it there." She indicates a mortar stone beside the fire. Hari hesitates, then reluctantly lays the token down.

"You'll be sorry when that lands in your neck," Ward says.

"If these are your Topsy's people, it's more likely to home in on you," she says.

"You and your bleeding heart."

But as they move on, the wealth of food in the foliage around them becomes evident, and the Jarawa's cane turns out to be a woody vine filled, like coconut, with water. Even Ward has to admit that the Jarawa camp was a lucky find and, whether because of Hari's charm or not, they proceed unmolested.

That night they reach a hill from which they can see the signal crane shape of Mount Koiob silhouetted against the lavender sky to the south. Ferrargunj is now just a few hours away. And, Claire calculates, Behalla is due east from the spot where she now stands.

Ward lays out his plan. "We need to make sure that Pandu's still there—and Tojo isn't. Four's too many for recon. Besides, this hill should give you decent reception."

Marching orders. It's more than a role she is playing, though too often Claire forgets that. Especially now, so close, the temptation to bolt and risk everything nearly overwhelms her. But other than filling her arms and heart—and quite possibly getting herself killed—what could she accomplish alone? Between the lines of his terse instructions, Ward is constantly warning: Shep and Ty are only two of the five who now rely on her—and vice versa.

So, while Ward and Luke slip off in the dark to Ferrargunj, she and Hari set up the TBX. Hari hand-pedals the generator, and she focuses on the crackles coming through her headset as she locates frequencies and adjusts the man-pack's antenna. The signals are mostly in Morse, but in their second hour a man's voice breaks through the high-pitched pulses. Her hand flies off the dial as the unmistakable tonality of Japanese barks through her headset. The clearer the signal, the closer the operator.

Alarmed, Hari stops pedaling.

The most difficult thing is to remember that the enemy is human. She pulls herself together and motions him to go on.

The voice is too indistinct to represent a direct threat. It has to be coming from Port Blair, but it belongs only to an operator, not anyone who'd have direct contact with Allied prisoners. She listens, rapt, as the quiet, halting intonations sign off and pictures this Japanese soldier boy in the seat vacated by young Tom Lutty. Not literally, of course. Colonel Hastings said the North Point wireless station was destroyed, per protocol, on the eve of occupation, now ten months ago.

But where did her jitterbugging partner go? Ten months. An eternity.

She and Hari do not set up camp. Nor do they discuss their orders to retreat should Ward and Luke fail to return. But Hari does offer her one of the Jarawa fruits, which he's peeled for her. The flesh is gelatinous and astringent. Naila would say it tastes green. Ty would purse his mouth like a fish.

To ward off the ambush of memory, Claire concentrates her thoughts on Hari, squatting now, elbows on knees, looking past her into the darkness. Only inches away, she senses more than she sees or hears him. His smells mostly meld with the rawness of the earth, but she is always aware of the sharp essence of his sweat, distinct from Ward's fishy odor and Luke's darker, gamier scent—and her own stink of jungle rot. More than that, though, she's aware of Hari's internal balance, like a coin poised on its rim, attuned in equal measures to past and future, the present a movable fulcrum.

Once, during their training in Colombo, she asked about his family. No children yet, he confessed, but then beamed with pride as he described his wife, a girl by his report of exquisite beauty who at eighteen consented of her own free will to marry him, but only on the condition that she first complete her studies at Calcutta University to become an oculist. *She means to give sight to others. That is something rare and wonderful, I think.* Claire told him his wife was a lucky girl.

Now through the leaning treetops a band of galaxy glitters, and a cuticle moon. *Child of ours,* Claire recites to herself. *Friend's shelter in the deep forest. Men thire mele ing nola timiukoon.*

Hari places his hands together against his cheek. When he turns his wrist, the luminescence of his watch reads three o'clock. She's about to tell him to go ahead and sleep, when the headset rasps: *Bobulu.*

This Biya word for *ghost* is their code for safe return, the signal from Ward's Handy-Talkie insurance against mistaking the returning men for an enemy patrol. Minutes later he elbows through the screen of thorns. Luke follows, breathing as if he's just climbed Annapurna. A building storm and the swaying forest gave them cover.

It's too dark to see, let alone read, Ward's face, and before he can say whether they made contact, the sharp wind trailing them unleashes its torrents. He points to a depression where they can bivouac, hidden from anyone climbing the hill, and they all set to moving the gear.

The downpour quickly liquifies the mud. Claire has to wrestle her mat flat as she digs in her poles, yanks the tarp over, and secures it. When she tosses her pack inside, Luke and Hari are still fighting the wind. Ward, however, has made quick work of his own tent and vanished inside it.

She pushes back the flaps to find him on his back. In the darkness she can just make out the forearm across his face. When he refuses to move, she drops and knees him in the hip. His hand finds her thigh, and she nearly throws it off but is stopped by its utter lifelessness.

Ward's breath deepens as he sits up. "They're gone." His voice sags under the weight he carries. "Shep and Alfred, both." The words, disembodied. "In front of the Browning Club." In the absence of light. "Pandu's brother saw it. Claire, I—"

No! The word pounces, landing hard at the back of her skull, then begins to repeat. *No. No. No. No.* She peels away from the tent and staggers out into the wind.

Water immediately fills her ears, her eyes, her boots. It pastes her clothes and hair to her skin. The night, she notes with abrupt detachment, has a plastic quality, one minute bending, the next breaking in two, then smashing to smithereens.

Shep stands in the darkness, a moonless night on Ferar Beach, as phosphorescence plays in the waves. More than once, he's saying, his father took him to see how barbarians administered justice. *How old were you?* Five, six. Old enough to learn a lesson. There by the gate to the old city, an executioner's block. *Don't look away, old boy, don't you dare look away.* The eyes had turned white rolling back in the rolling skull, but the severed head was still that of a man. *I didn't know which was more unspeakable, the execution, or the father who'd take his son to the execution grounds.*

Unspeakable.

Ward behind her, Claire spins and demands, "What about Ty?"

"He wasn't there. No one's seen him or the girl. Not since before you left."

A cicada screeches and the world goes dark. One light on an island burns. The mother who would leave her son at the execution grounds.

Luke pulls her to silence. He's come into her tent and taken her by the shoulders, and when she opens her eyes, his expression threatens to drown her.

"Sorry," he says and lets go at once.

She lies back, more exhausted even than she felt last night.

"Dr. Durant," Luke says. "He was one of the best."

"You believe it."

"I am so sorry." He lowers his gaze.

But he flinches when she grabs his wrist. "Were you there? Did *you* hear Pandu say it?"

Luke stares at her hand. "I was keeping watch outside the village."

"Then I'm sorry. I won't believe it."

He gently pries her hand off his wrist as he murmurs something about God. And then he's gone.

Outside, the forest is screaming, the day's heat already throbbing. Ward let her sleep, a dangerous concession, for she sees now what she couldn't last night. This is Ward's doing, his word only. He refused to let her come and meet his informant, refused to mention Behalla. He even made her surrender her L-tablet. As if she'd kill herself because of his lies.

It's a matter of will now, not faith. With or without Ward, she'll get to Behalla. But he'll be watching. She has to be careful, play the good soldier, the secret agent. Yes.

When she comes out of her tent, Ward glances up with a look of resignation and motions for her to finish the nuts and dried fish that pass for breakfast. He's laying out next steps.

Pandu's promised to scout the enemy installations around the port. He suggested a hollow rain tree north of Ferrargunj as their "postal drop." Ward and Luke will return in a week for a pickup. In the meantime, Bolger I will proceed northwest in search of a signal hill on the coast.

For Claire, the west coast is the wrong direction. She only knows how to reach Behalla from the east, from waters most likely seething with enemy patrol boats.

But Ward and Luke are trackers. They found their way to Ferrargunj, and the only signs of Japanese they've detected in this approach so far are those outliers in the Strait. None in the interior. Which means that Ty—and Shep, she insists—should be safe where they are. Safer than she can keep them until the O-boat returns six weeks from now.

They're in Behalla. They have to be. And when the time comes, Luke will know how to get there, with or without Ward's blessing.

❧

Leyo insists on calling her Yulu, and this no longer annoys her. She's as changed as if she were reborn, and this name seems to suit her new form, movements, and longings. Before, she didn't understand the logic of taking the name of a tree coming into bloom. Now she can feel herself blooming each time Leyo touches or even breathes beside her.

Ty Babu, too, notices the change, at once jealously guarding his place between them and smirking at their dazed expressions. For the first time, she feels modest around the boy, which is ridiculous after having gone nearly naked for months, but everything seems to have turned upside down. She even sees their abandonment in a new light. If the others were still here, would she dare to lie with Leyo each night? Would she dream of taking him inside her? She thinks with disgust of Ekko's lewd finger movements, but not even the memory of that awful day can destroy the joy she feels now.

The change reminds her of Teacher Sen's spectacles. One day when she arrived early for school Saar had been standing at the window rubbing his eyes, and she picked up the glasses from his desk and tried them on. She cannot remember what she expected, only her shock at the world's sudden transformation when she looked through his lenses. The classroom's crisp clean lines suddenly appeared as blurs, and the view from the window collapsed into a painful kaleidoscope of color and light. Teacher Sen laughed when he saw her, then gave her a private lesson on optics and the human eye.

Without these, he said tapping his spectacles, *I am virtually blind.* And yet with them, he could see the same things she saw, but in an entirely different way.

Now, as she moves between Ty and Leyo, she feels as if she's continually putting on and taking off different lenses. One minute the two of them look as familiar to her and to each other as brothers; the next they appear as father and son. Then a cloud will pass over the sun, or a flutter of light ignites the green of Ty's eyes, and all she can see is a white boy standing beside a black man with whom he has nothing but nakedness in common.

She is confounded and also, in these moments, profoundly grateful that she cannot see her own length or face.

Behind a camouflage screen on a bluff overlooking Constance Bay, Claire points her antenna due west. Ward and Luke have completed their first trip to the postal drop.

Okojumu, she signals. *Medicine man* means they're in business.

And the test now is real. The glossary she spent five years compiling sits for reference in front of Culman in Barrackpore—and simmers in her head. No written keys in the field. Dangerous enough to have it recorded to memory. More dangerous now if memory fails. *Birds for guns. Fish for boats. Footed things for land vehicles.* Translations upon translations.

For herself she creates a tablet of sandy loam in which she can draw her backward rebus puzzles, from intelligence to transmissible code.

Destroyer anchored off western coast of Bluff Island: shark + Bluff Island + oceanside = LAYE LURUA OTLE

Three major artillery installations on summit above Mayabunder Bay: three + big + hawks + summit + bamboo bay = ONDAFOL ELEOFO CE-TEL MUKHU RETFER

Japanese troops swim each morning at Rangachang Beach: little cock-roaches + swim + morning + long sandy beach + Port Blair = TAAHU LILE AMBIKHIR TOREBURONO DIUTEMEC

After each transmission, Claire erases the sand slate, picturing the words as carrier pigeons and willing their safe passage to Culman. She saves the most important news for last, once she's gained confidence. According to their informant, the Emperor's Third Destroyer Squadron is due to arrive in Port Blair in a week.

She taps out *ITARAIN JERO DULOTHIRE*: *third dugong comes next quarter moon.*

Every now and then a grumble sounds high above their ceiling of leaves, or a flash of silver crosses overhead. On overcast days it's impossible to tell if the aircraft are Allied or Japanese, whether they'll be chased down island by anti-aircraft fire or welcomed on the landing strip that was first bombed when Shep and Claire were still fool enough to believe what they were told.

She pictures her husband, down on one knee beside the unscathed tarmac, cradling a wounded sapling. *What did this little fellow ever do to Tojo?* Shep's notion of a joke, though also serious. At times she thought he loved his plants more than he loved her and Ty.

But when the skies are clear they can spot the red, white, and blue bullseyes of the RAF. Ward claims the Headquarters pilots are "keeping the Nips on their toes, monitoring their behavior."

They're also providing Balderdash cover. If and when Bolger I's intelligence translates into action, the history of flyovers could lead the Japanese in Port Blair to think the spies are in the sky.

One morning Hari clutches Claire's arm and points through the camouflage net at three Flying Fortresses soaring eastward above the ocean. The enormous planes pass over them to the south. A few minutes later, as Claire holds her breath, she can just barely detect a rhythmic concussion, like the dropping of distant coconuts.

Within the hour the same three Fortresses fly back unmolested toward Ceylon. She and Hari hug each other like children, gazing in wonder at those gleaming avenues of cloud.

The next day they spot their first Japanese patrol boat circling the bay. It speeds past their bluff and does not circle back, but it puts them on notice. They'll need to move the wireless to avoid signal detection.

Claire wants to help Luke scout alternative positions, but Ward preempts her. Their respective roles have solidified. She's the wireless operator and cryptographer, Hari the cook, generator, and camp guard.

"We play to our strengths," Ward says. Which makes him and Luke the hunting and reconnaissance team. Period.

She tries appealing to Ward's ego, asking him to show her on the map where exactly they've found evidence of new roads, bunkers, working plantations, and building. She does need to encode this information for transmission, but in the process, she also means to pinpoint any and all barriers between her current location and Behalla.

It would be easier getting these details out of Luke, but Ward sees to it that she never has solo access to his recce partner. So, she hedges her questions. How extensive is the Japanese presence around the settlements? Any sign of refugees fleeing Port Blair? Any more close encounters with the natives?

Pretending to keep it light, she makes Luke promise not to let Ward shoot anyone who's not Japanese.

The exceptions, the tracker apologizes, must be Ward and himself, since they've made a pact to kill each other rather than be taken prisoner.

She confronts Ward that night.

"I had a close call," he admits.

"When?"

"That first night with Pandu. Before I got out, a squad of Nips came into the village."

"Why didn't you say anything?"

"Figured it was too early in the operation to spook you." And, he might have said, would you even have heard me after I told you about Shep?

"What happened?"

"They were drunk and horny as toads. Pandu hid me in a silo of rice and covered the thing with gunny sacks. He'd gotten his wife and daughter out to hide in the forest, but the Japs had heard his wife was Burmese—hot stuff—and they went on a rampage searching for her. I could hear them smashing the place up, figured I was done for if they tipped the silo. Instead they stuck it with bayonets." He rolls up his left sleeve to reveal a smooth patch of skin near the wrist. "Shaved me like a razor. If they'd drawn blood, I'd be dead. But not necessarily right away. After that I made Luke promise to kill me and said I'd do the same for him."

"You must have ice water in your veins."

He smiles. "If only it were Dewars."

"There must be something you care about, Denis."

"Oh, there is. Right now, I care very much about getting us out of here alive. But we have one more month to take down as many Japs as possible before we go. And I care about that, too."

When Ward and Luke go out, they keep mobile communication to a minimum, but any failure to contact Claire at the appointed hour is to be construed as a signal to abort the entire operation: she and Hari, theoretically, will retrace their route to the hidden folboats, return to the original landing zone and call for extraction. In actuality, her emergency plan, should Ward vanish, is to head straight for Shep and Ty.

But Denis Ward is never late. And one week after their Flying Fortress sighting, he and Luke return a full hour early with a lengthy note from the safe drop.

"They've been rounding up suspected spies." Ward's voice breaks. "They've reopened the Cellular Jail."

For once, Luke has to tell what needs telling. Ward's former deputy, Narayan Rao, has been the nominal superintendent of police in Port Blair since the invasion, but after a whole squadron of destroyers was sunk without warning, Colonel Buco became convinced that there was a mole in the police department. The Japanese have been picking up Bolger I's wireless transmissions, but they can't decode them or locate the source. In retaliation, Rao and his associates—all the men who worked most closely with Ward—were accused and tortured, then executed.

Ward weeps as if his own children numbered among the dead.

Allied planes also have bombed several villages where Japanese troops are billeted to the south of Port Blair, and one bright morning, according to Pandu's report, a submarine surfaced off Rangachang Beach, mowing down several hundred soldiers as they bathed there.

Ward now worries that their informants might be compromised, especially since the Japanese have placed a former convict named Dipak

Patel—a notorious liar and schemer—in charge of the roundups. Naila's former teacher, Sen, is among those reportedly arrested, his accusers some young thugs he expelled from his class who now "serve" as police informants. They've also locked up the schools superintendent Dr. Diwan Singh, a Punjabi poet who was held in high esteem by locals and Europeans alike.

Then they learn that Luke's brother-in-law, a forest officer named Prasad, has also been detained. He is not an informant, could have no idea that Luke has returned to the island. But this is no consolation to Luke. "What difference, whether we pull the trigger ourselves, or signal for the relay to begin?"

Hari ventures that Pandu has too much to lose and nothing to gain by confessing. Hari the company optimist.

"Who says he has to confess?" Ward replies.

Through the tops of the trees, wind drums at the darkness.

Claire says, "We need sources that no one will even notice, much less suspect."

For once, Ward listens.

New roads being built to the north of Mount Harriet force them to take a circuitous inland route that adds two days to the march. Luke, having calculated Behalla's location from Claire's description of the trail she used to take, assumes the lead, but she follows so closely, craning over his shoulder for signs of patrols or the telltale column of smoke, that by the third day her neck has seized into a permanent cramp.

Then, around the sixth noon out, she smells it. The Biya call it the firewood tree, a type of padauk that produces a sweetish smoke, which she's only ever smelled in Behalla.

An hour on, and they're there.

The huts have been thatched recently, and Claire can see sleeping mats and cooking utensils, but only Kuli comes forward. He looks unchanged, though he seems to be here all alone.

"*Maia*," she says, barely breathing as she weeps and embraces herself in greeting.

Despite everything, Kuli is smiling, upright, strong and steady. Smiling. He hardly even seems surprised as, nodding, he takes her in.

She scans the empty camp again. And then she realizes. *Friend in the forest.* Of course, he's not surprised. Smiling. He's smiling.

But where are they?

Kuli pats his heart. Wherever they are, they're safe.

She reins herself in and reaches into her rucksack, walking herself through the rules. The first thing the Biya do when greeting an old friend is to exchange gifts. She's planned for this and brings out a Punjabstick jackknife that's served her well.

As the men of Bolger I look on, the Biya chief holds the knife to his nose as if it were a fine cigar. Then he glances to his left.

A small shape detaches from the main hut, and Claire lurches. She sobs as she opens her arms, but after a split second of suspension, she catches herself.

The approaching figure is not Shep or Ty, but a rail-thin figure with bloodshot eyes—the port vagrant Porubi.

Kuli trades the jackknife for an object cupped in Porubi's palms. Then he presses this gift on Claire: Naila's gold chain with the moonstone globe.

She stares in confusion. The clasp is broken. Another charm has been added, a star so dirty that she can't see what's embossed in the metal.

Kuli nods for her to look closer, so she rubs it on her pants until the surface comes up. A ring in the circle is inscribed, SHANGHAI VOLUNTEER CORPS.

She searches Kuli's face until he reaches up and lays his hands on her shoulders. "Ty Babu," he says, and grins with unmistakable reassurance. "Naila."

Alive, his grin insists. Ty and Naila. *Alive.*

Overwhelmed by gratitude and dread, she touches the star and braces herself. She must speak the words. She must ask. "*Bo eboe tiko?*" And my husband?

The old man looks away to Porubi. Both of them lower their gaze.

Over the next hour, conferring separately and together, Kuli and Porubi rejuvenate Operation Balderdash and force Claire to shutter half her heart so she can go on. The camp where Naila, Leyo, and Ty are hiding—she assumes for safety—is due north. Kuli gives them precise directions, and Luke pinpoints the spot on his geologic map. Perhaps a week's trek.

Take the children across the water. This is Kuli's instruction, as if they were gods with the power to come and go as they pleased. No questions asked. No doubt.

Claire wants to throw herself at his feet like a supplicant. Instead, she clasps his weathered hands and bows her head.

Porubi, meanwhile, delivers to Ward and Hari a trove of new information—delivered in near perfect English—about Japanese naval stations, barracks, gun emplacements, and weapons caches around the south islands.

At one point, Ward looks up at Claire with an expression that Shep most definitely would describe as *gobsmacked.*

Shep—

She clutches the stone and the star to stop herself. Grief is a luxury she cannot afford.

Ty is alive. She has to go on.

Ward's saying, "You're the perfect spy." Porubi bulges his eyes and slobbers his tongue in agreement. And laughs.

The world, Claire thinks with desperate hope, has turned inside out. In twelve days, the *O-24* is scheduled to retrieve them on the far side of Constance Bay, and they will meet it with treasure.

IX

March 1943

Dawn is flickering behind a wall of dark purple clouds. Naila yawns and rolls over, reluctant to leave the cool openness of the ledge, but she can feel the threat of rain. She opens her eyes. Leyo has risen already.

"Yulu!" He beckons from the front of the round house. "Ty Babu," he says.

Only then does she hear the moaning.

Leyo tells her he was mopping the sweat from Ty's face when the child vomited. Naila kneels beside the boy, touches his chest. Ty's eyes open, but they are empty. His skin is hot and wet, his breathing shallow. She covers him with her sarong, bunches her blouse into a pillow for his head. When Leyo brings her the medicine bag, she locates the serum Doctor *saab* instructed them to use for fever.

Ty doesn't react as she measures the dose onto his tongue and drips water into his mouth, but a minute later he gasps. His body goes rigid. Then he begins to shake.

Leyo holds the boy's head and instructs her to add a drop of the amber oil that stops convulsions.

Instead of daylight, lightning cracks over the forest. Thunder heaves in waves. The child's eyes roll back in his head, his arms and legs go limp. Naila's clothes swim around him, and his sleeping mat soon is soaked through.

"The fever will break," Leyo says, and their vigil begins.

Through the next days and nights, they take turns, one bathing Ty's head and body while the other rests and eats from their dwindling food supplies. The skies clear, but Naila and Leyo do not leave to hunt or forage. They do not touch one another.

On the third morning Leyo shakes Naila awake. A crusty rash, like a red sea dotted with white islands, covers Ty's upper body. He's begun to bleed from the nose and mouth and is uttering sounds that seem eerily coherent—not quite words, but as if some spirit were trying to speak through him.

This near speech frightens Naila even more than the sickness. Doctor Shep gave her no warning of such symptoms, and she is afraid to experiment with the few remaining remedies in his case.

Leyo says, "Hurry and get him ready. Kuli will know what to do."

Half the sky is still blue-black. He's filling her gathering basket with their tools and the last of their food.

"But what about the Japanese? Behalla will be too dangerous for Ty."

"Then we go somewhere else." He points out past the ledge to the west. A tendril of white smoke rises from the forest less than a mile away. "Maybe it is Jarawa. Maybe Japanese. But we cannot stay here."

❧❧❧

As Bolger I plunges toward the island's center, Claire focuses on the top of Luke's pack, bobbing like a cork in front of her. *Make the best*, Shep counsels her. *A bad situation, yes, but—*

His voice rises in bursts, filling her throat. *Is gumption your strong suit?*

It wraps like a hand around her heart. *Steady, old girl. A boy needs his mum.*

You're right, she thinks. All we have now is Ty. But a full year has passed.

How much do you s'pose he's grown?

And how much has he suffered? Kuli says Ty's happy and well. She has to believe this still is true.

If it is, we owe Naila and Leyo more than we can ever repay them.

A troubling thought occurs, and she combs her fingers through her shorn hair. Her skin is the color of cordovan. Until today her appearance had evaporated, of no more interest than the reek of her body or the men's matted beards—like grief, the less attention paid to it the better. But now it seems a different kind of liability.

Be still my soul, Shep's voice persists so that she nearly snaps aloud, But will Ty even recognize me?

She stumbles, puts a hand to Luke's back, and both of them jerk in alarm. Luke half turns and meets her eyes. She shakes her head.

A fraction of a second and they go on.

The whipping cry of a serpent eagle now softens with Shep's accent. *If Viv's right, and Ty can talk, what language will he speak?* And Claire finds herself trying to suppress the questions that trump his. What words could any son find to greet a mother he no longer knows? To defend himself from a mother who, for all he knows, abandoned him?

Naila and Leyo are Ty's family now. Take the children across the water. There are no words for the distance that divides them. All of them.

Ward issues a low hoopoe's cry, and everyone freezes. They shrink into the undergrowth.

Below, perhaps two hundred feet away, a small river snakes east. Claire scans the banks, the rotting trees, the tapestry of growth. Each flare of brightness reads as a threat, the most familiar yellow and orange bromeliads imbued with danger. Above, the canopy shifts and sways. This must be, she thinks, how a kelp bed looks to a small fish hiding from a passing shark.

When she finally spots their shark, though, it already has its kill. Across the river, four Japanese in combat gear flank four local men in dingy sarongs who carry between them on bamboo poles two large dead pigs. The officer at the head of the line takes off his cap and swats the mosquitoes that fog the slow-moving water. Then he reaches into his pocket and brings his hand down to the muzzles of two beagles. In a frenzy, the dogs begin barking and jerking at their leads.

Claire stinks. The days without washing, the beat of her blood, her running nose and seeping welts, every pore betrays her. *The pigs*, she wills the man to think. *A frenzy over the pigs.*

She presses deeper into the muck. Then she glances to her right and stops breathing.

Freeze, Shep warns as the flattened head hovers, less than two feet away. The viper lies switch backed. Maybe a yard long, it is mottled, with pale brown and black scales as distinct as mosaic tiles. Luke taught them to look for the telltale pit between eye and mouth, a heat-sensing organ that helps the venomous reptile locate its warm-blooded prey.

Stay cool. Lower your pulse. Good girl, you haven't moved a muscle.

The yapping dogs and their enemy handlers preclude any sudden escape, but with her left hand she feels for the knife in her belt.

You gave it to Kuli, remember? Just stop. If it senses—

The viper whips forward and sinks its fangs into her forearm.

Claire clenches her jaw. *Don't move. Don't* move. But the pain is obliterating, an injection of acid. A volcanic spasm shoots from her heart to her throat, and her whole body bucks with the effort to stay silent.

At some point her eyes shut. When she gets them open again the viper's retreated to a low-hanging limb to wait, coiled there, until she dies. Its vertical pupils dilate as the noise of the hunters intensifies, near enough now to serve up jokes chased by howls of male laughter and the frustrated whines of the dogs.

Claire's heartbeat whirls, and the puncture wounds scream. Her mouth fills with an alien taste, at once metallic and menthol.

Breathe. Breathe slowly, in and out, in and—

Her shirt is drenched, and she senses rather than sees the blood streaming from her arm. Her pulse wails over Shep's voice as her flesh begins to burn. Time speeds up and stops altogether, and she soon loses any sense of reckoning.

Only the viper remains within her scope. The viper and the finally diminishing echoes of the Japanese.

Ward appears through the thorns. "Imagine if we'd had your boy with—"

"Snake," she grunts and tips her head to his left.

Luke, who has the keenest hearing of the team, lunges for the viper before Ward has even processed what she's telling him. With a single slice of his *dha,* he severs the snake's head and sends it flying into the brush.

"Shit," Ward says when he sees her arm, but he's now fumbling with the first aid kit.

Hari crouches beside her and makes a garter of his hands below the elbow as Luke positions the rubber dam over the fang marks. Then Ward goes to work suctioning and kneading the site with his teeth.

Claire closes her eyes again and tries to picture Ty. Flames swallow her arm, but they have to get to him today and then cross the island.

"Stop," she lies. "I think it was dry."

"The pain?" Worry etches Luke's voice.

"It's swelling." Ward spits out the residue of rubber from his mouth and turns over the dam. "How do you tell the venom from the blood?"

"Best to let it ooze for a day or two," Hari says. "If you can do with the pain."

"You have a bandage in there?" she asks. "Just wrap it and let's go."

"You could be dying."

Steady on, darling.

"I've never felt more alive."

A wedge of light finds Ward's face, igniting the brackish blue of his eyes. He shakes his head but shoulders his gun. As Luke and Hari bandage Claire's arm and secure it in a sling, the forest roars down on them.

As Kuli promised, they approach the camp by a steep and narrow passageway. The front of the incline screens them from below but leaves them at the mercy of anyone who might be positioned at the top. Boiling oil was designed for just such approaches, so they climb cautiously, faces turned skyward, though Claire hallucinates not horror but a small round silhouette vying with the clouds. Each successive blink brings disappointment.

When they step at last onto the ledge where Kuli said she'd find Ty, the sky ripples with late scarlet and gold, but the stone underfoot is black. Her foot twists on the sludgy surface, crunching splinters of carbon beneath her heel. Her arm is on fire. Her mouth tastes like chrome. The men around her cast shadows onto shadow.

Scorched earth, Shep spits in her ear.

But he was talking about war in China. The evidence she sees and smells and tastes here doesn't compute. Ash. Cinders. Singed tree limbs stretch as if pleading. Is this the venom's work? She turns in circles, her senses careening.

Where is everybody? The voice isn't hers, isn't Shep's.

Is it Ty? No.

Come out, come out wherever you are!

Robin.

"Claire." Ward grabs her by the shoulders. "You'll want to see this."

He steers her past an uncovered cistern. Mosquito larvae squirm across rainwater. Robin is dead, but Ty was here. He made this climb, watched this sky and listened to these same moaning trees.

And then?

"Over here." Ward points at Luke, who's holding up a blackened mat. He and Hari bend to stare at the rock underneath.

She spots a chalkboard blooming with diagrams of flowers. Elaborate pink, white, yellow, and green drawings, fading but clearly distinguishable. A puzzle of blossoms shaped like elephants, dogs, trumpets and stars, and above each picture, in a child's print, the names that Shep and Som taught them. *Aerides odorata. Jumellea fragrans. Acampe praemorsa. Eria Kurzii.*

I love you, Shep whispers. *God save us all.*

"Luke. Hari."

The men move past her like ghosts as she sinks. With her good hand she strokes each line, rolls the chalky grit between her fingers, places it on her tongue. She kneels forward and kisses the colors, the stubborn softness of her son's hand. She finds a shard of umber, the color of his hair.

She squeezes her damaged arm against her ribs until the pain promises to eviscerate everything else. When the men return, she refuses to
look up.

"We can't be sure," Ward says, "but I think we've found him."

He kneels beside her. And for the first time she remembers the syringe
in Shep's fist, the actual slow-motion shock of the needle, the paralysis
and confusion as the guards held her down so her husband could knock
her out. And light. Blinding, desperate light. The force of his love. The
monstrosity of his terror.

"Show me," she says with what feels like her last shred of strength.

Hari and Luke hang their heads, but Ward stands and helps her, holds
onto her arm.

She doesn't fight him. If she did, she'd fall. So, she thinks about nothing but the effort of holding her body upright and placing one foot in
front of the other.

The plot is about sixty feet beyond the ruins of the camp, down an
incline cornered by two steep cliffs. Overhanging vines and palm debris
form a natural bower. Centella, moss, and toadstools cover the ground—
right up to the oval gash the men have dug.

"We could see the growth was more recent," Ward explains, as if needing to justify himself.

She turns before she can see what they've exposed. "How recent?"

"In this climate it's difficult to say. Weeks, perhaps months, but not
many."

"All right."

He still has her by the shoulder. The men were neat, turning back the
soil like a collar around the grave. Inside, the small skeleton lies on its
side, arms between knees as if playing with toes. The stubborn fibers of
whatever plant matter it was wrapped in form a slit cocoon.

It. The bones, though picked clean, still have the density of life. And
the hair—

Claire checks herself. She's never seen a real human skeleton before,
certainly never one that belonged to her own. Is it only that?

No. She looks closer. The waning light flickers and rolls. She covers her nose, though the smell of decomposition is hardly more than a whisper—the smell of turned earth more pungent. She squats to see if what she suspects is true.

The dome of the skull looks too broad, the chin too recessive, but the head of a child would be constantly changing. After ten, eleven months apart is it possible she can't recognize the shape of her own child's skull?

Yes, she warns herself. It's as possible as believing he is still alive. But the hair is another matter. Black, short, stiff and kinky as steel wool. Even in death, it could never be Ty's.

Scenarios buzz her brain now, warring with hope. He could have been shaved first, this hair used as some sort of ritual trade. But the skeleton is intact, undisturbed, and something about the pelvis and legs, too, tell her it's all wrong.

Ward has let go, freeing her, so she shifts forward onto her knees and takes hold of the skeleton's uppermost femur.

"Claire!" He's back on her, but she elbows him away.

"It's not Ty," she says. "This is not my son. It's—"

Artam's mischievous face appears, and the bowed leg falls from her hands. Claire squeezes her eyes shut and says through chattering teeth, "I knew this child." I loved her.

"Claire," Ward repeats, more gently now.

She lays the femur back into its original position and begins with her good hand to restore Artam's grave. With Hari and Luke's help she replaces the bed of earth, then whispers through tears a prayer of sorrow.

"*Molen thi ekjirake.*" Please forgive me.

When Claire looks up, Ward and Hari are black silhouettes against a violet sky. Ward has his maps out. They have just five days to reach the takeout on the far side of the island. She tests her arm. The swelling and burn are subsiding, the pain beginning to numb around the perimeter. If not a dry bite, at least not a lethal one.

She surveys the camp's charred ruins. How long does ash remain? How long for the rains to wash the stone clean? A new chill seizes her as she realizes just how recently this fire must have happened. Certainly, long after Artam was placed in her grave.

Luke would know. She pushes back on her heels and sees him rooting through the undergrowth above camp. When she approaches, he holds out a scrap of green fabric the size of a gecko.

She examines it. "Naila had a skirt just this color and weave."

"Where'd you find it?" Ward asks Luke.

"There's a path up there. A back way out." Luke motions away from the boiling oil approach. "There would have to be."

Claire touches the threads. "Recent, you think?"

The tracker fingers his beard and raises his eyes to meet Ward's. "Three days. Maybe four."

Three days. "Can you tell if they were followed out?" she asks.

"Not by Japanese."

"But . . . ?"

"Jarawa cover their tracks even better than we can."

"I won't do it," Ward says flatly. "I'm sorry, Claire. Time's run out. There's no telling how far afield this could take us . . . or what we'd find even if we caught up with them."

"They could have been taken prisoner," she says. "He's four years old, and he's my son, and we know he was alive when Kuli last saw him."

"You're in no shape—" Ward starts, but Luke interrupts him.

"Major, this path starts us in the direction we need to take. There still is light to gain some distance. If we find that the boy and his people have turned south, then we decide, but for this moment we have no cause to disagree."

It is the first time either of Ward's men have opposed him, but now Luke and Hari stand shoulder to shoulder like two small grizzled mountain men. Claire watches Ward consider his options.

Luke is right. *The boy and his people.* The words burn into her.

Leyo carries Ty, along with his bow and arrows. Naila follows with the last of their medicine and food. They steer clear of established trails, but even so, from time to time they hear distant voices and motors, the tramp of boots, the chopping of axes. Each time, they change direction, lengthening the journey. They are mute with exhaustion.

At night they sleep under giant ferns. Leyo plucks the youngest fronds, which they eat raw with the last of their dried meat. When they pass a grove of green bamboo, he fills their canteens with clean water from inside the giant stems, but Ty can barely rouse himself to drink unless Naila tricks him by gently working her fingertips into the soft spots just under his jaw. To ease the pain and itching of the rash, they wrap his torso in the pleated leaves of the orchid Doctor Shep called *Spathoglottis*. Leyo says this will heal the sores, and perhaps it does reduce Ty's agitation, but the child's eyes still stare dully, his mouth has gone slack, and the fever, now surging on and off, is shriveling his body. Terrified as she was of returning to Behalla, Naila is more terrified that her boy will die before they get there.

"We must give him the Last Resort," she tells Leyo. These drops Doctor Shep told her to use only if the fever lasted longer than five days. The clear and bitter tincture, he said, might make Ty see and act strangely.

Leyo knows the plant that Doctor used to brew this medicine; the Biya call it Spirit Leaf for the visions it causes. *Psychosis*, was the word Doctor used to warn them. But Ty's fever is in its sixth day now. Leyo agrees that a few visions are a small price to stop the child from burning to death.

That night Ty thrashes in his sleep, but by morning, the fever has come down and he stops pawing at his sores. They must continue the drops for three days. Leyo rubs Naila's back in encouragement.

The next day they reach a swamp. Its waters look like black glass crisscrossed by mossy berms. Mangroves dip their legs along one side of the water, pandan trees the other. Behind them rotting trunks of ironwood and padauk form a tilted wall. The smell of decomposition hangs over the water like a fog, yet despite it, brightly colored dragonflies dart through clouds of mosquitoes. A white heron perches, immobile, on an upright log that blooms with a brilliant pink and yellow orchid that Naila has never seen before. The surrounding branches, too, host spots of bright color, and prehistoric-looking turtles and frogs blink from the foam green algae at the margins. Water snakes whip across the darkness.

"Are there crocodiles?" Naila whispers. Though she's never seen a crocodile, she's heard they plague swamps like this.

Leyo catches her arm. "We are too far inland. Here." He rummages in the side pocket of her rucksack and hands her his pouch of clay and turtle fat. "Both you and Ty Babu. If we cross the swamp, Behalla will be only one more day . . . and no Japanese will come here."

She has neither the courage nor the strength to oppose him, but dread stalls her hands as they smear the waxy substance over Ty's exposed skin. Her own is already so covered with welts, the exercise seems pointless.

"Eyes," Leyo directs her. "Ears. The swarm will make you crazy, and you won't be able to balance." She sees then that he means for them to cross the swamp by walking those berms, each no wider than a foot. And even if there are no crocodiles, plenty of other perils lurk in that black water.

The thick green light and stench seem suddenly to converge in a high-pitched throb, and a wave of nausea bends her double, nearly causing her to drop the pouch.

Leyo grasps her elbow and pulls her upright. He presses her forefinger into the pouch and instructs her to paint his face. Ty lolls on his back. Leyo's bow rests against his leg. The swamp threatens to suck them into an underworld too terrifying to imagine, yet as Leyo's brown eyes study her, as her fingers trace the wide bones of his cheeks and encircle his brow, his quiet confidence seeps into her. Leyo's breathing, his long slow blinks, the unflinching muscles beneath his dark skin, his refusal to look away—all of this steels her.

"*Accha.*" She releases him.

They are halfway across the first berm when a flicker of white from the opposite bank reflects in the water. The movement is so quick and darting that it reminds Naila of the spotted deer that her father told her once lived in the islands. No one he knew had ever seen them, and perhaps they were mythical, but he showed her pictures drawn of the animals and said as a boy he searched for them. Now the memory gives her a surge of hope. She raises her eyes.

But this white belongs to no deer. It paints a face. And not just one. At least five men stand among the pandanus on the far side of the water. She can't see their bodies, but she can make out the red of their bows, the glint of their poised arrows.

In front of her, Leyo has stopped. "Jarawa," he says under his breath.

The berm offers no cover. A step in either direction will plunge them into that deadly ink. Naila prays for some kind of diversion, but though a hornbill swoops overhead and far off a rooting pig sounds, those arrows hold their aim.

Leyo is slowly turning even as the white-masked figures creep closer. Their chests and arms bear a painted armor of white lines, and their small lean frames look as tense as their bows.

Suddenly she realizes that Leyo is reaching for his own bow. "No!" she cries. One against five is folly.

But her cry is answered by a streak so close to her shoulder that both she and Leyo jerk backward. The movement rouses Ty and he lifts his face—a ghostly white mask in itself.

And out of him rolls a voice so impossible, it sounds as if a loudspeaker is bellowing across the swamp.

"GIVE US A KISS, OLD BOY!"

The voice catches Claire in mid-step, arresting her even before the surreal sound has time to register. Human and not, familiar and not, the words tremble high and clear in the canopy, then fade without an echo.

She must be delirious. It was an animal's shriek, the call of a myna or owl distorted somehow by the venom in her veins. Another of Shep's visitations.

But Ward and Luke also have halted in front of her, Ward peering through the foliage to a brighter murk ahead. And Hari's sharp, panicked breathing taps at her back.

"Did you hear?" he whispers. "It is a *bhut*."

Claire cradles her arm. A ghost.

"Get back." Ward turns, looking as if he's seen it. Even under all the layers of dirt, behind two months' growth of beard, his face is ashen. Whatever he actually has seen floods his eyes with tears.

"What is it?" she demands.

"Claire, no—" But Ward's breaking voice betrays him as Luke reaches past to wrap a hand around her arm. Fingers to lips, he draws her forward to the place where Ward was standing when he halted.

They're on the verge of a swamp. Peering through the scrim of leaves, her eyes take several seconds to adjust to the ribbons of light that filter down through the expanse ahead. At first, all she can make out are two misshapen stumps rising from the middle of the water, maybe half a mile away. Only gradually do the motionless shapes resolve into shoulders, two closely shorn heads.

She takes Luke's field glasses and searches back to the figures. She sees bare legs, a patch of dirty red, and then, slung across—

Luke claps his palm over her mouth before she can cry out, and the shock of his touch does its job. Far too soon, she wrenches her gaze away from her son's haunted eyes—his *living* face . . . and allows Luke to turn her toward the figures emerging from the pandanus, their arrows pointed straight at Leyo and Naila. And Ty.

The hunters are small as Pygmies, naked but for red waist bands, with hair like Brillo pads and skin the color of swampwater. The white paint, red adornments, and their hostile stance mark them as Jarawa. But they advance slowly, which suggests an intent to capture, not kill.

Claire glances back and sees Ward wielding the pistol, Hari with one of the stens. They're easing on behind the mangroves in the direction of the standoff, and she reads in their stealth Ward's intention.

She bolts after them. An attack will lead only to slaughter, most certainly of her son. "You don't know how many there are," she hisses.

Then she gives the field glasses an imperative shake. "The leader's arrowhead is Hari's charm."

It's a ploy. Impossible in this light at this distance even with binoculars to see any such thing, but Ward must not be allowed to shoot. Whatever triggered that voice also has spooked the hunters, or they would have taken the children already. But they still have Ty in their sights.

Ward keeps moving, no tears now. He has his own history with the Jarawa. "Do you want your son, or not?"

Claire glances through the foliage, makes a hard calculation, and plunges away on her own. She frees her right arm from its sling as she pushes with the other from trunk to trunk. The obstacle course lands her in a bed of mud with mangrove spikes piercing the soles of her boots, and she clings to an overhead limb for balance, but the noise she's making works.

The Jarawa, out in the open now, turn their arrows on her.

Knowing their vision and focus are far more acute than her own, she stretches her arms wide, then embraces herself.

"*Eneengeeya*," she yells, raising mosquitoes like stardust.

The surprise of the closest hunter is inaudible, but she thinks she sees his bow twitch.

Taking another hobbled step, she closes her right hand to her heart. Then she invokes Bathana, that heartbroken mother whose sole wish was to escape and take her child safely home.

Louder now, she shouts, "*Eneengeeya*." And then, "*Eykwota*." Her voice rings through the swamp as she sweeps her arm slowly in a motion meant to convey maternal connection toward the figures on the berm. Then she beats her fist on her chest again, bows her head, and prays.

The five painted figures waver briefly. For these and the next interminable seconds as the hunters recede, Claire wastes precious brain cells willing Ward to hold his fire. *They're going.* **Going.** *Do not shoot.*

Then the Jarawa are gone and Leyo begins, impossibly, to run across the water. Bringing Ty back to her.

His eyes stare, hollow, glassy and sightless from the shrunken well of his face. When Leyo transfers him into her arms, there is no cry of protest, not even a murmur of pain, and the thought that she's reached her son just in time to watch him die nearly buckles Claire.

Still, she cradles his weight and length, the physical feel of Ty's skin. His face is clammy, moisture beading around his neck and mouth. His shorn dark hair clings to his scalp, and his lips draw back in an unconscious grimace. The whites of his half-closed eyes are veined and yellow as ancient ivory. She presses her face to his sickness as if to drain it into herself, but except for the heart-stopping rasp of his breath, Ty does not respond.

Claire lifts her head and blinks as if she might wake to a different dream, but the heat, the exhaustion, the incessant swarms of insects and the continuing burn of venom in her arm belong to no dream state. The patch where they've taken cover is solid underfoot and screened from the water by liana vines.

Ward and Hari stand with their backs to her, guns raised on watch while Luke rummages in his pack. Naila and Leyo squat a few feet away.

They wrapped Ty's torso in soft green leaves. They greased his suppurated skin. They kept her son alive.

"How long," she whispers at last, "has he been like this?"

Leyo comes over and strokes the boy's forehead. The eyelids flicker and the hint of a smile relaxes Ty's mouth. "Eight days. The fever dropped only two days ago. Now this." He floats his palm above the visible rash and the loose poultice covering Ty's chest.

"Dengue," Hari breathes over his shoulder, but Luke's ahead of him, advancing with a tube of Prontosil and his canteen.

"If the fever is down, then infection is the next worry. That rash. Can we make him to swallow?" Luke asks.

Leyo nods to Naila, who approaches as if treading hot coals.

"Naila." Claire's throat aches with the effort of these two syllables, the confusion they engender, but the sound breaks the barrier between them, and in the next instant the girl lifts half Ty's weight and works her fingers along his neck until his teeth part and his tongue dances.

She signals Luke to administer first the water, then the pills.

"What have you been giving him?" Luke asks.

A muscle twitches in Naila's cheek. "Doctor Shep gave us medicine."

Claire stares at her. "Shep?"

Naila bends to her canvas rucksack—the same that Claire last saw in the breezeway on Marine Hill—and holds out a small clear vial for Luke's examination, but her hand shakes as she asks, "Did you hear him?"

Ty inhales sharply, shuddering, and Claire comes close to dropping him, but when in the next breath he yawns, the rolling pinkness of his tongue, those small white teeth, the familiar innocence of this unconscious reflex at once undoes and restores her.

She rubs the lobe of his ear and feels him surrender. "Hear him," she repeats.

"Ty Babu." The girl's weary young face lights with awe. "*Give us a kiss, old boy.*"

Ward turns back to them. "That was the *boy*?"

Naila and Leyo both nod. "This medicine." Leyo looks at the vial that Luke is inspecting. "It makes dreams to speak."

Naila kneels with her palms pressed in front of her heart and prostrates herself.

"Please. Don't. Get up." The words fall from Mem's mouth like glass beads.

"Please," she repeats more urgently when Naila fails to move. "Leyo, help her."

But it is the policeman, Major Ward, who insists. Slapping at his swollen neck. The same policeman that Naila has seen beating convicts in the streets of Port Blair. Now he would beat her.

"We'll all have dengue," he says, "if we don't get out of this hellhole." But he does not touch her.

She sets a hand on Leyo's knee to steady herself. The midday heat has turned the swamp into a buzzing cauldron, and she wants nothing more than to get out, but suddenly she realizes that the policeman is not talking about her. Or Leyo. Mem has just told her as much.

Major Ward and Mem both left Port Blair, then came back through all this danger to search for Doctor Shep and Ty Babu. Something has wounded Mem under that bandage. And now they care only for Ty.

You stupid, stupid girl. Doctor Shep died for her stupidity. Ty Babu yet could die. Perhaps Mem, too. And it is all Naila's fault.

The thin man named Luke is now treating Ty's rash, while Mem cradles her son's heel in her hand. The sole is so thickly calloused that Naila knows the boy can't feel her touch, but she also sees that Mem cannot stop herself from touching him.

"You're all coming with us," Mem whispers. Then she turns to Leyo and repeats, "A boat is coming. To take us to safety. All of us."

Naila's eyes well with hope, but Leyo's flare. He glances at Mem, then Naila, then out into the forest.

Mem turns abruptly to Major Ward, who is conferring with the small man named Hari. Mem says, "We can take them."

But the major replies as if Naila and Leyo were not there. "You've no idea what you're asking. Even if there were room."

"Captain van Dulm told me he never carries a full passenger load—in case he needs to pick up shipwreck victims. That's exactly what we have here."

"You're not thinking straight."

"I owe my son's life to these people."

Leyo shifts uneasily and motions with his chin. Ty's eyes have opened. His head has turned. The boy studies Naila as if trying to remember her name.

Her body tenses with the longing to hold him and with the equal effort now of holding herself apart. "Sorry." Her voice breaks, and tears coat her cheeks. She doesn't even know who she means to hear this.

"Don't," Mem says. "There's no need. You'll come with us."

Major Ward squints at the glittering swamp. "It's not up to me. If you want to take it up with the captain, be my guest. But first, we have to get to him." He turns back. "Leyo—that's your name, is it?"

Leyo's stunned expression has not left his face, and Naila realizes now the impossibility of Mem's order for him, even as he faces the policeman, who continues, "You know your way through the interior? How to get around the swamps and ridges and up to the coast above Constance Bay? The *fastest* way? Will you guide us?" The major glances at Ty Babu. "So, we can get him to safety."

Leyo winces at the *firenghi's* last words, but he nods his assent, and minutes later, after a brief discussion over the map, they're on their feet. Ty restored to Leyo's back, they slip deeper into the forest to the north, away from the swamp, away from Behalla now and from the danger of the Japanese. Together and away.

Their march back across the island goes so smoothly that Claire feels certain the Jarawa are watching over them. With each day both she and Ty get stronger. Healing, however, brings other challenges.

The child's return to consciousness makes him wary of strangers—his mother included. He clings to Leyo like a limpet, or rolls into Naila's arms. If Claire tries to hug him, he cringes. If she combs her fingers through his hair, he shakes her away.

He's still too weak to walk, and there have been no more outbursts, in his voice or anyone else's, but every so often she can hear a barely perceptible rumble deep in his throat, as if he were talking to himself. When she leans close and hums in his ear—Mozart's lullabye, "The Eensy Weensy Spider," "The Grand Old Duke of York," even "Goody Goody"—he does not bat her away.

"He will come, Mem," Naila promises.

The girl astounds her. One year has transformed her from child to young woman, from Indian to Biya, from victim to survivor. Now, in the deadening hours of their struggle over the island's central ridge and down toward the promised sea, as she watches Naila sometimes trailing and sometimes preceding Leyo and Ty but never more than an arm's length from them, Claire struggles to reconcile herself to these new impressions.

On the third day Hari stops in front of her. "Ahh." He throws his head back. "Can you smell?"

Twenty minutes later, she does. The ocean glimmers between the trees. The surf's hushed roar adds its bass to the symphony of the forest, and they can almost drink the scent of open water and clean, fresh air.

At moonrise, Claire and Ward stand surveying the beach that both pray will be their final campsite together. Contained at either end by rocky headlands, the white cove stretches in a shallow crescent for about a mile. The surf here is calm, a reassuring pulse. The sand looks undiscovered. No visible bunkers, no moored dinghies or passing launches. If all goes as planned, the sub will extract Bolger I around daybreak.

On the highest point above the beach, Claire and Hari set up the wireless and signal the ready code: *kada.* Luke and Ward climb out on the point and secure two white canvas signal squares where they can be spotted by periscope.

Meanwhile, Leyo and Naila distract Ty with a feast of beach plums, coconut, and sweet palm. When Claire rejoins them, she's stunned to see her son, who seemed near death just forty-eight hours ago, gnawing on his length of cane with gusto. And for the first time, in this loose talcum of light, she can see the new person he's become in her absence.

His skin is peeling and mottled and his energy still diminished, but he intermittently squirms and stretches his arms and legs, and she marvels at their length. The low tender catch of his breath and the barely audible hum of his throat still remind her, as they did in infancy, of the voice of a conch shell, but his scent has deepened, fused with Leyo's through their long hours, skin to skin. The two of them wear only breechcloths. Black and tan, they might be mistaken for father and son, Naila now more young mother than sister.

Claire sits on her hands to stop herself reaching out to all three of them.

When she and Naila look through the darkness at each other, their eyes fill with questions, but sound still must be kept to a minimum. There will be plenty of time for talk, Claire tells herself, when they are finally safe.

After everyone has eaten, they bury the remnants in the sand and move from the edge of the forest down to a cluster of date palms just below the headland. The half-moon makes this exposure risky, but they can't take the chance of waiting farther back, in case the sub arrives early. To avoid the visible profiles of tents, they dig sleeping pits in the beach.

When she looks up from this task Claire sees that Ty has fallen asleep in Leyo's arms. She signals him to lower the boy onto her bedroll, then motions for Naila to stretch out beside her, sandwiching Ty between them.

She takes Naila's hand, forming a bridge across her son's sleeping form. "Thank you," she says.

Above them, the palm trees shoot like black fireworks into the sky of stars. Naila gives her a squeeze and holds fast, and Claire remembers Ty swimming in the pool on Ross Island, stroking and kicking and coming up laughing. How Shep always caught him in confident hands.

The gales of delight. The miracle of peace. A man, a woman. Their glorious boy.

The sun rises behind the forest, stippling the sky with magenta and gold and turning the white beach black. Over a hasty breakfast of coconut meat, they kneel in the palm grove and scan the sea. The day brightens. The mist burns away. The surf grows louder with the rising tide, but there is no sign of the O-boat.

Ty rouses slowly but, once awake, grows restless. The swiftly climbing temperature makes the waves inviting. Ty paws at Naila's shoulder and glances distrustfully at Claire. When the girl places him on his feet he sways and starts to sink. Leyo catches him.

They are teaching him to walk again. Claire holds out her arms, but he spins away and instead grabs Leyo's knees. Without a sound, Leyo pries the boy's hands off, steadies and turns him. Claire will not look away. She will hold him with her gaze if nothing else. But though she can see his intelligence, she still cannot read his thoughts.

Abruptly Ty rockets sideways, intent now on making for the water. Leyo pulls him back, and the boy startles them all with a perfect trill that breaks the tension and sounds more authentically birdlike than any of Bolger I's calls.

Luke whistles and whispers, "We should have a contest to see how many birds he knows."

"Many," Naila replies with a smile.

"Absolutely not." Ward's reprimand bristles with exhaustion.

Claire notices the way everyone talks about Ty rather than to him. That much hasn't changed. But now Naila keeps her face averted from the boy, and Claire wonders if this is to avoid the silent exchanges that once excluded everyone else.

"Ty," she whispers. "Do you remember how to swim?"

He gives her a quizzical frown and paddles his arms in the air.

"Good," she says. "When the boat comes, we might need to swim to it."

Leyo nods as if her claim requires confirmation. Ty's gaze returns to the breakers below, but suddenly he raises his head. His face ignites as he looks down the beach.

Look! Claire hears his excitement, his innocence. She hears *him*, though he hasn't spoken aloud. *Bibi dogs!*

But she has no time to react. The others have followed his pointing arm and already are up in a crouch. From the far end of the beach two small black animals are charging along the water's edge, and fast on their heels come the crack of axes from the south end of the cove. A mile without cover is far too close.

Claire and Naila both reach for Ty and shrink deeper into the palm grove. When the boy squirms toward Naila, Claire lets go and turns to Ward for direction.

He has his field glasses trained down the forest. She angles her palm to shield the lenses from reflection. "Loggers," he says, still scanning. "Locals."

Then he draws in his breath. "Nips."

The wind is at their backs, and the dogs begin to bark. "Everybody, hold still," Ward says, but the animals keep coming. He glances at Claire, down at the boy, and his face stretches in a wholly new and terrible dimension of feeling.

Luke touches Ward's wrist. "Major." With the muzzle of his sten gun he indicates the other sten at Ward's hip.

Ward reads him. "Right. The rest of you, grab the packs and get ready to pull back up into the forest. Stay low but move quickly."

He glances at Ty, back in Leyo's arms and alert to the tension. "Not a sound. If they start coming, we'll create a diversion. Now, *go*."

The dogs already have halved the distance, and a dozen figures in mustard fatigues now jog in their wake. Leyo swings Ty onto his back and scuttles crablike from one leaning pillar of shade to the next. Naila and Claire follow, with Hari hesitating at the rear.

Ward lets them gain about twenty yards, almost to the gap between palms and forest. Then, as they pause there to gather their nerve, Claire hears a rifle shot down on the beach. Another, and she glances back to see Ward leap to his feet and plunge out into the open and down toward the water, screaming gibberish and kicking up clouds of white powder.

"Come on, you son of a bitch!" he yells, "Get your bloody ass down here and let's have this out once and for all!"

Luke releases a sob and springs after him, and the two men stand at the tideline with their weapons pointed—at each other.

Apparently, the tableau confounds even the dogs, now just a few hundred yards away, for the animals wheel back toward the soldiers. As Ward and Luke's farce escalates, Claire positions herself to shield Ty and Leyo, who are set to dash for the forest. Then a new round of gunshots sounds—this time coming in over the water.

A volley of loud pops, then a staccato of Bren fire.

"Wait!" Hari shouts behind Claire. "Come back! Quick! Quick!"

Naila glances back to find Hari hunching under his pack and madly, wildly, gesturing at the surf, where a shadow creature is rising, like a giant frog perched on the back of a porpoise.

"Come!" he cries again. "Now!"

He points past the many strings of smoke suddenly playing over the waves, and Naila watches in mystification as sunshine and a light ak-ak-ak ricochet off the water. The frog is spraying a chaos of pops and explosions at the dozen soldiers now running and falling backwards among the dogs along the beach. She can't see the men clearly from this distance, but she shares their astonishment and fear. *What is this beastly thing*?

Yelps from the closer, dying animals blur into the sputter of nearby gunfire. Luke and the policeman Ward have halted at the edge of the sea and are shooting over the dogs as they scream for Hari to bring everyone down to the water. Then the sky begins to pulse. Ty Babu's face flashes past, a sliver of brightness in a sandstorm, and Naila realizes as if in a spell that Leyo is running with him to the water. Only then, at last, does she, too, wake up and move.

When she reaches the surf, the shock of water braces her. Following Leyo, she dives under the swells, and her head ignites with the ammonia sensation of brine, the sting of salt in her eyes and skin. The tide takes over, yanking her down and folding her in, the force of Biliku raging. The cutting of wood infuriates the Biya goddess. So must this incessant noise, like steel cicadas beating the water. Naila rolls and is pummeled, the breath in her kneaded like dough, and when she comes up, Leyo kneels on the surface, Ty clasping his neck.

Looking up, she sees that the porpoise is really a huge metal shell, the frog a turret from which a fat gun keeps shooting, shooting back toward the beach. Her feet find the sandbar where Leyo and Ty and now Mem are waiting, but before she can pause, a voice yells, "Swim!" A high breaker bearing down on them.

They dive together, Naila staying close to Leyo, in case he loses hold of Ty. The blue-green water churns so thickly that her only directional clue is the pop-pop-pop of gunfire. They must swim toward the porpoise.

Then suddenly Ty is on his own, paddling in front of her. Like a long-limbed puppy, he paws the current, kicks at her face, and pulls himself forward and up. She pushes at his soles to propel him, and he turns his head. She sees the ring of his teeth from this angle, lit by sunbeams through water. He thinks she's playing. He comes up laughing, his hair a dark halo, like seaweed encircling his face.

The porpoise is a gray ghost now, the frog looming above them.

"Heads down!" The policeman Ward is treading water. Back along the beach, gunfire continues to send up puffs of sand around the bodies of soldiers and dogs.

"This way!" someone shouts. Leyo's shoulder glitters, and the swells lift into a roll, and then they are down below again where Biliku offers forgiveness.

Ty glides now between Leyo and Mem, each of them holding one hand, and Naila swims behind. She feels that she's watching some already ancient memory of herself.

Now when they surface, a man with orange hair and spotted skin reaches down to them from the frog's hatch. Leyo lifts Ty Babu up, and the boy in an instant vanishes. When the spotted man reappears, he beckons for Mem.

"You come next!" Mem yells at Naila. Then she grabs for those reaching arms, and she, too, is gone.

A cry lodges in Naila's throat. She glances back and realizes that Leyo has pushed away, as if to let the policeman and Luke and Hari go first, but Naila knows better. She knows the truth. She knows Leyo as he knows her.

She signals Hari to go ahead while she swims back toward Leyo. The submarine's throbbing surrounds them. In Leyo's eyes she reads both sorrow and offering, but there is no time. The policeman Ward and the gunner from atop the porpoise are the last to disappear.

No time to think. Only to feel, and what she feels makes her choice for her.

You, her heart speaks to Leyo. *You are my only home.*

Mha tumhare picche aye. I follow you, she cries aloud.

Dong abilak. I carry you, Leyo shouts in reply.

Their voices echo over the waves as they kick away from the metal beast, swimming alone and together.

Once down the ladder, Claire squats with Ty curled against her watching, waiting as first Hari, then Luke tumble in after them. Waiting for the others and for the adrenaline to stop. The midget's compartment has the capacity of a jeep, and with the Dutch crew, they're filling it quickly, but now the danger is over. They just need to squeeze a little tighter, make a few inches more room. Safe. All of them. *Safe.*

Ty's gaze is riveted on the top of the ladder, where Ward appears next, then the gunner's bare calves.

"Your arm," Luke says, and Claire glances down. The bandage is gone, her flesh a red tarmac of blisters and festering wounds, but before she can register any pain, a gasp from Ty thrusts her focus back up the ladder.

The gunner is in and pulling the hatch.

"Wait!" she cries. "Two more—"

Ty jerks away from her, staggering as the boat lurches into a dive. Eyes raised, he tries to push past Ward, but the gunner keeps turning the lock.

"Stop!" Claire raises her voice. "We can't leave them!"

Ward swivels into a crouch, blocking the child from the ladder. "They swam away," he says. "They didn't want to come."

"That's a lie!" She shoves him so hard that Ward falls backward, and Ty clambers over his chest, up the rungs, but already the boat is sinking. The gunner catches the child by the waist.

Ty's mouth forms an O, and the sound that emerges is a furious beating, like the wings of a butterfly trapped under glass.

Then the glass breaks, and he's howling, pounding, pounding against that sealed door.

"Naila!" He screams at the top of his lungs. *"Naila! Naila! Naila!"*

X

March–October 1943

They swam away of their own accord. Denis Ward swears it, and Claire has to believe. She holds Ty after his strength gives out and whispers into his ear. *"Molen thi ekjirake."* But her plea for forgiveness does nothing to console him.

Then, less than an hour later, the midget is reunited with the *O-24*, and something of a miracle occurs. Ty is still sobbing in her arms when Captain van Dulm receives them. "Here, then," he says. "You must be the boy that all the fuss is about." And the boy stops crying.

The captain has the imperturbable grace of a monk. When he lifts his eyes, Claire sees unveiled pain and joy. If Ty wanted, she knows this man would take him under his wing, never mind the demands of navigating enemy waters.

But Ty refuses to let go.

For all the fight in her son's eyes, all his terror and loss, and even though he barely knows her after all this time, she now is all he knows. So, while he won't let her bathe him, he nevertheless shrinks against her hip when the tattooed coxswain offers him a biscuit. He won't let her hug him, but he watches from her elbow as the sub's taciturn medic disinfects and tapes her forearm and injects her full of antibiotics. Ty won't let her kiss him, but he clings to her sleeve while the same medic examines him as Ward and Luke trade birdcalls.

Claire remembers how still and quiet Naila was with him, receiving and sheltering like a shade tree that always brought him back. At night when it was time for bed, she'd stroke her thumb across his forehead and extend her arm, waggling her fingers as Claire does now.

Ty lifts his grief-stricken eyes, his gaze quiet, and in a moment that seems to Claire to resound with grace, he slips his fingers into her pocket. She memorizes the sensation of his knuckles pressing through khaki into her thigh. *Dong abilak.*

Days unfurl as they wait to resurface. Ty comes up to her waist, frowns like a little man, still her son yet so changed, and she so foreign to him that a whole new distance appears between them. The difference now is that she knows better than to run from it.

Let the shower's warmth be enough to lure him. There being no clothes on the submarine small enough to fit, let Hari teach him how to fashion a dhoti from a muslin half-sheet. Let the boy's hunger announce itself, his curiosity distract him. Let him go but trust him to need her. And have faith against all odds that she will forever now be present when he does.

At night in their bunk she lets him lead. The captain has given them his quarters, his single bed, and Ty recoils from her, hugging the metal lip and turning his body away in the closeness. He shivers with the impulse of a thousand tantrums but seems instinctively to understand they will no longer bring him relief.

And softly she begins to sing. The same ditties from infancy that he accepted in the forest. He won't turn, but he grows quiet.

Then she calls up the stories. Fragments, really. *Remember the day Babar went to the beach and wore little crabs as earrings? That naughty Peter Rabbit, digging in Mr. McGregor's garden! Don't you think it's funny the way Ganesha rides a mouse?*

Each scene tugs them back to Ross Island, to his nursery, the veranda, the sitting room where Naila read him these tales at least as often as Claire did. As the words now penetrate Ty's mind, she can feel his breathing quiet, the resistence ebb from his shoulders.

Within seconds his sleeping body steals his will, and he wriggles into her. She sleeps at once on guard and more soundly than she has in years. Which means that the first time she hears him, she can't tell whether she's asleep and he awake, or vice versa.

It turns out to be something in between.

"Bol, Artam! Bol! Kha debe, jululu bidoteclao!"

He's running in his sleep and clutching the bedclothes. Syllables tumble, half murmurs, half shouts, and it takes Claire several minutes to realize these are fully formed words and pleas.

He's begging Artam to hurry. The ghost monster is coming. He's dreaming—and speaking—in Biya.

When awake, Ty remains as mute as ever and becomes irate if Claire tries to speak Biya. But one evening, in the wardroom after supper, when they find the captain sketching in his large white pad, Ty sidles over to sit where he, too, can reach the colored pencils.

An almost imperceptible signal passes between Claire and the captain, and within minutes Ty is drawing pictures like those Bolger I found the day they thought he was dead. Faces with petals large as elephant ears, curling tusks and open mouths. Winged blossoms like butterflies. Blue flower dragons.

Ty never lets go of her arm with his right hand. He sketches with his left.

Could she really have forgotten his left-handedness? Did she never even notice?

In the journal that Captain van Dulm provides, she saves the moments that seize her.

> *The miracle of his voice in the darkness, bright as mercury. A little boy talking in his sleep, some nights positively jabbering, others nearly wailing. I wrap him in my arms and press my ear to his throat. I don't want him to stop, but when he grows too agitated, I rub his earlobes as Naila used to do, and it soothes him.*

> *"We are your uncles," Hari and Luke say. "You can call us Chacha."*

> *Ty gives them a solemn once-over, from their scrubbed fingernails to their newly trimmed mustaches to the glossy black thickets of their hair. And nods.*

Surface. An open hatch. Dove gray sky and quicksilver clouds. On the bridge we stand eye level with the lunging swells. I wrap my arms around Ty, and he doesn't protest, but some of these men trot out over the deck as freely as lizards scurrying up a clay wall. In New York they call the Mohawks who build skyscrapers Skywalkers. I told the Captain he should call his men Seawalkers. He laughed and said so far, he was glad to have been able to call them all Lucky.

Turtle curry for supper. Ty tasted it first and stared at his bowl as if it could talk. The Tamil cook grew alarmed. I took a bite and reassured him, but it took me almost as long as it did Ty to go on eating. The last time we tasted these particular flavors we were still living on Ross Island and Jina had prepared this dish as a special monsoon treat.

Today is your birthday. I've told no one. Not even Ty. I want to. I want to bawl and scream and weep for you, but I cannot speak the words. I miss you, Shep, more than I can say. You would have been thirty-five today. How can you be gone?

They watch from the bridge beside Captain van Dulm as Ceylon thickens the horizon. The skies are murky, but clear of enemy bombers, as they've been the whole way across. The contours of their future are hazy, but free of imminent danger. The churn of the O-boat drenches them with spray, and Ty leans into it.

He wears a lifejacket, dhoti, no shoes. Hari's lessons in winding the dhoti intrigued him, but the steward's barber shears did not, so his wet hair falls in a scramble.

"Mowgli on the high seas," the captain says, cupping a hand to Claire's ear against the ambient roar.

The sensation of breath inside her head, compounded by the vibrations of engine and surf, makes it seem as if multiple voices are speaking. She clutches the straps of Ty's life vest, though the parapet rises to his shoulders.

"You too?" she asks the captain.

He shakes his head, puzzled.

"Kipling."

His gray eyes widen. "Guilty." A moment. "Why *too?*"

"My husband."

He glances at the promise of land, the ripples of brightness escaping the clouds. Sailors scamper from the forward hatches. The sea air shimmers with life.

"Guilty," Maikel van Dulm repeats, lowering both his hand and voice as if to dare the wind. She hears him, nevertheless. "And honored."

No drums roll. No bands play. No flag-waving crowds gather on the jetty.

"Remember." Denis Ward leans perilously close as the ropes are secured.

She's scarcely seen him the past two days, and now his pasty whiteness tells her why. Sweat glazes his jaundiced skin.

She repositions herself to lengthen the distance between him and Ty, who is scanning the wharf with the captain's field glasses.

"What is it?" she asks, gesturing at his face and weakened state with genuine concern.

"Never mind that." His voice wobbles. "Not a word about Balderdash to anyone outside the Executive. We'll doubtless be debriefed here, perhaps again in Calcutta. But otherwise—"

"I know, Denis."

"Yes, but now . . ." The vessel rolls over a breaker and he stumbles against the parapet.

Claire turns, in case Ty loses his footing, though the boy's agile as the sailors. The gangway is being positioned, and he's following every step of the process.

Ward is saying, ". . . a civilian, it makes no difference. Everything we did over there, everywhere we *went* is top secret."

A civilian. How bland and simple that sounds. Her chest constricts at the prospect, and she turns to Ward with a sudden welling of gratitude. His eyes are bloodshot, his lips chapped, his body bent with parasites that he must have been concealing for days, while saving her and Ty.

Here is a man who's always been more human than she acknowledged, who was never her enemy.

"Denis," she says, and rests her hand on his trembling shoulder. "I took the same oath you did."

But it isn't simple. Captain van Dulm was right that Ty is a modern-day Mowgli, and this makes them a spectacle. From MPs to rickshaw pullers, British lieutenants to Ceylonese dockworkers, everyone who catches sight of him gawks.

And the more they gawk, the more he glowers and hunches into himself.

Let him figure it out, she hears Shep counsel. *He's confused, not stupid.*

Van Dulm intercepts them before they cross the gangway. He points to a jeep at the end of the jetty. Ward hangs back with Luke and Hari, as if new lines have been drawn. The captain will accompany them, his uniform whites giving cover.

Steady on his feet, van Dulm takes Ty's hand and places a palm at Claire's back to brace them against their sea legs. As they step onto the pier, the gawkers part. Claire signals one last thank you to Denis and Luke and Hari, and the pang of grief that follows sears her.

"Galle Face Hotel," van Dulm instructs the driver.

He opens the passenger door for Claire to get in first, then Ty, and shuts the door before leaning in through the open window. "I have something for you," he tells Ty, who's drawn his knees up to his chin.

The boy scowls up at him.

The captain pulls from his pocket the binoculars that Ty dutifully returned to him on board. "There's a lot of world yet for you to see, Ty. The next time we meet I hope you'll tell me how it looks to you."

Without a sound, Ty takes the glasses, faces front, and fixes them to his eyes.

"Thank you," Claire says.

"Do you mind?" He rests his hand on the window frame. "I mean. Am I being presumptuous?"

She bites back a smile. "Captain, you once told me you could be your own worst enemy. I honestly can't imagine it."

"Maikel," he says, and reaches across Ty to touch her hand in parting.

As the car pulls away, Ty lowers the binoculars, turning to the street. Just tall enough to see out the window without getting up on his knees, he takes in the parade of bullock carts, bicycles, ambulances, and uniformed school children, tram cables running overhead like sideways kite strings. They pass a squat brick church with windows shaped in the same arch as the hoods that shade the carts. Some men wear turbans, some brimmed hats. Everyone, it seems, wears white khadi cloth and holds a black umbrella. The umbrellas float above the midday crowd like circular bats.

Not one of these images exists in the world where Ty has lived for the past twelve months. Even if he could speak, words would fail him.

All those hours when he was little, days of pointing, naming, shaping sounds he seemingly ignored. Would she make that mistake again? Was it a mistake? In so many ways they're starting over.

But not in every way. As the jeep approaches, the Hotel Galle Face's palatial edifice is dwarfed for Claire by the sight of two familiar figures, one tall and one short, seated on a marble bench by the entrance. With a dog at their feet.

"Ty!" she cries. "It's your uncle Roger and Aunt Viv."

As soon as the jeeps stops, Ty goes straight for the little Jack Russell. Eye to tan eye patch, boy and dog growl and whine and yip with immediate affection.

Viv grins. "This is Milly," she says.

"No." Ty enunciates ferociously and looks up as if he and his aunt have been having this argument for years. "Bibi."

Ty's voice emerges low and solid. How on earth, Claire wonders, did Vivian do it?

Playing through, Viv thrusts her lower lip in feigned consternation, then tosses a conspiratorial glance at Claire and Roger as she says in a plaintive voice, "All right. I guess since she's yours, you call her what you like."

Ty presses his cheek to the puppy's smooth coat as she licks his shoulder.

Is it the dog? More likely, it's the matter-of-fact way Viv addresses the boy, dares him, *gets* him—or gets his goat. As Naila did, but on a whole new level. Then again, maybe it's just time, after all he's been through, for the poor child to assert himself.

Or maybe, Claire thinks, she'll never understand. Be grateful, she admonishes herself. *Learn* simply to be grateful.

"Master stroke," she mouths.

Viv doesn't even drop her voice. "A gamble after what you told me about Wilkie."

"Wilkie?" Again, Ty speaks without the slightest hint of difficulty.

And again, Viv replies as if conversing with her nephew were the most natural thing in the world. "I heard how much fun you used to have with your old friend Wilkie, so I thought you might like having—um—Bibi around."

They all wait expectantly, but this seems to satisfy Ty for the moment, and he returns to dogspeak.

"So much for Top Secret." Claire laughs as Roger pulls her to him. "You two are always on hand to pick up the pieces."

But by the time Vivian hugs her, she's dissolved.

Steady on, darling. Shep rolls through her. *No apologies, no regrets. Off you go, then.*

May 25, 1943
Make Believe Cottage, Kalimpong

Dearest Mum and Dad,

Ty surrendered finally. The promise of a refuge called "Make Believe Cottage" did help, but really those daily triple-digit temperatures in Calcutta were unbearable even for him. So, we've at last beat our retreat to the hills, like so many "Ingrezi" of the Raj before us.

Roger and Viv wanted us to come with them to Simla, where most of the Government decamps during the "beastly months," but when I told Ty we could take a train up into the mountains, he immediately asked with great excitement, "Kalimpong?"

As you can imagine, every word that falls from his mouth is a jewel, so I sat up and took notice. How did this place come to be planted in his brain?

He insisted, "It snows in Kalimpong."

How did he know even what "snows" means? He folded his arms and thrust out his chin. "Naila said."

So that settled it.

Colonel Hastings, who's become a kind of godfather to us both, learned of this cottage with its magical name and made the arrangements with the old India hand who owns it. He also arranged for Nebu, my kindly bearer from Barrackpore, and his wife, Prana, to accompany us. And our beloved Bibi, of course.

You'd love this place, both of you. The smell of pine and evening woodsmoke, terraced tea plantations and racing glacial streams. The wild monkeys mesmerize Ty and drive the poor dog to distraction! But best of all are the Himalayas presiding snowily in the distance. Ty just stares and stares.

Our cottage is a Victorian confection with gingerbread trim and a red tin roof, rudimentary plumbing but furnishings so heavy and old, they create the illusion that time has no effect here. Would that it were so. By the time this letter reaches you, this place might be a distant memory, but I'm pretending we'll be here forever.

Meanwhile, of course, the war presses on, and in India it's gotten increasingly tangled with the fight for independence. Viv says that, unless we all wind up under the yoke of the Japanese, India is bound to become a democracy within months of war's end. It seems the shield of Empire is finally smashed, or at least too battle-scarred to keep polishing. Viv and Roger obviously are privy to information the rest of us mortals are not. I only hope that the letting go occurs peacefully.

On a lighter note, one of our unexpected pleasures is that Kalimpong's relative proximity to Calcutta may make it possible for Maikel to visit us here. His leaves in India may be few, but they matter enormously to both me and Ty. One way and another, we are building a new sense of family with Roger and Viv, Nebu and Prana and Bibi, Maikel and Colonel Hastings.

Nothing and no one can replace all we've lost, and Ty's exacting memory and moods assure me that he's not fooled by the surface calm of our life any more than I am. But we are mending. Little by little.

❧

He lurks behind the field glasses. In the garden. On the veranda. Across the road and down by the river. Kites and falcons, his targets.

He watches them rise and float on the updrafts, circling the sky, biding their time and sometimes hovering like malevolent stars, then diving at speeds of more than a hundred miles an hour to seize the prey they've been stalking from on high. A snake. A rat. A lizard. A newborn macaque or pye-dog. Always small, unsuspecting, and weak.

He can't see the kill but waits for the lumbering flight that follows, the extra muscle required in the wings, the dangling silhouette of a lifeless tail or paw or head skimming just above the trees. When at last he lowers the glasses, his face is calm and solemn as if to say, *That's why.*

And she wants to gather him into her arms then, to close his green eyes with kisses, to smooth the cool heel of her palm against his unsuspecting brow. Instead, she smiles and nods and extends her hand. Increasingly, he takes it.

Though he'll still go whole days or more without saying a word, she understands now that Ty is in constant communication, his voice working even when inaudible. Nightly he beats her at chess while humming along to the old records that came with the cottage's Victrola. Isham Jones and His Orchestra, Eddie Cantor, Al Jolson whistling "Toot, Toot, Tootsie (Goo' Bye!)" and Fanny Brice crooning "My Man". His perfect pitch has not waned, any more than his perfect recall of every melody he's ever heard.

Numbers, too, inform his language. They've brought a parcel of orchid roots and pseudobulbs from Shep's specimen trove to try growing at this elevation, and Nebu and Bibi help Ty pot and tend them in an open shed at the side of the house. Each day Ty counts the shoots and nodes and leaves. He records the counts in a small bound calendar that Maikel gave him. He also records his sightings of lizards, the time it takes a snail to cross the yard—any measurable progression.

When Claire joins him in his inspections, he sometimes rewards her with a cryptic remark.

"Five hawks, one nest. Rain."

"Tomorrow Bibi ate lizard for breakfast."

"That tree is too alone."

One morning in the bazaar as she's selecting mangos, Ty tugs hard on her arm. He points to a line of perhaps a dozen little boys and girls trudging silently through the mist down to the train terminus. A spry gray-haired European woman leads the line, and a morose Indian youth in white livery brings up the rear. The children wear maroon and gray uniforms, hold each other's brown hands. None is older than Ty.

With rare urgency he asks, "Where's their ma and pa?"

Claire touches his small square shoulders. "I don't know."

She has to fight to steady her voice. "Maybe they're waiting at home."

All these weeks, like the years before, he calls her nothing. He knows various words. *Ma. Amimi. Mother.* None seem to fit her. Not yet anyway.

For now, it has to be enough that he'll grip her hand or speak to her at all. Trust grows between them like spider silk, in microscopic gasps. And with the swell of the monsoon she fears that confinement will strain these tender filaments.

Fortunately, most of his books survived the evacuation, and Ty has lost none of his affection for them. On afternoons when the gorge fills with fog they curl up indoors with Bibi and read their way through *Babar* and *The Story About Ping. Caps for Sale. The Wind in the Willows. Now We Are Six. Peter Pan. Mary Poppins.*

At first Ty reads along under his breath, and she pretends not to notice. Then one day he reaches up and places his palm across her mouth.

Once she is mute, he picks up from the exact point where she left off.

From then on, he does all the reading, his new voice half growl, half song. Consonants still don't come easily, but she knows better than to correct him. He has his own timetable, his own peculiar and miraculous ways of knowing.

In September they're granted a day's reprieve from the rains that have lashed them for nearly three months, and Ty makes straight for the garden. Claire finds him alone, hugging the fence and looking out to the end of the gorge, beyond the Teesta Valley and the yellow plains.

Ty turns his torso clockwise until he can look between the fence rails with his head upside down. When she asks what he's doing, he answers, "This way the sky is sea."

He stretches one arm through the fence. His palm rises and falls. "I see Naila."

He waves again. "I see her. She says hello."

Neither of them wants to leave the hills, but by mid-October the rains have ceased, temperatures are dropping, and the worst of the mudslides have been cleared from the passes. Regular train service is now restored, but in another month, they could be snowed in.

Besides, Colonel Hastings has promised Claire a riverside bungalow and a place at the local primary school for Ty, if she'll return to the Signal Centre. Another Bolger team is due to depart—absent Ward, who's still in and out of hospital with the parasitic ailment he contracted during the first expedition—and her codework was so successful that Hastings wants the new team, as well as others in Burma, to use it.

Also, Claire thinks, it's starting to feel as if she and Ty actually are playing make believe. *The war hasn't stopped just because I've lost a husband and reclaimed my son*, she writes Viv. *I can still make a contribution. We have you and Roger back in Calcutta. And Ty's six now and needs to be in school with other children.*

Her sister-in-law replies simply, *Come.*

This next step is anything but simple for Ty, however. He still teeters on the brink between verbal expression and intuition. Claire's fear is that he'll be pushed off this precipice repeatedly and brutally at school. But what alternative is there?

Their interview with the school's headmaster takes place in an office whose shelves are lined with Darwin's Geological Observations and botanical treatises. Mr. Holcomb, a starved-looking Welshman, folds his yellowed hands and tilts his head like an egret as the young American widow strains to explain her son's unpredictable intellect, passions, habits, and history.

"Ty's not so different from his father," Claire says, as if this revelation will mean anything to a man who knows nothing of her husband.

Ty, who's been reviewing the summer's entries in his bound calendar, looks up inscrutably and blinks.

"Can you tell me, young man," Mr. Holcomb asks, "what you'd like to learn in school?"

Ty's gaze slides sideways to a large black ceramic pot from which a chartreuse plant climbs a bamboo pole to the ceiling. A trapezoid of orange light reaches into the office from the west, and the philodendron's broad heart-shaped leaves arch as if trying to drink the color. Ty points with one arm toward the pleading foliage, with the other toward the light.

Then he brings his two pointers together and says plainly, "Why?"

Mr. Holcomb rests his chin on his knuckles and studies his prospective student for several long seconds. When he turns at last to the boy's worried mother, the headmaster's eyes have gone glassy.

"It's all right," he says softly. "Bound to be a few hiccups with the others, but I'll look out for him."

December 1943

Three o'clock now. Measured hours. Soon there will be company. Cedar boughs drape the doorway. Red and white poinsettias seem to amplify the scents of cardamom, mace, and cinnamon drifting from the kitchen, and a small live sprig of casuarina shimmers in the corner.

Shep's service medallion, a Burma star polished to a fare-thee-well, crowns the little tree. Tiny ornamental cones stud the tinseled branches, and red and green ribbons suspend colored pictures of orchids, each one drawn and labeled by Ty's exacting hand.

Claire turns in the saffron light flooding through the window and locates Ty out by the banyan tree that canopies their new gate. His slight frame stands erect, binoculars trained on a silver Lysander lifting off from the nearby aerodrome. His lenses, Claire knows, melt the distance. He can count the Lizzie's struts and read the pilot's face, recognize in its complete concentration an aspect of his father, of himself.

Ty has studied the principles of flight. He reads the wobble of the ear-like wings as the plane twists upward into and through the slanting rays. Lazily the plane threads the clouds, climbing and floating on the updrafts as if in an avian dream.

The pivot comes without warning, the dive almost equal to a falcon's. One dizzying swoop, and Ty waits, so motionless in his silence that his mother can feel his held breath suspended in her own heart.

Then the flier catches himself and, unburdened, rises again.

Number 3 Riverside is their third residence in eight months if you count their first weeks at the Fairhaven, and the fourth if the Galle Face suite they shared with Viv and Roger qualifies. But these days everyone's a nomad. Within his first week at school, Ty had outstayed his rank as

New Boy. Within a month he was no longer the only boy who'd survived evacuation into the jungle. Twin brothers arrived who'd been orphaned during the trek over the mountains from the Hukaung Valley.

After their French parents died, the twins were borne along by Anglo-Indian neighbors, then deposited with a Parsi aunt. The ordeal left the seven-year-olds mute and withdrawn, and the rest of the class initially shunned them, as they had Ty—as if they were contagious. Mr. Holcomb said Ty was the only one who would even approach the twins, and he did so silently, signing with his hands a covert message that won a nod. Soon the three had their own gestured language, which made the other boys want in. The twins and Ty all started talking then, rather than give their secret away. Unfortunately, the Parsi aunt decided that Marc and Jean-Louis would be better off with their French cousins in Pondicherry. They left last night.

Claire flicks on the Philips and spins the dial until the static clarifies. "Canadian First Division has surrounded Ortona, cut off German retreat, and is currently engaged in a savage battle with house-to-house fighting."

She spins again as if gambling, and lands on a slide trombone. Tommy Dorsey. But a moment later the power cuts out.

She's too ready. The table is set with bowls of white waterlilies. Prana is putting the finishing touches on her best mutton bindhiwala. Nebu has polished the tin cutlery as if it were fine silver. Ty's even submitted to long pants and a sweater vest, and Claire herself is done up in a fitted green raw silk number, combed and rouged and slippered like a teenager on her first date.

Who's she kidding? The corrugated scars on her forearm, the diamonds from Shep winking in her ears, are all it takes to set her straight. She might be twenty-eight, but she's twenty-eight going on eighty.

Only when she turns back to the window and watches Ty bend down to rub foreheads with Bibi do the numbers truly gladden her. A decade more and the war would have pinned him again in its crosshairs. Viv has written about such boys, fresh off relief ships from Singapore and flung into uniform on the eve of their seventeenth birthdays. Not all of them reluctant.

But not Ty. God willing, never Ty.

Bibi's barking crescendoes outside and the grackles fling themselves skyward as Roger's clattering green Austin turns in the drive. Claire gets outside just as he and Viv and their terrier Billy are greeting Ty under the porte cochère. The dogs, already well acquainted, take off in circles, and the driver heads for the nearby car park spewing diesel and dust. Roger comically waves his arms as if drowning in the mayhem.

Viv, as usual, drops to Ty's level before asking if she might hug him. He nods gravely, then hugs her back, and when she lets go, he's smiling at whatever she's whispered in his ear. Viv and Roger he calls *Chachi* and *Chacha,* as he does all his honorary aunties and uncles.

Claire is collecting her own embraces when Colonel Hastings and Mr. Holcomb arrive, their bicycles stretching long shadows across the sunlit drive. They look like aging brothers, both raw-boned and a little florid. Shep and Ty have brought them together. Though neither has time to spare, they somehow manage to eke out several hours a week with Ty poring over Shep's notebooks, identifying the plants he referenced, and transcribing his findings and formulae so they can be verified at the Medical College.

Now Mr. Holcomb pulls a handful of peppermints from one pocket and two whips of goat jerky from the other. The dogs go into a frenzy over the dried meat, but he holds it over their heads and delivers the candy to Ty before demonstrating how young Bibi and Billy must be trained to sit and lie down before receiving their reward.

The adults applaud, but Ty stands with his peppermints, scowling.

"What is it, Ty?" Colonel Hastings asks.

"It's not fair."

"What isn't?"

Ty lifts his cupped hands, the red and white candy. "You don't make me do tricks."

Mr. Holcomb bends from the waist. "I beg your pardon, Ty, but I watch you do the most extraordinary tricks every time we're together."

Ty's not convinced, but Roger squeezes his shoulder, the dogs get their treats, and the tension of injustice ebbs as everyone moves inside.

Claire composes a hostess voice. "When everyone's got a drink, what say we go straight to presents? Ty, would you hand them out?"

She points. "Start with that one. The tag will tell you who it's for."

He gets up from the dogs a little grumpily. Two years without Christmas, and he's lost the taste for it. "But it says Ty."

Laughter circles the room. He eyes the package with suspicion, and Claire reads his mind. He can tell it's not a book, which he would enjoy, and the size and weight of the box are just about right for a new pair of leather shoes, which he'll refuse to wear.

"Oh, for heaven's sake!" Viv cries in exasperation. "Open it, Ty!"

But suddenly the dogs raise their heads and spring for the front door. A second later Maikel van Dulm appears, cap in hand.

"Any room at the inn?" he jokes.

Claire sets down her glass. "But how—"

"Top secret!" The captain turns with a bow to the others. To Ty he extends his hand.

Instead of shaking it, Ty gives him the present.

"Shall we open it together?" The captain folds himself down on a footstool while Ty drops cross-legged beside him.

"You didn't!" Viv exclaims as the tissue falls away, and the circular red and white emblem on the box presents itself. "You extravagant mother, you!"

Viv is the only one who recognizes the logo, though. "Isn't *Leitz* a German name?" Colonel Hastings muses.

Ty still hasn't reacted. He's studying the curled script, the skaterly swoop of the lower stroke of the L inside the white circle. Nothing happens in a hurry for Ty. Not if he can help it.

"It's a 1937," Claire reassures the officials in the room. "From Biswas in Crawford's Market. You know how things are there, never used and never new."

"It's all right, Claire," Roger assures her. "Even if it was smuggled yesterday, it's not strictly c-c-contraband if it's coming *out* of Germany."

"And like it or not," Viv says, "the Germans have no equals when it comes to cameras."

Ty swivels to stare at his aunt, and Viv claps her fingers to her mouth. "Oops!" She hoists her eyebrows like a silent film star. "Did I give it away?"

Ty gets down to business now with considerably more enthusiasm. Claire has watched him watching his aunt crank her Rolleiflex, adjust the dials, and finger the shutter button. The expression on his face last month, the first time he stared down into the aqueous images playing across the viewfinder, reminded her of the way he gravitated all those centuries ago to the lion and the lamb in the library on Ross Island.

Unfortunately, Viv apologized, the prohibitive cost of film stock and development took photography out of the realm of child's play. But Claire decided in that moment, rationing be damned.

Ty takes the streamlined Leica from the box and palms the leather and metal framework, studies the glass eye.

"It's more your size than a Rollei," Claire says. "It'll fit in your pocket. You can carry it with you."

"Is it loaded?" Viv asks. "There's still enough light out, if we go quickly."

"A group portrait!"

"Capital idea!"

"Your first photo, Ty! Just think!"

The kindness these people shower on her son.

Viewfinder glued to his eye now, Ty lets Maikel raise him up and Roger guide him out the front door like a blindfolded birthday boy toward his surprise. But he has his prize in sight the whole time: The marbled pink clouds above the treeline; the shadow-striped lawn. A full moon, like a wafer of bone, suspended high in a china blue sky.

"Nebu and Prana," he calls out, suddenly in command. "You too."

Viv reminds the boy about shutter speed and resolution, helps him correct the f-stop and adjust the lens as the others arrange themselves facing west.

"But he won't be *in* the picture," Roger suddenly realizes, and Viv tells him to hush.

The captain steps from Ty to Claire. He smells of shaving soap and wool, and she lets herself lean into him. "It's perfect," Maikel whispers. "You know him so well."

She shakes her head. "If only." But she's smiling.

Ty stands, eye to camera, elbows out like wings. His mouth opens, tongue unconsciously probing incisors as the party of adults arrange themselves, and the dogs flop down in front.

"All right, Ty," Viv calls out. "Quick now, light's fading."

But in that moment a cloud shifts, like a curtain being drawn back. The garden is bathed in sudden, incandescent gold. The air quickens, electric with such a mystical concentration of life that they all look up, bedazzled.

And that is how Ty captures them, grinning at the unseen director just above his head.

XI

October 1945

Code name 'Popcorn' offers a deceptively upbeat label for reoccupation, like a postwar reference to innocuous pleasures: a mission in a wish. Unfortunately, the flagship *SS Dilawara*'s depar-
ture was delayed for nearly two months after armistice, following by a full
two weeks the mercy ship sent to Port Blair in September. As frustrated
as Claire was by this postponement, which officials blamed on monsoon
conditions and the priority given to reclamation of Burma, Indonesia,
and the Malay Peninsula, Roger and Maikel credit it, along with the invisible influence of Colonel Hastings, for their success in slipping Claire
and Ty onto the passenger manifest.

From the start, Operation Popcorn included Roger in the delegation
of government and military brass assigned to witness Port Blair's official
handover. The ship would also carry reoccupation forces, plus a host of
press and newsreel photographers, Viv among them, to cover the belated
ceremony. In fact, it was Viv who devised the winning case that Colonel
Hastings passed up the chain of command: the power of the press de-
pends on the power of narrative, and what better story could there possibly be to dramatize the human toll of war—and the moral superiority
of the victors—than the return of the last civilians to escape from the
islands, a war widow and her son embodying the restoration of peace.

"We laid it on a little thick," Viv admits as she and Claire stand on deck
watching the Indian mainland shrink. "You'll forgive me."

Claire thumbs the gold wedding band, which she's resumed wearing
for a whole web of reasons, not the least of which is a recurring dream in
which Shep stands on Phoenix Bay Jetty to welcome her home.

"Claire?"

"I know this is the right thing to do. I owe it to Ty and to Shep, and maybe especially to Naila. But I'm terrified."

It sounds idiotic even to her own ears, after all they've been through, but Shep's sister seems to understand. "That's why we're doing it together."

"There you are!" Roger and Ty come at them, race walking down the aft deck. Roger has stride in his favor, but Ty beats him with velocity, arms pumping as if the camera permanently attached to his left hand were pulling him forward.

"Whew!" Roger pretends to wipe the sweat from his brow. "You p-put an old man to shame, lad."

"There's a darkroom on board! Come see, Mum. They said I can help!"

"Play your cards right," Viv says as she bends in a conspiratorial whisper, "and I bet they'll let you make some prints of your own."

Claire recalls her son's wonder the first time they stood together in the dark room in Barrackpore watching her face resolve beneath the surface of developer. *It's you, Mum, look!* And just like that another barrier fell.

"Excuse us." Claire leans back and kisses Viv's cheek. "Yes, I do forgive you."

They were also in the darkroom seven weeks ago, their third summer at Make Believe, when Nebu shouted the news outside.

"Memsaab! Ty Babu! War is over! War is over!"

She stood inside that Martian glow, unable to move. They'd been expecting, of course. Hoping. Hitler had been dead since April, the war in Europe over since May, but in Asia the fighting seemed to have spiraled beyond anyone's control, island to island, sea to sea, the geography of battle incalculable. Yet Nebu kept shouting, soon joined by Prana's interrogation, their excitement whirling into Hindi.

Imperturbable, Ty pulled from the fixer the last print of a series he'd shot of light and bird formations at sunrise and sunset over the Teesta Valley. Tears coated Claire's face as she scanned the majestic images.

War is over! War is over! Ty would not be rushed or distracted, but when they'd finished clipping the print to the drying line, the first words out of his mouth were, "Can we go home, now the war's over?"

The days that followed confronted them all with the horror of the particulars. Incineration. Vaporization. Erasure. Human beings reduced to featureless negatives in pavement and stone.

In India, Japan's ghastly defeat only intensified the drumbeat for independence, the white race's use of the "cruel bomb" against their Asian brethren adding moral gravity to the perceived heroism of Indian National Army leaders who'd sided with Japan and now sweltered in prison under the British authorities in Delhi.

Inquilab Zindabad! Do or Die! Quit India! As the firestorms of resentment escalated throughout the country, foreign civilians and military personnel schemed, fought, and bribed their way onto any seaworthy vessel out.

Come home, Claire's parents' now frequent and unstoppable letters pled. But America never was Ty's home.

The cameras begin rolling with their first glimpse of land. The sun has just risen, and its dimpled shafts hit the eastern coast of the Andamans lengthwise, giving the beaches and forest the appearance of a long empty stage flat.

The shoreline doesn't stay empty for long, however. Shabby thatched villages and encampments appear every few miles, and though most look abandoned, Ty points his lens at each new cluster asking, "Is that it?"

Claire shakes her head, no. Not Behalla. Not Port Blair, either. All of these structures have been built in the two and a half years since they left.

She has to remind herself over and over that Ty has no memory of this vista. The O-boat didn't surface until the islands were long out of view. It's this approach today that he'll remember for the rest of his life—a sequence of impressions scarred unmistakably and irrevocably by war.

The morning light lands hard on the low square bunkers that guard every significant harbor. Around these inlets much of the terrain has either been denuded of timber or cratered by Allied bombs, or both. They also pass the beached wrecks of minesweepers and picket boats, and as they near Port Blair, they begin to see ghostly figures of survivors wandering the shore.

The prow of Mount Harriet has just risen in the distance when the *Dilawara* is met by a flotilla of small blue boats rowed by cadaverous men dressed in tatters. Their chests and cheeks are sunken, arms like switches.

"How could they starve?" Viv asks. "These waters must be teeming with fish."

"Mines," Roger says. "No petrol for the outboards. And I'll w-wager the Japanese had a zero-tolerance policy for any local who kept his ca-catch for himself."

"But the Japanese were defeated two months ago."

"You think these fellows know that?"

The haggard faces turn up to them, fingers to lips in the universal gesture of hunger. They're rewarded with a rain of cellophaned sweets and compo rations pitched from the stern of the ship. The men swarm and dive, elbowing each other out of the way in competitive frenzy.

Ty laughs at the spectacle. Of course. To him it looks like a game.

"They're mainlanders," Claire says. "Former convicts. They've no idea how to hunt or forage, or fish, for that matter, without manufactured equipment."

Silent in this remark is her prayer that the native Andamanese have escaped the fate of these villagers.

Beneath her hands, Ty's shoulders twitch in anticipation, but the clouds to the south are darkening. The air grows thick and heavy, and distant lightning etches the sky.

The shoreline, too, begins to change. The beaches, gray with dead coral, look as if they've born the brunt of successive meteor showers. The bunkers multiply, and larger concrete fortifications mark strategic cliffs. The North Point lighthouse appears unscathed, if lightless, but virtually every other visible structure has been destroyed. Roofs gape open. Walls lean sideways. Dense black plumes of smoke rise from beachfront pyres.

Then Ross Island appears portside, green and wild on the rising tide, not a soul in sight. Claire looks away, grateful that Ty has his camera trained on the harbor ahead.

A hush descends as the *Dilawara* nears Phoenix Bay. The crown of the prison has held its shape atop Atlanta Point, but like the boatmen, the populace crowding the jetty and foreshore hardly look human. The whitish gray light only adds to the ghoulish effect of eyes sunk back in their sockets. Arms and legs poke like twigs through faded rags. A few children wave, but they too look shell-shocked, their skin drumtight over stunted bones.

Claire draws Ty against her.

"What?" he asks looking up and out, but the scene, for her, defies description.

Thunder cracks and the light turns electric as the square in front of Phoenix Bay Jetty fills with uniformed men in surreal formation. They wear either tan khaki drill or dark blue sailor uniforms and stare straight ahead with robotic discipline. On the jetty, apart from the others, two Japanese officers stand at attention, arms raised in salute, their white gloves bright as flags.

Claire turns the band on her finger round and round and round. Ty has the enemy commanders in his viewfinder. Her impulse to stop him wars with his clear desire to shoot and capture them. Finally, she untethers her arms from his neck and steps back.

The men on the jetty represent the enemy, but according to Roger these commanders have been here only since '44.

Brigadier General Salomons, in his own full-dress regalia, receives the officers' salute from the bow of the *SS Dilawara*. As commander of Operation Popcorn, Salomons is charged with officiating over tomorrow's formal surrender and, more broadly, with rounding up the Japanese troops and collaborators who remain throughout the Andaman and Nicobar Islands. The cameras follow his martial strut as he makes his way down the jetty to receive his prisoners.

The civilians on board, whose presence the General has done his best to ignore, are instructed to wait to disembark until he and his men have interned the Japanese outside of town. It's mid-afternoon and raining hard by the time Roger helps Claire and Ty off the tender.

Instantly, they're mobbed. Hands reach out to shake and touch them. Voices cry in recognition. "Doctor Memsaab!"

Faces made alien by shock and deprivation appear and disappear, many weeping. *Mister Dass Pati Pandit Ali Nabi Bux Appalswamy Mister Chengappa Dahwood Jan . . .* The names wash over, eyes and mouths moving in and out, blurred to gray by the downpour, streaming with need, insistent and desperately strange.

Claire grips Ty's hand and pulls him close under their umbrella. Viv already is out among the survivors, talking and listening, inhaling their stories.

For Claire it's too much, too fast, but Ty's excitement matches his aunt's. Eight now and strong, he strains against her with a ferocity she hasn't felt since he was four.

She thinks of Kim, whose story they've read together twice in the past year, the story Shep loved as a boy. If she let go of Ty in this moment, he'd fly out like Kim among these people, into this world, and he'd find his way. She knows that now about her son, but what he can't know, has no possible way of comprehending, even with his extraordinary mind, is that these people are in no condition to receive him.

"Stay close, Ty," she says. "We need to get out of the rain. As soon as it stops, we'll go out and explore." She squeezes his hand, their signal a vow.

He looks up, and she registers his impatience.

She squeezes again. *Trust me.*

He has his father's quiet regard then. He nods, and as they continue through the tattered, fetid crowd she tries to imagine his experience of this homecoming. The smells of abject poverty and hopelessness are new here. Piles of raw sewage line the streets, and the stink of rotting garbage mingles with the pervasive odor of sickness and death. She quails against the stench, but Ty sniffs the air as if the malignance were a minor irritant.

And then she smells what he's after, that still familiar mist of brine and forest, irrepressible life overlapping decay. He inhales and closes his eyes.

A jeep, just off the ship, pulls up, Viv already inside, and they pile in for the bone-clattering ride up through Aberdeen Bazaar, which has become a miserable caricature of its former self. More than half the street's paving stones are gone. The shop fronts sag, crumbling and faded, broken windows of the surrounding buildings not even papered over—where would anyone find a luxury like paper?

But then, just ahead, the cool broad edifice of the Browning Club appears through the mist, and the jeep makes a herky-jerky beeline for it.

The Japanese must have used this compound for their officers. The once rose-colored walls have been whitewashed, patched, and the garden let go, but the open corridors receive them just as they did after the earthquake four years ago. A few of the club's original servants are still on hand. They salaam as Claire and Ty enter.

Ty stares at them. Then, without warning, he yells. "Naila! *Naila!* NAILA!"

The cry fills the courtyards, soars through the rain. Eyes wide and expectant, body taut with anticipation, he peers down the corridor, into the dining room, off toward the stairs.

Claire sees his misunderstanding. This house represents reunion. He remembers staying here with Naila. He thinks his voice can hasten his wish. Before she can console him, however, he reads her face.

"Where is she?"

"I don't know," she says. "I hope with Leyo and Kuli. Remember, Ty, she's no idea we've come back to find her."

"In the forest?"

"I don't know. We'll go there to look for her as soon as it's safe. But first we need to ask if anyone's seen her here in town." She thinks. "It's like a puzzle, Ty. We have to gather clues before we can find her."

"Like Kim and his lama."

She speaks over the knot in her throat. "Yes, Ty. Like Kim's search for his Holy One. Exactly."

He accepts the rules of this game then, as he always accepted the rules of the games that Naila laid out for him, and they follow the others into the room that used to be the club library.

The shelves have been denuded, the comfortably overstuffed furniture and teak armoire that once graced it replaced by splintering camp chairs on which they are urged to sit. Roger has invited a group of local citizens in to tell their stories, and they squeeze tightly, creating a steam of warm wet bodies, everyone talking so urgently that Roger holds up his palm. "Speak slowly, one at a time."

They are men and women and a few older children, harrowed but also lit with fury. Claire searches their faces, recognizing none.

So many horrors, so many deaths, but the worst, they say, came just months ago. Had anyone known, it was only days before the Japanese defeat.

Everyone in Port Blair was starving. Men had been set on fire for stealing a teaspoon of sugar or rice. Fishing—even setting foot on the beach—was forbidden, except in the company of armed guards who confiscated all catch. All the bullocks and water buffaloes, even elephants had been slaughtered for food. Hindus were made to kill the last cows, and cultivation ceased. So, when an offer was made to resettle families and let them fend for themselves on Havelock Island, more than seven hundred men, women, and children volunteered.

They filled three ships and sailed at night, but before they reached shore the guards set upon the passengers with *lathi*s and *dha*s and flung them into the sea. Then they opened fire. Those who couldn't swim drowned. Those who could swim were shot or mangled by the ships' propellers. The returning Japanese sailors swaggered back to their quarters, boasting that no one had survived.

The excitement of outrage heats the room as rain shellacks the windows. No one knew when the war ended! The Japanese admitted nothing! The voices again rise out of control.

Roger promises that General Salomons will dispatch a search party to Havelock tomorrow. Then he asks for names of the missing.

Cacophony.

Ty shouldn't hear this, Claire thinks, and yet she can't move. The other children in the room have lived through these nightmares. Naila might well have succumbed to them. How else to explain to him? What are the rules?

Ty, for his part, ignores the hysteria. In his own focused fashion, he is approaching each of the strangers individually for clues. But no one here knows or has heard of Naila.

About an hour of daylight remains when the rain lets up. The air has turned soft, a pale melon color, its human stench rinsed by the downpour. Food distribution is proceeding in a godown near the main jetty, so they have this side of the ridge pretty much to themselves, except for the new guard of Indian MPs, stationed at every major intersection.

The captain of the first mercy ship told Roger that Shep and Alfred Baird had been cremated, their ashes buried in the Gymkhana Cemetery. It will take just a few minutes to walk there. The decision to go is made without discussion, the destination a foregone conclusion, and yet Claire can't seem to pull herself together. Her hat. Her shoes. Her notebook. Does she need her notebook to visit her husband's grave? And what does she tell her son?

She tells him, "We're going to see where your daddy's buried."

And Ty, being the child he is, says, "Yes, I know. Let's go, Mum."

Roger strides ahead with Ty, leaving Viv and Claire to their own pace. Banyans and mangosteens grow thick along the upper reaches of the Gymkhana grounds, and the uncut grass seems more alive than anything Claire has seen since they landed. A bank of crepe ginger tilts its many red heads beneath white petals like parasols. The Biya used the rhizomes of this plant to treat fever, rash, asthma, and snakebite, but Shep's early researches found that the Kama Sutra also recommended it as an eyelash enhancer. One night while Claire was still pregnant, he brought a bunch of these glowing flowers up to the bedroom on Ross and daubed a bit of the sap on his forefinger, then gently, gently painted it onto her lashes. She feels the sensation now and watches him leaning back, naked in the moonlight to study his handiwork. *Ravishing.* She guffawed at his heart-throb delivery, but then he did. Beach ball belly and all. Ravish her.

"You all right?" Vivian asks. "We could do this tomorrow."

"No. I'm fine." She pats Viv's hand on her shoulder, gives it a squeeze. "I couldn't live with myself if we waited."

"Me neither."

Up ahead Roger and Ty have found the gate, where a boy just a little older than Ty and an old man sit in attendance. They wear shredded gray sarongs and look hollowed out by the questions Ty asks. Claire reads their answers in their dipping chins and wavering hands. Maybe they remember long ago seeing two who matched Naila's and Leyo's descriptions, but not since the Japanese. So many have disappeared.

Ty seems to take their responses in stride and makes his next request. The watchman's boy has a lazy eye that keeps drifting toward the setting sun, but he grins obligingly.

When Claire and Viv catch up, Ty's made his portrait and is lowering his camera. The boy helps his grandfather up, and both bow their heads to Claire.

"Doctor Memsaab."

She salaams and searches for words. These two have survived. Gravediggers? Watchmen? What did they do—or not do—to still be here?

Easy, old girl. Shep's caution brings her up. *Since when is survival a crime?*

Since you died, she thinks savagely.

And what does that make Ty?

He has her. He always will.

The old man's face is pitted from smallpox, his body beaten by more than age, but he straightens with authority as he leads their procession into the cemetery, which one way or another has become his pride. They pass the prewar gravestones and arrive at a patchwork of mud and grass beneath a large banyan tree. Each plot here is marked with a rudimentary wooden stake, carved initials and dates. No crosses. No stones. No epitaphs.

The boy translates his grandfather's apology, explaining that the Japanese allowed no funerals or reverence for the Christian dead. Burial alone required much *baksheesh* and had to be kept secret.

They stand before two stakes that read, SD 5-5-1942 and AB 5-5-1942.

Claire wonders what she'd expected. Her husband's ashes lie in the ground in front of her. Shep and Alfred suffered together an experience that, even before it killed them, would have taken them to a realm beyond her imagination. Like all the victims of this war, they have disappeared, and she feels no closer to them standing here than she did looking out from Make Believe at Ty's upside-down ocean.

And yet, there is a kindness about this darkening place that makes her grateful.

Ty and Viv are struggling with the light settings on Ty's camera. Vivian weeps as she works, making Roger kneel as a human tripod, so Ty can steady the Leica on his head and lengthen the exposure. The lazy-eyed boy watches, enthralled.

Claire turns to the old man and asks in Urdu, "Who brought my husband's ashes here?"

Leaning on his stick, he starts visibly at the sound of his language in her voice, but it doesn't take him long to remember. "Abraham Chakraborty."

"Abraham!" The last man she expected. "Are you certain?"

The grizzled beard sways right and left.

Freed from his tripod duties, Roger comes over, brushing off his knees. "What is it?"

"We owe Shep's burial to our cook, Abraham. The thing is, he was an ardent INA supporter. I always suspected he hated us. And this wouldn't have curried him any favor with the Japanese."

She switches back to Urdu. "Do you know if Abraham is still alive?"

The man's eyes drop, and he points to a row of mounds so recent, the earth is still raw.

Early the next day they join the entire town on the Gymkhana maidan for the ceremony of surrender. In the clear morning light, people look less sad and a little livelier. Many of the women wear bright yellow and green saris, and some of the men sport crisp white shirts and blue sarongs, orange turbans—all newly supplied. They still have sunken cheeks and rickety legs, and there are no trappings of celebration other than the insistent playing of the *Dilawara*'s bugler and the Union Jack snapping in the breeze, but the air smells fresh, and the palm fronds glitter.

A long wooden table has been erected on the pitted lawn. Viv is busy filling her notebook, and the newsreel crews have their cameras in a row. Claire, Roger, and Ty are ushered to a set of chairs for special guests.

Ty hasn't spoken all morning. Now, using his camera like a telescope, he's surveying the crowd when two familiar vehicles round the bend of the foreshore road. One is a mottled yellow with a big nose and a tattered gray top, the other more compact, shaped like a knob in a dull pinkish color, faded from red. On the hood of each automobile waves a small British flag.

"Narinder!" Claire speaks the name fervently, like a prayer, but both cars turn out to be driven by uniformed Indian soldiers.

General Salomons steps out of Wilkerson's old saloon. The two white-uniformed Japanese emerge from the back of Shep's Morris.

The reporters and photographers surge, and within moments the official surrender is underway. General Salomons reads the proclamation that formally ends the Japanese occupation and reclaims authority of the islands under the Government of India. The Japanese commanders sit immobile and expressionless, white gloves pressed to their thighs.

When the reading of terms is concluded, each in turn signs the document. Then the Japanese surrender their swords, salute, and are marched, to the hoots and catcalls of onlookers, back to the old faded coupe. They are driven away.

The ceremony takes just fifteen minutes, but the General's aide de camp now signals the cameramen to keep rolling. Then he motions for the throng at the far end of the parade ground to make way.

"No." Claire stands. She raises a hand to shade her eyes.

"I can't believe—Ty, look. There—" She points across the field to some coral trees beyond the crowd, where a cluster of small dark figures has gathered.

Ty lets out a trill and leaps from his seat. Fortunately, the General's guard is at ease, or he might have gotten himself shot. Instead his outburst is rightly chalked up to the joy of the moment.

He runs at full tilt, dodging adults and pushing children, Claire dashing behind him.

It's Leyo. *Leyo!* Grinning, ebullient, their beloved friend raises both his arms as he spots Ty tearing through the crowd. Beside him Kuli leans on his staff, and Porubi squats there, too, cheeks still round as a bullfrog's.

Now Claire makes out Imulu and Sempe, Mam Golat, Ekko and even the brooding Obeyo. But where, where is Naila?

She's slow to notice the official commotion, as General Salomons himself summons Kuli forward. When Claire does glance back at the signing table, she registers startled chatter and suspicious mutterings among the locals, but the General waits with respect. It dawns on her only then that the Biya are going to be recognized for their service.

As well they should be. Kuli and Porubi became indispensible through the successive Balderdash missions. If only one of these missions had yielded intelligence about the person who mattered most to Claire and Ty.

But then Leyo scoops Ty into his arms. He cups the boy's face in his hands, and Ty wraps himself around those shoulders. The two of them touch their foreheads together, laughing and warbling, swaying with emotion. For several seconds they remain inseparable.

Then Leyo turns. He reaches toward the shade behind him.

Claire stops short, as a child toddles into view. For a split second she mistakes the tiny girl for Artam, but no, this child is barely old enough to walk.

Leyo kneels to receive her and lifts his face to take Claire in. "Anya, our daughter."

"Where's Naila?" Ty demands, all but batting away the child.

Again the bugle sounds. Leyo looks past Claire, as if to the clouds, but his face is beaming. She feels a hand at her elbow.

Mem. Please. She senses the words without hearing them. *No see-ums.* She opens her arms and turns.

And there, at last, is Naila. The same bright dark eyes. The same broad nose and cheeks but with tears gilding them in the sun.

Naila has grown into a woman. A mother and wife in her own right. She wears Leyo's old coral sarong and her hair sheared close to the scalp. A star composed of tiny pale scars blooms on her left shoulder.

Claire crosses her arms over her aching chest, but before Naila can return the gesture, Ty comes barreling back between them, his whole being electric.

As Naila falls with him into mid-air, his shouts soar in exultation.

EPILOGUE

1967

The clock tower has shrunk. At least that's how it seems. I remember craning my head back to puzzle out those two black needles inside the white circle. I don't think I learned to tell time before the war, and when we came back, the clock had stopped. It's still stopped, and the plaster around it is cracked and bleached.

The trees around the tower, though, they have continued to grow. Twenty-two years taller, and Aberdeen Bazaar, too, has swelled, closing in on old landmarks like the Browning Club. The tower square now is crowded with newcomers, mostly Bengali refugees fleeing East Pakistan. With them have come full-color posters for Fanta, Titan watches, Kwality ice cream, and Dalda cooking oil. Bollywood music whines and wiggles through the din of two-stroke motorbikes zipping around the memorial.

Little boys cry, *"Uncle!"* and come at me with open hands. When I ask to take their picture, they pile onto each other like puppies. The result is as winning as photographs in India always seem to be, but it is today's India that catches my lens, not the birthplace I recall—the birthplace that I've come to recover, if I can.

It may be an impossible mission. How can I expect to recapture the past of this place when I myself am so changed? I mind the insect welts that cover my elbows and knees as I never did when I was these boys' age. I recoil from the ammoniac fumes of urine, the pervasive petrol haze, and I stoop to meet the eyes of adults who should be looking down on me. The disorientation only grows when I try to find someone, anyone, who remembers my parents.

It takes an hour or more for me to be passed around the square from elder to elder until at last a matron selling crisps from one of the stalls tells me that Dr. Durant cured her son of the typhus in 1940. That boy now is a doctor himself in Nairobi.

"Africa," she stresses, as if her son lived on Mars.

When I tell her that Dr. Durant was my father, she salaams and mumbles a prayer. When she looks up, the creases of her wide face glisten. "I was there, Saar. I saw, that horrible terrible day." She points at a bullock cart piled with yellow jackfruit, parked at the foot of the tower. She lowers her head.

I take a step back and raise the Leica, the one my mother gave me all those years ago, preserved and refurbished especially for this trip. I photograph not the spot she's indicated but the woman herself, her pity and horror thrown into relief by the banana yellow and cherry red images of the adverts that adorn her stall. Such contradictions.

I'm still debating whether and how to ask for details about my father's execution when the woman's memory computes.

"You are the boy! I am remembering. They called you Jungle Boy." She squeezes her eyes and taps the scarlet bindi between them. "You came back, and we all saw your picture in the newspaper."

"That's right." I talk while continuing to shoot the changing planes of her face. "When the Japanese surrendered. We stayed for several weeks to find our friends and help with the relief efforts."

"And your ma. She was not like the other *memsaabs*."

I laugh and lower the camera. "No, indeed she was not. What do you remember about her?"

"They say she also stayed with the naked people. By her own self . . . even before the war?" Her slow question says, fine for a boy to run naked through the wild, but an American *memsaab*?

"Both she and my father studied and loved the forest." I want to ease her embarrassment. Forestry has a long and respected history in the Andamans. Orchid conservancy and botanical medicine, too, have gained currency in recent years. Respect for the "naked people" apparently has not.

My explanation allows her to sidestep my question with one of her own. "Is she living?"

"Very much so." I picture Mum and Maikel striding through the autumn light of Central Park the morning I left. "In New York City."

"Accha!" Now *that* thought definitely brightens her, and I expect the usual drill about Times Square and the Empire State Building.

Instead, she scolds me. Hands up, fingers dancing, her voice still musical with the tones of her youth. "Why you do not bring her *with* you?"

I laugh. "Believe me, I begged her. But I'm here, at least partly, to work, and she thought it best I come on my own."

"You're older now than I was then," is what she said. "You don't want my memories interfering." I tried to tell her it was far too late for that, but Maikel took her side. "You own this assignment," he said. "Reconciliation is not our story anymore. It's yours."

Without taking her eyes from me, my inquisitor adjusts the purple folds of her sari as if fingering a violin. "What work you are doing?"

I point to the camera with which I've just captured her hand gestures. "I take pictures for a magazine in America."

She giggles, coyly baring paan-stained teeth. "My photo in America?"

But the pose does her no favors, and I explain that I, too, am mostly interested in the forest. I've come to document what's become of one tribe in particular that I knew as a child, the people who took care of me during the war after my father died.

Suddenly I'm reluctant to say any more. It's too personal and complicated, and there are far too many unknowns, so I pay for a sleeve of crisps, thank the woman, and move on.

At the top of the square the Browning Club looks as if it's been frosted in mildew. A plaque beside the door now marks this building as "The Local Borns' Association."

I'm tempted to apply for membership, but the door is locked, so I sit on the steps to wait. If my last letter reached its intended destination, Naila's daughter will come to look for me here and guide me to Behalla. Twenty-two years. I've no idea what to expect.

We did used to talk about coming back together. Especially after Mum published her book about the Biya. It wasn't exactly a bestseller, but whatever it earned she sent to Naila and Leyo. Mum created a scholarship fund for Anya and was so proud when Naila wrote that her daughter had matriculated at Calcutta University and planned to be a doctor, *just like Doctor Shep.*

Not me. I weigh the Leica in my palm, considering the irony, that this phantom sister now may have more in common with my father than I do. Is that a function of chance, or of Naila's influence? Mum says Naila's the one who was supposed to go to college in Calcutta. Her parents' dream, my mother's offer. Instead, she sent her daughter.

Mum also insists that my father wouldn't have wanted me to be a doctor. He always knew, she says, that light was my first love. I find this touching and probably true of me. I just wish I had clearer memories of him. My hope is that this visit will bring him back—and that whatever story emerges will pay tribute to him and Mum, as well as to Leyo and Naila.

A muezzin's call to prayer rises from the Jama Masjid. I've no memory of this song in my childhood, though I must have heard it often. Muslims, Buddhists, Hindus, and Christians have lived for ages in these islands together, their common heritage of fighting the British overpowering sectarian rivalries even when Partition was causing carnage elsewhere. We were long gone by then—in 1947 I was ten years old, chasing poor old Bibi around my grandparents' Connecticut garden—but when Margaret Bourke-White's photographs appeared in *Life* . . . vultures and corpses, trains dripping blood, a black hand reaching from a shallow grave, Mum wouldn't rest until she had it from four different sources that nothing like that was happening in the Andamans.

The liquid cry ripples on and on, merciful and commanding. Why didn't we come? There was school, of course. Then the years of my grandparents' declines, followed by the back and forth to Europe after Maikel divorced his first wife. By the time he and Mum married, I was applying to college and she, belatedly, to graduate school, where she followed in Ruth Benedict's footsteps, traveling no farther for her later field work than the Algonquin nation.

Then my apprenticeship at the *Milwaukee Journal* and the trial run that launched me at *Geographic,* and I was off to Alaska, then the Amazon, then Yemen. I could have lobbied for this assignment years ago, but

I didn't. What I've always loved about photography is its paradoxical eloquence, each picture a silent story. I'd show up with my camera and not say a word. "Blend in," Mum would tell me, "make yourself as inconspicuous as an ethnographer." The truth is, I take after my mother. But how could I do justice to the story of the Biya with images alone? Or, be inconspicuous with Naila and Leyo? I owe my life to them, and yet we never came back. How do I shoot that story?

The *adhan* ceases. The devoted pray. We all parted willingly. We had no choice. Both we believed to be true.

My father was beheaded just one hundred feet from where I now sit, and no plaque marks the spot. I take his medallion from my pocket and finger it like a rosary. It's the closest thing I have to a direct memory of him. I can't see him, but I can feel his breath on my cheek, his palm on my back, the size of him kneeling wet beside me in the sun, on the sand, between the forest and the sea.

I never looked back that day, either. I didn't need to. I had Naila and Leyo. And then I had Artam and Kuli. I had everyone I needed until, one by one, they all vanished.

And then I had my mother.

When we found Naila and Leyo after the War, we all laughed and danced and cried and hugged. But they had created a new life, and young as I was, I knew that changed everything.

Before we left, Naila insisted I keep the moonstone globe that she'd worn during our time in the forest. I've brought this back, too, its cool green surface smooth as a marble after all these years, the etched lines of longitude and latitude long since rubbed away. When I hold it up, the stone's pale center still glows like magic.

"Ty Baba?"

I slide my childhood charms back into my pocket and rise to greet the slender young woman striding toward me. She wears a coral sarong and a bright white blouse, bouncy black corkscrews framing a heart-shaped face. Her skin is the color of pekoe tea, her dark eyes large and amused. A few feet shy of me she stops, balancing on one leg as the opposite foot slips from its chappal and her free toes flick a pebble away. One hand goes up to the gold stud in her ear as I move forward.

I tower over her.

For several seconds I can't speak. It feels like déjà vu, as if the mute little boy I'm told I once was has reinhabited me. I glance away, fighting inexplicable tears, and then, just as quickly as the spell seized me, it flees, prompting me to laugh.

"Baba!" I protest. "Am I that old?"

"More than I expected!" She's unabashedly cheeky. "It seems I've been sent to welcome you home."

"You must be Anya." I salaam.

She grins and returns the gesture. "But you may call me Yulu."

Author's Note

This novel is a labor of many years, and I owe an enormous debt of gratitude to those who have guided and indulged me along the way. For the spark that lit my initial fascination with the Andaman Islands I must thank Sharon and Ed Jay, who also introduced me to our beloved friend, the late Bandana Sen, and her son Akash Premsen and his wife Himani Dalmia. All were invaluable resources throughout my research.

I owe a special debt of gratitude to the team in Port Blair assembled by Sunshine India, especially Sunny, who procured the arsenal of publications on Ross Island that first alerted me to the unique history of the Andamans and their indigenous tribes during World War II. I would also like to thank Pankaj Sekhsaria, Madhusree Mukerjee, and Survival International for their work on behalf of the indigenous peoples of the Andaman and Nicobar Islands.

I should acknowledge these extraordinary islands themselves and the true events that inspired this novel. The South Asian archipelago known as the Andaman Islands is, in fact, home to a host of tribes that date back 60,000 years to the first Great Coastal Migration out of Africa. After thriving in isolation for millennia, these tribes began dying out after the British arrived in the mid-1800s to build a penal colony on South Andaman, and many were already extinct by 1936. The Biya people in this story are based on the Aka-Bea tribe, which once flourished in the forest near Port Blair. The Jarawa people still survive in South Andaman, though their forest preserve is under assault by poachers, tourists, and other outsiders who threaten the tribe with violence, disease, and pressure to "mainstream" into Indian society. As in the novel, the indigenous

Andamanese did weather the actual earthquake of 1941 without casualty, as their descendants did the tsunami of 2004.

It is important to stress that this novel is a work of fiction, as is each character in the story. Several of these characters, however, are loosely based on historical figures. The portrait of Dr. Ruth Benedict, for example, is drawn from her own writings and from her well-documented relationship with Dr. Margaret Mead. Several of the characters in Port Blair also are inspired by individuals noted in Rabin Roychowdhury's *Black Days in Andaman and Nicobar Islands* (Manas Publications), as well as other historical accounts of the Japanese occupation of the Andamans.

The convicts of Port Blair were almost all political prisoners—Indians fighting for independence from British rule, and many of the local residents did initially welcome Japanese occupation in 1942. At the time, British Commissioner C.F. Waterfall and his assistant Major Alfred G. Bird were waiting for a final evacuation that never arrived. The public executions described in the novel, as well as the justifications given by the Japanese officials, are based on the actual killings of Major Bird and local resident Zulfiquer (Sunny) Ali.

The stories of resistance here are also based on historical fact. In 1942 Port Blair's British superintendent of police, Denis McCarthy, escaped by motorboat across the Bay of Bengal and returned less than a year later to lead the first of what would be a series of secret intelligence missions code-named Operation Baldhead. Among the operation's island informants was the man on whom Porubi is based.

As for the boy at the heart of this story, his character is a work of fiction, but his condition is not. The Einstein Syndrome is a well-documented pattern of developmental behavior that was shared, as were the attendant family tensions and misunderstandings, by Albert Einstein, Richard Feynman, Arthur Rubenstein, Edward Teller, Clara Schumann, and countless other bright, late-talking children.

My own sons, Graham and Dan, inspired many moments within this story, but I am most grateful to them for the support they've given me over the decades as I've disappeared into the creative vortex to research and write my various books. An encouraging family is the biggest boon a writer could ask for, and I have a large and wonderful one. Jane, Marc, Mary, Rachel, Christina, and Emily, thank you all. And to Marty, you are my one and only.

Thanks also to my Goddard College family, particularly my colleagues Elena Georgiou, Darrah Cloud, Micheline Marcom, Victoria Nelson, Rahna Reiko Rizzuto, and Beatrix Gates. To Deborah Jones, Deborah Keehn, Florence Phillips, and my beloved YWLA writing group, including Laura Brennan, Deborah Cohen, Nan Cohen, Debbie Ezer, Danelle Davenport, Dominique Dibbell, Shari Ellis, Margaret Grundstein, Kellen Hertz, Charity Hume, Melissa Johnson, Robinne Lee, Amy Ludwig, Swati Pandey, and Colette and Lisanne Sartor, I am forever in your debt for the vital feedback you all provided on multiple drafts of this novel. My writing family also includes my endlessly patient agent Richard Pine and everyone at Inkwell, the indefatigable Megan Beatie, and of course Kate Gale and Mark Cull and their brilliant team at Red Hen, with an extra salute to Natasha McClellan and Monica Fernandez for shepherding *Glorious Boy* over the final hurdles and out into the world. I stand in gratitude.

The author gratefully acknowledges the following public domain sources of previously published material reprinted in this book:

Kim, by Rudyard Kipling, first published serially in *McClure's Magazine* from December 1900 to October 1901 and in *Cassell's Magazine* from January to November 1901, and in book form in October 1901.

"The Lost Legion," by Rudyard Kipling, first published in *The National Observer*, May 13, 1893, under the title "A Banjo Song".

About the Author

Aimee Liu is the bestselling author of the novels *Flash House*, *Cloud Mountain*, and *Face* and the memoirs *Gaining: The Truth About Life After Eating Disorders* and *Solitaire*. Her books have been translated into more than a dozen languages, published as a Literary Guild Super Release, and serialized in *Good Housekeeping*. She's received a Barnes & Noble Discover Great New Writers Award, a Bosque Fiction Prize, and special mention by the Pushcart Prize. Her essays have appeared in the *Los Angeles Review of Books*, the *Los Angeles Times*, *Poets & Writers*, and many other periodicals and anthologies. A past president of the national literary organization PEN Center USA, she holds an MFA in Creative Writing from Bennington College and is on the faculty of Goddard College's MFA in Creative Writing Program at Port Townsend, WA. She lives in Los Angeles. Learn more at *www.aimeeliu.net*